BRIGHT AND DEADLY THINGS

Lexie Elliott grew up in Scotland,
at the foot of the Highlands. She graduated
from Oxford University where she obtained
a doctorate in theoretical physics.
A keen sportswoman, she lives with her
husband and two sons.

Also by Lexie Elliott

The French Girl
The Missing Years
How to Kill Your Best Friend

BRIGHT AND DEADLY THINGS

LEXIE ELLIOTT

CORVUS

First published in the United States in 2023 by Berkley, an imprint of
Penguin Random House LLC.

Published in hardback in Great Britain in 2023 by Corvus, an imprint of
Atlantic Books Ltd.

This paperback edition published in 2023.

10 9 8 7 6 5 4 3 2 1

A CIP catalogue record for this book is available from the British Library.

Paperback ISBN: 978 1 83895 050 7
E-book ISBN: 978 1 83895 049 1

Printed and bound by CPI (UK) Ltd, Croydon CR0 4YY

Corvus
An imprint of Atlantic Books Ltd
Ormond House
26–27 Boswell Street
London
WC1N 3JZ

www.corvus-books.co.uk

MIX
Paper | Supporting
responsible forestry
FSC® C171272

At the risk of repeating myself…

For Matt, Cameron and Zachary,
always and forever.

1

There's someone in the house.

I know it as soon as I'm inside, though I couldn't say how. Some indescribable change in the air, perhaps, or a sound I hadn't consciously registered. A wave of adrenaline sweeps over my skin, prickling all hair follicles on end. I stand frozen, just inside the still-open front door, a layer of warm air and sunshine pressing at my back and the shadowy cool of the terraced house silently waiting for me. But it's the wrong type of silence. I stand motionless, staring, my ears straining to catch any sound above my own racing heartbeat, which is thumping in my ears, thumping in my throat; waiting for a moving shadow or the thud of a footfall or even just the tiniest of creaks—but nothing comes. The house, the intruder, me: we are all holding our breath.

I squint down the corridor that leads to the open-plan kitchen/living area at the back. Beyond the rectangle of the doorframe, I can see the bright saturated green of the back garden's lawn through the floor-to-ceiling windows at the rear of the house, verdant in the sunshine after the rain we've been having. *Call the police,* I think. *Call the police, call the neighbors and scream until somebody—anybody—comes* . . . But even if I scream, no one will come: the residential street outside is quiet, drowsy with the heat; and anyway, most of my neighbors will be either at work or away for their summer vacation. And what can I tell the police? *Come quickly because I have an absolute conviction that there's an intruder in my house, even though I haven't actually looked?*

But I know it's true: there's someone in the house. I can sense it with a pressing urgency, as if there's music playing at a pitch that's below my range of hearing, but nonetheless felt.

Do something. Find something, some kind of weapon. Wait—I know . . .

I check that my phone is easily accessible in my pocket, then slide my rucksack off my shoulder, easing it to the floor as quietly as possible—though surely whoever is here must have heard me come in—before reaching out slowly, silently, to the coat cupboard that is just beside me. My heartbeat is a hammering thud that must be audible streets away. I know the cupboard door will squeak, regardless of whether I open it slowly or fast. *Fast*, I decide. *Fast, and use the noise.*

I take a deep breath. *Go.* "Get out of my house; I'm calling the police right now!" I yell, and keep yelling as I yank the screeching cupboard door open with one hand and reach in with the other to grab a club—any club—from the golf bag that languishes beneath the coats. Words keep tumbling out of my mouth, though I have no real idea of what I'm shouting as I yank the club out, briefly entangling it with a navy rain jacket that slips off its hanger and falls to the floor as I charge with my improvised weapon toward the back of the house. Surely the intruder will head straight for the open front door? I don't want to be in the way when they do. I reach the living room, with the afternoon sun streaming in through the French doors, and whirl around so my back is to the sunlight, holding the club diagonally in front of me with both hands on the shaft,

2

no longer yelling and poised to spring. *Where is the intruder? Upstairs?* I strain to listen. The house is silent, but I'm not fooled. *Something is coming, something is coming, something is . . .*

A dark shape explodes out of the small study to my left, running straight for me. For a moment I'm frozen, staring blankly at the man—for it seems to be a man, though his head is covered by a black balaclava—who is heading directly toward me. *Why is he not heading for the open front door?* Belatedly, in blind panic, I swing the club viciously, but too late; he's almost upon me. Only at the last minute, he veers, planting a foot on the seat of one of the armchairs and leaping over the back, and my clumsy swing connects only in a glancing blow on his lower back, the club continuing in an arcing path. I hear, rather than see, it smash through the crystal vase that was on the sideboard, because I'm whirling round to keep the intruder in my vision; he's at the sliding doors, yanking one open to run out into the garden, where, without any hesitation whatsoever, he sprints across the small lawn to scale the cedar-planked back fence and disappear into the lane behind.

I'm left staring at the red-brown horizontal planks of the cedar fence, the club still gripped tightly in my hands. A small breeze slips in through the now open sliding door, carrying with it the shouts of children playing, a car starting somewhere, a bee buzzing round the lavender in the garden—the lazy sounds and smells of summer. I'm alone now; the insistent press of danger has receded. I am very much alone.

The police—an officer and a forensics specialist—come quickly. Perhaps there's less for them to do in Oxford in summer, when the bulk of the student body has melted away. The tourists more than make up the numbers, but I imagine they're less

3

troublesome: nobody comes to visit the city of dreaming spires for the nightlife.

The forensics specialist takes out some sort of kit and starts to look around while the officer and I sit on the sofa. He's a spare man with a no-nonsense attitude, but his eyes are kind when they meet mine. I sip from a cup of tea while I answer his questions, though what I really want is something much stronger. The golf club is on the floor now. It feels like a talisman, like I shouldn't ever be without it; I keep one foot pressed on it as I try to describe the intruder. I assume male, given build; somewhere between five foot ten and six foot; lean and obviously quite athletic; Caucasian, judging by the small patches of skin visible around the balaclava. Wearing dark clothing of the sporting variety: black joggers and a long-sleeved top. Gloves? I'm not sure on that. I find myself saying *It all happened so fast*. The cliché doesn't do the experience justice. That moment when he exploded toward me, when I was frozen in his path . . .

"He must have accessed from the rear," says the colleague, stepping carefully over the navy rain jacket that's still strewn on the floor. Nick's jacket: a good one, but too big for me. I ought to do something with it; it shouldn't go to waste. She crosses to inspect the sliding doors. "There's no sign of forced entry at the front door— Ah, here we go. There are marks here on the doorframe, and the lock is damaged. We won't get a print, though." She looks across at me, mild disapproval edging into her tone. "You really should think about an alarm system and additional locks on these sliding doors." I nod, though I'm thinking that it's a little late to lock the stable door after the horse has bolted. Though I suppose horses can always bolt again.

4

"And you're sure nothing is missing, Mrs. Rivers?" asks the officer.

"Doctor," I say reflexively. "Dr. Rivers."

"Dr. Rivers," he repeats. "Do you work up at the JR, then?"

He means the John Radcliffe Hospital. I shake my head. "I'm not a medical doctor. I'm an academic." My eyes move inadvertently toward the shadowy entrance to the study—only an alcove, really—as if the intruder might burst from there again.

"Ah. But you're sure nothing is missing? Bikes, electronics, money, jewelry, passports, other valuables?"

"Nothing that I can see. I had my passport with me, and I'm wearing most of my jewelry." I see them both eyeing my minimalistic adornments. "As I said, Oxford academic." I make an attempt at a wry smile. "We're not known for our disposable cash."

"Well, I would think it was an opportunist thief and they couldn't have been here long," says the officer in a tone that suggests he's bringing his questions to a close. "Probably just got here when you disturbed him. Or her." They are not convinced, given the balaclava and genderless clothing, that the thief is necessarily male; in their eyes, that may be an assumption of mine that has stuck in my head, tainting what I really saw and remember. Unconscious bias. I suppose it could be; they're right to keep an open mind. But nevertheless I can't shake the feeling that the intruder was male.

"He—or she—must be local," I muse. "Not everyone would know about the access to the garden from the lane at the back." Nor about the study either, in fact, though I suppose he simply looked for a place to hide when he heard me come in.

"Did the intruder pick up and smash the vase?" asks the

5

specialist. "If we're lucky I might get a print off one of the larger pieces."

"No, I did it. With the, um"—I lean down to pick up the golf club and look at the head of it properly—"seven iron." I see Nick deep in conversation with someone—who? Does it matter? And where were we anyway?—his beanpole figure hunched over like a shepherd's crook so that his words could be safely delivered to the ear of a smaller man as he said earnestly, *If in doubt, use a seven iron.* Nick, who had only taken up golfing six months before, giving golfing advice; I teased him about it mercilessly all the way home. *None so fanatical as a convert.* Even in those first moments, in the grip of that sweep of adrenaline, like a hand stroking an electric shock across me, I didn't consider that it could have been Nick in the house. I've moved beyond denial, I suppose. I know it will never again be Nick.

"I'm sorry?" asks the officer.

I don't know what I've said to prompt that. "It's nothing. Just something my husband said."

He looks up from his pad. "Is he at work?"

"No. No, he died a few months ago. A traffic accident." I've learned how to say it: the right amount of information to impart, and the right pace at which to do it. Not so rushed that the listener might miss what you've said, but not so drawn out that they become terrified you might dissolve on the spot.

"I'm sorry," he says again, though this time it's not a question and his expression is appropriately grave. I expect that in his profession, he's learned a few things too. I incline my head briefly; the social contract has been completed. He eyes the rucksack in the hallway. "Just back from a holiday?"

I shake my head. "About to go, actually. Well, not a holiday exactly; a reading retreat at a chalet in the Alps. I wouldn't have been here, except I missed my flight. I'm booked on tomorrow's instead now." I look around the room, somehow surprised afresh to find myself here. I was never the sort of person who missed flights. But then, I was never the sort of person who couldn't get out of bed in the morning or found themselves in tears at the supermarket cash register either.

The police wrap up shortly after that, promising emails with victim-of-crime information, but nothing more; we all know they won't catch him. And why should they expend resources and time on a thief who ultimately appears to have stolen nothing and done no harm to anybody or anything except an inexcusably flimsy door lock? I turn the key in the front door after they leave, and use the sliding chain for good measure, all of which seems rather pointless, given the unfettered access at the rear of the house on account of the damaged lock. Then I lean my back against the secure front door, the club still in one hand, and slide down to a seated position, wondering what I should be doing. Calling a locksmith, probably. I also have nothing in the fridge, given I hadn't expected to be here; I should call for takeout too. I look at the head of the club, at the grooves across the face of it. *If in doubt, use a seven iron.* It's a long time before I move.

Sofi

August 10th

Dear Mimi,

I've been at the chalet for a day now. Mike is here too; I hadn't expected that he would be. He's not in the slightest bit interested in me, which is fine—except, no, to be honest, it rankles; it's like he's been warned off or something. Maybe he has, come to think of it. Maybe James has been mouthing off about that stupid bet again.

Anyway, Mike's here; and a postgrad called Olive, who I'd guess is a bit younger than Mike, probably late twenties. There are two other undergrads besides Julie, James and me (although technically I suppose I'm not an undergraduate anymore), and Julie was right: the other two—Caleb and Akash—are nice enough, if deeply in the geeky camp. Everyone is very gung ho about the no-electricity, no-running-water malarkey, so naturally I'm very gung ho too, whilst secretly thanking the powers that be for the invention of dry shampoo. I don't think I have the right clothing either; it's only been twenty-four hours, but it's apparent already that it's absolutely de rigueur to wear battered hiking shorts or trousers in a gruesome shade of khaki or blue or dusty brown—anything the color of a bruise. My Daisy Dukes are raising eyebrows; I can feel myself stiffening in that half-defiant, half-awkward way when I spot the sidelong glances. But so what if I don't have the right clothes: I'm here. Just like you always said: turn nothing down. Julie has all the right stuff, of course. I guess you acquire it without even trying if you grow up spending all summer in Cornwall and three weeks every winter in Verbier.

Will is coming later today—with his girlfriend, apparently. That was something of a surprise. Ha! I like my understatement there: something of a surprise. (Oxford has taught me that: the power of understatement. See: I'm learning!) He'd certainly failed to mention her. I wouldn't have approached him if I'd known. Wait; a qualifier might be appropriate: I probably wouldn't have. Screw it, at least I can be honest here: even the probably isn't quite right. The best that can be said is that I might not have. It's not like they're married or anything.

Nick Rivers' widow was supposed to be here already, but she hasn't arrived. Prof. Herringway said she'll be coming today too, now. I liked the prof in Oxford but I like him even more now; he's so very kind to absolutely everyone. Anyway, Nick Rivers' widow—poor thing. I can't imagine wearing that label at her age. She must have thought her life was sorted: supersmart, great position at a top university, equally clever husband. And she's kind of beautiful too: tall and willowy, with all that glorious hair, though the last time I saw her around college, she looked awful, like she'd subsisted on air since he died. They'd been married a while apparently; I

10

wonder why they didn't have kids—I mean, why get married at all except to crack on with that?

I don't think kids are going to be part of my future. Julie will have them. She says not, but I can see what's ahead of her, even if she can't. She'll walk into a good, solid career—accountancy or something—and make good, solid career progression, and then she'll meet and marry someone from a good, solid background who probably also spent their childhood summering in Cornwall and wintering in Verbier—oh, to be someone who casually uses a season as a verb!—and then they'll have kids and a dog and she'll regretfully give up work and find herself making lunches and packing gym bags, taxiing the kids to ballet and music lessons and running the PTA. I mean, I love her to bits but she's not exactly going to break out from her mold. And it's such a waste: she's so very, very smart and articulate and she's had every opportunity in life, all handed to her on a plate with a cherry on top, thank you very much, and yet all she'll end up doing is reinforcing the cycle.

Somehow I don't think that's what's ahead of me. There's a feeling that I get when I think about this stuff; it's like the swell of the music in a movie for that crucial moment—you know, when the epiphany hits the main character—and you feel such a longing, so piercing that it hurts, to be that person, to be living in that instant, and to know you're living it, to know how important it is. I want to be out there, living it, breathing it, saying yes to everything. I won't turn anything down.

Love you. Miss you.

Sofi

2

Emily! I thought you were flying out yesterday."

I'm at the departure gate at Stansted Airport, where I've been for hours, anxious to avoid a repeat of yesterday's fiasco; I look up from my book to find Peter in front of me, his overly long sandy hair unkempt as ever and the smile on his long face a little wary, as if he's uncertain that it's safe to approach. I can just imagine his thoughts: *Grieving widows are dangerous beasts. Best handled with care and, if possible, at a distance.*

"Hi, Peter." I smile and gesture to the empty seat beside me, trying not to let his caution nettle me or, at least, trying not to let it show. "I missed the flight yesterday, so here I am."

He shrugs off his rucksack and sits down, his pale eyebrows rising as his body lowers. "Missed the flight? What happened?"

What did happen? I couldn't honestly say. There was plenty of time, and then suddenly time lurched and there wasn't, and I couldn't say what happened or how I lost my grip on things. I reach for a believable excuse. "Oh, it was silly of me: I misjudged the traffic." And then, rushing past the lie, "But it's just as well I did. When I got home, someone was trying to break in."

"No!" An announcement starts, and we both pause to listen, cocking our heads. "Yep, this is us," says Peter, unfolding to his feet again. "But tell me: the break-in? Did you actually see the intruder?"

My account of the events of yesterday takes us all the way through the boarding process and onto the plane itself, neatly plastering over the oddness of being in Peter's company without Nick. I've known Peter for years—he'd always been a close collaborator of Nick's in the Oxford University engineering department, and I'd absolutely consider him one of our closest friends, but it occurs to me that I can probably count on one hand the number of times I've spoken to him without Nick at least being somewhere in the room. And it's odd, too, to see him in such casual attire. Not that we academics necessarily dress formally; it's just that Peter, like Nick, usually prefers to wear a shirt, not a T-shirt, with his jeans; both of them joked that it was the only thing that differentiated them from the students. Mid-thirties is a difficult age for faculty staff: not enough gray hair; far too easy to be mistaken for a graduate or even, God forbid, an undergraduate.

We're not seated together on the plane, but we're only a row apart, and when the kindly man seated next to me sees us talking, he offers to swap with Peter so that we can sit together. *He probably thinks we're a couple,* I realize, and then feel even more awkward when Peter settles himself in the middle seat beside me, in the cramped economy quarters that are so space constrained that our elbows can't help but brush. He busies himself adjusting his seat belt as he says, "You haven't been to the chalet before, have you?" The chalet: Chalet des Anglais.

"No. You?"

"I went two summers ago. It's really something." He's finished with the seat belt now and is bent forward instead, pulling something out of the battered messenger bag under the seat in front of him. "One of those Oxford experiences that has you feeling like you're actually living in a slice of history."

"On account of the lack of electricity and running water?"

"Well, there is that." He straightens back up, a sheaf of research papers in his hand and a quick grin on his mobile face. Perhaps it's his animation, rather than the lack of gray hair, that makes him seem younger than his years. *Puckish*, I think. As if there are electrical currents of thoughts and ideas crackling beneath his surface, just waiting for an opportunity to reveal themselves. "But it's the whole thing: the seclusion, the academic aspect to it, everybody mixing in from undergraduate through to Robert himself. When you look through the chalet diaries, it really does seem like the experience is untouched by the hand of time."

"How does Robert decide who to invite?" Robert is Professor Robert Herringway, one of the trustees of the chalet. The chalet itself is jointly owned by three Oxford colleges, which take turns week by week to use it during the summer; invitations are extended, by whoever is leading the party, to staff and students of their own college. It's considered a privilege to be invited—it's an introduction to a very traditional part of Oxonian history, something that not everyone gets a chance to experience.

"Alchemy and witchcraft, I think. Somehow it always seems to work and everybody gets on—or at least, nobody has killed anyone yet. It's a rather science-heavy group this time, though, which is unusual." His eyebrows knit in a quick frown, gone almost as soon as I register it. "Robert is usually more careful to balance it: he always says it's a strength of Oxford that is underutilized, that each college has members spanning all academic departments; we ought to have more interdepartmental cross-pollination of ideas. Anyway, do you know when Jana and Will are getting there?"

"Today at some point." That's one benefit of having missed the flight—I won't have to spend any time out there without Peter or Jana and Will. It feels like a weakness to admit, even to myself, that I had been anxious about arriving twenty-four hours before my friends. "They're coming by train from Vienna." I smile as I think of the text conversation I had with Will.

Hey you. Missed my flight. Arriving today instead x

Hey yourself. Us too. Race you there . . .

You're on.

Then later, from Will:

I should have known better than to mention a competition to Jana. She's relentless now. If we miss our connection she may actually combust.

But I won't tell Peter about that. He'd become just as unbearable to travel with as Jana must be right now.

"Vienna?" Peter says. "Holiday? Will didn't mention that."

"Not holiday; a conference. Will was the key speaker." Alongside his work at the university, Will—disarmingly enthusiastic on his subject, and blessed with a decent head of hair and a beautiful speaking voice—has somehow managed to recently become a household name, presenting a popular science-for-laymen television program called *How the World Works* and publishing books that actually sell. I've known Will far longer than I've known Jana or Peter: he and I were in the same undergraduate year at the same college, and quickly became part of the same friendship circle. In our last year, we had adjacent rooms and nursed each other through the pain of finals; nothing cements a friendship quite like surviving panic, despair, caffeine overload and sleep deprivation together. But now it's Jana that I see more—often daily—as she works in my department.

"Ah, yes, the poor man's Stephen Hawking. And all this time I thought research papers were the key to career advancement." Peter shakes his head with a grimace that turns quickly into a grin: a theatrical display of mock enviousness meant to amuse. Though I rather suspect there's a streak of genuine envy there too: Peter is nothing if not ambitious, and he absolutely keeps score.

"Jana messaged me to say that the gala dinner last night was a ton of fun. I expect they're traveling with hangovers." Jana loves the attention and the perks. It wouldn't occur to her to pretend otherwise, though given the pair are deep in IVF struggles, perhaps only Will is likely to be suffering from overindulgence.

"Well, that's some consolation, I suppose," Peter says, tongue deliberately in cheek.

"The next leg of the journey is a train to Saint Gervais, right?"

"Yep, with a change at Annemasse; we should reach Saint Gervais midafternoon. Then we have a choice: short taxi, then long hike up, or longer taxi, then _télécabine_, and then a very short hike down."

If I were Jana, I would ask which is quicker, but I really don't care enough. "How long is long and how steep is up?"

"At least two hours, and decently steep in places."

Two hours uphill, carrying my rucksack all the way. It doesn't appeal. "Short hike down, please."

"Oh, thank God." That quick, mischievous grin again. "If you'd said the other, I'd have had to do it without complaining to preserve my male ego, but really I'd much rather take the easier route." He cocks his head, attempting to inspect my footwear—Converse All Stars—in the confined space. "Those should be fine for the walk down since it's dry." He sounds a mite doubtful. "Do you have anything sturdier with you?"

"I've proper hiking boots in my rucksack."

"Ah, good." Then he pauses; I can see he's steeling himself. I've gotten used to this too: the fear people have of even mentioning my husband's name. "Was, um, was Nick supposed to be coming too?"

"Yes, but only for a couple of days. It was kind of Robert to invite him, given he was at a different college. I was going to stay on whilst he went to visit his mum."

Peter's mouth twitches. "I bet you were quite happy to leave him to do that on his own."

I adopt an angelic expression. "I couldn't possibly comment."

The twitch explodes into a laugh now; Nick's mother is legendarily difficult. I'd had plenty of material for mother-in-law jokes, though secretly I'd wondered if we might have forged a bond if kids ever came along. *I should call her,* I think, though I can't imagine anything I could say that could be of any help. She had surely been looking forward for months to the visit from her cherished only child; she was expecting a whole week of him to herself, and now she has exactly what I have: a hole where he ought to be. Words can't fill that. *But still, I should call her from France.*

"Emily?" says Peter, so hesitantly that I wonder what expression is on my face to warrant it. But when I glance at him, it's not concern I see, but something else. Anxiety,

17

perhaps. "I, erm, I wanted to talk to you about something."

"What?" We are taxiing along the runway now, picking up speed and noise.

He blows out a breath. "It's nothing, really, except . . ."

I stare at him, bemused. It's clearly not nothing to him. "What?" I ask again against the backdrop of the high-pitched whine of the engines.

"The last time I saw Nick, the last time we spoke—well, we argued. Properly argued, not just academic discussion: raised voices and everything. And I feel so wretched about it." Indeed, his expression is the very definition of *wretched*. "It was silly, really, just something about work, but it's so hard to think that our last words were in anger." He's staring down at the papers held in both his hands. I don't know what to say. Nick never argued with anyone, ever. He was simply far too logical for that. Peter risks a glance at me. "Did he . . . did he tell you about it?"

I shake my head. "No." His face clears a little, as if that's some small kind of absolution, as if it couldn't have mattered so much if Nick hadn't bothered to tell me. I don't have the heart to tell him that Nick would have had to take the time to process the conflict internally, to turn it over and analyze and classify it, before he felt capable of presenting it to me. We're in the air now; I feel that extraordinary moment when the aircraft suddenly becomes light, as if shrugging off all tethers to earth, including gravity. Peter, though, still has the weight of the world in the lines of his face. "Peter," I say gently, "you and he were friends for years. He wouldn't have let a minor disagreement color what he thought of you."

"You really think so?" He looks as if he daren't quite accept the secondhand forgiveness I'm offering, as if I might snatch it away at any moment.

"I do," I say firmly. I have no idea of what this skirmish was about or what Nick thought about it, but Peter shouldn't have to carry this through life. He looks at me for a second, then closes his eyes briefly with a nod. His face is visibly lighter. After a beat, I can't help but ask, "Nick really raised his voice with you?"

Peter makes a sound that sits precisely halfway between a laugh and a sob. "Well, the balance of the raised voices may have been entirely on my side," he concedes. The laughter that escapes me dances along a knife-edge; if it treads too heavily, it will rent and tear. After a moment, he says, "He really didn't say anything?"

"Nothing."

"Huh." He stares at the papers in his hand for a moment, then visibly shakes himself. "Well, back to keeping up with the competition," he quips, picking up the top one to read. I catch a glimpse of the first few words in the title: *Van der Waals Heterostructure Polaritons with* . . . The book that's in my lap, a thriller that has had everybody abuzz but somehow can't hold my interest, looks rather lightweight by comparison. I pick it up anyway, but my attention is on the window—not the view through it, but on the three thin panes themselves. Such a thin, seemingly fragile boundary between life and death. I can't imagine why we allow planes to have windows.

By four p.m., we've successfully navigated the train journey and reached the *télécabine* Peter mentioned. There's not a cloud in the vaulting blue sky and the snowcapped mountains that rise from the valley floor are astonishingly close and extend much farther toward the clear blue heavens than seems possible. It's a vista that stretches one's field of vision, that forces a reassessment. The world seems bigger here. Bigger and wider and startlingly open.

The Prarion lift building is a brown wooden structure that appears to be suspended over the whirring mechanics of the lift itself, as if the Perspex bubbles shuffling in their semicircle beneath it were holding it up rather than the other way round. Given the time of day, most people are descending, either under their own steam or via the *télécabine*, and they're all dressed for hiking; it's an extraordinarily wholesome picture. If I'd closed my eyes in Geneva, I could have convinced myself I was in an English summer—hazily, drowsily warm such that even the image of it in one's mind blurs at the edges—but it's different here. Everything is cleaner, clearer, sharper. I can't feel an edge in the air, but I know it's there, just waiting for the sun to abate.

We pay at the desk and climb into one of the *télécabines*, which Peter assures me is meant for eight people, though I imagine that must be a squash. And then we're skimming up over the mountainside, rising steeply over a carpet of dark green pine forests, rent in places by raking scars of pale green open meadows that are clearly ski runs and the occasional gray-brown gash of a gravel track, as if some mythical beast had gashed at the mountainside with its talons.

"Can we see it from here?"

"What? Oh—the chalet." Peter has been oblivious to the landscape we're speeding over, instead checking his emails on his mobile and typing replies at a comically rapid pace. He looks up briefly. "No, it's the other side of the mountain. You should check your messages; the chalet has virtually no reception. Last chance and all that."

I nod, but he's already focusing on his mobile again. I don't bother fishing out my own; there's nobody waiting to hear from me. It occurs to me that all my threads have loosened, the ones that keep me in place. It's a terrifying realization, how easily I've become untethered. I'd had ambition too, hadn't I? My own intentions and goals? What has been the point of the life I've built up to now if I can shrug it off so effortlessly, like an unwanted jacket? I'm suddenly unnervingly aware of my own pulse beating away beneath my skin, hammering in my very core. It's trying to take over, to bully me, hurry me, to race my breathing and ravage my heart—

Stop it, I tell myself. *Breathe. You've been spending too much time alone. You're overthinking everything, and it needs to stop.* When I glance at Peter, he's still focused on his emails and hasn't noticed my discomfort at all. I breathe carefully, evenly, again and again, concentrating on each inhalation and exhalation, and gradually feel myself calm.

The *télécabine* is approaching the top station. I twist myself sideways on the bench seat to gain space to pull my rucksack onto my shoulders, and think carefully, resolutely, about nothing, but the pulse is still there, deep inside my chest, beating away implacably. Trying to ignore it is like trying not to hear a dripping tap; the obsession with it could become as maddening as the noise itself. But I don't know how to stop either.

21

3

The chalet seems to conjure itself into existence from nothing. One minute I'm focusing on picking my way, my gaze flitting between the ground beneath my feet and the faded blue of Peter's technical rucksack ahead of me, and then the next minute I look up properly and the chalet is somehow right there, bathed in late-afternoon sunshine, at the end of an incongruously well-cleared lawn—boasting cricket stumps, no less. Despite having seen it in photos, the rectangular two-story building, glowing reddish brown in the sunlight, is larger than I expected, but just as old and rustic. A terrace wraps around the upper floor, topped by a disconcertingly basic steeply pitched gabled roof made of, as far as I can tell, corrugated iron. I recall that the original building burned down in the early twentieth century and was replaced by this one; it looks every bit of its one hundred or so years.

"Here!" says Peter completely unnecessarily, but with such triumphant relief that I realize he'd been worried about his navigation. The walk down the broad main path was, as advertised, fairly easy, despite the loose rocks and stones, but the final section involved a turn onto a tiny trail, barely more than a rabbit track, that would have been all too easy to miss. The narrow path wended its way through stretches of tall wild grasses, over a tiny wooden bridge spanning a small stream and through a woodland, leaving me thankful for wearing jeans, which, despite being a little hot, at least protected my legs from the tough grasses and bushes.

"Ah! Welcome!" The small, stout figure of Robert, in utilitarian hiking shorts and boots and with a pinkish tinge of sunburn on his balding head, is ambling across the lawn to greet us. "Peter, welcome back, I should say." They shake hands enthusiastically. "And Emily; excellent, excellent." He reaches out and clasps my outstretched hand in both of his, his pale blue eyes assessing me keenly from behind his small circular spectacles. "How are you, my dear?"

It's a genuine question, full of kindly concern. I want to answer him properly, but not here and now. "Good, thanks." I wince internally: my words are bright—too bright, almost dismissive. I hurry on. "I'm so sorry to have been delayed. You got my message?"

"Yes, but not until this morning." We start back across the lawn. "We weren't too worried, though—you wouldn't have been the first to decide to enjoy an impromptu overnight stay in a hotel in Saint Gervais before joining the melee. Still, better late than never. We're only short of Will and Jana now."

"Yes!" Robert raises his eyebrows at this unexpected passionate response from me. "That means I beat them here," I explain. "Jana gets very competitive."

"You didn't tell me we were in a race," grouses Peter.

"As does Peter," I add to Robert, my lips curling up in amusement at Peter's chagrin, "which is why I didn't tell him; the journey would have been unbearable. But I'll take the bragging rights nonetheless."

Robert's lips are twitching too. "The bragging rights are indeed all yours."

"Tanner's here already too?" Peter asks.

"Alas, no. His wife has been unwell—nothing serious as I understand it, but he's likely to be delayed by a day or two, as he doesn't want to leave her on her own." I murmur something sympathetic. I know Tanner quite well—Professor Tanner, whom absolutely everyone calls by his surname; I'm not even sure I can recall his first name—as he's rather senior in Nick's department: he's lined up to be the director of the newest, swankiest engineering lab in all of Britain, and had been pushing Nick to apply to be his deputy. Robert switches tack. "Now, I posit a cup of tea wouldn't go amiss?"

"Lovely. Thank you."

"Same, thanks." Peter is looking around. "Where is everyone?"

"One or two are taking a nap. The rest went up to the Hotel Le Prarion, foraging for chocolate and phone reception, I believe, so you might have a quiet ten minutes before they return and disturb your peace. Sit out here and enjoy the sunshine. I'm pleased to say that the weather is set to be fine for the whole week; the Alps are having quite the summer this year. Dare I say it, but they'll actually be hoping for rain if they don't get some soon."

Five minutes later I'm seated in a deck chair in front of the chalet, enjoying a cup of Earl Grey in a somewhat battered tin mug. Peter and Robert settle into deck chairs beside me. I ought to be sociable—perhaps asking about the rest of the party, trying to imprint their names onto my mind (never my strong point, despite years of practice through teaching)—but the view is simply too breathtaking. I hadn't taken it in properly on the walk down. Once again, I think there's something incredibly *clean* about it all: the verdant greens of the slopes before the gray alpine cliff faces emerge majestically, topped by pristine white snow. Up here, I can feel that sharp fresh edge to the air that I sensed on the valley floor, even as the sunshine warms through to my very bones. I close my eyes for a moment, savoring the feel of the rays on my skin, though I don't feel at all sleepy. If anything, I feel like I'm waking up.

"Jeez, is that—" Peter mutters, then stops. I open my eyes, blinking in the light. He's looking across the lawn at something, a slight frown on his face. I follow his gaze: it's not possible to see clearly because of the low-angled rays of the sun, but it appears that an enormous bear of a man is approaching us. I hold up a hand to shield my eyes. It's not a trick of the light: this man must be at least six foot three and built like an American football linebacker.

"Ah, yes," says Robert, yawning. It occurs to me that he looks older, and more tired, than I've noticed before. Is he seventy? I've never thought to pinpoint his age before. "The triumphant hunters return. I'll put on another pot of tea. Oh— Akash there is our treasurer for the week, so give your kitty money to him at some point, please." I belatedly realize that the giant is followed by a gaggle of youngsters, strung out in a line on the narrow trail. It puts me, rather incongruously, in mind of a mother duck with her ducklings.

Peter has extracted himself from the deck chair and scrambled to his feet. "Mike, I had no idea you were coming." It's not the most enthusiastic of greetings, but he reaches out a hand to shake the other man's with a friendly enough smile. Peter is not small, but this man genuinely dwarfs him. "Were you a late addition?"

Mike glances at me. "There was a free spot." *He knows who I am*, I realize. *Or more to the point, he knows who my husband was.* "No, don't get up." But it's too uncomfortable to twist my neck to look up that far; I keep struggling awkwardly in the deck chair and he reaches down to offer a hand to me. "Mike Shepherd," he says, pulling me up smoothly with no visible effort, then turning the grip into a handshake. "Visiting fellow, engineering."

"Thanks. Emily Rivers. Research fellow, theoretical physics." His hand is quite simply enormous. My own feels tiny and as light as air when he lets it go. Suddenly, I make the connection. "You must be Big Mike, Nick's squash partner."

"Guilty as charged." He smiles, and it's like watching granite rearrange itself: until I saw it happen, I wouldn't have thought it possible. *Craggy*, I think. Jana would be less kind; she would say, *Neanderthal*. Mike's smile fades. "I'm sorry I couldn't be at the funeral; I was in Canada. I heard it was incredibly well attended." His gray gaze is steady and clear; there's something calming about it that gives me license to answer freely. I don't have to worry that anything I say might rock this man.

"It was." I shrug. "It was a good day, I suppose, in as much as it could be," I add, almost surprising myself. "And also completely and totally awful, of course."

He nods. "I can—" But the ducklings are among us now, chorusing welcomes to Peter and myself. We all shake hands in an awkward dance of crossing arms and shifting positions, and I attempt to attach faces and names inside my head; I vaguely recognize the five undergraduates—three men and two women—from having seen them around college, though they all look rather more disheveled than normal, as if the chalet has already rubbed off on them. *Caleb, Julie, Akash, James and Sofi*; I repeat inside my head like a chant. *Sofi. Hmm, I've heard of her*, I think. The staff members are not completely deaf to the undergraduate gossip; we only pretend to be. If it's loud enough, it always reaches our ears—and the young woman in question certainly looks like she could make some noise. Her long brown legs, almost entirely bared by the shortest of cutoff denim shorts, could spark a clamor all by themselves. I can't quite remember what I've heard about her: a prolific sex life, yes, but that's not so very uncommon. It would have to have been something more than that for the noise to reach me.

Julie—an athletically built jolly-hockey-sticks type from the home counties, with straw-colored bobbed hair, and shoulders and nose so heavily freckled that her milk white skin is almost entirely camouflaged—offers to show me where I'll be sleeping. I follow her, asking about her subject—chemistry, as it turns out—as the easiest of all icebreakers, with Sofi trailing behind us. We cut through the dust motes that dance in the sunlight just inside the doorway to the chalet, and pass onward through the salon and up the stairs to the bedrooms. A long corridor runs the entire length of the chalet on this upper floor, with rooms on either side, giving something of the impression of a dorm.

"This one," says Julie, pushing open a door at the far end that protests audibly. The room beyond it is simple and small, wide enough only for its two single beds with a gap of perhaps three feet between them, and dim, given the lack of electrical lighting. The only light comes from the windows of the top half of a pair of doors that open out onto the terrace, but even that is partially blocked by the steep roof, whose protection extends as far as the edge of the terrace itself. The width of the room is such that, if the terrace doors were opened wide, the beds would partially block the egress. I place my rucksack on one of the beds and glance through one of the windows. A game of cricket is commencing on the lawn.

"We kept it for you," Sofi says, pulling my attention back into the room. Her accent is intriguing; Scottish, I think, though I haven't quite heard enough; it could actually be Irish. "It's small enough that you ought to be able to have it to yourself." There's something feline about the way she moves, the deliberate grace of each motion, even if it's only to push her ink black hair behind one ear as she does right now.

I look at the pair of them hovering in the doorway. *Poor Julie*, I think. Even with her startling coloring, does anyone ever notice her with Sofi around? "Thank you both. That's kind of you."

"We'll leave you to get settled, then," says Julie, and they do, thoughtfully pulling closed the door behind them, though it's slightly warped and doesn't quite catch. I have to give it a hard shove afterward to get it to close properly. There's a feeling of dry wooden dustiness to everything I touch; I worry that the wood might splinter and crumble on my fingertips. I'm beginning to understand the disheveled look of the rest of the party after being here for only a day: the hundred-year-old chalet is literally rubbing off on us. Eventually there will be nothing left of it at all.

More noises float up from outside. There's a key in the lock of the terrace doors, so I turn it and venture out, cautiously leaning my forearms against the wooden balustrade; it seems sturdy enough, despite appearances. Peter is winding up to bowl from the far end of the lawn. He starts his run toward the chalet, unleashing the red ball in an unexpectedly coordinated cartwheel of limbs. I don't quite see where it goes, but I don't need to: he thrusts an arm in the air in triumph as a collective groan breaks out. "Who's next to face the firing squad?" he calls.

"Me, but I'm not going in without protection," calls a voice below me. I look down to see Sofi sitting on the grass, long legs akimbo as she attempts to put on some very grubby cricket pads. She's struggling to secure one of the straps around her leg, the smooth, dark, vulnerable skin of her inner thigh exposed beneath those shortest of shorts. "Mike, can you help me?"

"Nope" comes a cheerful reply. I look for the man behind the voice; he's over near the chalet door, by no means the closest helping hand. He moves farther toward the chalet, presumably to go inside, and my view is cut off, but the voice floats up nonetheless. "I'm on dinner duty with Robert."

"I'll help you, Sofi," says Caleb (or is it James?) with deliberate comical alacrity.

"And me! And me!" chorus Akash and James (or is it Caleb?), and Sofi laughs, having finally got the reaction she wanted, if not from the man that she wanted it from. It's all so very transparent, watching from up here. For an instant, I remember being her age, or perhaps I'm remembering being younger, a teenager: the destructive, chaotic, ravenous storm of every emotion, be it desire, despair, jealousy, ambition; the pin-sharp hurt of every minor slight or rejection. When did I change? Was I still like that when I met Nick? Yes: I wanted things then. I wanted him, and I wanted other things too; I remember the wanting. Now I can't think of a thing that I have the energy to want.

It's not just the grief. Even before Nick died, I'd begun to feel like I was going through the motions: teaching courses that I could cover in my sleep because I'd taught them several times before, collaborating with the same people on ever-similar topics to publish in the same journals. I remember Nick standing behind me with his hand on my shoulder as I turned from a research paper to look up at him. "Are you . . . are you happy?" he asked me cautiously. I must have said yes, I suppose—that's the only possible answer that wouldn't have alarmed him, and I certainly didn't want to do that. I wasn't *un*happy.

Sofi is in front of the stumps now, bending herself awkwardly to the cricket bat in front of her. I should go down and join everyone; I don't know why I'm hesitating. It will be easier when Jana and Will are here, though waiting for them feels a bit like cheating, like taking the easy way out. *The whole point of coming here was to try and find a way to climb out of the rut of grief. So start climbing.*

I leave the small room and go downstairs, meaning to go straight out to the lawn, but as I cross the salon, my attention is arrested by a shaft of sunlight that illuminates a large object I hadn't noticed before: a clock. A grandfather clock, in fact. It's almost as tall as I am, in a rich brown oakwood case, with ornate ironwork decoration around the clockface in the upper section. But it's the pendulum that has stopped me in my tracks. It's a deeply burnished brass color, with an intricate pattern etched into the surface. I lean forward, trying to get a sense of the swirls and twists and whorls of the lines, but the pendulum is of course constantly moving, with the light rippling across it, running like liquid along the different etched channels, such that it almost seems to be a living, changing thing; I can't get a sense of it.

"It's an odd beast, isn't it?" It's Richard: I jump a little at his voice. He's surprisingly light-footed for such a stocky man.

"How old is it?"

"Probably mid-eighteen hundreds, but it's an odd mishmash of styles—the hands suggest even earlier, but they may have been salvaged from another clockface. *Horloge comtoise*." He rolls the words across his tongue, relishing the feel of them. *"Horloge comtoise,"* he repeats. "That's the French for *grandfather clock*. Ordinarily the pendulum would be embossed in enamel with a country scene—a horse pulling a cart, or a man at work in the field, that sort of thing. This is quite the oddity."

"It's . . . it's hypnotic." It could be a floral pattern, or musical symbols, or some long-lost script—or all three, or none at all, as mesmerizing as the flames of a fire. *I could be lost to it,* I think. Those lines and swoops could cast out and ensnare me in their intricate, dancing net of light, dragging me into time itself.

"It's actually quite famous around here; some of the older locals call this *le Chalet de l'Horloge*—the Chalet of the Clock. As far as I can gather, it was one of the few things salvaged from the original building after the fire. The wood needed some restoration work, but the clock mechanisms were entirely unscathed. We actually thought it had been lost." He pats the side of it as if petting an animal and falls silent, his eyes on the pendulum.

"Lost?" But Robert doesn't reply. "Lost? How so?" I prompt.

"Oh." He visibly pulls himself out of his reverie. "Well, it went missing for decades, but would you believe it? It was in the loft the whole time under some moth-eaten blankets. It was found when the roof was inspected at the beginning of this summer." A bemused look crosses his face. "I can't imagine why anyone put it there. Anyway, we had it cleaned up and here it is; it arrived back only a few days ago. It's working just fine, albeit in its own fashion."

I check my own watch reflexively. "It's fast."

"Sometimes. And sometimes it's slow. But somehow, over the period of a day, it's pretty much bang on. As I said, it works in its own fashion."

"What?" I stare at him, then back at the clock. His eyes crinkle in mild amusement at my consternation. "Surely that's not possible." I don't have any detailed knowledge of timepieces, but I know that they work on repetitive motions, such that the timekeeping is standardized: a clock can be consistently fast, or consistently slow, or consistently accurate, but not all three.

"Yet nonetheless it's the case."

"Is it down to temperature changes?" I can imagine that if the ambient temperature were to vary considerably, the pendulum rod might expand or contract enough to noticeably affect the timekeeping.

"Seasonal temperature changes can be expected to affect a floor clock such as this; they tend to run slower in summer. But one wouldn't expect changes on an intraday timescale."

"Has anyone examined it to determine the cause?"

He shrugs. "Not to my knowledge. And anyway, I prefer to leave it as one of life's little mysteries. There are more things on heaven and earth, and so on." He looks at my expression. "I can see that doesn't sit well with you." If anything, his amusement is increasing. "A scientist through and through?"

"I don't . . . I just . . . I would want to know. I *do* want to know." It's almost a wail.

"But in not knowing, you might open yourself to all sorts of possible solutions you wouldn't have otherwise considered." He smiles again at my discomfort, but not unkindly. "Consider it an experiment, my dear Emily. If you fling the windows of your mind wide-open, who knows what might blow in?"

4

Ems, come on, it's not fair—you are even thinner than when I left you last week," Jana pronounces. We are sitting together at dinner, practically hip to hip at the dining table; twelve fit, but only just. The table itself is a polished dark wood, with sinuously curving carved legs; earlier I thought it looked a little forlorn, sitting incongruously in an isolated chalet when it's clearly more suited to the dining room of a grand English pile, but it's certainly being put to full use this evening. "Maybe what I need to do to lose ten pounds is bump off Will."

"Jana!" But I'm laughing. Jana's directness, and absolute lack of apology for it, is always so utterly refreshing. "And anyway, you really don't need to lose ten pounds." It's true, she doesn't. Her curviness is exactly right for her.

She ignores my words. "Or I suppose I could stop with the cheese and the red wine." She picks up her glass and eyes the deep burgundy contents, then sighs. "No, bumping off Will would definitely be easier."

"Do I hear that my life is under threat?" calls Will from across the table.

"Yes, but it's nothing personal," I assure him.

He quirks his eyebrows in mock alarm. "That doesn't make it any more palatable." James—blond, boisterous, public school manner and manners—laughs more than is strictly called for. If Sofi is also equally enamored of the television personality that is Will sitting between them, she is handling it with much more aplomb. I glance again at Jana's glass: she's definitely drinking, not just pretending. I feel a pang of guilt: I must have lost track of where they are in their IVF process. Another unexpected side effect of grief: it turns you into a bad friend.

"Coming through, coming through." Mike enters from the kitchen with five plates of the starter stacked efficiently up his arms, with Robert just behind him, a measly two plates in his hands.

"Show off," calls Peter to giggles around the table.

"Misspent youth catering events at the rugby club," Mike explains as he starts to off-load his cargo. "Pass them down, folks."

"Wouldn't you have been more useful actually on the pitch?" I ask. For some reason, laughter breaks out. "What? What am I missing?"

"I take it you're not a rugby union fan," says Robert as he passes me one of his plates. "Our boy here played for England."

"And for the Lions," adds James. *Lions.* That rings a bell, though I don't quite know what it means; James makes it sound as if it's even more significant than representing one's country.

"Oh. Good to see my finger is nowhere near the pulse, as usual." My self-deprecation kicks off another wave of hilarity. *I'm almost having fun,* I realize. The realization throws me out of myself as if I'm suddenly an observer of my own reality. I watch my fork in its path to the honeydew-melon-and-ham starter on my plate. I watch it spear the melon; I watch it lift toward my mouth.

Suddenly Mike squeezes into the chair next to me, a space that I hadn't even realized was empty, and I'm shaken back into my own self. With his bulk beside me, the table feels rather overcrowded after all. Jana begins a conversation with Robert on her left, and Mike turns to answer a question from Julie on his right. I sit quietly in between, eating and sipping the red wine—not what I would have chosen, but perfectly drinkable—and let my gaze roam around the table. *Be present*, I tell myself. *Be here*. Sofi has changed since the cricket game and is now wearing a flower-print top that sits entirely off her shoulders, revealing the sweep of delicate collarbones beneath skin so perfect that it seems polished. As she makes a gesture to emphasize her point, one of those bare, burnished shoulders lifts. I see Will's eyes rest on it, then flit quickly away.

"People watching?" asks Mike in a low voice, drawing my head round to him.

"A little. Don't you think it feels a bit like a social experiment?"

He catches on immediately. "With different social strata of academia? I suppose."

"Exactly." My eyes have moved back to Sofi. In truth, it's hard not to look at her in any room she occupies. But for all the looking, she's a closed book tonight—no, a blank surface: it's far too easy to project whatever one chooses onto her. Yet earlier she was so very transparent; I wonder what has catalyzed the change. "It's an odd setup when you think about it. Not exactly under university rules, but not free of them either. It must be hardest for the undergrads to navigate."

"Harder for some than others." There's an edge to his voice, and he too is looking in Sofi's direction. But before I can ask what he means, he's reaching across with a bottle. "More wine?"

I put my hand over my glass. "Oh, no, I'm good, thanks. I'm out of practice, truth be told."

"You might be the only one." We survey the table together. There will be some sore heads tomorrow morning. "Water instead, then?"

"Yes, please. I seem to be inordinately thirsty."

"Same." He pours a glass, which I promptly drain, and then pours again. "It's the altitude, I think. I expect it will calm down when we acclimatize."

I look around the table again. "It's a shame that Tanner is missing out," I say. "You haven't heard any more about when he might arrive, have you?"

"Nothing, though if he doesn't make it out at all it will rather scupper his beauty parade."

"Beauty parade?" I'm not following.

He's about to answer, but Jana is flapping a hand animatedly on my other side to get my attention. "Oh, oh, Emily! I forgot to tell you!" The rest of the table falls quiet too, and she pauses, a glint in her eye as she draws out the moment; Jana loves nothing more than a crowd to play to. "There was a break-in." For a moment, I'm confused—she already knows about my home intrusion—but she's still speaking. "At your department. At the theoretical physics building."

"*What?*"

"It's true." She pauses to enjoy the ripple that passes through the table. "Elena rang to tell me." Elena is the secretary for the head of the theoretical physics department, and happens to come from the same Estonian town as Jana. I'm not exactly sure that they have anything other than their origins in common but it seems to be enough, and anyway, Jana is an inveterate networker. "She's been trying to get hold of you, but what with you traveling . . . I meant to tell you earlier, but I got distracted by the starters." She picks up her glass again, and makes a show of inspecting the contents. "Or perhaps the wine." She gets some laughs for that.

"Why is Elena trying to get hold of me in particular?"

"Yours is one of the offices that was raided. Yours and Dr. Carver's." Her accent is becoming a little more evident as the evening, and the alcohol consumption, progresses.

"Mine?" I stare at her. A break-in. *Another* break-in: break-ins, plural. A small curl of unease has settled in my stomach. "What did they take?"

"She's not sure they took anything at all, actually. Did you leave any valuables in your office?"

I try to think. "No, I don't think so. No money to speak of—only small change for tea and biscuits at eleven. I had a very nice Montblanc pen in a drawer, but that's about it. Did they take any of the computing equipment?"

"No. She's going to email you pictures so you can see if anything is missing."

"Who on earth would bother breaking into the theoretical physics building? It's not like there's lots of expensive kit just lying around in that particular department. Unless they were planning to steal blackboards." This is Caleb. I know which one he is now, and I'm coming to appreciate his dry sense of humor. I had thought him shy, but succinct is probably more accurate. Akash *is* shy, but very polite. James I have yet to get a handle on. Everything about him screams entitled, privately educated posh boy, not overly burdened with academic ambition, but surely there's more to him if Robert deemed him worthy of an invitation. Or maybe he's simply here on account of being fun to have around. Like a Labrador.

"You're assuming the culprits actually know what theoretical physics is," Mike interjects.

"Very good point, Mike. I barely know what theoretical physics is, and I'm the physics outreach manager," says Jana. This is rewarded by a loud burst of laughter around the table; a quick satisfied smile creeps briefly across her face.

"Two break-ins," Peter says. "You're pretty much the unluckiest person in the world right now."

"Or the luckiest. Seems like literally nothing was taken each time." But the cold knot in my stomach belies my upbeat response.

"Attagirl," Peter says approvingly. "Loving the glass-half-full approach. Good job you didn't leave your laptop there."

"I know. It's actually off being fixed right now."

"Is that a new one I saw in your rucksack then?" asks Peter with obvious interest. "Which one did you get?"

"Sorry, tech head. That's Nick's. No exciting new purchases, I'm afraid."

"You're able to access it?" asks Peter.

I'm about to say, *Yes, I know all his passwords*, but then it occurs to me that that's absolutely against the university digital security policy, even for privately owned laptops that access the network, so instead, I say, "I've got my own profile on it." Which is true too.

The conversations are starting to fragment again. The light is failing now; we light a multitude of candles and a couple of gas-powered lamps. From my seat, I have a view through the open door to the salon, but I can't quite see the clock with its intricate swirls and swoops; still, I'm acutely aware that it's there, ticking off the time that has passed and marching implacably into the unavoidable future. The candlelight will be running liquid gold along those etched channels, drawing fiery hieroglyphs in the air as the pendulum passes back and forth. I eat and I sip cautiously and I smile and I talk into a babble of background noise that rises as the levels in the wineglasses fall, but I can't quite dissolve the ball of unease in my abdomen.

"Earth to Ems," says Jana, making me start.

"Sorry," I say guiltily. We're past dessert and onto the coffee now. I turn my full attention to Jana. "It's just . . . this break-in at the department. It seems a little strange, is all. Mine isn't exactly the easiest office to access." It's on the second floor. Surely the ground floor offices would be the low-hanging fruit?

"Doesn't that depend on where they entered from? They probably didn't saunter in through the front door." Her movements are very deliberate as she puts down her glass. Jana is smashed, I realize. I see Will looking at her across the table, his face oddly closed; then he turns back to his conversation with James.

"Yes, I suppose so." But I can't think of a possible access point on the second floor without a very long ladder, and surely lugging a ladder around would be rather inconvenient, not to say conspicuous? "Still, it's strange."

Jana looks at me skeptically. "You mean, given the break-in at your house? Come on, that's just a coincidence." She's right. I know she's right, but I still can't quite shake off the *oddness* of it. She eyes my face, and her expression softens. "Honey, shit just happens. Bad things happen to good people; Christ, you must know that more than most at the moment." Her lips twist ruefully, and I feel mine do the same. *Bless you, Jana,* I think. It's such a relief to speak with someone who doesn't make Nick an elephant in the room. "The shit doesn't have to be part of a grand conspiracy. It's just life."

"Wow, that's a really uplifting philosophy. Or does good stuff just happen too?"

"Nope. The things you want, you have to work for." She shrugs and I laugh. "Such is life. Now, come on, eat cheese," she orders, pushing the cheese platter toward me. "Lots of it. We need to spend this week putting some fat on your ridiculously twiglike bones."

Much, much later, I'm alone in the kitchen, looking for some water to take up to bed with me, as my thirst has not abated much. I have a candle stuck in an empty wine bottle for illumination; it's not terribly effective as a searchlight. Everyone else has either headed for bed already or moved to the salon for some kind of parlor game; intermittent bouts of laughter and shouting emanate from that direction. There's a door in the corner; I open it, holding the candle in front of me, and am confronted by a very small walk-in pantry. The shelves are stacked with dry goods and candles and cleaning products; their labels loom at me alarmingly when I move the light toward them, then fade just as suddenly when the light moves on—but there's absolutely no water.

There's a sudden noise behind me; I turn. It's Sofi. "Are you looking for something?" she asks. I can't quite tell if there's a slur in her words or if it's just her accent. She also has a candle in a wine bottle; she places it carefully on the table. The flickering light makes the red-and-white-checkered squares of the plastic tablecloth swim.

"Just bottled water."

"I think there's some under the table." There's definitely a slight slur, but her accent is stronger than I've heard it too.

I twitch up the tablecloth; the plastic is slightly tacky to the touch. On the floor underneath, there are a couple of pallets of two-liter bottles. "Bingo. Thanks. Do you want some too?"

"Yes, please." She's moved to position herself in the frame of the open back door, despite the fact that the outside air is decidedly chilly now. I put down my own candle and take a couple of tumblers from a shelf and fill them up. She turns to take one as I approach, half of her face touched by the moonlight and the other half painted by the flickering yellow candlelight; then she moves past the doorframe, leaving the yellow light behind. I have the strangest sensation that she's stepped through a curtain into another world, something eldritch and dangerous. She might be a wraith now: an echo of the past or a promise of the future. "You can see the stars really clearly tonight," she says over her shoulder, though all I catch of her face is a glint of light from one eye. "Come and have a look."

I step closer to the door. She's folding herself to sit on the edge of the large concrete slab that acts as a doorstep. I hesitate for a moment, then step through the doorframe into the dimly lit outdoor world to sit down beside her, carefully placing my water behind me. The concrete slab is cold through my jeans; I draw my legs in and wrap my arms around my knees to ward off the chill. We're at the back of the chalet, facing the mountain rather than the view of the valley, which must surely now be sprinkled with clusters of lights from villages and roads, like galaxies of stars but on land. Here, though, there are no such lights. There are no colors whatsoever; they have bled away to leave only grades of darkness.

"Look at the stars," Sofi murmurs encouragingly.

I unfold a little, wrapping my arms around my middle instead, and look up at the cold lights piercing the black velvet of the sky. *This ought to be beautiful,* I think. *I ought to be stunned by the wonders of nature.* Maybe if I look up enough, if I go through the motions for long enough, eventually something will break through.

"Are you sad?" Sofi's voice is not more than a whisper beside me.

"What?" I'm not sure I've heard her properly.

"At dinner, you looked happy from time to time." Apparently I wasn't the only one indulging in people watching at dinner. I look sideways at her. Her dark head is tipped up to the stars. "I was wondering if you really were, or if the sadness is just *there*, all the time."

It's such an unexpectedly frank question that it jolts me into answering with matching honesty. "I think you can be more than one thing at any one time. Feel more than one emotion."

She nods slowly, her eyes still on the heavens. I don't think she's aware that I'm looking at her. It occurs to me that it's extraordinarily intimate to be sitting here in this gray-black world, cloaked in shadows and moonlight, close enough that I can feel the heat from her body crossing the mere inches between us; and as if it has just occurred to her also, she turns her head and I realize I was wrong: she's utterly aware of me. Her eyes gleam darkly liquid as she studies me. I am years, decades, eons out of practice: by the time I realize that she's moving toward me, by the time I realize what's about to happen, it's actually happening. Her lips, impossibly soft, are touching mine, warm velvet imbued with wine brushing gently against me. For the merest of instants, I'm frozen, in shock at what is happening, and at the sensation, so different to Nick—

Nick. I'm married. She's an undergrad. Everything that's wrong with this floods my brain at once. I jerk backward. "Sofi—no."

"Sorry. I'm sorry." She's scrambling to her feet, in a tangle of elbows and limbs that suddenly resolves into an upright figure—an upright figure that's fleeing.

"Sofi—wait—," I say helplessly, but she's gone, she's slipped away into the world of yellow candlelight, leaving me in the gray shadows on the cold, hard step, wondering what just happened. I sit on the step until my bones ache from the cold of it, trying to puzzle it out. Her kiss still rests on my lips. Is this my fault? Am I so out of touch with the rest of the world, so grief deadened as to have entirely missed signals from her along the way? And when I did react, my instinctive reaction was *I'm married*. In truth it was that—rather than the fact that she's an undergraduate, and what's more, an undergraduate at my own college—that shocked me into action. *I'm married*. But I'm not now.

Eventually I pick up the tumbler and stand up, slow and stiff from the cold, and turn for the door, then stifle a half scream. James is standing just outside the doorway, lolling nonchalantly against the wall of the chalet, his eyes gleaming as he looks at me. His sharp cheekbones are painted silver by the moonlight. For a moment I'm afraid that I'm seeing the skeleton beneath.

"James." My heart is still hammering. I'm clutching the glass so tightly, I'm suddenly afraid it might break; I deliberately loosen my grip. "I didn't see you."

"I know. Did I scare you?" There's none of the apologetic note one would expect, nor the respect for someone in authority. The puppyish enthusiasm of his persona at dinner is gone; this version of James is altogether sharper.

"I just didn't know you were there." *How long has he been there? Did he see Sofi try to kiss me?* "Did you need something?" I ask briskly. *If he did see, what will he do with that knowledge?*

43

"Why would I need anything from you?" I can see from the reflected gleam of silver light that he's smiling, the same smile as at dinner, but in this odd light, I can see only menace in it: a deliberate show of teeth.

He's mocking me, I realize, shocked. But why? Because of what he's seen? "Then good night," I say. My tone is as sharp as I can make it, but I haven't the practice; the cutting edge has never had much whetting. I take the few short steps to the doorway, determined not to alter my path because of his presence, but equally taking care not to trip over his outstretched legs. Passing through the doorframe takes me back into the normal world, where color sits in the pools of light around the candles—mere stubs now—in the two wine bottles: the red and white of the checkered tablecloth, the green glass of the bottles, the gleaming gold of a crest on the wine labels. Sofi's kiss, soft and secret and sweet, crosses the divide with me; I feel it on my lips still. So too do James' parting words, said in a smiling, languid poisonous drawl: "Sweet dreams."

Crossing through the kitchen to the stairs, I can feel the hammering of my heart, an uneven and ragged tattoo above the low murmur of chatter from the remaining revelers in the salon. I have one foot on the first tread of the stairs when a loud, ringing chime stops me in my tracks. The sound, a single peel of a discordant bell, reverberates into absolute silence as if even the darkness outside is holding its breath. I turn slowly, one foot still raised on the step; from where I'm standing, the occupants of the salon are hidden from sight, but the clock is in full view, facing me squarely, standing tall and upright, like an unwavering justice that sees and considers all. *It's judging me,* I think nonsensically. *Me, and everyone else.* The pendulum swishes back and forth, implacable and fierce, golden-red skeins of light rippling across its surface. Half of the plate glass protecting the clockface appears darkly mottled, and reflected light has cast a red hue on the other half as if from a fire banked in the belly of the timepiece. As I stare at the face, I could swear I see wisps of shadows moving beneath the glass. *The shadows from the world outside*, I think absurdly. *The netherworld: it's inside, too. It's crept inside the clock.*

"Jesus, I haven't heard it chime before. Is it going to do that at twelve fifteen a.m. every night?" someone remarks in the salon, breaking both the silence and the spell that has kept me in place. My feet are released from their involuntary freeze and I take the steps two at a time toward the sanctuary of my room, with nary a care for the noise I'm making.

Julie

I feel completely stupid writing this. And I am stupid; it thoroughly serves me right. If I hadn't felt that irrational, awful flash of jealousy last night when James looked so bloody impressed that Sofi keeps a diary—if I hadn't felt that, I wouldn't have pretended that I do too, and then found myself having to go through this ridiculous charade of actually being seen to write in this stupid notebook. The only thing it's ever held before is my shopping list, but now it's supposed to be the depositary of all my dreams and ambitions, as if writing those things down will suddenly transform me from a chemistry student who dropped English after GCSE into the next Jane Austen. Stupid. Stupid, stupid, stupid.

And I have a hangover. That was stupid too. I always feel so maudlin the morning after a big night. In the true spirit of the chalet, we're having a reading morning, which basically means any academic pursuit—and I did try: I sat in the salon, staring at that molecular spectroscopy chapter, but my brain simply wouldn't function and the relentless ticking of that bloody clock was like fingernails down a blackboard. If

47

I'd clenched my teeth any harder, I'd have broken them. So I escaped outside and here I am, writing a fake diary. I'm not even sure it really is a diary anyway—Sofi's, I mean. I've caught glimpses before and it seems more like a collection of letters. But why would she be writing letters that she never sends?

I hate feeling jealous. It's mean and unkind and just so much effort. And I love Sofi; truly I do, which makes me feel even worse. It's just . . . does literally everyone else have to love her too? Really, she's so beautiful that it's inescapable—you can't not notice it. Even the men who pretend she's not their type are only saying it because they know she would never look at them twice. Except Mike, maybe—that's an interesting one. I'd almost say he's avoiding her like the plague, though I can't think why. She hasn't done anything with him that I know of. Unless she has and didn't tell me? I guess that could be possible, perhaps for that awful bet with James? I still can't quite believe he even suggested it, let alone that she took him up on it—though, to be fair, it was a couple of years ago; they've both grown up since. I suppose I would feel hurt, if she had done something with Mike and not told me, though I'd have no right. Everyone should be able to keep secrets. Not that I have ever done anything worth hiding. There's an ambition for you, fake diary—I want to do something that's worth keeping secret!

Anyway, my point is, I like it best when you really love someone and then they become beautiful to you; you know that hardly anyone else would see it, which makes you feel privileged, like you've been gifted the ability to see them how they truly are. I'll never forget how pretty my mum's green eyes were or how the laughter lines around them only made

them lovelier. Probably tens of people saw those eyes every day,
but I was granted the gift of appreciating them; I was special.
Everyone's been granted the gift with Sofi, and if everyone's
special, then nobody is.

It's strange being here. The dynamics are all weird, like
magnetic field lines gone awry. All the normal college rules of
engagement have been erased and it makes it kind of awkward.
I don't want to be calling professors by their first names; it feels
too false. And for all we're supposed to be a homogenous soup
of people on equal terms, that isn't really how it's shaking
out. All the undergraduates—Sofi, Caleb, James, Akash and
myself—are sticking together, even though I barely knew Caleb
or Akash before. They're nice, though. Caleb has a quiet, sly
sense of humor that a lot of people might miss. I'm not sure
he cares if people do miss it; I think he says the things he says
purely for his own amusement. Akash doesn't say much but he
seems sweet. And of course, I knew James before. After all, it's
his bloody fault that I'm writing this thing.

Except it's not; it's mine. Mine and the green-eyed monster. I've
made a decision, fake diary: I will not be jealous again. I've
decided. It's done.

5

Someone has been in my room.

I stand frozen in the corridor, eyeing the door—the door that I carefully yanked closed to ensure the latch had caught, that is now sitting a couple of inches ajar. It sticks so stubbornly on the frame that I can't believe it could have come open accidentally: someone has been in my room—might even still be in my room. I can hear my accelerated heartbeat in my ears, feel it in my throat. *Calm down,* I tell myself in exasperation. *You're completely safe.* Unlike with the intruder incident in Oxford, if I yelled now, at least half a dozen people would come running.

I approach the door carefully, silently, swaying my head from side to side to see as much of the room as I can through the small gap. There's no sign of anyone: the room is as empty as I left it. I push the door open and enter warily, looking around to see if anything has been disturbed. On the left-hand bed, my sleeping bag is stretched out as I'd left it, unzipped and thrown open to air. My rucksack looks untouched too, resting on the right-hand bed, an open bag of toiletries spilling out of its yawning mouth. Everything looks as it should. I look around again, running a mental inventory. Something is off. I know it, but I can't quite see it—and then I do. My laptop has been moved.

It's roughly where I left it on the bed, but rotated through ninety degrees; I'm not sure I'd have noticed the difference if I hadn't been primed by the door being ajar. I step forward to lay a hand on it and find it's warm to the touch, which can only have been generated internally; there's certainly no sun slanting into the room at this hour. I look around again, as if the very walls might offer up some answers, but if this dusty old wooden room knows something, it's not telling. Instead I sit on the edge of the bed and flip up the lid of the laptop—or, more accurately, Nick's MacBook. It comes to life with a low whirr that I feel through my thighs as well as hear, showing the log-in screen, with Nick's profile autopopulated, patiently waiting for a password.

Nick's profile. Not mine.

The log-in screen should default to the profile of the last user. When I used it last, I had of course been using my own profile. Someone has been trying to break into Nick's profile.

I find myself glancing around as if the weight of an unknown pair of eyes is resting on the back of my neck, but of course there's nobody there. Still, someone here, someone in the chalet party, must be targeting me. The gnawing unease that I felt at dinner returns, only magnified a hundredfold. An urge to bolt back to Oxford, to my terraced house with its newly mended rear lock, floods through me and my fists ball up; I feel them pressing at my mouth though I wasn't conscious of raising them. *I brought it with me*, I think bleakly as panic rises. *Everything I was trying to escape, I've brought with me. The grief, the solitude, and now this too.*

Stop, I tell myself sternly. *Think.* And anyway, if I brought it with me, what's the point of bolting? It could all just follow me home again.

51

Think it through. Is there a way to know if they succeeded in accessing Nick's profile? I think, *I bet Will or Mike or Peter would know*—and then I stop. I can't ask Will or Mike or Peter. I can't ask anyone here, because I don't know who the culprit is. *Can I narrow it down, though?*

I take a deep breath, then another, and try to think of everybody's actions through the morning, but it's not immediately obvious whether anyone at all can be discounted as a suspect. I'd set myself up in a corner of one of the salon sofas and right now others are spread out variously through the salon and the dining room; some, like myself, are working through research papers or holiday reading, though Sofi, Akash and Julie are outside, doing little of anything as far as I could tell. People have been moving through the chalet all morning, climbing up and down the stairs, getting drinks or sweaters or books or other sundries; I haven't exactly been taking notes, except perhaps in respect of Sofi and James. The former hasn't quite met my gaze yet, managing to pass me with her head a little too high, her focus a little too fixed on something else. James, on the other hand, has been far too keen to catch my eye, with a malicious humor lurking in the back of his own. *He did see*, I think again resignedly, dropping back into the endless loop my mind has been stuck in all morning—and all night, if I'm honest. I had found myself slipping into a half-waking, half-sleeping dream where I was hunting desperately for something—I didn't know what, but I knew beyond a shadow of a doubt that its loss was all my fault—with someone or something watching my every move. The part of me that knew I was dozing actively tried, repeatedly, to wake up, but every time I managed it, the dream reached back for me and dragged me down again; even now, I still feel a lingering cold dread. *He did see. But really, what can he do with that knowledge?* She tried to kiss me, and I turned her down: that surely couldn't be used to destroy my career? But that assumes what actually happened is what's reported, and there's no guarantee of that; it never takes much to cast events in a different light, if one is so inclined. Of course, he might not report anything; perhaps he didn't see after all.

He did see, though. I'm sure of it. And I rather suspect he's the sort of person who might be so inclined.

I shake myself in annoyance: the laptop is my immediate concern. That, and the fact that someone here—in this very chalet, someone with whom I share meals and a roof to sleep under—is targeting me. I look at the laptop resting on my lap. I doubt it would hold its heat for long; whoever is to blame, they hadn't long left before I came upstairs. *Not Jana, then*—not that I thought it would be, but she came down late and immediately stretched out on a sofa, a thriller covering her face, and hasn't moved since. But really, can I definitively rule anyone else out? It's patently ridiculous to consider Will or Peter and Robert, all of whom I have known for years, but if I'm being strictly scientific about it—*a scientist through and through?*—then I have to admit that I can't truly strike anyone other than Jana off the list.

That's right: you can't, so don't waste time on it. Back to the first question, I tell myself. *What can I check to see if whoever it was actually succeeded?* I type in Nick's password and am duly granted access. Activity Monitor: would that tell me anything? I scan the processes that are running—lists and lists of activities that are, in the main, utterly meaningless to me—and I manage to find the CPU history, but even that doesn't seem to answer my question; it's just black boxes with tiny green and red squares popping up. Ordinarily I'd google the problem, but of course there's no Wi-Fi for googling. I sit, frustratedly tapping at my teeth with one fingernail while I try to think of another course of action, but nothing presents itself. Finally, at a loss for what else to do, I change Nick's password to usea7iron; that at least seems fairly unguessable, and I won't have to write it down to remember it.

I close up the laptop and look around the room for a hiding place. The room is remarkably ill-suited to secrecy: apart from the beds, there isn't another stick of furniture in it. After a moment's deliberation, I pull up the end of one of the mattresses and place the device underneath, sandwiched between the wooden slats and the thin mattress. It's not exactly a hiding place that would stand up to a thorough search, but it's the best that I can do, short of carrying the thing around with me all day. For a moment I consider actually doing that—emptying out the rucksack and carrying the laptop in it for the afternoon's walk—but I'm sure someone will challenge me on it; Peter at the very least knows that I have a much smaller (too small for the MacBook) day pack with me for walking. In any case, as far as I know, the entire party is intending to walk. I survey the room again, trying to ignore the continued uneasy scratch at the back of my neck, that sense of being watched. It's pure paranoia, of course, though from now on the line between caution and paranoia is going to be a hard one to tightrope walk. I'm about to leave the room when I realize that I've forgotten the reference book I came up to fetch. I fish it out of my rucksack, and then, after a moment's hesitation, I grab my toiletries bag and arrange it carefully on the mattress above the laptop so that it looks carelessly dropped, unzipped with some items poking out. Then I take a quick photo of it: nobody could possibly access the laptop without disturbing the toiletries, and now I'll know for sure if they have. At last I leave the room, very carefully pulling the door closed until I hear the latch click securely into place. I'm turning to go downstairs when I'm brought to an abrupt halt by the presence of Sofi loitering in the corridor.

"Oh," I say, and then can't think of anything to follow it.

"Can I . . ." She gestures awkwardly to my room. "Can I talk to you for a wee minute?"

"Um, sure." I turn back and open the door that I have only just so very carefully closed, then usher her ahead of me into the room, looking around the corridor before I enter myself. I'm half expecting to see James watching again, but there's nobody there. Still, I intentionally leave the door slightly ajar behind me when I enter, in a Regency-era declaration of no illicit behavior. Inside, I suddenly panic that Sofi might sit down on the bed, right above the laptop—whilst she's only a slip of a thing, I can't imagine it would be very good for it—but she walks between the beds, turning just before the terrace door and remaining standing, her arms crossed protectively in front of her stomach.

"What can I do for you?" I ask briskly.

"I . . . um . . . I wanted to say I'm sorry for last night." The words come out in a rush; she doesn't risk a glance at my face until they've been uttered. I wait. She has more to say, I think. "I didn't mean anything by it. I was just drunk—"

"Don't *do* that." My response is sharp, sharp enough to produce a flush in her cheeks.

"I'm sorry; what—?"

"You're not a child. Take responsibility."

She looks at the ground. Then she collects herself. "Okay. Then . . . I am sorry about last night. I made you uncomfortable."

I incline my head ruefully in acknowledgment. "I *was* drunk, you know," she says, looking at me this time. She has a hand at the ready, fingers already splayed, as if to ward off anything I might say, but I don't interrupt. "But that isn't why I"—she stumbles on the words as if it's harder to say the thing than do it—"why I kissed you." Now she's looking steadfastly at her trainers.

I let a few seconds pass before I say anything. "Thank you." She nods, still inspecting her trainers, which are plain white, mildly dusty and unworthy of all this attention. "But why did you do it?"

"Oh." Her gaze swings up, then quickly away. "Well, I wanted to. You're . . . you're someone I admire and . . ." She shrugs, an elegant ripple across her narrow shoulders. "And I suppose I misread things. I thought you wanted me to."

"I suppose people usually do." She darts a questioning glance at me. "Want you to, I mean."

She flushes. "Well, that's not quite—" She stops, seeing the warning again in my raised eyebrows: *Be honest. Take responsibility*. "Yes. Often they do."

"You're an undergraduate, Sofi. You were putting me in a very awkward position."

"I'm not, actually."

"Not what?"

"Not an undergraduate. I just graduated—PPE is a three-year course."

"But—but Julie said you're sharing a house together next year." Naturally I'd assumed that meant they were both still undergrads. Julie must be; chemistry is a four-year course. I hadn't thought about the fact that PPE (Politics, Philosophy and Economics) takes only three years.

"Yes. I'm staying in Oxford next year for the GDL." GDL: Graduate Diploma in Law. A one-year conversion course for aspiring lawyers who didn't study law as an undergraduate degree.

"Oh." *Not an undergraduate.* I breathe out a little: that really is a somewhat better fact pattern, though still not ideal. I regroup. "Nevertheless, a staff member involved with a student, even a former student—you must see how it would look in the current environment—"

"I don't see why it should look like anything." She's visibly nettled. "You've never taught me. And we're both adults."

I am, I think. *But you're not; you're still just a child, for all you think otherwise.* "Sofi," I say as gently as I can, "don't be naive."

Her face shutters abruptly. I wonder if that was the worst possible thing I could have said to her. "Well, anyway." Her voice is as tightly closed as her expression. "We'll be leaving soon for the walk. I have to get ready."

I stand aside to let her go and ignore the temptation to say something, anything, to smooth the situation: it *should* be uncomfortable for her. She can't continue to career through life ignoring the impact of her actions on others. And it should be uncomfortable for me too. I'm very much aware that my reaction last night had nothing to do with her student status, although it ought to have. What might I have done, on another occasion? What might I do at a time when Nick no longer lingers so close to me? Already he is drawing away, or I am drawing away from him. Is it being here that is causing that? It's what I need to happen—what I was hoping for, even—but nonetheless there's a sadness in it.

But Sofi . . . A door opened is a difficult thing. The urge to take another look inside is powerful; I can't allow the opportunity to arise again. I leave the room, closing the bedroom door with great care to ensure it catches, and start to descend the stairs. I make it all the way to the bottom before it occurs to me that the encounter with Sofi has derailed my analysis of the laptop situation. I've avoided the most critical question: *Why?* Why is someone targeting me? I can't even imagine—but no, I'm being stupid. Of course I can. *They're not targeting me. They're targeting Nick. Or something Nick knew.* A cold wave sweeps over me. *Maybe it wasn't a mistake that the intruder at home was lurking in the study alcove. Maybe the intruder was exactly where he—or she—wanted to be, looking for something of Nick's.* In which case, it must have been someone here, someone who knew us both—

"Everything okay?"

I startle at the voice and realize I'm standing stock-still at the bottom of the stairs. Mike has paused in his path from salon to kitchen, practically midstride. *We must look like a photograph,* I think distractedly: a snapshot of stillness presumed to have been taken from an arc of motion, only neither of us is moving. "You look like someone walked over your grave."

"Yes . . . I just . . . Yes." It's not the most articulate of responses, I realize.

He eyes me calmly. "Come help me in the kitchen." It's a suggestion, not an order, but it's a relief to have someone else take the lead. I nod and then look blindly at the book in my hands, then back at Mike. He turns back to call generally to the occupants of the salon, "Emily and I are making baguette sandwiches to take on the walk with us. We'll do a selection of ham, cheese and both. Shout if that doesn't work for you."

"Do you need any help?" calls James. I find myself tensing and wishing his manners were a little less impeccable. But to my relief, Mike replies, "Thanks, but I think we'll manage."

In the kitchen we set up a production line, with him slicing and buttering the baguettes before I pack them with some combination of ham, cheese, tomato and lettuce and wrap them in kitchen foil. It's reassuringly mundane work that I can manage perfectly adequately, despite the distracting loop of thoughts in my head. *What did Nick have that someone wants? And who exactly is it that wants it?* The list of people here is running though my head, but not all of them would have known Nick; I can't imagine that any of the undergraduates would have known him, nor the postdoc Olive. Robert, Peter, Mike, Jana and Will did know him, obviously. *But they are my friends,* I think. Well, not Mike, though I expect he will be, in time. I can't truly be suspecting them, can I? *It's that bloody home intrusion,* I think. *That and the break-in at the department. I've lost all sense of perspective and plunged into paranoia.*

"Okay?" asks Mike again, and I realize my hands have stilled.

"Yes, sorry." I resume packing lettuce onto a baguette. "I'm clearly a bit distracted today. Anyway, what have you been working on this morning?" I ask, mainly to head off any possibility of him asking me about my strange behavior, though he doesn't seem the type to pry.

"Statistics. Specifically, Bayesian inference."

"Oh, Lord." Bayesian statistics. Conditional probability, but more than that: treating probability as an expression of a degree of belief in a theorem, and using outcomes to update that theorem. It's important, but not exactly fun. Statistics rarely is.

"I know. Not my favorite either." He grimaces. *Not Mike,* I think. *He couldn't have been the one in my house. He couldn't hide that bulk; it's unmistakable.* "But I offered to teach a course on it in Hilary term for the first-year grad students, so I'm brushing up."

"You offered? What on earth possessed you to do that?"

He huffs out an exhalation that might be a low laugh, but before he can answer, a head pops round the kitchen door: Olive the postgrad. "Remember I'm vegan," she says, her corkscrew curls bouncing.

"I thought you were vegetarian," says Mike. It's possible he's startled by this pronouncement, but given his usual granite equanimity, it's hard to tell.

"No, vegan," she insists.

"Right," he says neutrally. "Lettuce and tomato for you, then?"

"Fine. No butter, though. Thanks."

"Right." His tone is neutral again. Olive exits the kitchen and Mike looks at me. "Oops. Last night's dinner was dripping in butter."

"What she doesn't know won't hurt her." I'm trying not to laugh, and I sense he is too; I see traces of it lurking round his eyes. Those eyes are what you have to read, I'm realizing. If you relied on the rest of his face, you'd be utterly lost as to what he's thinking.

The walk that's planned for today, Peter informs me, is an easy-ish route to break us in on the first day, descending from the top of the Prarion *télécabine* to the bottom, via Col de la Forclaz and Vaudagne, and returning via the *télécabine*. The names mean nothing to me; I nod at the right places without making any effort to remember what I've been told—it's not like I'll be leading this expedition. As Peter talks, I survey the group milling on the lawn, and guess that everyone here, bar Jana and Olive perhaps, will be fitter than me. The sheer quantity of technical clothing is mildly intimidating; it's as if I've woken up in a Patagonia brand advert. My tan shorts, which are neither *lightweight* nor *durable water repellent* nor *UV resistant* are clearly not up to scratch. Thank heavens for Jana, who is dressed in black three-quarter yoga leggings and a sky blue vest top that wonderfully frames her ample cleavage. And for Sofi, I suppose. Her endless legs are topped once again by her Daisy Dukes. I look everywhere else.

Jana catches my eye after Peter moves on to share his knowledge with others. "Do you think there will be a test later?" she asks, tongue firmly in cheek.

"If there is, I'll fail."

"Rubbish. You've never failed anything in your life. Bless him, though," she says fondly, her eyes following Peter. "He does love it here; even I'm in danger of finding his enthusiasm catching. Oh—we're off." She's right; the group is starting to move. I shrug on my small day pack and follow. We pick our way carefully along the narrow path, strung out in a line until we reach the main path up to the hotel, but then, released from that single file, groups begin to form: undergrads with undergrads, staff with staff. Like tending to like. Robert had a quiet word with all of us staff members earlier to encourage us to speak to everyone throughout the day, as otherwise cliques might form, but nobody is following his instructions just yet.

"How's the hangover?" I ask Jana as we start up the stony path. It's certainly much more of an ordeal to climb it rather than descend; I can already feel my calf muscles working. I suspect that soon I will be very thankful not to be carrying the extra weight of Nick's laptop. Hiding it was the right option.

"The hangover I can cope with; it's the sulking that's hard to take." She tips her head toward Will, who is just ahead of us on the path. James has hung back deliberately to engage him in conversation and they begin to talk animatedly, though I can't hear the topic.

"I don't understand," I admit. I really have been a bad friend; I have no idea why Will should be cross with her.

She sighs. "We're in the midst of another round of IVF. Round five, but who's counting . . . ? Anyway, we're waiting to see if it has taken, so to speak. I shouldn't be drinking at all."

Ah. I'd assumed, when I saw the glass in her hand last night, that I'd got the timings wrong. Now Will's facial expressions of last night make sense. "But?" I prod gently.

"There isn't a but—not one that's defensible. I absolutely shouldn't have been drinking. It's just . . ." She pauses, as if trying not to say it, but the words burst out of her nonetheless. "God, I fucking hate this stage. It's torture. I mean, the whole thing is torture: I'm about a stone heavier than I should be with all the drugs for the egg harvesting, with this ridiculous moon face—"

"You don't have a moon face." I look around, checking that nobody can hear her, but we've lagged behind and are out of earshot.

"I absolutely have a moon face, and I feel like a fucking elephant and don't even talk to me about sex, because there's zero chance of being in the mood for that—but this part, this waiting, is the absolute worse. Waiting and waiting, and the longer it goes on, the more excited I can see Will getting, and then I know he's only going to be even more disappointed with me when it doesn't work—"

"Not disappointed with *you*, surely." I glance sideways at her, dismayed. "Disappointed with the situation."

"Yes." She takes a breath. "Yes, you're right. With the situation, of course. Only . . . only it feels like with me, too.

62

He won't even talk about marriage; he keeps saying we can discuss it when this is all over, which makes me wonder: Is one dependent on the other? The first time, during that first round, it was kind of exciting. Every time since, it's like waiting for the guillotine blade to drop." She's chewing at the side of her lip, a nervous habit that I've seldom seen from her, her eyes on her footing as we trudge along.

"Oh, honey," I say helplessly, sticking out a hand to halt her, "I'm sorry."

She looks back at me, hands on her hips, breathing a little hard from both her outburst and the climb, and tries for a smile, her eyes overbright. "It's not your fault."

"I know, but I feel like I should have been there for you. I've been too wrapped in everything with Nick—"

"Ems, your husband died. You get a free pass. Come here." She pulls me into a hug. There's a light sheen of sweat on her neck. It's not at all unpleasant; she smells warm and earthy. There's a comfort in the softness of her, the give in her waist. After a second she releases me, pressing the heels of her hands briefly against her eyes. "Though if you're planning a return to Planet Normal, I would definitely appreciate it."

"Done. I'm here. Planet Normal. Or normal-ish, at least."

She smiles, a stronger effort than before. "Normal-ish will do. Come on, we'd better catch up."

Normal-ish. I think of Sofi, of that not-so-secret kiss, and of what James may or may not choose to do with whatever he saw. I think of my hammering heart and of the strange clock; of the break-ins and the warm laptop and the fact that someone in this very group must be responsible. *Normal-ish*: I should know better than to make promises I'm not certain I can keep.

6

After ninety minutes of walking, we stop to eat our sandwiches, settling in clumps on boulders by the side of the path. In keeping with Robert's forecast, the sky is gloriously cloudless; there's already an uncomfortable tightness in the skin across the back of my neck. I apply some more sunscreen before I start to unwrap my sandwich, glancing up to find Sofi's eyes on me; she jerks them quickly away. I sigh inwardly. If this awkwardness hangs between us all week, someone is bound to notice, but I can't see that talking to her again is going to help.

"Who has the chocolate?" asks Peter.

Robert starts to fish in his rucksack, then hands a slab to Peter.

"Save some for me. I haven't even started my sandwich yet," I say.

"You snooze, you lose," says Peter, but he breaks off a line and hands it to me. I place it carefully in the shade of my rucksack.

"So, Sofi, are you planning to specialize in any particular aspect of law?" asks Jana, turning to the younger woman. I suppress a smile at Jana's rather transparent attempt to curry favor with Robert.

Sofi nods. "It's probably a little premature to have a fixed idea, given I haven't had a broad experience of all practice areas yet, but I'm thinking intellectual property. I've been doing some work with the university IP rights management team, and I've found it really interesting."

"I've never had to worry about it—there are scant few patents coming out of my line of work," I say wryly. "But Nick was always rather against patents, even though his projects often resulted in patent applications. He used to wonder what could be achieved if everyone just shared their work."

"Yes, but Nick was an idealist and a purist," Peter says, rueful admiration in his voice. A silence falls on the group: a respectful reflection. Peter shakes it off before it can grow too heavy, too difficult to shatter. "I, on the other hand, am a moneygrubbing little cockroach who is absolutely in favor of any and all patents that might make me very, very rich."

"We know," says Jana, reaching out an arm to affectionately tousle his hair. "It's almost endearing."

"It's a valid debate, though," Mike offers. I hadn't noticed him join the group, but somehow all the subgroups have merged into this one. "How do you encourage research and innovation if there's no reward for those who put the time and money into R and D? But equally, for the sake of mankind we want the fastest advancements possible, and that means quick and effective sharing of data and ideas—but you would need everyone to buy into that model."

"It's like the escalator argument," Julie puts in. "You know, on the Tube."

"What's that?" Caleb asks her, saving the rest of us, myself included, from having to ask.

Julie's cheeks are filling with warmth as the group's attention focuses on her. *She's the opposite of Sofi, and not just in coloring*, I think. *An entirely open book.* "Well, if everyone stands on the Tube escalators, instead of walking, then everyone gets there faster. It's counterintuitive but it's true; there's been research on it."

"Ah, I see," I say, catching on. "An individual might get there faster by walking or running, but on average everybody gets there faster if they all just stand."

She's nodding. "Exactly. You need altruism for it to work. Everybody has to forgo their own advantage for the sake of the greater good."

"That's a great example, Julie," Will says, and there's a general chorus of agreement. She flushes a little at the praise and the general goodwill. Only James' face is oddly closed, I notice.

"But . . . altruism? Really?" Peter says. "Isn't it just a little like socialism: great in theory, but a disaster in practice? I mean, everyone wants something for themselves, right? And that's a good thing: it keeps us striving for more and better."

"I suppose it's a good thing if kept in check. But I'm now imagining Peter stomping on the heads of all the obedient souls standing on the escalator as he makes a mad dash for the exit," says Will. That draws some laughs, not least from Peter, who throws up his hands, palms forward, as if in surrender. "Now, who has that chocolate?" Will was originally sitting almost as far from Jana as possible, but now he comes to join her, resting his back against the same rock. She places her hand on his leg and he covers it with his own. I wonder if that is all it takes for them to solve an argument. Or is this just the first tentative olive branch? I can never quite understand conflicts between other couples; I haven't had the experience. Nick simply didn't operate that way.

"Here," says Sofi, handing over the much-depleted chocolate slab. Will has to lift his hand from Jana's to take it, his eyes flitting to the young woman, then quickly away. *I'm not the only one who finds her difficult to ignore,* I think wryly.

"You should speak to the rights management team, Emily, if you haven't already," Mike is saying. I turn my head to him gratefully, away from the tableau that is Will and Jana and Sofi. "Any patents that Nick had, either in his name or through the spin-off companies he founded, or any that are pending, will be part of his estate. Which I expect all goes to you, right?" I nod. "Well, then, it's worth a call."

"Shouldn't we get going?" asks Peter generally, unfolding himself. "If we get down too late, we won't be able to get a *télécabine* back up."

"We're doing fine for time," says Robert, unruffled, but nonetheless he too stands up.

"You'll have phone reception when we get down into the valley," Mike says to me. "You could call the office then."

Peter breaks in before I can speak. "I think Emily came here to escape all of that for a bit," he says with a meaningful look directed at Mike. I hadn't expected Peter to be quite so thoughtful about what might or might not upset me; it's unexpectedly sweet of him, though unnecessary. Then he turns to the rest of the group. "Come on, slow coaches. I want time for a large *pression* at the bottom. Possibly two."

"A cold beer is definitely worth moving for," Will says, scrambling to his feet, and pulling Jana up too, the latter yawning and groaning. Everyone is stirring now, grabbing their bags and struggling to their feet.

"Damn it," I hear Sofi mutter, and glance across. She's standing too, her neck bent as she scrapes at the front of her shorts with one hand. "I've got chocolate all over me."

"No worries, I've got spare shorts back at the chalet you can use," Julie offers.

"Don't be silly, Julie. They'll swamp her," says James dismissively. "You must be at least three sizes bigger."

A flush spreads across Julie's cheeks. "Charming, James," she says tartly. "Thanks for that."

"What? Oh, God, I didn't mean . . . Sorry," he pleads, both palms raised in surrender. "I'm an idiot. Julie, you're gorgeous; that came out completely wrong. Ignore me. Sorry." But as he turns to grab his backpack, I wonder if I see the barest hint of a smirk lurking by his mouth; I notice that Will is watching him too, a slight crease between his eyebrows. Then I glance back at Julie. The hurt on her face is laid bare for all to see before she manages to collect herself, making herself busy with her rucksack straps.

"Ignore him," Sofi says in a low voice to her friend. "He really is an idiot." *Possibly,* I think. *Or possibly he's much more dangerous than that.* She raises her voice. "Some men can't judge measurements. Mostly the ones with really tiny pricks," she says mock thoughtfully—loud enough to be heard by James too. "It's because they think this"—she holds her thumb and forefingers around three inches apart—"is six inches."

James' head snaps toward her as Sofi and Julie giggle, though Julie's smile is a little watery. I see the briefest flare of anger before he takes hold of himself; then he laughs ruefully, shaking his head at Sofi as if to say, *Good one; I deserved it.*

Interesting. Sofi's response was so hard and fast: did she too think James was being deliberately mean? If so, this can't have been his first infringement. I glance at Will, who has shouldered his rucksack and is helping Jana with hers; I'm wondering whether we ought to be remonstrating for what is after all not the most grown-up of put-downs—though remarkably effective nonetheless—but he shakes his head minutely at me. Instead, he calls out, "Julie, come and enlighten Jana and me on archaeological chemistry—Robert tells me you're doing

68

your fourth-year project in that area. I really think it could be an interesting topic to do an episode on." He gives a self-deprecating grimace. "I started trying to explain it to Jana, but I was hampered by the fact that— Well, in truth, I know almost nothing about it."

"Never stopped you before," I tease.

"Harsh but fair. But, Julie, do come and help me out here." Julie turns to him with a smile—albeit a little forced—and she and Will and Jana set off down the path together. *Bless him*, I think. He's always been a kind man. I think back to our finals week, grabbing a kebab together at two a.m. from the van on the high street; our lives had shrunk down to the absolute basics—study, food, the bare minimum of sleep—but Will still took the time to speak to the kebab seller about which A levels his daughter ought to do to pursue a degree in engineering. Here in the present, though, James watches them go, his face unreadable, and then turns to Robert with a carefree grin, saying something I don't catch, which makes the older man's shoulders shake as he chuckles.

I thread my way to Peter's side as we set off. The path is narrower here—no more than two abreast is possible—and the ground is uneven and strewn with occasional large rocks; I have to keep my eyes on my footing. "You know, Peter, I've never asked. Has Nick's death left any ongoing projects in the lurch?" I'm pleased to hear that I barely stumble on *death*, though it's not said without cost: on its exit from my mouth, the word trails little hooks behind it that catch and drag at my insides. "With whom was he working mainly?"

"Oh." Once again, he's a little awkward, as if worried about upsetting me by saying the wrong thing. *I will have to brazen it out*, I decide. *Exposure therapy*. I like Peter: I like the way his mind leaps and races, the way he owns to his own flaws such that they become, as Jana put it, almost endearing. We can't have the topic of Nick sitting as an unmentionable black hole between us; it would bleed our friendship dry. "Well, you know what Nick was like. He always had fingers in lots of different pies. You must know that—he said you proofread everything he did." He glances at me with raised eyebrows as if it's a question.

"Well, yes, and vice versa. God, the number of times we disagreed about punctuation . . . Nick was largely against." My wry words pull a laugh from Peter. But I'm thinking about Peter's statement: Could I reliably say that I knew what Nick was like in a professional context? The work was generally done by the time it reached me. Sometimes we talked about his projects, just as we sometimes talked about mine, but not in great detail; by the end of each day, we both preferred to just switch off. "But in terms of current projects, the only thing I knew for sure was that he was working with you on . . . What was it? Power trains for electrical vehicles?"

He flaps a hand dismissively. "There's a few of us working together on that; we'll get it finished up without him." He adds quickly, "But I'll make sure his name is on anything that comes out of it, of course."

"But was that what your argument was about? A project?"

"Well." I risk a glance at him and see him grimace. "No, not really. Or at least, only tangentially. It was just something silly." I glance at him again. The words sound right, but the body language doesn't match; his mouth is strained, tight. *There's something he's not telling me. Something he doesn't want me to know.* Or am I being paranoid again? Perhaps it's just that talking about Nick is so hard for him, particularly with Nick's wife. He rushes on. "But anyway, in truth, he's much more of a loss to the doctoral students that he was supervising and to some other, larger-scale collaborations. Actually, if I'm perfectly honest, the biggest loss might be all the work he had yet to do. He had such an inventive mind. He'd have got the deputy position at Tanner's new lab for sure, and then he'd have been a dead cert for the directorship and the chair once Tanner stepped down; with those facilities and that kind of funding, I can't believe he wouldn't have come up with *several* great things over the next few decades." He pauses, a ghost of a grin on his mouth. "Of course, I would never have told him that."

"Of course." I smile back, but I'm seeing the space where Nick should be like a ripple of darkness, a void moving forward through time, spreading wider as it travels—the effects of all the things Nick should have done but won't now, compounded over years . . . Suddenly I realize what Mike meant by Tanner's beauty parade. Having been robbed of his intended deputy, Tanner must have been planning to spend time with the likely candidates in a social context. I can't exactly blame him, even if it's not a strictly orthodox process—after all, he's going to be working very closely with whomever he chooses. "The deputy job: I take it you'll apply?"

Peter blinks. "I—well, yes. I was going to anyway, even though nobody stood a chance next to Nick. But now . . ." His eyebrows quirk half apologetically as he lets his sentence trail off. It's too stark to say it out loud, that someone will profit, career-wise at least, from Nick's death.

"And Will? And Mike?"

He knows what I mean. "Yes, I imagine they'll apply too." He's controlling his expression carefully. "I expect that's why they're here; if you recall, Tanner and Robert are old friends, which is how Tanner was able to influence the invitations. I can't speak

71

for Mike, but I don't recall Will ever voicing an overwhelming desire to hike the Alps before now." There's the slightest trace of bitterness in his tone, but he catches himself and throws out one of his quick grins. "Anyway, may the best candidate win."

When we return to the chalet, all of us a little sweaty and some of us sunburned in places, I check first of all that the laptop is untouched—though, really, how could it be anything else, as we were all out together?—and find that everything in my room is exactly as I left it. Then I grab a towel and toiletries and head off to brave the waterfall shower with Jana; we've made a pact to act as lookout for each other, seeing as it doesn't exactly have a door and neither of us are keen on any undergrads stumbling upon us in our birthday suits.

I wade into the pool below the fall, awkwardly finding my balance on the rocky bottom; it's around thigh deep, not quite enough to support me. When I step into the main flow, the water, cascading from a ledge perhaps a foot above my head, is shockingly cold. It's as if I'm being frozen from the inside out, starting with my bone marrow; I have to arch my head out of the flow to alleviate the instant ache. My skin, and the scant layer of fat beneath it, is as nothing to the relentless downpour of the glacial stream; all that I am are the bones that hold me up. I am scaffolding, nothing more.

"Well, I'm never doing that again," pronounces Jana afterward, disgusted, as we head back across the lawn to the chalet.

"Really?" The sense of exhilaration flooding through me now is startling. "I think it's worth it for the afterglow." I have the sense that I'm coming fully, truly awake for the first time in months.

Jana puts a hand on my arm, stopping me. "I meant to tell you, I spoke to Elena this afternoon. She said the thieves probably came in through the bathroom window on the second floor—you know, right next to your office? That's why they went through your office and Carver's: they were the closest." Jana's eyes are examining my face, gauging my reaction. "Come on, Ems, I know you've had a lot to deal with of late, but be rational. It's a coincidence."

The implication in her words, that I'm letting my grief cloud my judgment, delivers a sharp sting, though I know she didn't mean it unkindly. I force myself to nod. "Yes. I'm sure you're right." I'm not, though—not entirely. Two offices hit: a coincidence or part of a targeted campaign? The former would be simply unfortunate, but the latter? The latter could mean I'm in some kind of danger . . . But Jana is correct: I should be rational. I should consider the evidence—only the data set isn't large enough; one could make it fit either narrative. *Conditional probability,* I think as we begin walking again. What are the chances of experiencing a burglary or intrusion in any year? Low, surely. One percent, perhaps? So the chance of three (counting the warm laptop) statistically independent events in a year is minuscule: one percent cubed, quite literally one in a million. Tiny. But not statistically impossible. There are approximately sixty-seven million people in the UK. Six or seven of them can reasonably be expected to be exactly that unlucky in a year.

"Did you see the photos from Elena?" Jana asks.

"Yes." I'd checked my emails in the valley as we sat, tired but virtuous, outside a café, the table in front of us laden with perspiring glasses of beer and soft drinks. The photos—an extremely thorough catalog of ransacked drawers and shelves, and of the book- and paper-strewn floor—were a world away from that; one might have imagined that the room had been hit by a hurricane rather than thieves. I had winced when I saw them, my natural sense of order and tidiness thoroughly affronted: every single book had been pulled off the shelves, every drawer opened. "They made quite a mess, but I couldn't see that anything was missing." I'd inspected the images carefully, and try as I might, I couldn't think of anything that wasn't there. I even spotted my Montblanc pen in a heaped pile of chargers, change and assorted stationery by the desk; presumably the culprit simply pulled the drawer out of the desk and turned it upside down. "Did they take much from Dr. Carver?"

Jana shakes her head. "Nothing, really. They didn't even make much of a mess in there. Elena said he thought they'd taken a book he'd written on condensed matter physics, but then he remembered he'd lent it to someone."

A small giggle escapes me. "That sounds like Dr. Carver. And I know that book; only he would imagine that thieves might be interested in it. It has a natural audience of less than one."

We giggle together, and it occurs to me how good it feels to laugh. *I must laugh more,* I think. *I must allow myself to laugh more.*

"What are you two giggling at?" We both turn at the voice; Will is coming toward us, a towel over his arm.

"Nothing much. Do you need a lookout?" Jana asks him.

"Or you could come in too," he suggests, waggling his dark eyebrows in a pantomime leer at her.

"Not a chance. Once was more than enough," she says emphatically. "And I promise you, sex is the last thing you'll be capable of when you get in that freezing water." But she flaps a vague hand at me and turns to join him, linking her arm through his. He angles his dark head to smile down at her. I turn away, aware that I've become absurdly sensitive to the small interactions between couples—a touch of hands, an exchange of glances—as if I might nourish myself on what I see. But a vicarious diet is no nourishment at all.

On the lawn, between myself and the chalet, Mike is occupying a deck chair with a glass of wine, with Olive on the ground in front of him, performing some complicated yoga poses and, if I'm hearing correctly, earnestly delivering a brief summary of Canadian politics. Mike sees me approaching. "Find yourself a glass—two, actually, since you probably want water as well—and come join us," he says with just the slightest inflection of tone to suggest that he needs to be saved.

"Will do. Shall I get you a glass, Olive?"

"No, thanks. I'm just finishing up, and then I'm going to shower in the waterfall after Will. Have you tried it?"

"Yep, just now. That's why I need the wine—to warm up," I joke.

She looks up at me from the downward-dog position. "Alcohol is a depressant, you know. It can't warm you up."

Perhaps humor is not in her repertoire. "Um, indeed," I say lightly. "Well, the sun can do that instead." I return a few moments later, having tied up my damp hair and swapped my towel and toiletries for two glasses and a deck chair. Olive has already departed for her shower.

"Is it just me, or is she rather . . . ?" I ask as I arrange the chair next to Mike's, both of us facing out to the view.

"It's not just you," Mike assures me, taking both glasses and filling one from the wine bottle and the other from a bottle of water I hadn't spied. "She's *very* intense and quite possibly bonkers, though apparently she manages to combine that with being incontestably brilliant in a particular field of medicine. Tropical diseases, maybe? I forget."

I lower myself into the deck chair and accept the glasses, and we both look out at the incredible view. I should be getting used to the extraordinarily beautiful scenery that confronts me whenever I look around, but somehow it surprises me every time. I feel curiously detached from it nonetheless: I don't belong to it, and it doesn't belong to me. Is that what I'm looking for? Somewhere to belong? But surely I belong in Oxford?

No. There's nothing to keep me in Oxford now. The clarity that sweeps through me seems as if born out of the lingering cold of the waterfall, out of the cleansing sweep of adrenaline that came with it. When Nick died, I abandoned my teaching and lecturing schedule, or it abandoned me: it was clear to everyone that I was incapable of arriving at the right time and speaking for an hour, let alone making sense. I should be returning to it after the summer, but the thought comes without any accompanying enthusiasm. *If I'm brutally honest, the only thing keeping me in Oxford for the last couple of years was Nick.* I think of the night we met, at a Christmas drinks party in one of the big old Victorian houses on Rawlinson Road, hosted by some department bigwig or other. I had had plans for dinner in Summertown with friends afterward; Nick found me fishing my long winter coat out of a pile in a back bedroom, intending to make a surreptitious exit. "Leaving already?" he asked, his expression genuinely crestfallen. "I've been plucking up the courage to come and introduce myself; did I leave it too late?" His complete lack of artifice was utterly disarming; I'd stayed for another drink and ended up inexcusably late for dinner. Where would I be if we had never met? Where might I go now, and what kind of person might I become there? Once again, I find I'm hyperaware of the endless tattoo inside me, every beat marking time that's passed, that's lost, that can never be regained. I feel the pace of the beat accelerate as if to hurtle me through life faster and faster, rushing me to the finish line before I've even had a chance to answer those questions—

Take a breath, I admonish myself. *And another. Those questions don't need immediate answers.* I tip my head back against the deck chair and close my eyes, forcing myself to breathe slowly and concentrate on enjoying the warmth of the sun on my skin with no fear of burning at this time of day. Though if I'm honest, I'm fighting against irritation at my persistent thirst and the slight headache that's traveling with it. "This is lovely," I say defiantly, as if my words might make it so.

"Mmm." The sound is a low rumble beside me that could have come from the mountain beneath us. "Very relaxing."

"At least until Tanner gets here and the beauty parade begins," I tease, still without opening my eyes. "Right now you can just be yourself."

"I was planning to do that anyway." He sounds a little amused at the idea that he might have behaved otherwise. I think of granite again: he's not a man who's easily rocked. "Though if he doesn't come at all, I expect Robert will still feed his thoughts back to Tanner."

"You're right. I should have thought of that, given the lifeblood of academia is gossip." *Oh, dear Lord,* I think wearily. I can think of nothing more exhausting than Peter, Will and Mike all jostling for either Tanner's or Robert's approval or both. Well, not Mike—I certainly can't see him jostling, though I do wonder now if his offer to teach Bayesian statistics might have been a subtle attempt to curry favor. "How *tiresome* for the rest of us."

Mike gives a small huff as an approximation of a chuckle, then falls quiet. I open my eyes, lifting a hand to shield them and blinking as the spots in my vision clear. Beside me, Mike is entirely relaxed on his deck chair, his legs stretched out in front and one arm lolling down to the grass. He could be asleep but for the glass in his hand. "Can I ask you something?"

He doesn't open his eyes. "You can always ask." The second half of the sentence is implied: *I may not necessarily answer*, but his tone is lazily playful.

"Sofi." I pause, glancing sideways at him to gauge any response, but his profile gives nothing away. "You seem to be actively avoiding her. I've been wondering if there's a story there."

Now he opens his eyes and his head inclines a fraction. "Yes." He takes a sip of his wine and I wait while he savors it. The evening sunlight is picking up a hint of ginger in his stubble. I wonder if he will grow a beard while he's at the chalet. The male undergrads were talking about doing so earlier on the walk, though James seemed less than keen, possibly on account of the fact that it looks as if a beard may be beyond him, whereas Akash and Caleb are already sporting considerable shadow. Though perhaps I'm being uncharitable to James. I'm certainly predisposed to be.

Mike begins to answer; it's been so long that I'd wondered if he might not bother. "I'm not sure you're going to like hearing it," he warns.

"All the same, I think I'd better."

He sighs. "Well, then." He looks around, checking that we are alone. Several of the party are playing cards on the benches just outside the front door of the chalet, but they're far out of earshot. "There are rumors of a bet." His voice is low, despite the fact that nobody else is close by; I have to lean toward him to hear.

"A bet?" I'm puzzled. This is not at all what I was expecting. "What sort of bet?"

"A fairly salacious one." Distaste is evident in his tone. "In the version I heard, someone bet her that she couldn't sleep with ten dons by the end of her time in Oxford." I take a sharp breath in. "The details are sketchy." He waves the hand that's holding his glass very gently; the deep red liquid is barely disturbed. "It might be six; it might be ten. It might have been staff members rather than dons. It may even have included anybody above postgrad level."

"This is . . . this is for real?"

He waggles his head equivocally. "Well, it's all hearsay, but"—he grimaces reluctantly—"on balance I'd say yes. I've been privy to certain corroborating events, shall we say."

"She . . . she actually took that bet?"

"Apparently so. Or at least, people think so. I hear some enterprising soul is even running a book on it."

"Jesus," I say faintly. Surely my cheeks are betraying me, but mercifully Mike has his eyes on the vista before us as I think again of that kiss in the strange nocturnal netherworld. Not special, then. Something bestowed on many others. But it didn't feel that way at the time. It still doesn't, though I suppose that would be the trick of it: to make each person feel they were special. "How many has she notched up, then?"

"Rumor has it she's more than halfway there."

"Halfway to *ten*?" He nods. "Jesus." Five people, potentially. Five men with secure, enviable positions at Oxford throwing caution to the winds. No, not necessarily men: there could be women too; I'm surely proof of that. "Do you know who they are?"

"Some, yes."

"You're certain?"

"Certain that she's been shagging a plurality of faculty members, yes. I'm not certain of the wager angle."

I stare at him. *How does he know these things?* But I can see how: he's exactly the person one would choose to share problems with. I imagine his broad shoulders simply absorbing them all; I imagine him forging onward with unwavering equanimity. "But . . . but regardless of the wager angle, it could destroy a career if it got out."

"Yes." His lips move in a grimace. "Especially in the current climate. I'm sure it's nothing more than a game to her, really, but it's hardly a level playing field of risk. I for one am determined to steer well clear."

"Yes." My cheeks have cooled now. "If the media got hold of it, they'd characterize her as the victim of an abuse of power. She's not stupid—she must see that." Except even as I say it, I realize she doesn't feel that way. *We're both adults*, she'd said. Jesus. I want to grab her and shake some sense into her, though given the growing sense of anger inside me at having been targeted, I might never actually stop.

"I doubt she sees herself as a victim," Mike comments, unwittingly confirming my own thoughts. "And she isn't, from what I understand; quite the opposite."

Indeed. "But why would anyone risk . . ." He turns to me as I trail off, his eyebrows raised as if to say, *Come on, you know why*, and of course I do. I know it rather better than he might think I would. What was it I had said to her? *I suppose people usually do. Want you to.* I switch my focus to my wineglass, lest my eyes betray my inner thoughts. "Who is on the other side of that wager?"

"That's almost the more interesting question, isn't it?" he says thoughtfully. "That, and whether it was her idea in the first place or theirs."

"Yes." I pause. "If it's true, that is."

"Yes." He shrugs, both shoulders lifting slowly. He's the opposite to Peter, I think. Peter is all quick motions and darting thoughts; Peter is electricity. Mike is due consideration and deliberate movement over time: gravity.

We fall silent. I look out at the clean, fresh landscape in front of me. It seems ludicrous in the face of such wholesomeness that anyone could even contemplate what we've just been discussing. But even as I'm sitting here, the shadows from the trees at the end of lawn are growing ever longer. Soon, they will creep up over our feet. I pull mine back from their outstretched position.

"It could be all rubbish," I offer. I feel obliged to labor the point, not to convict without due evidence.

"It could be." There's nothing combative in his response, but I know what he really thinks. "More wine?" Mike suggests.

I shake my head. "I'd better go slow, or I won't even make dinner." He refills my water glass instead and we lapse into silence again. He's a comfortable presence to be around, Mike. He doesn't feel the need to fill a silence, but perhaps that's because his bulk does it for him. I'm finding that when I'm in his company for a time, I get used to his size, as if my perception of normal has been recalibrated; but then the next time I see him, it's a shock all over again.

"Did you call the IP rights team?" Mike asks.

"Yes." I'd called from Les Houches, while the others were finishing up their drinks. I called Nick's mother first but she wasn't in; I left a stumbling, awkward message promising to try her again soon. The rights team call was no more successful; the relevant person wasn't at their desk. "Someone will be getting back to me." It suddenly strikes me as odd that he's following up so diligently on this point. I glance across at him. "Why? Do you know something?"

"I don't, not really. I know Nick was talking to the IP team recently; he took a quick call from them after we played squash once. But I don't know what the project was, and I wouldn't be expected to; most of his stuff was bound by an NDA."

An NDA: a nondisclosure agreement. Common enough when working on projects in conjunction with a commercial enterprise, which happens a lot in many fields, including engineering.

"He took a call, though," I muse. "So there ought to be something."

"I'd say it's a fair bet. And he works a lot with Peter, who, umm . . ."

"Likes to throw in patent applications at the drop of a hat?"

"You might think that, but I couldn't possibly comment." He looks across at me, wry humor warming his gray eyes. "But I would go so far as to say that, given your husband's field and known collaborators, one could imagine there might be a benefit in speaking to the IP rights team."

I reach out an arm to clink my almost empty glass against his. "Nicely done. Beautifully navigated."

He actually laughs. It sounds exactly like I would have imagined: a low rumble as if starting from beneath our feet. "Thank you." While we've been talking, the shadows of the trees have advanced inexorably, claiming our knees and inching up ever higher, minute by minute. I think of Sofi, of that disturbing kiss. I shouldn't apportion any blame for it to the shadows, but nonetheless I do—for in truth it would never have happened in the sunlight. I stare at the approaching line in a kind of horrified fascination: on one side, vivid color and warmth, and on the other, a chilling absence of both, a creeping dark gray sickness relentlessly claiming all in its path. I have the oddest sensation that rather than the shadows advancing, the bright veil of sunlight is being dragged back to reveal what truly lies beneath . . . I jump up hastily to return to the safety of the chalet. I can't be outside when the netherworld comes again. I'm not ready to face what lies beneath my own skin.

7

I take advantage of the lull in the rhythm of the chalet in the half hour before dinner, when everybody seems to be tending to themselves—showering, changing, otherwise getting organized—to sit down with Nick's laptop to try to understand what on earth someone might be looking for. Though whatever it is might be on the university computer network rather than this private hard drive, and I certainly can't go rooting around in there without setting off all sorts of red flags. I've been wondering what might have happened to those files, Nick's files on the university network; technically I suppose they must be the university's property. Did someone have to go through them? Did that someone expect to find something in particular, and when it wasn't there, did they resolve to search his personal laptop? Or am I looking for a pattern that simply doesn't exist?

The files that Nick had saved on his hard drive are beautifully organized, a testament to his meticulously cataloged mind, but nonetheless I'm hampered by the fact that the project names—all rather grandiose: Titan, Nimbus and so on—mean nothing to me; certainly he would never have used a project name when we talked about his work. *You know, the battery thing*, he'd have said; or, *That semiconductor project*. I pull up Word and look at what was most recently opened: files in the folder structure of Project Mjölnir and Project Nimbus. One appears to be a half-completed grant application. The other is an (abysmally punctuated) early draft of a research paper, bearing Peter's name among others: the power-trains thing, named Project Mjölnir. I sigh. Without knowing what I'm looking for, I could be staring right at something vitally important and still not recognize it. I sit for a moment, idly tapping my teeth. It would have to be something valuable; otherwise why not just ask me directly? Why go to all this trouble? If I make the assumption that whoever was looking at the laptop was the same person who broke into my house and my office, then that limits the pool of possible offenders to those who are here. More realistically, it limits it to Peter, Will and Mike—surely it's not feasible that anybody else here would know what Nick was working on? But Peter or Will—I've known them so long, I can't believe that either wouldn't just approach me if there was something of Nick's to discuss, and I really can't imagine either contemplating breaking into my home. Or Mike, come to that, though I've only just met him. I type in a quick search for Mike Shepherd and I find him, both listed in Nick's contacts and also in calendar entries for squash games, but I can't see any documents related to him. And anyway, he's far too big to be my home intruder.

So in essence I have three suspects, none of whom I can convince myself are to blame. Isn't it more likely that the laptop thing is unrelated? Perhaps a naughty undergraduate snooping around? In which case, the pool of suspects for the intruder could be much wider; it wouldn't need to be anyone here— which I suppose means they could easily try again, with no chance of being interrupted by me. That should be reassuring: on that logic, I'm much safer where I am; perhaps I should never go home. But the idea of someone searching carelessly through my home and my things—our things, Nick's and mine—is so horrifying that it brings a cold sweat. It would be a violation—a desecration, even. Once the ripples of Nick's absence subside, those things will be all I have left to show of our life together.

Dinner again: twelve of us squished around the dark wooden table once more. Peter and Caleb are on duty tonight and have somehow whipped up a rather impressive curry, though Peter rather spoils the enjoyment, for me at least, by loudly asking Will (who is not known for his cooking prowess) what he intends to cook on his turn—but perhaps I'm being unfair, too highly attuned to any hint of one-upmanship. Robert directs the seating, adroitly ensuring that nobody ends up with the same neighbors as last night, and I find myself sandwiched between Will and Julie. Julie is good company, smart and straightforward, with a refreshing lack of affectation, and it's usually an absolute treat to sit next to Will; while I adore Jana—in fact, I was the one who introduced them—I do occasionally secretly lament the impact their relationship has had on my own, separate friendship with Will. But tonight it quickly becomes apparent that Will's capacity to hold up his end of the conversation is sorely lacking.

"Is everything okay?" I ask Will quietly, but he doesn't answer. I look toward where his gaze rested a moment ago, but it doesn't tell me anything. He could have been looking at any one of Caleb, Jana or Sofi, who are seated together at the other end of the table, though I suppose Caleb was unlikely to be the target. And I don't want to look at Sofi, not after what I heard from Mike. I can't help feeling like I've been made a fool of. It's a wound that's too raw to have scabbed over just yet.

I try again. "Is everything okay?"

"What?" He turns his head to me.

"Will, what's with you?" I'm not trying to hide the exasperation in my voice.

"Sorry. I— Sorry," he says guiltily. "I'm listening now, really."

"No, you're not. I know I haven't been doing anything too interesting of late, under the circumstances, but still . . ." He has the grace to look ashamed. "Look, never mind me; I think we need to talk about you. What's going on?" He glances again at the end of the table, and my eyes follow his. Jana has a wineglass in front of her—she prefers to pretend to drink rather than have people speculate about why she's abstaining—but I'm relieved to see that it looks untouched; I'm not sure she's up to another bout of disapproval from Will. "Is everything okay with you and Jana?" I press. "I know the IVF is pretty stressful."

He looks across to check that Julie is safely in conversation with Olive on her right before he answers. "Yes," he sighs, toying mindlessly with the wax at the base of one of the candlesticks. "It's really hard on Jana, and if I'm honest, I don't think I'm helping. She's ordinarily so—so *clinical* about everything; she just figures out what needs to be done for a successful outcome and gets on and does it. She bulldozes through every obstacle." He has a slightly bemused expression on his face, as if he still can't quite comprehend how she does it. I nod, my lips curling up in recognition: this is exactly how Jana operates. She may lack finesse at times, but her effectiveness is never in doubt. "I guess I thought this would be another of those things; I suppose I've just been expecting it to work." He leaves unsaid what we both know: *But it isn't.* It isn't working. This is, what, round number five? They must have the money for more, given the profits from Will's newfound popularity as the nation's favorite scientist, but really, how much more of this can Jana take?

Will's long fingers are separating the strips of hardened dripped wax from the candlestick, then breaking them between thumb and forefinger into ever-decreasing pieces. He goes on. "Drinking last night—they say best not to, so normally she just wouldn't. It wouldn't even be a question for her. Why pay the money if you're not going to do everything you can to maximize the chances? I mean, normally I'm the one who can't be so cut-and-dried." He turns from the pile of crumbled ivory wax in front of him to give me a lopsided smile. "It just seemed so out of character that she would drink. Like . . ." He trails off and stares at the wax pile again, poking it with an index finger as if unsure how it got there.

"Like?" I press gently.

"Like she's given up."

It's said with such quiet sadness that I feel my throat tighten. It's a struggle to force words past the constriction. "She hasn't given up, Will." A sudden guffaw from across the table causes us both to lift our heads: Robert is almost crying with laughter, and James, clearly the cause of the mirth, is grinning at him, his blond hair gleaming liquid gold in the candlelight, his cheeks ruddy with laughter and alcohol. I turn back to Will. "She hasn't given up. It's just the stress and the hormones from the injections. You know that." I think I'm telling the truth, that she hasn't given up. At least, not yet, though I don't know how much longer she can hold out for. Jana is so very practical. She would see no benefit in flogging a dead horse.

He blows out his breath in a puff, then turns to me with a weak smile. "Yes. You're right. I know. It's just . . ."

"Hard," I supply. "For both of you." He nods, meeting my eyes, and tries for a rueful smile, but the hopelessness within it worries me. "Have you talked about what to do if this route

88

is—" I'm about to say *a dead end*, but I catch myself. "Well, not forthcoming? There's always adoption."

He shakes his head definitively. "I won't do adoption." He hesitates, darting a glance at me. "It sounds like an awful thing to say, but I'm not sure I could love the child the same as if it were really mine." He risks another glance, checking for disapproval in my face, but there's none there. "Best to be honest about something as important as that," I say.

"Yes." Then he shrugs, adopting a self-deprecating grimace. "I'm a scientist to my core, I suppose. Legacy, a proper record of having been here is important to me. Passing on the genes and all that—isn't it what we're biologically driven to do?"

Is it? I don't feel qualified to answer; thus far I haven't felt that drive. Nick had begun to mention it a few times, and I suppose I'd thought I might get my head around the idea at some point, but I'd never felt any pressing sense of urgency. Will misunderstands my silence. "It must hurt that you didn't get that chance," he says quietly, covering my hand with his. I look down. His hand is wrong: the fingers aren't long enough, the nails too broad. "I miss him. You know we used to meet every Friday for a coffee. *Black Americano, extra shot, please,*" he says in a pitch-perfect imitation of Nick. A laugh escapes me even as my throat threatens to close entirely. It was always a source of pleasure to me that Will and Nick had hit it off so well right from the moment I introduced them. I'd initially worried that Nick might have felt uneasy about Will's affection for me, and mine for him, but Nick was refreshingly uncomplicated about it: I explained Will was like a brother to me, and that was that. "God, he was a relentless creature of habit," Will says. Another laugh breaks through the barrier, threatening to carry tears along with it. *Yes, he was certainly that.* "I still go to the same café at the same time each week. It feels like— Well, it feels like talking to him. He would love that he'd indoctrinated me into the routine to such an extent that I still go without him."

Yes, he would indeed have loved that. I look up at the ceiling, wreathed in shadow, and exhale slowly, trying to marshal my jumble of emotions into coherence, feeling Will's eyes on me and his hand tightening on mine. The table is starting to empty, with some drifting into the salon and others beginning to clear dishes. We sit among the ebb and flow until Jana comes to join us, breaking the moment and releasing me from the bubble of Will and myself and the memories. She slides into the empty chair next to me, putting her still full wineglass on the table. I wonder if that's a statement to Will: *Look, I'm not drinking.* "I'm exhausted," she says, yawning as if to underline her words. "All this healthy fresh air and exercise can't be good for me."

"Go on up to bed, then," Will says. "It'll be fine."

Jana looks doubtful, but I nod agreement. "Nobody will mind in the slightest."

"Well, okay, then." She pushes back from the table, skirting behind my chair and dropping a kiss onto Will's mouth, upturned to receive it, before leaving the room, empty now save for Will and me.

Akash pops his head round the door. "The prof is looking for us all to convene in the salon for coffee." He wrinkles his nose. "Though I'd bring your wineglasses; the coffee is pretty average."

In the salon, Robert has settled himself into the wicker chair nearest to the woodstove. "Are we all here?" he asks.

"I think Mike and Peter are clearing up in the kitchen," I say. Mike had offered to do it, triggering an almost Pavlovian response in Peter to offer too. "And Jana's gone up to bed."

"She didn't take a candle upstairs, did she?" asks Robert. Will shakes his head. "At the risk of laboring the point, any kind of naked flame upstairs is an absolute no-no."

"I know." Will is nodding. "You've got me paranoid about it: I could have sworn I smelled smoke last night—I even went hunting to check, but it was nothing."

"Well, always best to check. Most likely an unattended candle started the fire that burned down the previous incarnation of the chalet."

"When was that?" asks Olive, drifting over to join us.

"Let me think— Well, goodness." Robert's eyes widen in surprise. "Goodness, somehow I hadn't realized: exactly one hundred years ago. This is the centennial year. I suppose we ought to have a dinner in memory of those who perished."

"Wait—is this the fire? I knew the chalet burned down, but I hadn't realized anyone actually died." This is Akash turning from his own conversation to join ours.

Robert nods. "Yes: three people actually. One was a young student of mathematics. Another was an elderly professor of philosophy; Bellingham was his name. There's a bust of him somewhere in the senior common room. Quite an important thinker of his time, uncommonly fond of litotes."

"Erm—litotes?" asks Akash uncertainly.

"Double negative, sort of," I say. "Such as saying *a not-inconsiderable increase*, rather than *a considerable increase*."

"Precisely." Robert nods. "Affirmation by negation of the contrary."

"And what do litotes have to do with the fire?" asks Olive.

"Absolutely nothing," says Robert cheerfully. "But I can never resist a detour in the garden of the English language.

But returning to the point, the third was a local woman who had been employed to help with cleaning and cooking and so on. She raised the alarm and got everyone out—well, almost everyone; she died after going back into the burning building to try to help Bellingham."

"And yet I rather doubt there's a bust of *her* in the senior common room," says Sofi dryly. I hadn't realized she was listening.

"Indeed, and you're absolutely right: she's the very one we should be lionizing, by all accounts."

"She was probably overcome by smoke inhalation," comments Olive. "It's remarkable how quickly that can take effect; it takes only a few minutes indoors."

"And the young student?" asks Akash.

Robert grimaces. "Possibly a victim of his own love of port. The suggestion is that he was too inebriated to heed the alarm. And actually, there was a fourth victim, though somewhat indirectly and after the fact. The local woman's father, poor chap, took it very hard; she was his only child and much loved. He came up to the chalet some days afterward, completely distraught, and took an ax to the *horloge comtoise*—the grandfather clock—of all things."

"The clock?" Akash asks, voicing the puzzlement visible on every face. "Why the clock?"

"Who knows? Grief affects people in strange ways. And as I mentioned to Emily the other day, the clock holds a certain fascination for some of the locals here. There's a chapter or two on it in Bochert, if memory serves me correctly. He wrote a history of the chalet in the mid-1930s." He gestures to the bookshelf, but we have all turned to look at the clock instead. The pendulum is stirring the air with its steady beat, its strange hieroglyphs swooping to and fro, and suddenly I have the uneasy sense that the clock doesn't so much keep time as direct it.

Robert notices the target of everyone's gaze. "It's a survivor, that piece. First the fire, then the ax attack—and then banishment to the attic! A miracle it's here, really."

Not a miracle, I think. That word should be held close, dispensed to describe only good things, joyful things. The clock is something different. I'm not sure what yet. Robert goes on. "There was actually another fire in the chalet's history—1958, if I'm not mistaken—but that was put out before it could do much damage."

"What happened to the man?" asks Sofi.

"Hmmm?"

"The local woman's father?" Sofi presses.

"Oh, yes—before he could do much damage, he collapsed and died, presumably of a heart attack. Poor man." Robert waits a respectful second or two before adding, "Though of course that served only to fuel the clock's lurid reputation."

"A hundred years," says Akash, in a tone of some awe. His eyes are fixed on the ever-moving pendulum.

"Indeed. Well, well," says Robert, half to himself. "Yes, we should certainly mark the occasion."

"Do we know the exact date?" Akash asks, tearing his gaze away from the clock.

"I expect it's in Bochert if it's known."

Akash moves to the shelf, picking out a small off-white volume and flipping through the pages. "Let's see . . . Oh," he says excitedly. "It was August fifteenth. That's— Wait. That's just a few days from now." He looks at Robert. "We should have the dinner then."

Robert smiles at his enthusiasm. "Excellent. How serendipitous. We must make plans. But for now— Ah, Peter, Mike, there you are. Good, good." He clears his throat. "I have a suggestion to make," he announces mildly, somehow commanding the attention of the room without raising his voice in the slightest. He surveys the expectant faces turned toward him; I see the merest hint of a satisfied smile. Perhaps all the best tutors and lecturers are performers at heart. "It's a chalet tradition to nominate a diarist for the week, but in this particular week, we already have two accomplished private journalists: Sofi and Julie." He nods to them both, and a stain spreads across Julie's English rose cheeks. I wonder if her diary is a private thing or if she dislikes being made the center of attention. "Their sterling dedication has made me think about why we write. The playwright Edward Albee once said, *I write to find out what I'm thinking*. I would like to challenge each of us to keep a diary this week. No need to share it, of course, for your personal edification only—and there will still be an official chalet diarist, for which I nominate"—he looks over the group—"Olive!" A small burst of applause breaks out, at which Olive blinks in flustered surprise, then flushes with pleasure, smiling. Robert goes on. "I know we're an unexpectedly science-heavy group this week, so this is a little outside the comfort zone of many of you, but perhaps we might all surprise ourselves at the end of the week when we find out what we're thinking." I'm fairly certain the twinkle in his eye, when he turns his head in my direction, is meant entirely for me. The chuckle when I move toward his chair, shaking my head and smiling, confirms it.

"What's the joke?" asks Mike, looking from myself to Robert and back again. He's settled on the floor next to Robert's chair;

there aren't quite enough seats for the entire party if we're all in the salon at once.

"I suspect Robert has concocted this diary plan just for me. He thinks I should fling open the windows of my mind and defenestrate my inhibitions," I explain to Mike dryly. I lower myself onto the floor by them both, careful not to spill my wine as I do so. It feels a little like we have been transported into a renaissance tableau, with Mike and me as Robert's disciples, listening avidly at his feet.

Robert's eyes have lit up. *"Defenestrate,"* he repeats delightedly. "There's a word you don't hear often enough. You know, this woman is wasted on physics," he tells Mike with a confidential air, shaking his head sadly. "If only I'd got hold of her for PPE."

"You know, I never really intended to stay in academia at all," I say musingly. Around the room, conversations float and bob, though with less energy than on the previous evening; the walk and the fresh air have had an effect on us all. Julie's eyelids are half closed as she slumps back on the sofa, her straw blond hair spread out like a halo on the cushions. Beside her, Sofi is a dark contrast, but I won't look that way; I'm sure my face would betray me if I did. *That's not quite the sort of defenestration of inhibitions that Robert has in mind,* I think with wry black humor. I also don't look at James, though I feel his eyes following me as if just waiting for the chance to throw me a sly, self-satisfied, knowing grin. Instead I grit my teeth and focus my attention on Robert and Mike. "I was going to take my PhD into the City and find myself a ludicrously well-paid investment banking job." I take another sip of the wine, savoring the taste. It seems to be different to whatever I was drinking earlier, but it's very good. Peter has joined us, a tray of coffee cups in his hands. He pauses for a moment and appears to be mentally tallying up the occupants of the salon. "We're only down Jana," I say, tipping my head up to look at him.

"What? Oh, yes." He looks at the tray in his hands as if still trying to perform some mental arithmetic.

"What happened?" Mike asks me. I've lost the thread of the conversation, but he answers his own question before I'm forced to admit to it. "Ah, I know: the Global Financial Crisis."

"Bingo. Suddenly there were no entry-level quant jobs for people like me." Quant: quantitative analyst. Investment banks had lured many a math or physics doctorate into their quant departments. It wasn't hard to do given the remarkable differential in pay between banking and academia. "I was offered a postdoc, I took it and then suddenly I was on a different path." I take another sip of the wine.

"Emily, is there something in your glass?" Peter asks suddenly, an oddly urgent tone in his voice. "Apart from the wine, I mean. I saw something in the light . . ."

I look at the glass in my hand, then hold it up, squinting to see through the blood red liquid in the yellow light from the woodstove and the lamps. It does seem like there's something there, an unexpected glint of a much lighter color.

"Pour off the wine into a coffee cup," Mike suggests, getting to his feet to pick one off Peter's tray and handing it to me. I pour carefully, trying not to spill, though I daresay the wooden floor of the chalet has seen more than its fair share of wine stains. Then I gasp as what Peter spied becomes apparent to us all: glass. A dozen or so small, jagged pieces, the largest the size of a child's fingernail, are languishing in the bowl of the wineglass, still tipped sideways in my hand. The light glints along the edges of one of them, a perfect tiny isosceles triangle with every side a lethal blade.

"Good Lord," breathes Robert.

"Christ." Mike is visibly unsettled. "How the hell did that get in there?"

"You didn't ingest any pieces, did you?" Peter asks, his concern evident.

I shake my head, unable to speak as I stare at the fragments, surrounded by the remnants of the red wine, as if the liquid was blood spilled on account of their sharp edges. It so easily could have been. I can almost feel them sliding down my throat and esophagus, slicing my insides with their knifelike edges, so razor-sharp that it would have taken a second or two for the sting to be felt, for the scarlet blood to well up in those long slits . . . I cast around for my voice, but when I find it, it emerges jagged and raw, as if the glass truly has shredded my throat. "Thank you, Peter. Very well spotted." I try for a laugh, but it's shaky and unconvincing.

"Yes, well done, Peter." For once, I can't spot even the slightest hint of preening from Peter at Robert's praise. The older man goes on, his voice troubled. "That's most unsettling. I can't imagine how that happened."

"Somebody must have smashed a—I don't know, something—and the shards ended up in there," Peter replies. "We'll have to check all the glasses on the shelf." He looks at the tray in his hand again. "I'd better deliver these. Thank goodness you're okay, Emily."

Mike snags a cup from the tray as Peter turns away, dropping down onto the floor again and swapping it with the glass still held in my hand. Robert has the coffeepot and pours; my hands are shaking slightly but he's kind enough not to mention it.

"Thanks," I say. My voice is more my own again. My throat has not been sliced by those shards; my insides are not running bright with slick scarlet blood. Yet I'm still cautious when I swallow the coffee, as if waiting for pain to slash through me.

"That was a lucky escape," Mike says mildly, inspecting the fragments. He pokes a finger into the bowl of the offending wineglass, moving the glass chips around. "They're certainly sharp. How odd." His head is cocked, considering; then he looks across at me. "Are you okay?"

"Yes. Fine." I take a breath. "Though if Peter hadn't spotted it . . ." I look around. Robert has moved off to pour the coffee elsewhere; nobody else can hear me. "It was an accident, right?"

Mike's eyes jump to my face, his gaze suddenly whetting to become as piercing as the glass itself. Then he looks at the fragments again before refocusing on my face. "Do you have any reason to think it wasn't?"

Do I? I can't tell. Is it yet another coincidental event or an escalation in a pattern? "I don't . . . I suppose not." I try for a laugh; it's no more convincing than my previous attempt. "I suppose I'm just feeling paranoid, what with the break-ins and everything."

Mike tips his head minutely sideways and back, a thoroughly equivocal gesture, his steady gray eyes thoughtful. *This is how he does it*, I think. *This is how he encourages people to spill unto him their worries, their concerns, the very nature of what lies inside them: it's his steadfastness and utter lack of judgment.* I can feel it myself, the urge to vomit up everything. I'm about to open my mouth when—*dinnnnngggggg*—the clock gives another of those single, seemingly random chimes, instantly silencing all conversation as if a mute button has been pressed on the entire world. Every head in the room turns involuntarily toward the clock. The glass face is partially shadowed in mottled gray and black, as if the darkness of the netherworld outside has again snuck in to crawl slowly across its surface—or is it that the darkness is the truth and the rest simply a facade?

It's just the reflection, I tell myself, stamping on the urge to shake myself as if to knock crawling insects from my skin. *Basic geometry.* Given that I'm on the floor, I'm seeing the reflection of the dark, shadowy ceiling.

"I don't think I'll ever get used to that," says Olive, the first to break the silence.

Me neither. "Well, I think that signals time for bed, at least as far as I'm concerned." I unfold myself from the floor, flapping a hand in acknowledgment of the chorus of good nights that my words elicit. On my way out of the room, I feel the weight of Mike's eyes following me and the touch of James' sly gaze. And I feel the clock, with its constant *tock, tock*. I almost always feel the clock.

Akash

Aug 11th

How strange that, as part of my history education, I have read hundreds, thousands even, of pages of diaries and chronicles and letters as primary sources, and yet I'm uncomfortable writing my own. I imagine that, in the main, when those historical figures put pen to paper, they were aware that what they wrote would matter; they might reasonably expect, when writing to a king or a bishop or so forth, that their words could be read and analyzed by future generations. This won't, though, so it feels pretentious and self-aggrandizing to be writing at all: Who cares what I might have to say?

But the prof would say that I should care, even if nobody else does—even if nobody else reads this. Which they won't. But what to write about? I'm enjoying myself; everybody is interesting and friendly—apart from James, on occasion— which of course makes for an unspeakably dull account. The chalet itself is just as it was described to me. Its history is a classic tale of English eccentricity and white privilege, which my sister would demand I rail against on principle, but in truth I'm entirely fascinated by it. I brought Bochert up to bed and have just been reading the section on the grandfather clock. There's a (largely discounted) theory that the clock once stood in Bonaparte's study, though how it could possibly have traveled from there to here is conveniently ignored. The story might have come about because the clock's maker was a local man who moved to Paris for work and became an apprentice in Versailles to a family-run horology firm. Oddly enough, his name is never detailed in Bochert; he's simply known as the Clockmaker. He was mathematically gifted and rose through the ranks to be an important figure in the industry, but he also seems to have been an odd fish, with few friends and strange interests—most notably, in the occult. His feverish love of horology bordered on religious fanaticism, and he claimed that clocks, by "capturing time," allow a glimpse at the inner workings of the world; he even claimed the "perfect" clock could exert an influence on the world around it. It was an obsession that proved to be his undoing, as it ultimately led to a fracture in his relationship with the firm; he left for the Alps in high dudgeon after a particularly nasty dispute, with, if his employer is to be believed, valuable components from many different and notable clocks in his luggage. So it was the Clockmaker himself who traveled from Paris to the Alps, which may have seeded the rumor around the clock's origins, but the clock was most likely fashioned locally, here in the Alps. I haven't read far enough to find out how it was acquired for the chalet.

James and Caleb have just come up—that's it for tonight.

8

Back in my room, despite being bone-tired, I perform the now routine check of the careful arrangement of toiletries and find nothing has been disturbed; the laptop is still safely under the mattress. But once tucked inside my sleeping bag, I find it hard to drift off. My retiral has obviously spurred others to do the same, but the accompanying noise quickly dies away. I've left the shutters open and the darkness, which was total and absolute when I turned off my Maglite torch, becomes diluted in certain places as my eyes adjust, to give a suggestion of shape and form. Snatches of music float up from the salon, which is more or less directly below me, along with the occasional burst of laughter, but on the whole the vibe from below is much more mellow than the previous night. There's a feeling of safety and comfort, lying here with the faint strains of Lana Del Rey drifting up to me along with the murmuring of voices, like the feeling I had as a child upon waking and becoming aware of the muffled noises of my parents moving around the house. Can I really have been considering that one of these people tried to break into Nick's laptop and into our home? Or that the glass fragments were anything but an accident? It seems ludicrous.

Presently, the music stops midsong and I hear footsteps below, then the creaking groan of the wooden boards of the stairs and in the corridor, along with some stifled giggling. Before long, those noises subside too; there are no more protests from the stair treads or floorboards. The chalet is drifting into its own slumber. I drift too, but the ease and comfort don't follow me into my half-waking, half-dreaming state. Instead, the dream from the previous night slowly encircles me, pulling me deeper and deeper inside it, until I'm desperately searching for something, looking everywhere, in every room in the chalet, and I know whatever is wrong is all my own fault; I've done something awful, something that can never be undone, that can never be taken back. I'm searching in my own bedroom in the chalet now, tossing the sleeping bag aside to check beneath it, dropping to my knees to peer under the bed, while behind me something wooden creaks reluctantly in a drawn-out, ominous juddering, and I daren't turn to see it; I know that I can't look, I mustn't look—

Abruptly I'm awake, gasping for a moment or two to extract myself from the remnants of that desperate, awful dream, shaking my head to rid it of the creaking noise—and then suddenly I become aware that the creaking noise is in fact reality. I freeze, holding my breath, too terrified to make the slightest move as the noise judders again, a long protestation of . . . of—what? I must see, I must see; I can't lie here in the pitch-black with unknown horrors encircling me. I fight to extract an arm from the sleeping bag and reach down to fumble among the items on the floor beside me. My skittering fingers recognize the cold, thin tubular Maglite torch; I grasp it and sit up quickly, simultaneously twisting the end of the torch so that it spools out a circle of cold light, illuminating the wooden wall beside me. I quickly train the circle on the door, finding the black lever handle. For a moment, I can't quite make sense of the shape of it; the shadow it casts is almost as black as the lever itself, and surely the angle is wrong . . . and then I realize why. The lever is depressed. Someone is on the other side of that door trying to get in. I watch in horror, too frozen by fear to move, to even breathe, as the black lever handle rises slowly back to its resting position.

Where's a seven iron when you need one? I think semihysterically. Then, incongruously, a wave of anger rushes over me, galvanizing me into action: *How dare someone scare me like this?* I scramble out of the sleeping bag, hopping to free one trapped leg, and dash to the door, yanking it open and thrusting myself and the torch into the corridor.

There's nobody there.

I flash the light all over—walls, floors, up at the ceiling— as if the culprit might have temporarily flattened themselves against one of those surfaces, but no: there really is nobody there. The circle of light travels across the floorboards, walls, rafters, bringing instant color that winks out just as quickly when the torch moves on and revealing nothing but wood, wood, wood, occasionally punctuated by black door handles. Every single door is closed. I stand still for a moment, listening to my thudding heartbeat slowly returning to not quite normal, breathing in and out, in and out, again and again. I'm becoming aware that the back of my neck is clammy and cold; I must have been sweating in my half dreams in the sleeping bag. In fact, all of me is becoming cold; I'm only wearing a thin-strapped vest and cotton pajama bottoms, and nighttime gets very chilly at this altitude, even inside the chalet.

I look down the corridor again, flashing the torch around. Could I have dreamed the whole thing? I've heard there's a phenomenon of extremely vivid dreams at altitude, possibly as a result of the decreased oxygen levels. Or perhaps I hallucinated it? I'm not blind to the impact that grief can have—*is having?*—on my mental state. But no, I was awake and compos mentis enough to grab the torch before I saw that handle move. There was definitely somebody there. Could they have retreated out of sight, back to the safety of their own room, in the time it took me to reach the corridor? Almost certainly, I would think, and given the noise of my own movements—hopping to free my leg, the floorboards protesting violently under my weight—I wouldn't necessarily have heard them moving. What on earth would have happened if I hadn't woken with the creaking of the handle? I feel a wave of nausea hit me at the thought of lying defenselessly unconscious in my sleeping bag as some nameless, faceless individual creeps silently into the room, drawing ever closer . . .

Stop it, I tell myself. *Breathe. In and out. In and out.*

Gradually the nausea passes. I lean against the wall at the end of the corridor, the torchlight trained in a long splash down the center, and concentrate on the grain of the wood periodically broken by the heads of ancient nails. But part of my mind is still thinking, working through the threat. I'm not in a public space, and this intrusion was not due to some nameless, faceless individual. It was one of the chalet party, one of the people I sat down to dinner with tonight. What was the aim? To steal the laptop? Or . . . something else? Was this a threat to Nick's information or to me personally? Or is there a completely benign explanation? Perhaps someone went to use the chemical toilet and accidentally returned to the wrong room? Unlikely given my room is notable for being the last on this side, but not at all impossible, not for tired individuals, most of whom had had several drinks. I stifle a half-hysterical laugh, imagining the drama that would have ensued had I opened the door before they recognized their error.

That's if it was an error. There's no way of knowing. Both possibilities, the sinister and the benign, sit before me, overlaid on each other, bleeding into one another. I can't truly believe in the benign scenario; the unease of the other has stained it, but I can't truly believe I'm at risk either, not when there's such a plausible explanation right in front of me.

I turn to the door to my room to inspect the handle, wondering what made the would-be intruder—accidental or otherwise—pause. Was it the torchlight that spooked them? The backplate has a keyhole, though there's no key in it and I haven't seen one in the room. I stand in the corridor and reach around the door to shine the torch through; a keyhole-shaped cold white splash of light appears on my hip. Yes, I would have seen that; had I been trying to get in, I would definitely have noticed the light coming through once the torch was switched on. But of course that's not the right test: the torch wasn't shining at such close quarters. I go back into the room and, with some difficulty and with the aid of the rucksack, balance the torch on my bed at the right angle to shine on the handle. Then I go out into the corridor and pull the door almost closed; I don't want to wake everybody up by yanking it hard. The light filtering through the keyhole is faint, but enough to have been noticed. Particularly if someone was looking directly at the handle as they turned it gently, concentrating hard on trying not to make a noise lest they rouse anyone. Even in the dark, I would think the handle would be the natural place to direct your eyes.

I go back into the bedroom, shutting the door carefully and sit on the edge of the bed, pulling on a fleece. My phone screen tells me it's one thirty-four a.m. I can't imagine that I'll be able to sleep again in this unlocked room by myself. My eyes keep straying to the door, to that black handle. Even when I tell myself that I'm being ridiculous, the coil of unease in my belly says differently. For a moment I consider waking up Jana and asking to sleep on her and Will's floor: of course they would let me—in fact, Will would probably insist on taking the floor so that I could share the bed with Jana—but I know I won't ask. If I did, I would have to face the pity in their eyes. *Poor Ems,* Jana would tell Will later. *Like I told you before, she can't think straight anymore. Grief has reduced her to paranoia.* They would think I dreamed the handle movement; and really, who could blame them? After all, I considered that myself.

I play the Maglite over the room, looking for something to jam the door—a vain hope, given I already know it contains nothing but two beds. *A bed, then,* I think resignedly. I doubt it would actually stop anyone getting in but it would certainly make enough of a racket to prevent them getting in unnoticed. But on closer inspection I see that both bed platforms are actually bolted against the walls on two sides.

All right, then; something else, something not in this room. A chair, perhaps? One with a high back to jam under the handle. I remember seeing some spare chairs in the kitchen, pushed against the table; I could use one of them. I take the Maglite and pad softly out of my room and down the long corridor, following the circle of cold light that travels in front of me. The darkness yields and then reforms behind it as if liquid and living. The chalet feels awake now, even if the bulk of its occupants aren't, but it's holding its own counsel; the floorboards do not creak beneath my bare feet and even the stairs make no protest at my tread. As the bottom of the stairs,

I purposely don't look toward the grandfather clock as I pass almost silently into the kitchen, playing the light over the room. I have the oddest sense that I'm somehow spying on it, that the kitchen itself has been caught in the act of—what? I play the torch around again. It's the shadows that are unsettling me, I decide, in the way that they change size and shape and direction, depending on how I angle the torch; they make it seem as if the room itself is lurching and looming, or shying away. But I'm only here for a chair, and the torchlight catches on the legs of one of those; I run it up and down the wooden structure, considering. The backrest is taller than the handle on the door, I judge. If I tip it, it should work perfectly.

Some noise or movement spins me around, my heart thumping as the torch paints a moving circle of light that rushes over the oven, the wall, the table with its sticky red-checkered plastic cover, expanding and contracting according to the distance it has to cover. It settles in a dinner-plate-sized splash on the slightly ajar door to the walk-in store cupboard with the dull brass handle at its center. I suddenly realize there's a dim unsteady light coming from that cupboard as if someone has left a candle burning inside there, and as I hold my breath, I realize I can hear a faint snuffling animal-like noise. I'm squeezing the torch so tightly I'm peripherally aware that its ridges are digging into my fingers, every fiber in my body urging me to bolt as I shuffle silently closer. *It will be a rat,* I think. *Or a fox*—some kind of wild animal, at any rate. A small one, hopefully . . . I stop suddenly: *Surely there aren't bears here?* I hastily lower my torch, not wanting to startle whatever the creature may be, and take a slow, deliberate step to one side to better peer through the gap. The light is so very dim and uneven and there are moving, flickering shadows—for a moment, I can't make sense of what

I see, of what is substance and what is absence of light. There's black fur, about waist height—no, no, it's not fur; it's hair, long, dark hair; and above it, a pale shirt with thin pinstripes. And suddenly it all resolves itself, and I *can* make sense of it after all. A girl—Sofi, it can only be Sofi—is on her knees facing away from me, her dark head working busily, forward and back, again and again, at the crotch of the man in front of her. My eyes track upward over the man's hand, the front tails of his shirt crumpled within it to keep them out of the way, then up over the pale material with its thin gray pinstripe, climbing button by button to the open collar. It's the shirt that I recognize first. Even before my gaze reaches the collar, I know whose face must be above it: Will.

His head is tipped back against one of the shelves. His heavy-lidded eyes meet mine as I take in a sharp, shocked gasp. Then he reaches out slowly, deliberately, and silently pulls the cupboard door toward him with his free hand, his expressionless gaze not leaving mine until the door blocks my view, leaving Sofi apparently unaware they've ever had a spectator.

I stare at the door. *Will and Sofi. Dear God. Will and Sofi.* I back away silently, feeling to the side of me for the table and the chair. Then I put the torch in my mouth, grab the chair and hoist it up, scurrying backward as silently as I can manage. I make it all the way to my room unimpeded, shutting the door forcibly and jamming the chair, which is indeed the perfect height, underneath the handle before I even try to process what I've seen.

Will and Sofi. I slide into my sleeping bag without removing my fleece, suddenly aware that I'm shivering, and reluctantly switch off the Maglite torch: I don't want to waste the battery. *Will and Sofi. Poor Jana . . . How long has that been going on?* I wonder. Was it happening during term time in Oxford, when she was technically still an undergraduate, or has it just started? Jesus, did she simply move on to another faculty member when I rejected her advances? Did she deliberately target him as part of this bet?

And what on earth am I meant to *do* about it all? Tell Jana? But my loyalty is split: I care about them both, and in fact I've known Will for far, far longer. *For fuck's sake, Will,* I think despairingly. In all the years I have known him, he has never, to my knowledge, played fast and loose in his relationships; he's always been one of the good guys. And if it's merely a momentary lapse, should I really tell Jana and destroy their relationship?

The chair is enough of a security comfort for me to feel safe within the room, and as I warm up inside the sleeping bag, I'm surprised to find I actually feel sleepy. *I will have to talk to Will tomorrow,* I think drowsily. I see his face again as it looked when he drew that cupboard door toward him. No lingering expression of lust, no shame, no guilt—no surprise, even, at being discovered: he was simply expressionless. Closed. The message was clear: *This is none of your business.* The sheer self-possession of that reaction is astonishing; I'm almost more shocked by that than the act itself. It's a side of Will I have never seen before—no, that doesn't quite describe it. It's more as if there's something else—some*one* else—buried underneath the surface of the Will that I've always known. The sunshine veil has been pulled away to reveal the truth of what lies inside Will in the shadows. *The netherworld again,* I think just before I drop off to sleep. *It's inside the chalet too.*

9

I wake in the morning, surprised to find that I have slept—and slept properly, without dreams and half waking. At some point in the night, I must have become overheated and stripped off my fleece; I find it tossed on the floor. That and the wooden chair jammed underneath the door handle are enough to remind me of the events of last night. For a moment I squeeze my eyes shut and wish to be peacefully oblivious again or, failing that, instantly transported somewhere—anywhere—else. But the universe refuses to cooperate. I am here, and the day must be faced. It occurs to me, with a certain amount of black humor, that this is without a doubt the worst vacation I've ever had.

There are croissants and pain au chocolat laid out in the dining room, for which we apparently have Peter to thank—he is hoping to break the croissant run record of thirty-two minutes from the boulangerie in Saint Gervais back to the chalet during this trip—and plenty of people are already milling about, though none of them are Will or Sofi. Or Jana— *Dear God, Jana*. I haven't even thought about how I will face her, knowing what I know. Surely she will sense something is wrong: I've never been a good liar.

"What's this?" I ask the room in general, gesturing to two piles of assorted jotters at the far end of the table, safely distanced from the breakfast paraphernalia. Some of them look modern, the sort of things one can find in any newsagent, but others are unquestionably much, much older—and posher.

"Akash," says Caleb. I shake my head questioningly and Caleb expands on his answer as he reaches for a croissant. "They're the official chalet diaries. He's planning to work through them to see if there's any mention of why or when the clock was consigned to the attic."

My eyes involuntarily leap toward the timepiece, even though I can't see it from where I'm standing. "Clearly he hasn't been set enough holiday work."

Caleb grins amiably at my weak joke, and I snag a pain au chocolat and a cup of tea and slip outside, hoping to find a small moment of calm but that is not to be: Will is sitting on the bench just outside the chalet entrance, a cup of coffee in his hand. I stop abruptly in the doorway. He looks up at my footsteps, then sighs and moves along the bench to make space. For a moment I simply look at him. He seems tired and older. He's no longer the boy I met at eighteen; I can barely even see that person within him. *What does Sofi see?* I wonder. Someone charismatic, clever, funny and, most of all, grown-up—a finished product in her eyes, I expect. But we are none of us ever that, except on the outside. *The outside.* The facade we all construct for the world—for the daylight hours, at least. Nighttime is a different story. Or at least, it is here.

"Aren't you going to sit?" he asks.

"I'm not sure I'm keen on the company," I say tartly, but I do sit, balancing my tea on the bench between us. "Where's Jana?"

"Still asleep."

"Then I can safely say you're a fucking idiot and I hate you."

"I'm a fucking idiot and you love me," he says wearily.

113

I spread my fingers helplessly, unable to deny it. "Well, I hate the position you've put me in, then."

"Fair." He crosses one leg over the other and picks up his coffee, and there is something about that action, the pose that it puts him in, that I see him once again, the boy he was at eighteen; all he is missing are the rolled-up cigarettes he used to smoke. I take a bite of the pain au chocolat and chew it slowly. Mist entirely obscures the view; there's nothing for us to see, but we stare out regardless. *We're essentially in a cloud right now,* I think. How different the reality of that is to those towering banks of perfect white that I flew over in the plane. Looking at those peaks, like well-stiffened meringue shining brilliantly in the unimpeded sunlight, I had fancied them solid enough to take one's weight. And yet in fact one would fall through into this nothingness.

"How long has it been going on, then?" I ask in a low tone.

"Since Easter, give or take." His voice is equally soft.

Since Easter! At least four months: I certainly hadn't expected that. "And you came here with Jana, knowing that she'd be here too?"

"Jana wasn't supposed to be coming, what with the IVF and everything. Christ, even *I* wasn't coming until Tanner made a big deal out of it. And for Jana"—he twirls his hand around expressively—"all this rustic charm is not exactly her usual scene." He shrugs. "But then the dates of the cycle moved or something—I can't quite recall—and suddenly she was all gung ho and I couldn't exactly tell her not to come."

No. I suppose he couldn't. "What the hell are you doing, Will?" My volume has inched up a little; he makes a sharp movement with his hand, glancing round. I drop to a whisper. "Are things that bad with Jana?"

I see him shrug in my peripheral vision. "I could tell you they've been difficult—and that's true—but that's not it."

"Then what?"

"Ego, if I'm completely honest," he says thoughtfully, as if he himself is an academic project to be analyzed, as he does so well on the screen. He's the master of not only telling his audience about the science, but also about important historical figures in the field, and—in keeping with the present zeitgeist, where emotions are king—of making the audience *feel* what those scientists might have been feeling. "Ego and opportunity." I shake my head, not understanding. "I mean, have you seen her?" *Yes*, I think wryly. *I can't help but see her, even when I'm trying not to: a door opened is a dangerous thing* . . . "And she's smart and funny as well as so fucking sexy. She's . . . she's the real deal." He turns to me suddenly. "You and I were at college together. How many girls like that were beating down my door?" he challenges. I shake my head mutely. He'd had one or two girlfriends, but in truth he'd been the embodiment of the adage *nice guys finish last*. "Exactly. None. So"—he shrugs—"ego and opportunity, I think. Perhaps a sense that I owed it to myself to find out what it could be like with someone like her, which brings us back to ego. Or long-held insecurity, which is the flip side of the same coin."

He looks at me, waiting for a response, but I'm too nonplussed by his own surgical assessment of his reasons: he's completely aware of why he's been following this dangerous, self-destructive path, yet he's been doing it regardless.

He sighs into my continued silence. "It's not like I went looking for it. I can assure you, she's absolutely the one who instigated it."

"Oh, I can believe that," I say wryly, finally finding my voice. He glances at me, eyebrows quirked questioningly. "She tried to kiss me. The first night here."

He opens his mouth, then closes it again. I feel a small sense of triumph for having silenced him, though that's not at all why I told him. I hadn't thought I would tell anyone of it, ever; how odd that Will felt like the right person to tell. But now that I have, I can't divine what he's thinking. Is he hurt that she showed a sexual interest in someone else? Or has he come to terms with the fact that he can't possibly assert any right over her, given his own circumstances? After a moment he says, "I didn't know that was your thing." *That.* He means girls. *That's* the thing he chooses to comment on; I almost laugh.

"It isn't. Or it never has been." *Defenestrate your mind,* I think with no small internal amusement. "Do you think she's told anyone about you and her? I hardly need to tell you it would utterly destroy your career." *But I'm telling you anyway. So perhaps it does need to be said.*

"Yes, I know." For the first time he looks unsteady. "Jana would kill me for throwing it all away," he mutters, more to himself. Then to me: "No, she hasn't told anyone." He sighs. "I'm not an idiot—Well, I am, but not that kind of idiot. I know she's not in love with me, not really. I know she's not for me in the long run, nor I for her. But for now . . ." He shrugs. "I don't know. Clearly it's been giving both of us something that we need."

"But to risk your whole career—I could have been anyone last night— Christ, imagine if I had been Tanner—"

"I know, I know. I'd have torched any chance of the deputy job. Thank God he isn't here yet; Robert said he's planning to arrive the day after tomorrow. It was madness; I don't know what came over me."

I can see in his face the horror at how the consequences of his own actions might destroy him. "You really want it." I don't think I'd truly realized that before.

He nods sharply, a tiny but decisive bob of his head. "I do." He grimaces. "Much to Peter's chagrin; he keeps trying to bring up how much time I've been spending on the telly stuff in front of Robert." *Oh, Peter.* I make an exasperated sound. "It's okay. I'm not taking it personally; I genuinely don't think he can help himself. He's doing it to Mike too—not about telly stuff, obviously; it's the rugby angle there. Somehow Peter keeps managing to suggest that Mike's scientific career pathway has been eased by everyone being so impressed by his past glories on the pitch." He smiles at my evident vexation. "But yes, I want the job, and I'd be good at it." He would. They each would, in their different ways. "Which is why it—Sofi—can't happen again. I have to stop it." He glances at me. "You won't tell Jana, will you, if I stop it?"

I hesitate. In truth this is exactly what I've already decided: that if he cuts it off, I won't tell Jana. Saying it out loud is different, though; saying it out loud is an active betrayal. Would I have wanted to know if Nick had had a dalliance with someone? If it was over and done, and nobody knew of it, then on balance . . . on balance, I think not. I was happy. Not blissful, honeymoon-every-day happy, but happy enough in the sense of being content. I wasn't looking for more or different. I wasn't looking for disruption. *Should I have been, though?* The thought, rising sharply out of seemingly nowhere, makes me blink.

We look round at a noise to see Caleb exiting the chalet, shirtless, with a towel over his arm. "Morning," he says as he passes.

"Morning," we chorus. "Enjoy your shower," adds Will to his back. Caleb raises a hand in acknowledgment without turning round. I wonder idly if he rows; his back is much more muscular than I'd expected. The fact that I've even noticed shocks me. *Dear God,* I think in wry amusement. *You've had zero libido since Nick died but now you're looking at undergraduates? What on earth has Sofi's kiss unleashed?*

Will waits until Caleb has made it halfway across the lawn before asking, "Well?"

"I won't tell." *There. I am Judas now; pass me my pieces of silver.*

"Not Jana nor anyone else?"

Tanner, he means. I nod slowly.

He sighs, possibly in relief. "Thank you."

I poke his side. "You knew I'd say that," I grumble. He waggles his head equivocally. It rankles a little to be so predictable. "Though there is one other thing," I say carefully. "I heard a rumor about a bet."

"Oh, that," he says, completely unfazed. "She told me about it." He looks at me, mild outrage dawning. "Thanks a bundle, Ems. That's not why she's been—" He waves a hand rather than saying it out loud: *sleeping with me.*

"I didn't mean—" Though I had, a little.

"Look, she told me all about it. It was a stupid drunken thing when she was in first year; she never even properly agreed to it, but James won't stop banging on about it. You know, for all he's Robert's golden child, I'm starting to wonder if underneath all the smiles and good humor, he's actually a little shit."

"Yes, I'm fairly certain he is. But he also saw her making a pass at me."

He glances at me, taking in my anxiety but a little confused nonetheless. "But you said that you declined."

"I did. That doesn't mean he'll tell it that way."

"He wouldn't. Surely." But with every second, his certainty is faltering. "That would be—"

"The sort of thing a little shit would do?"

"Jesus. Yes." He thinks for a beat more. "Jesus. You're genuinely worried he'll tell someone?"

"I think he's exactly the sort of person who might, and then it would become a he-said-she-said kind of thing, and there would be all sorts of talk. People have been ruined for less, you know. Who knows what he would do if he knew about you?"

Will pauses. "He's Sofi's friend. He won't put her in an awkward position." But his words are uneasy; they can't carry their own weight. I don't need to disagree with him; I can see he disagrees with himself.

"Are you absolutely sure Sofi hasn't told anyone?" I press.

He shakes his head. "No. I'm . . . She . . ." *I'm sure of it. She wouldn't.* He can't say either with confidence. He tries a different tack. "I don't believe so. She says she hasn't."

"I hope that's right."

I drink my coffee, and he stares into the mist, which is already starting to clear. The trees at the far end of the lawn are gradually resolving into shapes rather than mere dark shadows. "It's going to be hot again," he murmurs.

A scuffing noise above us causes me to crane my neck, but Will just says laconically, "Squirrels."

"Oh." But something he said has needled at my brain. I glance around again to check nobody is listening, then ask, "What did you mean when you said that James is Robert's golden child?"

Will looks around too before answering. "Golden goose might be more accurate. James' father is an alumnus and, more

119

importantly, a very generous donor to the college; he's some kind of ruthlessly successful hedge fund bigwig now. I met him once." There's a faint twist of distaste on Will's face—Will, who is famously hail-fellow-well-met to literally everyone. "Didn't strike me as the easiest man to be the son of . . . But anyway, from what I understand, there might be another sizable donation if James is offered a PhD place."

"Is he good enough for one?"

"I don't think he's destined to set the world of history alight, but I'm told he'd probably muddle through with the right supervisor. The thing is, I don't think it's what he wants to do."

He pauses, a sardonic gleam in his eye as he waits for me to ask, and I oblige. "What does he want to do?"

"He wants to work in television. We're likely to have a couple of entry-level positions next summer on the new series; he's been bombarding me with questions."

"Could you keep doing the telly stuff, even if you got the deputy position?"

He shrugs. "I don't see why not. It raises the profile of the science we're trying to do, which can only be good for fundraising for the lab."

I suppose that's fair. It might even give him an edge. "Well, whatever you do, don't hire James; that would be a disaster."

"Yeah, you're probably right. And I'd much rather have Julie, if she's interested."

"I am right. About that, and the other thing."

He rubs the stubble on his jaw with the heel of his hand. "Yes. I know." I can hear the fatalism in his words; he must have always known this day would come. "I'll stop it. Right away."

I nod, but I'm thinking once again of stable doors and horses bolting. Putting the creature back inside its box doesn't mean it never escaped, and what kind of destruction might have been wreaked in that time? Whatever harm was done cannot be undone.

Last night at dinner, we collectively decided on a long walk today, so we set out soon after breakfast. Jana is feeling a little unwell and opts to stay at the chalet, without having emerged for breakfast, but otherwise we're a full complement. It occurs to me that that might give Will a chance to speak to Sofi without Jana present, but I quickly dismiss that: there are too many of us; somebody would notice. Will won't take that chance.

Before we leave, I tell Robert, at a deliberately high volume so that all can hear, that someone tried to get into my room last night. "Goodness." He frowns. "I can only imagine someone became confused about which room they've been assigned."

"Or maybe they were sleepwalking?" suggests Akash. "My brother used to sleepwalk. He peed all over my toy castle once; he must have thought he was in the bathroom. I was so annoyed."

"Ewww!" exclaims Sofi.

Peter laughs. "Sounds like it could have been a lot worse, Emily. Count yourself lucky there was no peeing involved."

I laugh too, and the moment passes, without anyone betraying nefarious intent with a guilty expression (had I truly thought they might?). But the lingering unease is not so easily dispelled. It coils in my belly, entwining sinuously around those two scenarios, refusing to let go of either.

Our route to the Bionnassay Glacier includes the Tramway du Mont Blanc, a rack-and-pinion train that will take us up to Nid d'Aigle on the slopes of Mont Blanc. It's perhaps a forty-five-minute walk to the Col de Voza, where we will pick up the tram. I'm pleased that I'm not at all stiff from yesterday's excursions, and in any case, any aches and pains would have been quickly forgotten in the sheer delight of seeing the dogged little red train come into view, making steady, stalwart progress against the fifteen-degree incline. Inside, the benches are made of wooden strips and pleasingly curved for comfort, facing front and back to create little booths for four to six people.

"My little brother would love this. It's like actually being inside a Thomas the Tank Engine cartoon," Julie enthuses as she peels off her rucksack and drops onto the wooden bench opposite me. Sofi goes to copy her, then sees me and hesitates for an instant before yielding and joining us.

"I know." I smile back at Julie, similarly charmed. "I hope they never, ever modernize."

"Peter said these trains were manufactured in 1957," offers Sofi. "But it all seems to work well enough; I don't see why they should replace them."

"At least not until they give up the ghost," I agree, "though what they decide to do then will be the tricky part. How to balance respect for tradition with the march of progress."

"Ah, the Oxbridge dilemma," comments Sofi slyly.

"Indeed." Will is right: she is smart and funny.

"Did either of you have parents who went to Oxbridge?"

Sofi shakes her head, but Julie nods. "My dad went to Cambridge."

"But you chose Oxford instead?" I'm genuinely curious.

She flushes a little; that pale skin can't help but always betray the strength of her emotions. "I have no idea if it would have helped at all that Dad was an alumnus, but I didn't want anyone to say that I only got in through his connections."

"Good for you." There's an impressive thread of steel inside Julie. It must have taken confidence to forge her own path

122

entirely on her own merit—though I doubt, in this day and age of entrance-policy scrutiny, that an alumnus parent would have made a difference. Nevertheless, I love that she wanted to remove any suggestion that it could have. "What about you, Sofi? How did you end up at Oxford?"

"There was a teacher at school who was really keen that I apply. I went to a state school—it was a good one, but it wasn't the sort of place that sent hordes of people to Oxbridge. But this teacher had been there, and she pushed me to consider it. I wasn't going to, but my grandmother guilted me into at least visiting. And of course, when I did, I was blown away." She smiles suddenly, a smile all for herself, as if seeing Oxford afresh once again, and it throws me back to when I myself saw the city for the first time. It was early evening in winter, and a light mist hung in the air, creating a fuzzy halo around the Victorian-style streetlamps and lending a sepia tinge to the scene. I walked down the deserted High Street to University College, my footsteps oddly muffled by the damp air, the beautiful old buildings towering over me in the dim light, and I felt a similar sense to that moment outside with Sofi: a sense of otherness, that this was a place that existed out of the normal channel of time, in the bubble of an alternative universe. I had understood then that it would be a privilege to be invited into it.

But Sofi is still speaking. "At the time there were all these media stories about lack of diversity at Oxbridge—well, there are always stories about that—but compared to my rural Scottish state school, Oxford is a cosmopolitan rainbow. At school, there was only me and two Pakistani kids, and that was it for people of color."

"Your grandmother must have been thrilled for you when you got the place," I comment.

"She was high as a kite, possibly even more excited than I was." There's something on the edge of her smile that doesn't quite fit. "She wanted me to get everything I could out of the opportunity. *Say yes to everything* was her motto. Don't turn anything down."

"Broadly good advice, though perhaps best taken in moderation." Both of them laugh at my deliberate schoolmarm tone; I'm not sure if I've imagined it, but perhaps Sofi winces a little too. "Is she still with us?" I ask Sofi gently, though I fear I know the answer. The edge of her smile has given it away.

"She died the term I started, actually. She'd been ill for a good wee while by then; the doctor said she was on borrowed time. She got to see my matriculation photo, but that was it." I wonder if she held on for that. I can imagine a fiercely determined old lady holding the photo with so much pride—enough pride to bank up the fires within her and eke out the last few days of her life until she saw the evidence of her granddaughter's achievements. My throat is closed tight. I look at Sofi, unable to express my sympathy, and her eyes meet mine without any hesitation. Her smile is achingly sad. The little train is starting to move now, the cogwheel mechanism clattering loudly and making any more conversation impossible. The three of us sit companionably—a vast improvement on Sofi's previous awkwardness around me—and take in the chocolate-box views. The light this morning is so clear that the mountains appear too pin sharp to be true. I stare out at those peaks and consider Sofi's grandmother's motto: *Say yes to everything*. It's a brave way to live a life. So far I haven't had that courage.

Caleb

Aug 12th

A diary. This feels weird. But I'm willing to humor the prof, and as Mike pointed out, most career scientists keep a daybook, which is really a cross between a to-do list and a diary of sorts.

To do:

- *Call Dad to check he remembered to get the flowers for Mum*

- *Call Mum to wish her happy birthday*

- *Finish the multivariate calculus questions (check question nine again; it's still bugging me)*

Went to see the Bionnassay Glacier today. Epic scenery, though the glacier itself was a bit disappointing—it basically looks like a heap of gritty mud; you can barely tell there's any ice in it.

Everyone's been passing around the Bochert book; there's a bit of a grandfather clock obsession developing! I can sort of understand it—I mean, I know it's just a clock, but it does freak me out a bit. It always seems to be watching, like those paintings where the eyes follow you around the room. If it was up to me, I'd move it to the kitchen or, better still, back up into the loft.

James was an utter prick again to Julie today. That's like the fifth day running or something. I can't even remember what he was picking on her for, it was so ridiculous. Not sure what's driving all this. I don't remember him being deliberately nasty at college; it's a bit weird. I always thought he was friendly enough. Not my crowd, obviously, seeing as he's one hundred percent focused on being one of the cool kids, but apart from that, fairly harmless, or so I thought. I shouldn't be complaining if it means she'll actually notice somebody else, but when I saw how upset she was, I could have seriously punched him. Though the last time I punched anyone was Steve Barker when I was eleven, and if I'm brutally honest that didn't go so well. Still, with all the rowing and the gym work, I'd back myself to take down James.

10

Sofi's not back yet," says Julie to nobody in particular.

I glance across at her. There's a crease of worry between her pale wheat eyebrows. We—Mike, Julie, Peter and myself—are sitting on deck chairs in front of the chalet, enjoying the late-afternoon sunshine.

"Shall I get us some wine?" Peter asks, also of nobody in particular, but this at least gets a response of a general chorus of assent, as does Mike's request of water too.

"Will do," says Peter. "Though isn't this thirst thing supposed to have abated by now?" he asks rhetorically as he extracts himself from his deck chair.

I look at Julie again. Peter's shadow crosses her as he moves off to get the drinks. When the sunshine is once again upon her, the crease between her eyebrows is still there, and she's looking repeatedly at her phone. "Where did she go?" I ask.

"Up to the hotel." Her tone is almost offhand in her effort to appear perfectly calm. I recognize the instinct: *Don't overreact, or they'll think you're a hysterical female*. They, meaning men. *Even in times of anxiety, we tailor our behavior to the male gaze*, I think ruefully. "She probably lost track of time." Julie looks at her watch. "Though she's been gone almost three hours now." The crease deepens.

An answering knot of unease is building in my stomach. "Is everyone else back?"

"Yes. I thought she might have been with Will and Jana but she didn't walk down with them. Will said he chatted to her at the hotel, but he assumes she left before he and Jana did. They've been back more than thirty minutes—I remember checking the time when they walked in."

"Do you have any reception to call her?" I ask. I'm doing it too, now: seeking to project calm.

She looks back at me, mute relief in her eyes at being taken seriously. "I've already tried that, but no luck. I've got reception—at least, I do at the end of the lawn—but maybe her network doesn't."

"She would if she was still up at the hotel," Mike points out. I hadn't realized he was listening. "Every network seems to work up there."

"True." Julie's crease deepens further. "I'll try again." She takes her phone out of her pocket and heads to the end of the lawn. I watch her go. The unease isn't contained in my stomach anymore. It's like the mist of the clouds: I've fallen through into it and now I can't see anything else.

"She might have missed the path here from the main track," I say to Mike. "It would be easy enough to do."

It would. *Or instead, Will might have broken things off with her and she's currently drowning her sorrows, or self-harming, or doing any one of the stupid, dramatic, attention-seeking things that people do when they're young and heartbroken.*

Something blocks the sun: I look up to find that Peter has returned, his hands filled with a wine bottle and a multitude of glasses, with a water bottle awkwardly jammed under one arm. He moves to open the wine, and then stops.

"What's up?" he asks, glancing from Mike's face to mine. Mike fills him in. "If Julie has no luck calling her, I'll head up to the hotel and check there," Mike finishes. "Someone else can maybe walk down for a bit instead, toward Saint Gervais."

"I can do that," Peter volunteers. I smile my thanks to him and he returns a quick, rueful grimace as he places the now unnecessary wine and wineglasses carefully on the grass. Laughter comes from the salon, where a card game is in progress, but we're a small taut band inside our cloud of unease. Even Mike's natural granite countenance has noticeable lines of tension. We drink the water only and watch Julie pacing up and down at the end of the lawn, her phone pressed against her ear. It's apparent that there's no response. After a time, she lowers the phone, then taps out a message, presumably to Sofi, before walking back across the lawn.

"No luck," she says unnecessarily.

"I'll head up to the hotel and check with the owners," Mike tells her, levering himself up out of his chair.

"I'll come with you," Julie says instantly.

Peter looks at his watch. "How long do you think we have before dark?"

"Maybe forty-five minutes?" I hazard. "You'd better all take torches, just in case. And I'll head out in about twenty minutes and wait for you on the track so you can't miss the path."

As they nod and depart to collect their torches and fleeces, I catch Julie's arm briefly, enough for her to turn back to me questioningly, and ask in a low voice, "How was she before she went up to the hotel?"

"What? How do you mean?"

"She wasn't upset about anything? Or distracted?"

"No. Why?" Julie's head is cocked in bafflement. "Did something happen?"

"No, no, I'm just—I'm just trying to figure out if she could have been in the state of mind to miss the path, is all." It's not the best cover, but it's all I can manage.

"Oh. Well, no, not that I'm aware of. She seemed fine—" She halts suddenly. "Well, she did have a bit of an argument with James, but when I asked her about it, she didn't seem too bothered by it."

"What were they arguing about?"

"I don't know; I didn't actually hear it. I just saw them and asked her later, but she said it was nothing and brushed it off." She flushes. "I thought maybe it was about . . . Well, there's been some tension between him and me, so I didn't really want to press."

"And she couldn't have come back and—I don't know—fallen asleep somewhere in the chalet without us all noticing?"

She shakes her head definitively, her yellow bob bouncing as she does so. "I checked. I even checked the waterfall." Then she looks at me directly, an appeal in her cornflower eyes. "It's not like her. She's sensible. People might not think—"

"It's okay. I know. She's got her head screwed on. It's why we're all taking it seriously."

"Yes. Exactly. Thank you."

I reach out and rub her upper arm briefly as reassuringly as I can. It's a measure of how deeply ingrained the university mantra is—*Don't touch the students!*—that even this small gesture of comfort, in this extreme scenario, feels awkward to me. "We'll find her. Go on now with Mike. I'll wait for you on the track."

Robert joins me as I'm watching the three of them head out across the lawn. "Mike explained," he says. "Dinner has been put on hold. James is being a trooper; he's leaped into the void and is sorting it." He looks at my face. "Emily, my dear—it's very unlikely that any harm has come to her."

"I know."

He's still examining my face. "My dear, is there something I'm missing?"

I shake my head. "No. No. It's just—I just have a bad feeling." I try for a self-deprecating laugh, but it emerges as a half-strangled gasp. "Not very scientific, I suppose."

"On the contrary. There's a lot of research on the science of intuition. It seems to fundamentally be a form of subconscious pattern recognition." He looks pensive. "I will have the others check through the chalet again and around the waterfall. Just in case."

I take my Maglite and my phone out to the track to wait. I'm not at all sure why I bothered taking the phone since I have no reception except up at the hotel—habit, presumably. I stamp on some of the long grass by the little pathway to flatten it and then sit there, my head swiveling to look up and down the main track, my ears straining for sounds. The jinks and curves of the route mean that I can see no more than ten meters in either direction. I try to be entirely dispassionate about the fact that the end of the day is approaching—this is absolutely not the time for my paranoia to surface—but I'm acutely aware that the shadows are growing so long that it's no longer clear what's casting them. The light has acquired a peculiar quality, oddly tinged with red, as if the infrared spectrum has become visible. I glance at the snow-topped mountains, the tips of which are still catching the remaining sunlight, turning from white to something more akin to pink. The pristine panorama doesn't help at all. It's too remote from the lives of mere mortals; it operates on a timescale that's too vast. Anything can appear immaterial given enough time and distance. Even a missing girl.

Not girl, I think. Around the university, I'm supposed to say *woman*—or nothing at all, for fear of offending a nonbinary identifier—and by and large, I manage to; I'd certainly hate to accidentally imply that these young women are somehow *less.* I don't think of Sofi or Julie as less, but I don't think of them as women yet either, though it's true to say they're beyond girlhood—which leaves them traveling through some kind of a hinterland, I suppose. We all went through it and came out something more like the person we were going to be.

That's assuming we survived it. *Come on, Sofi,* I think. *All you have to do is get through. Wherever you are, and whatever is going on, just survive.*

The light is almost gone by the time I hear footsteps and voices coming down the track from above and leap to my feet. Julie comes into view first. She's not close enough in the crepuscular light for her expression to tell me any news but her body language communicates for her. They haven't found her. The grim shake of Mike's head, when he rounds the corner too and sees me, reinforces it.

"Peter's not back yet," I say, forestalling their questions, and then we see that he is, crunching up the track at pace and breathing a little hard.

"Nothing?" he asks.

Mike shakes his head. "Nothing. Pierre—the owner of the Hotel Le Prarion—called the police to warn them of the situation. They'll check tonight if any of the lift operators saw her descend and let him know, but they can't do any kind of search now that it's getting dark; it's just too dangerous to be blundering around this terrain in the dark. But if we tell them she's still missing in the morning, they'll start one; I'll head up first thing and let Pierre know how things stand."

Julie is silent, her face pinched and her arms wrapped across herself. "Come on," I say generally, though it's mostly for her. "Let's go back to the chalet."

"Yes," she says. But she doesn't move. "Only—she'll never find the path in the dark. We wouldn't have found it without you waiting here and it's not even completely dark yet." She glances around, her gaze leaping from place to place as if trying to catalog the deepening shadows.

"Then I'll leave my Maglite here," I say. "I don't know how long the battery will last, though."

Mike is fishing something out of his pocket. "My head torch would be better; it's pretty strong and I just changed the batteries." He turns it on and fiddles a little with the settings until he's satisfied. The result is impressively luminous.

"Put it here," I suggest, showing him the flattened patch where I had been sitting.

He places the head torch down and steps back a few paces. It's not entirely dark yet, but even so it's clear that it would be hard to miss the light that it casts. We stand for a moment, looking at the head torch, at the green-yellow of the long grass stems that it's illuminating. *The very definition of a beacon of hope*, I think. Then I put an arm around Julie and tug her gently toward the overgrown path to the chalet.

Somehow we all eat, but it's a desultory affair. Conversation is stilted; there is nothing that feels right to say. Julie pops out to the end of the lawn every hour or so to check her phone; I see the glow of her head torch pacing back and forward. Periodically someone tries to come up with an explanation:

133

Surely she just . . . Perhaps she . . . But the sentences tail off. There's no acceptable way of finishing them. Will takes responsibility for organizing coffee and I offer to help, following him into the candle-lit kitchen.

"Did you speak to Sofi?" I whisper urgently.

He looks across at me from lighting the gas stove to boil the water. "About—?" He makes a flat, hard cutting gesture with one hand. *About breaking it off.*

"Yes, about that."

The stove lights with a *whoomf*, providing an additional circle of blue-white light. He nods. "I did. When we got back after the walk. Cafetière," he instructs, pointing to a shelf.

I grab the cafetière and put it down on the table. "How on earth did you manage a tête-à-tête without everybody noticing?" Even now, my eyes keep flitting to both doorways, the one to the dining room and the one that leads outside, to check that we aren't being overheard.

"Serendipity. Jana wanted some chocolate, so we walked up to the hotel. I stayed inside to make some work calls while Jana had a short walk, and Sofi happened to come into the hotel too."

"How did she take it? How was she when you left her?"

"If you're asking was she upset enough to do something stupid, the answer is no." He wrinkles his nose. "She was unflatteringly matter-of-fact, actually."

I can't help the acid that edges my words. "I daresay your ego will recover."

"Indeed." There's a wealth of weary sadness in that single word that I hadn't expected. I glance at him in surprise, but I can't see well enough in the dim light to discern his expression.

"Are you . . . are you okay?"

He shrugs. "I don't have a right to be anything else."

I don't know what to say to that. We stand in silence, watching the water begin to boil. For some reason I think of Nick, of the endless cups of tea that I made for him, which he was always genuinely delighted to receive but almost never finished. I think of the cold gray-brown liquid that circled the drain of the kitchen sink as I tipped away the half-drunk contents.

"I am worried, though," Will says after a bit. "I can't imagine where she can have got to."

Except he can, I think. We can all imagine, and none of it is good.

I take a tray with the cups and the cafetière into the dining room, just as Robert stands up to begin ushering everyone into the salon. "Why don't we just stay here?" I suggest, the words leaping from my mouth without conscious thought; all I know is that I don't want to be any closer to that clock. Even here, in the dining room, I can feel its insistent presence.

"Good idea," says Julie quickly. It's perhaps the only thing she's said all evening.

Robert looks as if he might push the point, but Caleb starts passing out the cups, so he settles back into his chair with a slightly discomfited air. The coffee doesn't improve the conversation at all; I find my teeth clenching at the startlingly loud sound of a spoon scraping on china, a sound that only this morning would have been drowned out by chatter. Even the ticking of the clock can be heard, as if the timepiece is demanding our attention. I fancy that if I were to step next door and let my eyes linger on the pendulum, those lines and swirls would cast out and ensnare me in their intricate net of light, dragging me into time itself. *I would be inverted*, I think nonsensically. *The beat, beat, beat would no longer be inside me; I would be inside the beat.* It's a relief to go to bed.

Back in my bedroom, I note that my careful arrangement of toiletries is untouched and I don't care in the slightest. Whether someone is or isn't trying to access Nick's laptop hardly seems to matter now. I do jam the door handle with the wooden chair, though—I don't think I would sleep otherwise—but even with that defense, sleep is a long time coming. I can't help imagining Sofi out on the mountainside in the darkness on her own. She's been gone too long; she's strayed too far; she's on the wrong side of the curtain between that other world and this and, try as she might, the shadows won't let her find the way back.

The next morning, I'm awake just before dawn, having set my alarm. Mike, Julie and Caleb are already in the dining room when I get there, mugs of tea and coffee scattered across the table. I look at Julie's strained face, then at Mike, who shakes his head minutely. Through the window, the sky is bleaching in front of our eyes. The world beyond is moving from black into shades of gray. In the improving light, I can see the dark shadows beneath Julie's eyes, starkly delineated against her almost translucent skin.

"Did you sleep at all?" I ask her.

"Not really. Not properly."

"That bloody clock chiming at odd times can't have helped," says Caleb, yawning.

"I'll go up to the hotel now," Mike says, draining his coffee cup and pushing his chair back. He hasn't shaved and looks rumpled and grimy; he probably hasn't had a chance to shower since the day before yesterday. I realize that I haven't either; the skin on my face feels uncomfortably greasy. "Whose mobile picks up reception here best?"

"Mine, I think," says Julie. They swap numbers and then Mike exits, catching my eye briefly before he passes through the doorway, in a mutual expression of grim sympathy, like the deep breath one takes before stepping into a funeral. *It is going to be an awful day,* I realize. I cannot think that it can be otherwise.

"We should put together a party to search the area round here," Caleb says. He's spreading butter on toast. "We don't have to wait for the gendarmes. My best guess is that she took a path that wasn't really a path and got lost somewhere in the woods."

"Yes, but we'll need to leave it a bit longer," I caution. "The light will be dangerously dim under the trees for a while yet."

"Yes," says Julie, but her shoulders are turned to the doorway as if to be ready to spring up and start searching at any moment.

Caleb passes Julie the plate with the toast. "Here. You need to eat something." She glances at her watch. "Emily's right; we have time," he coaxes.

"Thank you," she says, picking up the toast, but her actions are borne entirely of her ingrained politeness; she takes only the tiniest of bites before putting it down again. "We should wake the others. We need as many searchers as possible."

Caleb reaches out an arm and grabs the small mallet that rests on the sideboard behind him and, without pausing, strikes the dinner gong twice with a strong backhand. The sound reverberates through the silence of the chalet, perhaps through the whole of the Alps, echoing from each peak and returning tenfold to our ears. It's a remarkably decisive action; I'm both surprised and impressed.

Julie looks at Caleb, wide-eyed. "Well, that ought to do it."

He shrugs. "Subtlety is overrated."

There's the smallest of upturns at the corners of her mouth; then suddenly, all three of us are grinning. But it's like the sun peeking through briefly on a stormy day: it can't possibly last. Almost as soon as Julie realizes she's wearing a smile, it slides away from her.

"Emily, I wanted to ask you something." She's chewing her lip. "It's . . . it's a bit difficult." She reaches to one side and picks up what looks like a book from the seat next to her. But no, it's not a book. It's—

"Sofi's diary," I exclaim. It's a thick spiral-bound A5 notebook with a striped pink-and-blue cover: just the kind of standard item that one could buy in any stationery shop, with nothing to mark it out as being either Sofi's or a diary, but nevertheless I recognize it as such.

"Yes," Julie says. My eyes fly to meet hers, and she answers the question within them before I ask it. "No, I haven't read it. I . . . It wouldn't feel right. But Caleb and I have been talking, and we think that under the circumstances—maybe someone should?" Caleb is nodding supportively. I notice that his hand is on Julie's upper arm as if he is worried that he might need to physically hold her up at any moment. *By the end of the day, he may be proved right.* "Just the last few entries, perhaps, in case there's something important? Then if . . . Then when she turns up, we—her closest friends—don't have to feel uncomfortable for having violated her trust by reading it." She's pushing the notebook across the table toward me. I don't reach out to take it. Has Sofi written about me? About Will? I don't want to know. *Though if someone has to know, it might be better if it was me . . .* "Will you do it?" asks Julie.

"I . . ." I look into her eyes, into the clear blue of them, like a bottomless mountain lake—the same limitless blue that they've always been, yet somehow I can see the dread within her, the same dread that lies turgid in my stomach. I reach out a hand to slide the diary toward me. When I touch the smooth surface, I have the oddest feeling that time has lurched, has begun to accelerate, with the beat inside me quickening its pace in answer; I have to resist the urge to turn and look toward the grandfather clock. The pendulum must surely be gaining in speed, racing through its arcs, charging us headlong into whatever danger lies ahead . . .

I lift my hand away abruptly and then tap the book twice as a cover, as if my sudden movement was merely part of an intended gesture. "Of course. I'll look at it quickly before we go. I can spend more time on it after the search. If need be, that is," I add quickly.

If need be. If Sofi's still missing, if there's still the dual possibility that she might be either fine or . . . or . . . not fine.

11

The gong has the desired effect: a steady flow of bodies trickles into the dining room and within fifteen minutes everyone is downstairs, including Jana—though she looks truly awful, and even turns her head away in disgust at the suggestion of coffee. I take advantage of the crush to slip unnoticed through the front door to sit on the bench in the morning chill, the diary in hand. There's no fog to burn off this morning; the sun is already glistening on the dew on the lawn, and beyond, the peaks of the Alps are lit brilliantly white against the shadow that remains in the valley, but this is no time for admiring the scenery. I open the notebook gingerly and leaf through it, half expecting the same strange sensation as before, but nothing takes hold. It's immediately apparent that the layout is not that of a normal diary, but a collection of unsent letters, all addressed to the same person: Mimi. And every single missive is signed off with:

> *Love you. Miss you.*
> *Sofi*

Who is Mimi? Surely not anyone living; otherwise why write letters that are never sent? Sofi doesn't write every day, but nearly, and she includes the date every time; this notebook starts on February 1st and is around two-thirds filled. Some entries are only a few lines and some are several pages long, but most run to around a page and a half of her clear cursive script. Her penmanship is appealing to me: neither starkly utilitarian nor dramatically showy, with none of the loops and whorls that irritate me in some of my students' work. Instead, it is simple, functional, elegant—grown-up—and all written with the same fine-nibbed black-ink fountain pen; not for Sofi a standard Bic Biro. *It was a ritual,* I think. *The pen, the ink, the look of the thing—that was all part of it for her.* Whoever Mimi was, she was important to Sofi.

Where to start? How far back to go? There's a certain logic to focusing more on the entries written here in the Alps, so I search for the day she arrived. There isn't an entry that day, but there's one for the following day:

August 10th

Dear Mimi,

I've been at the chalet for a day now. Mike is here too; I hadn't expected that he would be. He's not in the slightest bit interested in me, which is fine . . .

I read on. A sentence jumps out at me farther down that same entry—*Just like you always said: turn nothing down*—and I realize whom Sofi has been writing to: her grandmother. Mimi was her grandmother, the lady with the brave design for life. It's so obvious now that I'm surprised I hadn't twigged already. I swallow, my throat suddenly impossibly tight. The ritual of it, the letter format—it all makes sense. She misses her grandmother.

But I have to shake myself and move on: there's a reason why I'm reading this. I grimace at the references to my own self—*And she's kind of beautiful too: tall and willowy, with all that glorious hair, though the last time I saw her around college, she looked awful, like she'd subsisted on air since he died*—and the cutting brutality of the youthful gaze. *I'm so much vainer than I thought,* I think ruefully. I really shouldn't care that she thought I've been looking awful of late—I know I have. *At least I'm still tall,* I think with dark humor. Was she right, though? Had I thought my life was sorted? It sounds so smug and unforgivable. Had I taken everything for granted? I suppose I had, to some extent; I suppose everybody does. One can't live every day with a crushing apprehension that it might all slip away.

I turn my attention to the references to Will. If someone other than myself was reading this, would it have been instantly apparent to them as to what was going on? I read those sentences again, looking for incriminating language: *I wouldn't have approached him if I'd known.* And *It's not like they're married or anything.* It's not definitive, but it's certainly suggestive.

I move on to the next entry, for the morning after our encounter in that netherworld, steeling myself for whatever I am about to see. There's a reason for the old adage that eavesdroppers never hear good of themselves; I'd much rather not know, especially given what I now understand of her brutal clarity, but I don't feel that I have a choice.

August 11th

Dearest Mimi,

I've made an idiot of myself. I'm not usually so stupid. I could blame the alcohol or the sheer bloody awful awkwardness of Jana being here and suddenly feeling so very fucking peripheral—and those were all part of it, but really I just read things wrong. Really astoundingly wrong.

Jana. Let's start there. I don't want to like her, but I sort of do, from the little I've seen of her so far. She's definitely a force: straight talking, no bullshit, smart and quite funny and in no way hanging off Will's every word. Not that I do that either, but, for some reason, I'd imagined that his girlfriend would be some pale (metaphorically, if not literally), insipid type who followed him around, gazing with adoring eyes. But no. The first thing I got wrong, I suppose. I didn't know about her in Oxford—I mean, I didn't not know; I guess I had assumed there was someone, but that's different to seeing her, and seeing them together as a couple IRL. So then I drank more than I should have, and tried not to watch her talking to Dr. Rivers— Emily—and started to wonder if all I have going for me is the superficial stuff? Because that's the only thing she doesn't have: she's not hot—she probably was, not too long ago, in that voluptuous, obviously sexy way—but not anymore. Now she's like someone who has just slipped the wrong side of it: a little too heavy, a little too old, a little too much makeup—you can see what they used to be, but they've lost their grip on it. So, really, why do I hold an attraction for him? Is it just that I look the way I look and I'm always willing to fuck? I never questioned it before and now I can't think why I didn't.

I wince. This is no longer merely suggestive; it's pretty damn clear. *God, I hope Jana never sees this.* Quite apart from the proof of her partner's infidelity, the clinical assassination of her attractiveness by a gorgeous twenty-one-year-old is something Jana can definitely live without ever seeing. But I have to go on.

So yes, I drank too much. And Emily—God, it's excruciating. I really thought we'd connected. I suppose I just really wanted to believe it. After all, she was married to Nick, who, bless his soul, was nobody's idea of an Adonis, but a sweetly enthusiastic giraffe-sized nerd with a wee bit of autism thrown in (I'm not being rude; he really must have been on the spectrum, everyone said so) . . .

I find I'm trying not to both laugh and cry; it's such an accurate description of Nick: *sweetly enthusiastic giraffe-sized nerd with a wee bit of autism thrown in*. Would he himself have laughed at it or been hurt? I'm suddenly unsure. The uncertainty rocks me, as if the world is tipping under my feet. *I would have known, before*. Before he died, when I lived with daily reinforcement of how he thought and felt. I clutch onto the notebook and force myself to read again.

I suppose I wanted to feel like someone liked me for me. Wanted me for me. Only she didn't. Or if she did, it was only for a fleeting second.

I've apologized. Of course I've apologized. And that was just as mortifying, really, as the rejection. It wasn't that she was nasty. She wasn't; she was just—I don't know—surgical. About everything. "Don't be naive," she said. I hate that word. I hate the suggestion of being that word. If James called me it, I would explode—it's not as if we've all had the benefit of his quarter-of-a-million-pound private school education to turn us

*into such sophisticated fucking pricks. But she's not James—
she's nothing like James—and I managed not to lose it with
her; I just left. Though it's been needling away at me ever since.
Naive: as if I've been a stupid little girl who needed to have it
laid out for me in black and white. I don't want to think that
she might be right.*

Love you. Miss you.
Sofi

"Emily? Oh, there you are." It's Jana, standing in the chalet
doorway with a mug in hand; I sharply snap the notebook shut.
"What are you doing? What's that?"

"Sofi's diary," I say with a grimace.

Jana looks surprised. "She kept a diary?" I nod. "I didn't
know," she says.

"Really? Oh, yes—you were ill on the evening that Robert
was making much of the noble art of diary keeping. Anyway,
Julie didn't want to read it, but she thought someone should.
In case there was anything relevant to . . ." I can't finish the
sentence. There isn't a word that fits.

"And is there anything relevant?" She comes out to perch
beside me on the bench. She looks tired, but better than she
did earlier.

"Not so far, but for now I'm just reading the trip entries. I've
got one more to go."

"Well, you'd better hurry up. We're starting the search in a
few minutes. Peter will court-martial you if you're late."

I flip open the notebook again, then become aware of Jana's
eyes on me, her head edging toward me, and close it again.
"Jana, stop trying to peek," I say severely.

"You're no fun," she says mock grumpily. "Why can't I too live vicariously through a twenty-one-year-old with pneumatic boobs and endless legs that apparently don't know how to close?"

"Jana!" I'm laughing as she gets up to leave, but with a twinge of guilt. The laughter is only because Jana expects it of me, because she would ask me what was wrong if I hadn't laughed, and I can't risk that for fear of somehow giving Will away; it dies away the instant I open the notebook again. Sofi is not something to laugh at; she's not a joke. Nor is she the cipher that I recognize I was guilty of viewing her as when I first got here: beautiful and inscrutable, with no agency of her own to act as anything other than a foil to those around her. I know her a little now: Julie, Sofi and I spent much of yesterday walking together, idly chatting, and on top of that, I'm now reading her private thoughts; she's no longer a blank surface on which to project my own preconceptions. I'm seeing the shape of her now: a little blurry and unformed still, like a photograph developing in the chemical tray, but she's increasingly resolving into focus for me with every entry I read. Nothing about her, or this situation, is a joke.

August 12th

Dearest Mimi,

Will is looking for an opportunity to talk to me. I can guess why. The store cupboard last night was beyond risky; in the cold light of day he must have wondered what the hell he was doing. The cold light of day changes everything, doesn't it? With candlelight and a drink or two I'm all look at me, I'm so cool and in charge, twenty-first-century independent fucking

woman, do what I want, fuck who I want, blah-blah-blah.
Then in the morning you're faced with their other half and it
occurs to you that you've never once stopped to look at it from
the other side. And then you wonder why you did it at all. So
I was attracted to him—really incredibly attracted, fantasize-
endlessly-over-him attracted—but so what? Did I ever think
we were going to be a proper thing, have a life together? Never
once. So have I just been scratching an itch because I could? Or
was it to make me feel better about myself in some way? I don't
know, though it seems like maybe I should have figured that
out before imploding someone's world. Hopefully she'll never
know, but he will. He'll always know. He'll promise to love her
forever, never to hurt her, and all the while it will be hollow in
his mouth because of what he's done.

Or not. People compartmentalize; they do and say all sorts of
things and somehow find a justification that allows them to
live with themselves. Maybe he'll be able to make those promises
without even blinking. That would be better, I suppose. It
would almost let me off the hook.

Love you. Miss you.
Sofi

That's the last entry. I flip through the remaining pages,
which are mostly blank, but some do have writing on them,
generally slanted across the page in blatant disregard of the ruled
lines: shopping lists and reminders, to-do lists. A telephone
number here or there, and on one page a four-digit code for
something unidentified. Nothing significant. Except—one page
catches my eye as I flick through. I stop and leaf back through

the pages. Surely I didn't see what I thought I did . . . But there, on a page of to-do items, I see it: *NR*, followed by a mobile number that is perhaps the only one, other than my own, that I know off by heart.

Nick's.

12

Nick's mobile number.

How on earth could Sofi be in possession of Nick's mobile number? *The usual way,* I realize bleakly. *He must have given it to her*. For any one of a number of perfectly normal reasons, I chide myself, and wait for examples to present themselves to me, but precisely none spring to mind. There's certainly no obvious reason why a third-year Politics, Philosophy and Economics student should be in possession of the personal mobile number of an engineering research fellow. *No obvious innocent reason, at least.* But I have no time to process, or even name, the tidal wave of emotion that floods through me, because Peter sticks his head out of the chalet impatiently, calling peremptorily, "Come on, Emily, you need to hear the plan." I shut the diary closed with a palm on each cover, as if clapping. The sound acts as a demarcation, a signal to pick up and move on. *People compartmentalize,* Sofi wrote. *Time to do just that,* I think grimly. A young woman is missing: anything beyond that is petty and insignificant. At least for now.

It's clear that Peter has once again assumed a leadership role. He's taken down from the salon wall a framed aerial photograph of the chalet and its surroundings and laid it on the dining room table, the detritus of breakfast pushed carelessly aside, so that we can all see the sections we are to search; everyone is chivied into the room to inspect it. Caleb takes out his phone to snap a photo of it and soon everybody is copying him.

"Now take care, everyone," cautions Robert. "The mountainside is very steep—particularly over here." He gestures to the rear of the chalet. "With all the greenery obscuring the ground, it would be frighteningly easy to step off a precipice."

There's a moment of awful, terrible quiet while I see, writ clear in every set of eyes, *Like Sofi may have done*. Then Peter clears his throat loudly. "Each of you take water with you," he says, breaking that unnatural quiet. "Lots of it, more than you think you need. We all seem to be drinking it like fish."

"And wear long trousers," adds Olive. "There are ticks in the grasses, even at this altitude, and plants that can sting."

Peter nods approvingly. "Absolutely. So: three teams of three. Team one: Julie, Caleb and Olive. Team two: Emily, myself and Akash. Team three: Will, Jana and James. Okay? Mike isn't back yet, and Robert will stay here at the chalet to act as a central point, so make sure you have his mobile number—not that anyone is likely to have reception once we're out there." He grimaces. "Julie, can you remind everyone what she was wearing yesterday?"

"Um, Daisy Dukes—that is, short denim shorts—and a navy tank top. Oh, and she had a navy fleece with her too. Also, she was wearing white trainers that weren't terribly white after yesterday's walk."

"Thank you, Julie. Now, Caleb, your team is searching here." He shows Caleb a swath on the map. I can't stop myself from bristling at his casual assumption that Caleb, as the only male in his group, will be in charge, but perhaps now is not the time to launch a challenge over gender-role assumptions. "Will, you're over here. Emily, Akash, we'll do this section."

I look at the sweep of map under Peter's fingers. Roughly speaking, he has divided a wide circle, with the chalet as the focal point, into three equal pizza slices. Our sector fans out across the steeply banked wooded land to the rear of the chalet: the area that Robert warned about. I shiver. It's easily the most difficult section to search: even in broad daylight, it would be all too easy to take a tumble. There would be a sickening cartwheel of limbs stopped only by a hideous thud against a rock or a tree trunk . . .

Stop it, I tell myself sternly. *Focus on the process. Focus on the search.* I grab my rucksack, checking quickly that my water bottle is full and that my cap is nestling inside. The diary is still in my hand too. There's no reason to take it with me, but I feel uncomfortable leaving it behind; I suppose, having been entrusted with it by Julie, I feel a duty of care to it. I stuff it in my bag, then quickly double-check that my water bottle is closed tightly and won't leak; Sofi won't thank me if I return a pile of papier-mâché to her. *God, I hope I can return this to her.* A small voice inside me adds, *And then ask her how the hell she came to have my husband's mobile number,* but I stamp on that. *Compartmentalize,* I remind myself. Outside the chalet, the milling crowd resolves into the three teams, with Jana giving my arm a small squeeze as she turns away. I can manage only a sketch of a rueful smile in return.

The main path up to the Hotel Le Prarion provides one of the borders of our sector; Peter suggests we climb the path a little, then start the search from there. Julie, Caleb and Olive, whose sector abuts ours, do the same. We trudge some one hundred fifty meters up the path and then stop, looking at one another in silence. "Well, good luck," offers Caleb awkwardly. I raise a hand in desultory acknowledgment and then we split into our two groups of three as if falling away from the knife blade of the path and begin to fan out. There's a stretch of long grasses, perhaps one hundred meters wide, before the forested area begins. I'm the closest to the chalet, with Peter about thirty meters from me and Akash roughly the same distance beyond Peter. We begin, moving painfully slowly, both on account of our heads turning constantly, scanning the ground, and because it's heavy going: the ground is uneven, with sudden hillocks and mounds erupting through the midthigh-level long grasses. There's no clear idea of what lies beneath from one step to the next and the gradient adds to the difficulty: we are essentially walking along contour lines, such that one leg is always stretched and the other bent; my center of gravity frequently threatens to drag me down the slope. Sometimes I hit my toes painfully on hidden rocks; at other times I have to detour off my planned line to skirt stubborn thorny bushes, rocky outcrops or unexpected drops. It's energy-sappingly slow going.

After some time, the sun begins to beat back the morning chill; I pause to take off my fleece, glancing up to gauge my progress against Peter and Akash. We're still broadly keeping pace with one another. I look down the slope, surveying it carefully. I'm confident I would spot a person sprawled below me, unless they happened to be hidden by a particularly large pile of rocks, but I'm also fairly certain a person could be lying prone among the tall stems between Peter and me, and I might miss them entirely. A person: *Sofi*. But surely Peter would see her from his higher vantage point, I reason. It's only the area uphill of Akash that we'll have no confidence over, though it will be worse when we get into the forest; I imagine the scrub under the tree cover will be well suited to thwarting any kind of ground search. But really, what else can we do? This is surely better than sitting in the chalet, waiting uselessly for the gendarmes to drip-feed us information—much better to be doing something, even if we're not doing it terribly well. So I keep moving forward, turning my head on a swivel, scanning left, right, left, right; running my eyes over the land, looking for something, anything—a flash of color or a dent in the grassland; something that seems out of place. But the only splash of color that catches my eye turns out to be a handful of perfect alpine daisies, with delicate pale blue-violet petals spreading from a golden center. I stare at them for a moment. They have no business being so perfectly, heartbreakingly, beautiful on a day like today.

I struggle on and I keep scanning: left, right, left, right. Nothing.

As we approach the trees, the slope is already becoming much steeper, with areas where it drops away in small bluffs of gray rock, and I'm beginning to question the wisdom of this venture. But I know we can't abandon the search; I know that our sector is the one in which Sofi's most likely to be found. As she descended from the hotel, she would at least have been certain that she had to turn off the main path onto a track on the right, so surely, if she got lost, it was somewhere around here. And then we're into the shadow of the trees, where it's noticeably cooler. Now that we're actually within the forest, I realize I was wrong: we actually stand a much better chance of finding her here than in the grasses, if she's in fact here to be found; but equally we have a much higher chance of hurting ourselves in the process. The tall grasses are no longer and instead the ground beneath our feet is a deep, springy carpet of needles from the largely coniferous trees, layered with green moss and scrub and veined with brown tree roots, like rib bones poking through the earth—and sharply banked, with ever more frequent small tumbles of rocky cliff faces: only a couple of meters in height, but nonetheless capable of inflicting serious damage. Every single footstep brings anew the fear that I will trip and slide, or my foothold will give. In trepidation I grab onto a tree trunk for balance, standing uphill of it so that it acts as a kind of gravity break wall for me, and consider whether to try to work my way from one tree to the safety anchor of the next, my mind skittering away from the image it held earlier of tomahawking limbs. The trunks are farther apart than I'd expected when viewing the forest from the outside; they're mostly spaced between nine and twelve feet apart—certainly farther than a step-and-reach method can span, but I can't think of any other way to do it. *Concentrate,* I tell myself as I push off. There's an uncomfortably long period where I have nothing to hang on to before my outstretched palm reaches the reassuring rough surface of the next trunk. *And don't forget to keep scanning.*

"Okay, Emily?" calls Peter after a mere ten or twenty yards under the trees, but his voice isn't coming from where I think it ought to be—have I deviated off the line already? I turn to look for the pale blue of his T-shirt, but the only colors I can see are brown and green, interspersed with gray granite. "I'm fine," I call back. "Where are you? I can't see you."

"About twenty-five meters above you. I can see you and Akash."

"Am I on the right line?"

"Yes, just keep going steady." I could swear his voice is coming from behind me rather than above me. Perhaps the tree trunks are playing havoc with acoustics. I turn back to the direction I think I'm supposed to be headed, surveying the area. If Sofi is here, surely her clothing at least would leap out among the green/brown/gray.

The sharp crack of a dry twig behind me makes me jump, but when I turn, I can't see what caused it. "Peter?" I call. But there's no response. Perhaps it was a bird or some kind of small animal—a gray squirrel, say, or a marmot. I turn again to plan my next tree leap, but I have the sudden uncomfortable feeling of being watched—though when I whirl round to check, there's nobody there. *Of course there's nobody there,* I chide myself. *Nobody in their right mind would be hiking through this section of woodland. You're being paranoid again.* But even so, I can't shake the feeling. And I'm aware too of that insistent internal drumming that never seems to be far from me these days; it's picking up pace and volume. Every time I reach the safety of the next tree, leaning with temporary relief against its reassuringly solid presence, I find I'm listening for the crack of a twig, the huff of a breath, the rustle of brush. And I hear them. I do hear them—every one. The forest is unnaturally quiet, but every sound that splits the silence is categorized by my brain as manmade, coming from somewhere slightly behind and above me. It's as if I'm being stalked by an entity that has the ability to turn invisible whenever I whirl round.

There's no need to cry for help. You're just imagining it, I try to tell myself sternly, but the drumbeat inside me is quickening second by second and any composure I might have claimed is fast deserting me. *Breathe,* I tell myself. *Breathe.* But in an embarrassingly short time I crack and yell, "Peter? Are you there?"

Silence.

"Peter, Akash, are you there?"

More silence. I have the uncanny sense that the forest is listening, waiting to see what I might do next. There's a sly malice in the absolute unbroken quiet.

I am done with this, I think with a ferocity born out of pure, primal fear. *I'm getting out of here.* Planning to cut diagonally back out of the forest, I turn and launch myself toward a tree that's downslope from me, but closer to the tree line. I'm moving with reckless pace, and as I launch, I could swear I hear a low laugh followed by loud rustling. My breathing rasps in my throat. I risk a quick glance behind when my hands hit the next trunk. There's a distinct shower of debris rolling down the gradient toward me. *Someone is above me and moving fast,* I think desperately. I don't stop to try to see more, I simply launch myself for the next tree, yelling, "Help! Help!" as loud as I can with my limited, rasping breath. But the tree I've chosen is a young one—too young. The juvenile trunk flexes under the onslaught of my weight, and the unexpected movement is enough to throw me off-balance. It's as if the ground drops away beneath my feet, or perhaps my feet lift up from the ground, but either way I'm pitched past the tree, scrambling to grab at its trunk and feeling the bark slide though my hands. And then I'm skidding on my side, feetfirst down the steep gradient on the bouncy lattice of fallen needles, flailing around with my arms for a branch to hold on to—surely a trunk will break my fall soon? There's no time to try to direct my travel; there's no time to do anything but claw ineffectually at the ground, trying to catch hold of something, anything, to arrest my slide. But my fingers rip through the mattress of needles and mossy cover without slowing my descent at all, and then my hip smashes jarringly on a rock and I'm suddenly terrifyingly airborne for a long second before thumping down again and sliding even faster, except now I'm rolling too, my vision a repeating cycle of arcs of the tree canopy punctuated with my face mashed into the ground, accompanied by a strange keening in my ears, which I only belatedly realize is coming from my own mouth. Now I'm not hoping for a tree to stop me: my head will crack open like an egg if it hits either a trunk or a rock at the pace I'm sliding. There's another moment of terrifying, stomach-lurching free fall, and then I thump down again, one ankle taking the brunt of it, but at least the rolling action has stopped. One arm finds some kind of scrub plant and I claw desperately at its prickly, knobbly little branches, my fingers closing on a clump and clamping down. My body pivots around my arm, and my shoulder is almost dislocated by the sudden jar, but remarkably, it holds: I've finally come to a blessed halt.

Jesus. I lie still for a moment, my breath panting and gasping through a mouthful of dead needles and leaves. I stare up at the canopy of tree branches that crisscross to obscure the sky. *Jesus.* I can't quite believe that I'm alive.

Well, congratulations, you are indeed alive, I think. *But where exactly are you?*

I start to gingerly assess my situation, spitting out the debris from my mouth and trying to regain some measure of control. I'm lying awkwardly half on my back, the water bottle in the rucksack I'm still wearing digging painfully into me. The arm that's clamped on the bush extends above my head, but now that there's no momentum, the weight of my body is largely taken by the slope itself. I try to bend my knees to dig my heels in, but my left ankle puts up a strenuous objection, forcing an involuntary cry from me. My right ankle holds, though, so I cautiously ease my grip on the bush and lower my arm. Then I twist my head to look back up the slope—am I still being chased, if that's what was happening? I can't quite see from the position I'm lying in, but surely not after that long, terrifying, tumbling descent? I must be close to a hundred meters farther down the slope from where I started. The forest quiet has a different feel to it now too; I can hear birds peeping to one another. The pulse inside me is slowing to an ordinary heartbeat. The malice has gone.

I roll over cautiously to scramble onto my hands and knees—facing up the slope, keeping my left ankle off the ground—and look around. What I see turns me cold. I'm in some kind of narrow, steep canyon. The gradient I've tumbled down, essentially the uphill wall, must be at least sixty degrees, split by a long gash of gray cliff face of perhaps five meters in height, but every other access point is a sheer drop. Where I've come to rest, the gradient is a much gentler thirty degrees, and when I look below, I see that in some five meters or so it's almost flat. If I had tumbled in at any other point, I would surely not have survived. I am amazingly—extraordinarily—lucky to be in one piece.

That's if I am actually in one piece. Now that the adrenaline is retreating I'm becoming aware that every single part of me aches. All exposed skin feels like it has been sandpapered, and every limb is bruised and jarred, but my shoulder and ankle worry me the most. I stay on all fours and try to wiggle my ankle in all directions, an exercise that, while painful, convinces me that it's probably not broken. I'm sure my shoulder won't be broken either; it's just badly wrenched from that jolting stop, but I'm not keen on the idea of moving it around to check.

What to do now? I'm safe here, I reason—I'm certainly not in danger of tumbling any farther. But I won't get out without help; there's no way I can climb back up with one ankle and one shoulder close to useless. Even were I in mint condition, it would be difficult: presumably the bottom of the gorge acts as a riverbed when there are heavy rains or snowmelt, as there are no handy tree trunks to cling onto in the gully itself—just tumbles of rocks and lots of ferns, all of it a little damp. The bush that halted my tumble was one of very few. I look around again at the canyon. It must have been carved out over time by snowmelt, the most patient of all processes. Not even hard rock can withstand the relentlessness of water: sometimes just endlessly dripping, sometimes pounding in torrents, but always, always finding a way.

"Peter! I'm down here! Help!" I shout, then pause to listen for a reply. The forest seems to act as a muffler; it swallows my cries without even allowing them to bounce and swoop around. I try again. "Peter! Help!" Nothing. I remember the phone inside my rucksack and move gingerly to sit on my bottom, unclip the waistband and extract my arms from the straps— an uncomfortable exercise for my right shoulder—but when I finally accomplish it, it's to find, rather predictably, that I have no signal. I try shouting again. The forest continues to be alarmingly unmoved by the noise I'm making. I feel like a toddler railing at a parent who is thoroughly ignoring the tantrum. The serene tranquility simply absorbs all my bluster impassively.

What next, then? Surely better to stay put and wait for someone to find me—though I wonder if there is any way out through the bottom of the canyon. I suppose it couldn't hurt to shuffle down on my bottom to the flatter section and have a look. I'm just starting to do that when a flash of white among the green ferns on my right catches my eye.

Daisies again, I think, my gaze passing on, but my stomach gives an odd sudden lurch and I freeze, squeezing my eyes shut. *Not daisies,* whispers a small voice in my head that I don't want to hear. *Not this time.* I'm going to have to turn my head and look.

Slowly I open my eyes and swivel my head toward that flash of white. Not daisies. There's too much solid white for daisies. I shuffle closer on my bottom until I'm only a few meters away, looking as I move at the ground, my legs, anywhere but that fateful patch of white. But soon enough there's nothing for it. I can't escape it. I have to look.

It's a trainer. I knew it would be. It's a white trainer that leads to a long slender brown limb half hidden by the ferns. *Sofi.* Now that I know it's her, I'm galvanized into action, scooting across as fast as I can, my breath coming in ugly gasps and gulps as I pull the ferns away from her to follow that limb up to her torso, to her neck and beyond, to her face, half cradled in a nest of mossy rock, with one open eye staring straight at me.

I scream.

Robert

August 13th

It is with deep unease that I must write that Sofi is still missing. Peter has organized a search party; I've remained at the chalet to be a central point, though without any form of working communication, I feel rather redundant. As I have been on this trip in general, I fear. I wonder if it was a mistake to come? Perhaps the desire for one last chalet adventure outweighed my good sense. Or perhaps not: I am coping well enough with the walking, even though I am so very tired afterward—it's the general administration and organization that I feel slipping out of my hands. But had I not come, I would have had to explain why not, and I would prefer that all my affairs were in order before starting down that road; though one sometimes has to consider whether the fear of acting extemporaneously might inhibit taking any action at all. The chalet trip is, and always has been, such a pleasure and a privilege to be part of. I was very aware of how much I would miss it when I was considering pursuing a chair elsewhere after my darling Susie died. On balance I think I was right to stay; I can only imagine that I would have alighted in the States somewhere, no doubt endlessly debating freedom of speech and no-platforming issues in much the same way we do here, but without the friends that I have built up over these many years spent among the dreaming spires.

I have been deliberating, and I have concluded that I will ask Peter to take over as trustee when the time is right—sometime during next term, I would think; I may well be too ill if I wait much longer than that. It is a decision that has been weighing on me, and there's some relief in having settled it in my mind. I am certain that he will accept, and I believe that his future will remain at Oxford for some years to come—an important consideration, and not something I am nearly so certain of with regard to, say, Will or Emily. He's also appropriately enthusiastic about the chalet and preserving its traditions—and its future. My only reservations have been around his judgment in choosing to whom to offer invitations. It takes such a lot of experience to find the right mix. But I daresay he will arrive at a formula that works for him, by trial and error—certainly I didn't get it quite right to begin with, and I fear I have not done so on this occasion either: Tanner's exhortations swayed me to invite far too many from the same department. I can't deny that I felt it unwise, given they are all shortly to be vying for the same prize, but Tanner was so very persuasive and continued resistance required depths of stamina that I fear are now and forevermore beyond me. Every trip has its own character and this one is defined by ambition—well, that, and the horloge comtoise! The buzz the timepiece has created is quite unexpected: in my experience, academics are perfectly capable of being unmoved by far more exquisite pieces than this one. Though to give it its due, it's certainly mesmerizing; I particularly enjoy, at present, the relief from pain that comes from allowing its hypnotic trance to take hold.

Still, I think every chaletite has read Bochert by now, or at least the chapter on the clock—I myself reread it yesterday. I'd forgotten the rather ignoble behavior of the chalet founder, Anthony Fraser, though I daresay a pinch of salt is required around the tale. In any case, according to Bochert, Fraser met the Clockmaker by chance, who boasted that he could produce a clock the like of which Fraser had never seen, and he and Fraser shook hands on a price for such a clock. The Clockmaker went to work and in due course produced a clock of such magnificence that the villagers were in awe of it. Fraser, however—presumably with an eye to penny-pinching, and with characteristically little thought given to the possibility of offending the locals—claimed that he had seen many similar clocks, and thus the Clockmaker had not held up his end of the bargain; consequently, Fraser refused to pay any more than half of what they had agreed. The Clockmaker flew into an understandable rage and would not sell the fine clock for that price, despite his own sunk costs in the making of it. For the next few months, he made a hermit of himself in his atelier and the villagers lived in terror of the strange noises heard and bursts of fire glimpsed in the dead of night. One day Fraser arrived back at the chalet to find that a different grandfather clock—presumably the very same that is in our salon today— had been delivered direct to the chalet, along with a note demanding that Fraser spend a month in its company before deciding whether to pay in full. A mere two weeks later, Fraser did indeed pay, and pay in full. Four weeks after that, he went missing and was never seen again.

So, a lurid tale indeed! And likely lacking in historical accuracy; Bochert was neither the most gifted nor most meticulous researcher. I'm quite certain the deeds of transfer of the chalet would disprove the never-seen-again part: never seen again in the Alps, perhaps, but I'm confident in my recollection that Fraser died at a ripe old age at his home in Hampshire, though had Bochert included that particular detail, it would have rather diluted the impact of the tale.

I am not unaware that I am writing this nonsense to avoid thinking about what might have become of our dear Sofi. She is an adult, of course, and I truly believe there is not a thing we should have done that hasn't been done to safeguard these students, but nonetheless I must take responsibility if somehow the worst has befallen her—though we must not assume the worst without any evidence of it. Whilst we can, we must continue to hope.

13

I scream and scream until I'm forced to take a breath, and somehow that very ordinary necessity pulls me back into myself and I stop, gasping and gulping for air. The canyon and the forest around me are utterly unmoved by my hysteria; not a hint of it returns to me in an echo. I look at Sofi, or at what once was Sofi. She's dead. I know this to be true: quite apart from the staring eye, there is something obviously wrong in the color of her face—but nonetheless I do the things I have to do, the things I would want someone to do if it were me or someone I loved, the things they must have done for Nick by the roadside. I check for a pulse; I check for respiration, all the while expecting and finding neither. She is very cold to the touch. She's already on her back, but with her head turned to one side on that pillow of rock and moss; I try to move it straight, thinking to attempt CPR, but her body is stiff and resistant. I try to lift her arm and find the same. Rigor mortis: she's been dead for a while. CPR can't save her now. Nothing can.

Through the ferns, I feel down the line of her arm from her shoulder to her hand and settle beside her, my own hand curled over hers, the temperature of which is so very unnatural. But I can't think what else to do, and she shouldn't be alone. Nobody should be alone like this. After a while I realize I'm shaking, although I don't think I feel cold; I don't feel anything. Even the bumps and scrapes and aches from the long, terrifying tumble feel oddly fuzzy, as if they're reaching me through a blanket of cotton wool. The trembling continues, though. It occurs to me that I could get the fleece out of my rucksack, but I don't. I sit among the ferns and hold Sofi's cold, cold hand.

"Emily? Emily!" Someone is shouting my name. Have they been shouting for long? It takes seconds (minutes? hours?) for me to realize I ought to shout back.

"Here." It's only a croak; nobody could possibly hear it. I try again, throwing my diaphragm into it. "Here! Here! In the canyon!"

"Emily! I hear you." It's Mike. The sense of relief that flows over me is astonishingly powerful. It's like the shock of a wave of cold water, or the waterfall shower; it wakes me up. "Keep shouting," he calls. "I'll follow your voice."

"Here," I shout. I let go of Sofi's hand and move to my knees. Pain jabs my ankle as I shift my weight. *So much for the cotton wool.* "Here, here, here, here." The word has begun to lose all meaning, but I keep shouting.

"I see you. I'm up here."

I look up, craning my neck to find him, and finally spot him silhouetted, perhaps ten meters above me, peering over the lip of one of the sharp walls of the canyon, where the fall is direct and unbroken. "Careful," I shout, alarmed.

"Don't worry. I won't fall."

"Well, I did." I sound peevish.

"You certainly did." He sounds almost amused by me. Or perhaps a little giddy with relief. "Are you okay?"

"Nothing broken, I think, but my ankle won't hold my weight." I pause. "Sofi's here. She's . . . she's not . . ."

I can't find a way to say it. I look up at the featureless silhouette and shake my head.

"Oh, God." There's a pause. I can't see his face but I can imagine it: the still grimness around his mouth as he absorbs the news, the steady unshakable gray of his eyes. "Right. God. Right. Hang tight for a bit; I'm just going to see if I can get down to you via the top of this little gorge, where it's not quite so steep." His head withdraws, and I hear him moving purposefully across the cliff top, foliage rustling and cracking beneath his weight; he's far too big to move silently. "Ah, fuck!"

"Everything okay?" I call.

"Fine." He sounds highly disgruntled. "Just the thickest patch of stinging nettles in the world."

After a few minutes he's back in his original spot, leaning over. "I think we'd best get you out from over there, where it's not so steep, but I wouldn't want to do it without a rope. I'm going to have to go back to the chalet to get one, and tell the police about . . ." He gestures to Sofi. I nod. "Can you hang tight while I do that?" I nod again, a little hesitantly. "Do you need water? I can drop some down."

"No, I'm fine." Am I? I suppose I am, if the comparison is Sofi. Though in truth I'd rather we weren't left alone again, Sofi and me.

"Okay. Hang tight," he says again. He seems as reluctant to leave as I am to see him go. "I'll be back as soon as I can, I promise."

"Much obliged."

I hear a small chuckle at my attempt at dry humor and then his silhouette withdraws. I look at Sofi, at her open eye. The iris is a beautiful, rich dark brown, the color of ancient polished wood. It occurs to me that I won't have any time with her after this. Presumably Mike will contact the gendarmes, and they will come to take her off somewhere—to the sort of place where I saw Nick after the accident, I suppose: a sterilized room of metal and tiles. It was hard to talk to him there, with the pathologist standing respectfully by and everything so hard and clean and shiny. All the things that I should have said got stuck in my tightly closed throat. If he had been laid out somewhere like this, with the green and the quiet and the occasional peeping of a bird, it would have been far easier.

"I'm sorry," I say to Sofi. "This isn't what your life should have been. I'm so very sorry." I settle down beside her and take her hand again. Mine is scratched and bloody, with dirt under every fingernail, and some of those ripped and bloody. Hers is spotlessly clean, with each oval nail painted a perfect liquidlike dark bronze, but the coldness of her skin is so very disconcerting—a constant reminder of the wrongness of her state. "And I'm sorry I had to read your diary, though I expect you understand why. I wish I'd known you better. I would have liked to know you better." My eyes rove over her. There's nothing to betray what caused her life to leave her: no open wound, no obviously broken bones. I expect it would be a different story if I could see through her skin, but the way she fell, it's as if she's just woken and is about to reach for something. Or someone. Whom would she pick if she had that choice? Will? Or someone else? *Perhaps Nick?* a sly voice inside me asks, but I slam it down almost immediately. I don't believe that. I won't believe it. Either way, I won't have a chance to ask her now.

Though . . . My eyes move back to her shorts. Tucked in the pocket of the hip that juts toward the sky is her phone; I can just see a corner peeking out. I suppose . . . I suppose I could check if she rang him or sent him any messages. I hesitate, reluctant. It feels wrong—even more wrong, somehow, than reading the diary; at least that was done with the purest of intentions. This has nothing but naked self-interest behind it. I shouldn't. I know I shouldn't . . .

But I'm going to. As soon as the decision is made, I move quickly—I have no sense of how long it will be before Mike returns. I drag my rucksack toward me to recover my fleece from its innards, then wrap my hand in the soft material to tease out the phone. It lights up as I bring it up to look at it, but it's locked: there's a padlock sign above the time stamp, with a photo of Sofi and Julie as a backdrop, arms slung round each other and tongues poking out at the camera. I look at it blankly for a moment: I should have expected it to be locked, but somehow I hadn't. Presumably it uses a facial-recognition system. I glance at Sofi's face. Just a little more than half of it is visible; will that be enough? I hold the phone in front of Sofi's silent staring face, then look at the screen. Remarkably, it has unlocked.

Quickly, I pull up her recent calls and scroll through, searching for Nick's number. There's nothing, but the phone shows only the last three weeks or so—of course there would be nothing in that time period. I pull up her contacts instead. There's nothing under *Nick Rivers*. There's a surnameless Nick, but the mobile number is wrong. I try *NR* and find myself staring at his contact card, with his work email address as well as office and mobile numbers on it. A wave of despair threatens to rise up inside, but I won't let it flood me. *This isn't new information. I already knew she had his number.* I leave the contacts menu and instead input *NR* into the main phone search box. The results suggest his contact card, the National Rail app and two calendar entries.

Calendar entries: they arranged to meet. I look at the dates. In the month before he died, they arranged to meet twice. No emails or text messages. It doesn't exactly suggest torrid passion.

The merest hint of an indistinct male voice floats down to me; I quickly rub my fleece all over the phone and shove it back in her pocket, then turn to peer up the canyon wall. The voice gets louder and splits into at least two registers: Mike has brought company. Within a minute, I see him leaning over the edge again. The sun has moved in the time he's been away; he's no longer a mere silhouette. Peter and Caleb flank him, leaning cautiously over too, chorusing hellos to me and their relief that I've been found. Their gaze flicks past me to search for Sofi. I see Caleb's face freeze when he spots her, his eyes suddenly huge dark pools in his lean face.

"How are you doing down there?" Mike calls.

"Fine." The false cheer in my voice makes me feel self-conscious: will they think that I'm acting oddly? But I'm hurt, at the bottom of a canyon, with a dead girl for company. If I broke into song or danced *The Nutcracker*, they would simply put it down to shock. "You brought reinforcements."

"Yep. Caleb is going to be the man in charge. He knows something about ropes and harnesses."

"Um, yes." Caleb shakes himself into gear. "I'm going to come down and talk you through it all. Just give us a few minutes to get set up at this end; I'll be coming down over there. Did you bang your head when you fell?"

"Many, many times," I say dryly. "But I don't think I'm concussed, if that's what you mean." *Though would I know?*

Caleb looks at Mike, who shrugs and mutters something that might be *We don't exactly have an alternative if she is.*

Caleb turns back to me. "Okay," he says. "Well, let's see how we go."

170

"And what about Sofi?" I don't want to leave her. She shouldn't be alone.

"Umm . . ." Caleb looks at Mike, nonplussed. "The gendarmes are coming," Mike says, stepping seamlessly into the breach. "They aren't more than forty-five minutes behind us. Let's get you to safety and leave the scene for them."

The scene: as if it's act one in a theater piece, as if, at the interval, Sofi will stretch, then climb to her feet and laugh behind the curtain with her fellow actors, full of the rush of the performance. I look across at her again. If it weren't for the odd ashen color of face, and the darker, almost purple mottling on the underside of her legs and arms, I might believe she could do just that. I crawl over to her to cup her cold cheek with one hand and press a quiet kiss to her hair. Her iris doesn't flicker. Then I crawl to where Caleb indicated he'd be coming down and settle on the ground to watch him; my ankle is going to suffer on the way out without me adding to it by standing unnecessarily. In fact, all of me is going to suffer: I am so scratched and bruised that I can't even sit comfortably, let alone comfortably ascend on a rope. But in what seems like mere seconds, Caleb is abseiling toward me down the uphill wall with its gentler gradient. He has a climbing harness on, and while he's moving backward, his head is twisted to survey the terrain below him and he's almost running, moving lightly and confidently with a speed that speaks of long practice.

"Hi," he says when he reaches me. I'm still sitting down; he hunkers down to my level, then winces as he runs an eye over me. "You look pretty beaten up."

"I feel it."

I see him glance over at Sofi and swallow visibly. He seems suddenly very, very young to me; he could be fourteen, not twenty-one. When he looks back, his expression is utterly miserable. "I don't know what to say." There's a note in his voice, halfway between hope and a plea, as if I might have some answer that will make the awfulness go away. *But I don't. Nobody does.*

"I know. Neither do I." I reach out to gently grip his upper arm as if to imbue him with some resilience through physical contact, though I don't have a surfeit of that myself right now.

He closes his eyes briefly, then nods and swallows again. "Okay. Well. Let's do this," he says. He stands and starts to loosen the harness straps before shucking it down his legs. "I need to get this on you; we have only the one. Here." He kneels to help me put my feet into it in my sitting position. "I'm afraid you're going to have to stand now." His tone is apologetic as he stretches out his hands to help pull me up. "You can lean on me if you need to. Here we go."

The rope that he attaches to the harness in a complicated knot is worryingly slender, but on close inspection I can see that it's densely woven. And I would think Caleb is heavier than me, and it evidently held for him, so there shouldn't be anything to worry about. But still . . . Caleb takes in my expression. "It's okay. All you have to do is sort of sit back into the harness and walk your feet up the slope. Will your ankle cope with that?"

"Yes." *It will have to.* I imagine the alternative is a complicated extraction involving the gendarmes or mountain rescue, possibly even by air, and I couldn't bear the fuss of that. Not today, not when all attention should be on retrieving Sofi.

Caleb calls to Peter and Mike to take up the slack, and I feel the tug through the harness. There's a level of trust involved in this endeavor that I might ordinarily have blanched at, but today I don't even hesitate. In fact, my head is oddly light

172

despite aching so much; it's a relief to leave the thinking to someone else, and Caleb's instructions are clear and calm. It takes a bit of adjustment from Peter and Mike to get the pace right, as my ankle is inhibiting the speed I can travel at, but we soon find a rhythm. Caleb is climbing nearby, spiderlike and ropeless, which would ordinarily make me anxious for him except I don't have the bandwidth for it right now. He gives me plenty of encouragement and repeatedly tells me not to look down, but I do. I can't help it. I'm moving away from Sofi with every step; she's a shrinking splash of blue material and tan skin among an increasing circle of green. Only . . . something strange is happening. The green is leaching out of the plants around her in a spreading circle of gray-black devastation. I gasp aloud and stare, horrified, at the expanding ruination, but then have to suddenly grab at the mountainside as my feet stumble; the harness is still yanking me up despite the fact that I've stopped moving.

"Are you okay?" Caleb asks anxiously. "Pause a moment, guys," he yells up to Peter and Mike. "Is it your ankle?" he asks me.

The harness pressure lessens to simply hold me steady. "I . . . Wait . . ." I peer down again at Sofi. Everything around her is green once more. *What had I seen then?* Caleb's eyes follow mine. "What?" he asks, squinting to follow my gaze. "Did you see something?"

"I don't know . . ."

"An animal, maybe?" He looks distinctly uneasy. "Would— would something try to . . ." *Eat her.* It's a truly appalling thought. An image crosses my mind of some kind of beast snuffling over Sofi, then settling down to gnaw at her perfect clean hands, its teeth tearing into her polished skin . . . I feel instantly nauseous. I say quickly, "I think most of the creatures round here are herbivores." I'm not at all sure that's true but I don't want him to worry about it—especially as that's not what I saw. I look down again. Once more the color is bleeding away in an expanding circle, with Sofi as the origin, leaving a sickly dark gray carpet of detritus behind; I glance at Caleb, but his expression hasn't changed. "Do you see anything?" I ask him, and he shakes his head; when I look down again myself, the green has returned. *It's me*, I think. *I am concussed after all. Or something worse.*

"All okay?" calls Mike.

"Ready to go again?" Caleb asks, and I nod. He calls up, "Yep, let's go," and we're off again, rediscovering our rhythm. I repeatedly glance back anxiously, but the foliage stays green and healthy. At my last glance, I can't even make out Sofi's face among the ferns.

As I near the top, Mike reaches out a hand and grasps one of mine, hauling me up over the lip, my legs scrambling to keep up with the speed of his pull—but he doesn't stop when I'm safely up over the edge; he keeps hauling until he's pulled me into a hug, stepping backward away from the lip as he does so. My face is crushed into his chest before I quite realize what's happening. Caleb reaches the top only seconds later and flings his arms around both of us, and after a second, Peter does the same. I smell the tang of their sweat, feel it on their skin; I feel their relief too, somehow, as if the arms around me are lighter for it. *They needed this*, I think. *After Sofi, they needed to feel like they had at least saved one person.* But it doesn't feel the same for me. I didn't save anyone; I'm the one who was saved.

We still have to navigate our return to the chalet, of course, and the ground is no less treacherous than it was when I fell.

Peter picks the way, choosing the flattest, safest route, but it's only a few minutes before Mike mutters under his breath in exasperation. "Right," he says decisively. "Piggyback or fireman's lift?"

"I can walk," I protest.

"I know you can; I just can't stand watching you do it. And it's going to take a lot longer than is good for your ankle. So which is it?"

I yield. "Piggyback, then."

He hunkers down a little, but he's so tall and his back is so broad that it's actually fairly difficult to climb on. When he straightens up, I worry that my linked arms will crush his throat, but we rearrange ourselves until we're both a little more comfortable. His hard bulk is so unfamiliar to me after Nick's gangly leanness—but why I am even comparing them? I wonder. Perhaps because this situation necessitates intimacy: his forearms are hooked under my legs and my mouth is near his neck; his scent in my nose. He smells of tropical holidays: *Sun cream*, I realize. At some point today, despite the horrors it continues to hold, he thought to stop and put on sun cream. How reassuringly practical.

"Okay?" asks Mike after a bit in a low voice meant purely for me. His words rumble through his chest before emerging, like the purring of an enormous lion.

"Not really." My head is really thumping now. "You?"

"Same, but at least I'm not bashed to buggery."

"Is that a technical rugby term?"

I feel the slight chuckle in his chest through my arms. We're out of the tree cover now, following Peter as he picks a path through the long grass. I can already see the track. It seems ridiculous that I can have been in so much danger only several hundred meters from the main path, and even more incredible that Sofi could have lost her life there. Mike doesn't miss a beat; he simply walks on, following Peter, who is helpfully pointing out any hazards for him. I close my eyes and turn my head sideways to lay my cheek against one of Mike's shoulders. The jolting of each step is sending shooting pains through my shoulder, my ankle, my head—but there's no point in complaining; there's nothing that can be done about it.

"Sofi," Mike murmurs. "How did . . . how did she look?"

"What?" My eyes fly open. *Did he see the green disappear too?*

"You know."

I don't, though. "Was there anything visible? Any clue as to what might have happened?"

No, he's not talking about the green, I realize. But he'd said, *What might have happened?* What does he mean? "But . . . she fell. She must have. She must have got lost and then fallen."

I feel a slight shrug. "You fell. You're still here. Bashed up, yes, but still here."

"Ye-es." I think of Sofi, of her hand in mine. I think of those delicately painted oval fingernails without even a smear of dirt underneath them. "You know, she wasn't bashed up at all," I offer hesitantly, lifting my head briefly, but it thumps too hard; I lay it down again hastily. I really must be concussed. That would explain what I saw. "There wasn't a visible scratch on her that I could see, though I didn't exactly search. She looked . . ." I swallow. *Perfect.* She looked perfect. And then I realize what he meant earlier when he said, *Leave the scene for them.* He wasn't thinking of the theater—of course he wasn't thinking of that. He was already thinking of a crime scene. "She didn't . . . she didn't look like she even tried to break her fall." Who wouldn't try to break their fall? I take a sharp intake of breath. *Someone who couldn't. Someone who wasn't conscious enough to be able to do it.* I have been very, very slow on the uptake here. Suddenly it comes back to me: the panic I was in before I tripped, the noises I was sure I heard. Am I concussed? Or have I been in such a state of shock over Sofi that all else was swept away? "Mike, I . . . Oh, God, before I fell, I thought someone was chasing me. I don't know if I was being paranoid—"

"Did you actually see anyone?" His voice is still a low murmur. It cautions me to rein in my own. I shake my head, which is wince inducing, then realize he can't see that, though maybe he can feel it. "No," I say quietly. "At first it was just odd noises. I tried to shout for Peter, but he obviously didn't hear me." Obviously . . . But another, dreadful possibility flits through my mind: *What if Peter was the one chasing me?* But of course not. Why on earth would he? Why would anyone? I try to slam down on the thought, but it's like the insidious water creating the canyon: even as I ignore it, I can feel it drip, drip, dripping into me. I rush on: "And then I saw a lot of rustling, and falling debris, and— Well, I bolted. And that's when I fell."

He's silent for several long, careful strides amidst the long grass. "You're not exactly the type to invent things."

I've just begun to suspect Peter, for God's sake. "Ordinarily, yes, I'd agree with you—except . . ." Even putting the paranoia and the strange hallucination around Sofi aside, I'm aware that at times I've been experiencing something that might fall into the category of an episode of anxiety or a panic attack, even if I've been loath to label it as such, even to myself.

"Except what?"

But there's no opportunity for me to answer, because we're almost at the path, where I can see Olive waiting, tucked in the shade provided by a hairpin in the path, and a little to the side of her is Julie, her face almost luminous in its ashen white color, her arms wrapped across her stomach as if she is holding the pieces of her together. "I'll tell you later," I say quietly.

"I'll hold you to that," he rumbles quietly back, and it doesn't strike me as a throwaway comment. He will indeed hold me to it. He's not a man to let things go.

Caleb pushes past Peter and goes straight to Julie, crunching across the dirt and gravel track to wrap his arms around her so that she is entirely encompassed within the circle of them, murmuring something too soft for anyone else to catch that causes her to sink against him as if she has lost the ability to hold herself up. I turn my head away; even my gaze feels like an intrusion. My eyes fall instead on James. I hadn't noticed him before, lounging against the banked curve of the path, but it's clear that he'd noticed me. His head is cocked to one side as he surveys me, still on my awkward perch on Mike's back; the golden grin arranged on his face is undermined by what's in his eyes: pure malevolence.

He's furious with me, I realize, shocked. *What on earth have I done to deserve that?*

Mike sets me down carefully at the edge of the path so that he can speak with Olive for a second; if I tried I might be able to catch the conversation, but I'm too exhausted to make the effort—*nothing broken, medic* and *meet the gendarmes* are all that register. I rest against the bank some meters from James, deliberately looking anywhere else. But still, I'm conscious of him unfolding himself and crossing the distance between us to stand right in front of me so that I can't ignore him. I tip my head to look up at him.

"I'm so relieved you're in one piece," he says, still wearing that awful parody of a smile. The words are the right ones for the circumstance, but his tone matches the ugliness that lives within his eyes.

"Are you really?" I ask almost meditatively.

He glances round. No one is paying us any attention. "No, actually. I really couldn't give a shit about your welfare." The arrogance of his rudeness, the vileness of his response, the way in which he delivers it through his trademark grin, threatens to steal my breath. He shrugs.

"What is *wrong* with you?"

"What's wrong with *me*?" He's visibly nettled, struggling to recover his nonchalance. "More to the point, what's wrong with *you*? You should be thinking of how you can be very nice to me, you know." He adopts his boyish grin again, though his eyes are still flat and angry. "Unless you want the police to hear all about your little affair with Sofi."

So that's his game. I draw in a sharp breath—I won't let him drag me into his schemes. He wants to play sly games in the shadows, but I want everyone to see that he's playing them. I stand up as straight as I'm able, ignoring the pain in my ankle, and say, loudly and distinctly, for all to hear, "Fuck off, you little shit."

14

There's a moment of silence, in which all heads turn toward James and me, swiveling in comical unison.

"Wow, Ems, calm down—," says Peter, wide-eyed in shocked surprise, but Mike is talking brusquely over him. "What did you say to her?" he barks at James.

"I—well—"

"Yes, James, what did you say?" I challenge him. Something has shifted inside of me. I feel reckless in a way I haven't for years—if ever. All this time spent saying the right thing, learning the right things, reading the right things; being diplomatic, protecting my career, my position, my future. All this time spent carefully not disappointing anyone. All it's left me with is nobody to disappoint.

"Nothing!" James bursts out. "Can't you see she's hysterical?"

"Well, Ems, you have had quite a—," Peter tries. I turn narrowed eyes on him, and he steps back, visibly alarmed.

"Not in the slightest." Mike is standing right next to James now, towering over him. "She's in no way hysterical."

"She's verbally attacking me! I'd say that's hysterical—"

"I'm hardly hysteric—"

"Wow, wow, calm down—"

"And I'm saying I'd like to hear what you said to—"

It's Caleb, surprisingly, who breaks through the cacophony. "Shut up!" he yells, his words ringing with unexpected authority. Then I think of him striking that gong this morning, his arm reaching out sure and true without even a glance; perhaps I shouldn't be surprised at all. "Shut up, all of you. This is not the time." He looks down at Julie, still tucked against his side. "We're going back to the chalet," he says wearily. "You lot can do what you like."

Mike scoops me up, one arm under my shoulders and one under my knees, without even giving me time to loop my arms around his neck, and sets off down the path behind Caleb and Julie. "Little shit," he murmurs. The tightly controlled anger in those quiet words is more intimidating than any outburst would have been.

"My point exactly," I say archly, and hear a reluctant huff of almost laughter. "I can't understand why Robert even invited him."

"James has a knack for just the right type of flattery; Robert seems to think he can do no wrong. What did he say to you?"

"It's a long story. Too long for this walk."

"Another thing I'm expecting to hear later." I can sense the tension that's still tightly reined within him; there's a sharp, staccato feel to his movements and words.

"You will."

It's a couple of hours before Mike comes to cash in on my promise of *later*. First I have to reassure an uncharacteristically tearful Jana and a shaken Will that I'm fine, and then I have to submit to Olive's very thorough medical examination. "Well, by some miracle you've avoided concussion, nothing's broken and you don't appear to have signs of internal bleeding—"

"Excellent," I murmur faintly. I hadn't even considered that as a possibility.

"—so on the whole I'd say you just need a lot of rest and a lot of painkillers," she pronounces at last. We're in my bedroom in the chalet. She tears a wrapper to reveal a stretchy crepe bandage and starts to wrap it around my ankle. "Though in the interest of full disclosure, I've been working in research for a while now; I won't be at all offended if you'd prefer a second opinion."

"I'm happy with yours," I assure her. "You were a surgeon, right?" She nods. "Why did you move into research?"

She goes quiet for a moment. Her head is bent toward my ankle; all I can see are chestnut corkscrew curls. "I killed someone. In Africa." Her tone is almost meditative. I stare at her, as if I might see through those curls to her downturned face. "It happens, you know. I was very tired; I'd been working twenty hours straight. And when you're tired and you can't find what you're looking for, you just cut deeper and wider. My boss came in and flipped the X-ray around; I was operating on the wrong leg. He sent me home to sleep and that was it, no other sanction." She's securing the end of the bandage now. I still can't see her face. "But the little girl got an infection in the cut she was never supposed to have had and died." *Oh, Olive.* I close my eyes briefly as if to ward off the futile wave of sadness that follows her calmly delivered words. "In the UK, I'd have been struck off."

"In the UK it wouldn't have happened at all," I say quietly. "You wouldn't have been working under such extreme conditions."

"Yes. Of course." Her head lifts, curls bouncing, and I finally see her face. There's no tension in it at all, no attempt to excuse,

182

apologize or dissemble. Her clear hazel eyes could be ancient. She smiles in response to whatever is on my own face. "My therapist would agree with you wholeheartedly; he tells me that the route back to the operating theater is to forgive myself." She shrugs. "That might be true, but I'm just not sure that's where I want to be or ought to be, which apparently is fear of failure, except that it could also be realism . . . It's really quite difficult to tell from the inside." She smiles once more and again I have the impression that the smile is for my benefit, to leaven whatever I might feel on hearing this story.

"Do you miss operating?"

"Yes." She starts to gather together the medical kit, the bandage wrapper, the used antiseptic wipes and other detritus from her examination. "But I miss my ex-boyfriend too, and he was most definitely bad for me, so I wouldn't set any store by that."

I start to laugh and, after a moment, she joins in, though I have the impression she has no idea what she's said that's so funny. Still, her story tugs at me: a life that's changed course through a single event. Where would she be now if that hadn't happened? Would she be happier in that other place, or is this where she's supposed to be? Then suddenly I remember that Sofi is dead and it's like the ground falls away underneath me, revealing an endless dark abyss; how can I have been laughing at all?

Olive leaves me, and somehow I fall into a light doze without quite realizing it; Mike's tap on the bedroom door brings me back to the chalet in a journey that rushes quickly from queasy disorientation to quiet despair when I fully comprehend where I am and what has happened. "Sorry," says Mike, hovering by the doorway. "I didn't realize you were sleeping."

I wave him inside, pushing myself up to a sitting position and shuffling until my back is resting against the wall, with my sore ankle stretched out along the bed. "It's okay. I didn't mean to."

"There's a policeman who'd like to talk to you if you're up to it?" I nod. "He's already talked to everyone else; you're the last. Shall I send him up, or do you want to come down?"

"Here is fine," I say through a yawn.

Mikes nods and disappears. I hear his heavy tread receding on the floorboards, then returning scant seconds later with another pair of footsteps. Mike introduces the French policeman, a slim man in his late twenties with a doleful expression, then he leaves us to it. The policeman settles on the opposite bed when I gesture to it and opens a notebook. The interview doesn't take long, though longer than it should have; the gendarme's understanding of English is very good, but his speech is so heavily accented that I have to keep asking him to repeat himself. His questions are routine, but they still catch at me: How did I know Sofi? When did I last see her alive? What were my movements yesterday afternoon and evening? What were the movements of the others in our party? And on and on; and all the while, I feel the gaze of that single iris heavy upon me. I have my own questions, but they aren't ones that he could possibly answer—questions like *Was there something I could have done? Did I fail her somehow?* I have no reason to feel any more responsible for Sofi than anyone else in this group, and yet somehow I do. That moment between us in that shadowy netherworld left its mark. A door was opened: that invitation was a link between us, even without any crossing of the threshold.

Eventually the policeman's questions peter out, and he flips his notebook closed. "*C'est tout.* Thank you."

"Are you treating it as an accident?" I ask.

He shrugs. "It is too early. I do not know." He pauses, his face growing even more doleful. "It is a shame," he says carefully, imbuing the words with unexpected gravity.

A shame. It is that, and so much more. I nod, unable to speak; and he nods back, rising to his feet. *"Merci,"* he says.

I answer by rote, *"De rien."* It *was nothing.* Except that it isn't nothing. Sofi wasn't nothing.

Later, Mike taps on the door again and I beckon him in.

"Did you manage to sleep again?" I shake my head. "You should. Best thing for recovery." He gestures to the other bed questioningly, then sits when I nod, facing across the divide. The bed creaks ominously, in a way it hadn't for the policeman; I'm mildly concerned for the health of the wooden slats. "How do you feel?"

Sad. Exhausted. Beyond weary with this day, with this world. "I'll live, thanks in no small part to you for finding me."

He opens out his fingers as if directing a breeze to disperse my words. "It was a team effort."

"What's happening now with Sofi?" Should I still be calling her that? But what else can I say? The body? Her body? That single iris continues to regard me unblinkingly. *It's still her,* I think.

"The gendarmes are working on the site. I don't know if they've taken her off the mountain yet." He stiffens slightly and turns his head toward the outer wall for a brief moment before turning his attention back to me.

"Do they know what happened?"

"If they do, they haven't said so yet. They're mostly liaising with us through Akash—his French is the best—and me. I've

185

been trying to keep Robert away from it all—he actually doesn't look too well—though he had to go up to the hotel to deal with the university and deliver the news to her parents." His gray eyes are assessing me. "I bet you would feel better after a shower," he says abruptly.

"That's a little direct, but I'll take the hint." Still, I'm somewhat taken aback by his bluntness—and then I realize that he has a finger to his mouth. He lifts the same finger and circles it in the air, then returns it to his lips. The message is clear: *someone could be listening.* Or is it more definite than that? Is he *sure* that someone is listening? My eyes dart to the door that's ajar. There's no sign of anyone there, but I suppose they could be pressed flat against the wall. Eyebrows raised, I move one finger to point outside, and he nods. "Uh, could you help me to the waterfall and stand guard?" I say, a smidgen louder than I might have otherwise.

He flashes a quick thumbs-up with one hand. "Sure. What do you need to take with you?"

Is it my imagination, or do I now hear creaks on the outside terrace? I direct Mike to grab toiletries and a towel, simultaneously twisting to peer out onto the terrace, but if there ever was anyone there, they've gone. They could have come from anywhere, though—the terrace can be accessed from every bedroom and wraps right around the building. All that time when I was worried about jamming the door handle, I hadn't even thought about the terrace access. A cold shiver runs through me: *What else haven't I considered?*

We leave the room together, moving slowly with me leaning heavily on Mike's arm (I refuse to be carried again), but when I look up, I stutter to a halt. The door of the room opposite mine is open, but the entrance is barred by a crisscross of red-and-white police tape: *Sofi's room.* And Julie's. *I wonder where Julie will sleep?* I think inconsequentially.

"But it's . . . it's not a crime scene," I say to Mike.

"No. And someone has already been through her things. I expect they just didn't quite get round to removing the tape." He tugs me gently and I start to move again, resisting the urge to look back over my shoulder. The door two along from mine is wide-open—*Akash, James and Caleb's room,* I think—and I glance in, clutching at Mike's arm to halt him again when I spot the unmistakable yellow of Julie's hair. She's on one of the single beds, curled awkwardly with her head on Caleb's stomach and his arms wrapped protectively around her. I can't see her face for the tumble of her hair. Caleb's eyes meet mine and he silently mouths, *She's sleeping.* I nod, and Mike and I resume our slow procession.

"Don't look so worried. He's a good lad, Caleb," Mike says quietly as we navigate the stairs, one step at a time. "He'll look after her; he's not the sort to take advantage."

"No. I know." But I hadn't been worried about Julie, or what she and Caleb might or might not do when teetering on the edge of that awful black abyss. Instead I've been trying to work out who could possibly have been creeping around, eavesdropping on the terrace: not Mike, nor Caleb or Julie, of course. And I can hear Robert, Akash and Olive in the salon, so not them either, unless they ran down quickly, which surely we would have heard. But it could have been anyone else out of the group—which leaves Peter, James, Jana and Will. And then it occurs to me that since we got back, I haven't checked if the laptop is still there. I clutch Mike's arm. "Can you do me a favor?"

He stops, his weight on one foot on the bottom step, for once only a couple of inches taller than me, since I'm standing one step higher. "What?"

"Can you run back to my room for something, please?"

"Sure. What did you forget?"

I tug on his arm and stretch up, and belatedly he catches on, leaning so that his ear is nearer my mouth. I catch the faint smell of masculine shower gel: something with *Sport* in the title, no doubt. "My laptop is under the mattress," I murmur quietly. "Can you bring it with us?"

He lifts his head. I can see confusion in those gray eyes, but he nods anyway. "Back in a jiffy."

He returns less than a minute later, the laptop wrapped inside my red towel with a corner of it just visible, and we head toward the waterfall at the end of the lawn, pausing only to reassure Robert and Akash in the salon as to how I'm feeling.

"Shower first," Mike suggests as we approach the waterfall. "We can talk after. I'll stand watch."

It seems silly to be unwrapping Olive's bandage so soon after she applied it, but now that I'm here I find I'm too eager to be properly, truly clean to mess around with trying to keep my ankle dry. The water is no less cold than I remembered it—a cold that steals inside, a cold one could sink into. Surely its icy reach is cold enough to wash away memories, to dissolve whole days. But when I'm finished, still gasping from the shock as I towel my goose-bumped flesh, that pin-sharp iris is still there in my mind, gazing sightlessly at me.

"It's all right," I call to Mike's back. "I'm decent now."

He turns, then shifts position to settle on a slightly closer boulder. "So: James," he says with no preamble. "Tell me."

"He essentially threatened to blackmail me."

"What?" He searches my face. "Over what?"

"A misunderstanding. Or perhaps it's more accurate to say a misinterpretation." I sigh and explain what James believed he saw between Sofi and me in that nocturnal shadowy world, while I sit on my own boulder in a patch of dappled sunlight and try to re-create Olive's dressing. Apart from a mild lift of eyebrows, Mike's expression doesn't change.

"That little shit," he says again when I've finished, though without quite the same intensity as before.

"I think we've already established that." I'm aiming for irony, but I can't keep the acid out of my tone. I reach for the towel and start to rub my hair.

He's quiet for a moment, idly stripping a stick of its bark, revealing the pale vulnerability of the green-white inner layers. "He can't truly think you had anything to do with what's happened to her."

"No, I wouldn't think so, but I think he'd be very happy to make my life miserable. I've realized I really don't much care if I lose my position at the university—not that James would know that—but I suppose I'd rather not go out under a cloud."

"Interesting." He continues working on the bark. "If she was still here, this would all be nothing," he mutters, almost to himself. "She could refute it herself."

My hands cease toweling my hair. *Still here.* As if she's just left to go somewhere else, which I suppose she has, though not anyplace where we can reach her. The abyss yawns in front of me. For a moment I feel a very real fear that I might suffer an instant of vertigo and fall in, tumbling back to those dreadful, despairing first days after Nick's death when there was not a single point of light in the world, when it would have been all too easy to lose myself for good. I force myself to put down the towel, pick up a brush. I learned that, somehow, after Nick: do one thing. Then the next, then the next. It turns out that life is really just a series of single actions. Well, not life exactly: survival. Life is something more.

For a moment Mike watches me work the brush through the tangled mess of my hair; then his eyes drop quickly away to the stick in his hands as if he's somehow ashamed to have been looking. It occurs to me that, ordinarily, the only person who would have seen me brush my hair was Nick, and perhaps anyone in the women's changing room at the gym, and I'm suddenly absurdly aware of the unexpected intimacy of the situation, the seclusion afforded by the trees. I find myself hurrying to break the silence. "Actually she wrote about it in her diary—both the incident and her apology. So there's proof right there, I suppose, not that I would really want to be using her diary in my defense."

His gaze swings sharply back to me. "You've read her diary?"

"Julie and Caleb asked me to this morning." I explain their thought process and he nods.

"Sensible." He pauses. "Was there anything in it? Anything that could have led to"—he makes a slight movement with his hand as if trying to pull the right word from the air—"well, this?"

I shake my head. "But I didn't have time to read it all. I just read the last few entries."

"When was the last entry dated?"

"Yesterday morning. So we have no idea if anything relevant might have happened during the day. And I suppose there could be something relevant from earlier on, before this trip; I can look later." I feel a small pang of guilt, but I can't bear to tell him about Will. If I tell him, I can never untell him; he can never unknow it. Loyalty to Will demands that I keep his secret safe—and loyalty to Jana, in a certain way: surely she would have to be the first if I were to tell anyone at all. But I won't. After all, Will has nothing to do with Sofi's death. *Maybe nobody has anything to do with Sofi's death; maybe she really did just fall . . .* Mike is looking at me oddly; I change tack quickly. "I did find out that it was James behind that bet, though. Not that it's exactly relevant."

"And once again, he proves that he's a little shit," says Mike sourly. Then: "Do you still have the diary?" I nod. "Who knows that?"

"Julie, Caleb, Jana. So we probably ought to assume Will too. And, I suppose, anyone who saw me reading it outside the chalet this morning." This morning. Only this morning. It seems further away than that. Who said, *The past is a foreign country*? It's another world, another universe.

"So basically everyone could know, but might not, depending on their levels of observation."

"Yes, I suppose. You didn't."

"Yes, but I was up at the hotel this morning." He's shredding a second stick now, methodically pulling off the bark in long strips. "What's with the laptop?"

The sudden change of direction catches me by surprise. "Oh. Well, I might just be being paranoid."

"Like I said before: unlikely."

I laugh a little. "Wait till you hear me out before you pass judgment." I tell him everything, starting with the break-in in Oxford, right through to the sense of someone chasing me on the mountainside. He starts in surprise when I explain about someone trying to get onto the laptop. "Why on earth didn't you say anything?"

I flush a little. "I couldn't tell if I was being paranoid; I still can't. I'm . . ." I think of the expression on Jana's face when

191

she said, *Be rational.* "I'm aware people don't currently see me as the most reliable of witnesses; I'm not exactly keen to go out on a limb publicly right now." The glances, the quiet whispers of *How is she doing, do you think?* as I left a room: I had endured enough of that when I went back to work. "If I did, pretty much everyone would chalk it up to me being overwrought or depressed or otherwise rendered unstable on account of Nick. And I have been all of those things, and more, at times." He tips his head briefly, not entirely conceding the point, but not arguing it either. "Even now, I can't tell if I'm being paranoid or if I really shouldn't be trusting anyone."

"You're trusting me now," he observes. I can't read his expression; his eyes are focused on the work of his hands.

I shrug. "You're too big to be the person who broke into my house."

"You're assuming there's only one person working against you." I stare at him. He's right. I have been assuming that. He looks up and smiles at whatever is displayed on my face. "Relax. Even if there's a multitude of people working against you, I'm definitely not one of them." His hands lift in a gesture that could be either placation or surrender, leaving the bare, barkless twig resting on his lap. "I know, I know: that's exactly what someone working against you would say. You'll just have to have a little faith."

"Mmmm."

He laughs, that gravel rumble that comes from deep in his chest. "Ah, a true skeptic." He picks up the now white twig, surveys it critically, then tosses it into the spring. It bounces along in the ice-cold water, then catches on a half-submerged rock. *It could be a bone,* I think, suddenly chilled deep inside, deeper even than the reach of the glacial shower—and then the current tugs on it, freeing it to tumble along with the water, out of sight. "We shouldn't assume the two threads are connected," he muses. "But we shouldn't assume they aren't either."

"Threads?"

"What happened to Sofi and what's been happening to you."

"But—connected? I don't—" I stop. *How slow have I been?* "You're saying . . ." I work it through. If Sofi's death wasn't an accident, then someone killed her. Even though my thoughts have got this far before, my mind still skitters to a halt: *Killed her. Are we really considering that?* It appears we are. And if someone did deliberately kill her, there must have been a reason. But what kind of reason is worth killing over? "How could there be a connection between Sofi and someone snooping through my things?" Except they weren't snooping through my things: they were snooping through Nick's. And Sofi did have Nick's number. They even had two meetings . . . I should tell Mike that. But I'm not sure I'll be able to hold myself whole if he assumes what I myself have considered, even though I can't truly bring myself to believe it; I mean, *Nick*—really? Is it even feasible that Sofi would have been interested in my *sweetly enthusiastic giraffe-sized nerd*? I certainly loved my husband but even I recognized that the pool of people who would find him an attractive proposition was limited. But still, I can feel it growing inside me, the urge to spill it out and have someone—anyone—reassure me.

Mike shrugs. "Maybe it's something simple. Maybe she saw someone doing something they shouldn't have been. Such as, well, snooping through your things. Or trying to get into your room."

"Yes," I say slowly. "I suppose."

He looks at me. "Spit it out."

"What?"

193

"Whatever it is that you're biting your lip and trying not to say."

Nothing, I intend to say, but that's not what comes out. "Sofi had Nick's number. In her diary."

"Ah." His brow creases marginally: a strong statement of emotion for him. "I can't imagine why."

"Yes, you can." My words are beyond dry; they're as parched as a desert.

He shakes his head. "No, I really can't. I do not for even a millisecond think he was cheating on you." He looks at me. "And neither do you, really," he says gently.

I look down at my hands, at the brush I'm still holding. I will not cry. Not now, not here.

"We should probably find out why she had his number, though," he says after a second or two. "It might help to shed light on whether there's a connection. Can you get into Nick's profile on his laptop, see if there's anything there that gives us a clue?"

"Yes, I'll have a look later." I'm grateful for his businesslike approach; it helps me to find the same. I wrap all my toiletries and dirty clothes in the wet towel, then stand, flexing my ankle awkwardly; I can't tell if I've applied the bandage too tightly. "We should head back."

Mike picks up the laptop, then offers me his arm to lean on; I smell his shower gel again. "Perhaps Jana should sleep in your room with you. You could play the invalid card and say that you might need something in the night."

"Yes." And I really might. In truth I don't fancy navigating the stairs alone by torchlight with a dodgy ankle. And I'm definitely not keen on falling asleep alone without extensive jamming of both the inner door and that inexcusably hitherto ignored terrace door, and I can't think how to jam the latter, since from memory it opens outward. But it has a key, at least; perhaps jamming is unnecessary.

We're crossing the lawn now. The sun is beginning to set; the peaks have taken on an odd syrupy orange tone, as if the surface is a semitransparent skin with the light of fire burning far beneath seeping through. Lamps have already been lit in the chalet. I think of the clock, of the liquid light running along the etched whorls and swirls of the pendulum, like blood coursing through its veins. I wonder if it's running fast or slow right now. I wonder what kind of time it was keeping when Sofi died.

As we enter the chalet, it's evident that the salon has become the chosen point of congregation; Will, Jana, Peter, Robert, Akash and Olive are all present, looking up and acknowledging us with somber nods and muted greetings. All but Jana have a glass of red wine in their hand, though Olive's looks untouched. Akash is leafing through one of the official chalet diaries, a small heap of others at his feet. Jana pats the empty spot on the sofa beside her. "Why don't you have a seat and I'll drop off your things and then come back down?" Mike suggests. "Do you need anything from your room?"

"Thanks; no, nothing," I say, lowering myself down onto the sofa next to Jana. We swap our burdens: the laptop for the towel-wrapped bundle. I rest the device on my lap, wondering if anyone is secretly eyeing it longingly, but if they are, I can't discern it. I'm conscious too of the grandfather clock's imposing presence some meters behind me, like an authority figure peering over my shoulder. I grit my teeth: I will not look. I do not need to see it dancing through its own mercurial version of time.

Jana leans against me, breathing out in a long sigh as she does so, like a tree yielding to the wind. I put my arm round

195

her and kiss the top of her head, feeling my eyes prickle. I've become practiced at handling my own grief; other people's grief is harder to witness. Julie and Caleb cross paths with Mike, entering as he's leaving; I see Mike briefly squeeze Caleb's shoulder on the way past. Olive gets to her feet and carefully shepherds Julie to a chair. She looks better than she did earlier: her skin is no less translucent but there's a touch of pink to her fair cheeks; the sleep must have done her some good.

A sudden thump and a shout from above rents the quiet of the room. Peter half rises out of his chair and Robert starts to say, "Wha—" but he's cut off by a clatter of thumping treads on the stairs. In the next instant, James comes into view, his face furiously indignant as he squirms and throws protests over his shoulder at Mike, who has him by the scruff of his hoodie, pushing him into the room. In his other hand, Mike is holding my backpack.

"What's this?" demands Robert with unexpected steel in his voice.

"Perhaps you'd like to ask James." Mike's voice is a whipcrack. "I found him in Emily's room, going through her bag. Perhaps you'd like to ask him what exactly he was looking for."

15

James?" asks Robert, blinking in surprise. Then he turns to Mike. "I'm sure this is all some sort of misunderstanding."

"You really can't grab me like this, you know," James complains loudly. His face is still red with indignant fury. "I could report you," he tosses over his shoulder to Mike. Then he turns back to the rest of us. "I could report all of you for passive bystanding."

I stamp down the urge to laugh. *Passive bystanding—really? When a girl is dead?*

"Relax. I'm not touching you, passively or otherwise," Mike says mildly. It's true—at least, it is now. Less so when Mike was dragging him down the stairs.

"James," Robert repeats, refusing to be derailed, "were you in Emily's room?"

James makes a show of straightening his collar before he looks around the room. Then he throws up his hands as if to say, *Oh, all right, if I must . . .* "Yes," he says, a touch petulantly. "Yes, I was."

"Why?" I ask, bewildered.

He looks at me. I'm certain the malevolence of earlier is there, coiled within him, but I see only calculation in his pale blue eyes. He scans the room again. *He's looking for allies,* I realize. *He's strategizing.* "For Sofi," he says quietly, respectfully. *Ah—so this is the part he's going to play.* "For my friend. She's . . . she's dead, and"—he grimaces as if reluctant to go on—"Emily has Sofi's diary—she stole it."

"I didn't—," I say mildly, but James barrels on.

"Doesn't that strike anyone as a tad incriminating? I thought we should get it back."

"James, I gave Emily the diary," Julie says wearily from her spot on the other sofa next to Olive. "Caleb and I both did." Caleb murmurs assent. "We thought someone ought to look at it, in case it had any bearing on . . ." She stops, wrapping her arms across her stomach, her gaze slipping to the floor.

"What? You gave . . ." James trails off, eyes narrowed as he absorbs that. Then he rounds on Julie. "How stupid can you be? You gave it to the very person who has something to hide."

"James!" says Olive, shocked, but Robert's voice cuts across her. "That's enough," he says sharply. "James, we understand you're grieving—we all are—but you will speak with respect to members of this party, or there will be repercussions— repercussions above and beyond the fact that you've been found going through a university fellow's private property."

Mike passes across my familiar gray rucksack. "Is anything missing?"

"I'm not a thief," protests James, but I notice he's more careful with his tone; he needs Robert on his side. Mike raises an eyebrow in the mildest telegraphing of disbelief. James can't resist a dig: "Believe me, she has nothing I would want."

I start to rummage through the rucksack, trying to remember what ought to be there. My phone and wallet are the most obvious items to check for; they're both there, and as far as I can remember, the contents of the wallet appear to be intact. And my cap and fleece, and the water bottle, and sun cream . . . The absent item is so obvious that somehow I don't immediately notice—until it suddenly hits me. "It's not here." I search through the bag again with increased urgently.

"What isn't?" asks Mike.

"The diary. Sofi's diary. I had it in the rucksack when we were out searching and I haven't taken it out since I got back. It ought to still be here." I go through the bag once again—conscious of all the eyes in the room on me, conscious of the relentless glare of the clock burning into my shoulder, of the pace of time starting to pick up—before frantically upending the bag to tip all its contents out on the sofa. But a bulging A5 notebook is not like a lost lipstick or pen. It can't have been hiding in an overlooked corner and it doesn't magically appear on the upholstery. I look up at Mike in consternation.

"James," Mike says warningly, "if you—"

"Don't look at me; I don't have it." He raises an eyebrow at Mike's now much more obvious expression of disbelief. "What, do you think it's hidden in my underwear or something? I'm fairly certain you'd notice." He holds his arms up as if surrendering and turns in a full circle. To me, his every movement is a calculated taunt, but I wonder what Robert sees. "Look, no diary. Or do you want to strip-search me too?"

"Shall I go and check your room, Emily?" offers Peter. He's standing now also, moving from foot to foot, the nervous energy that's always present within him responding to the tension in the room. "You never know. A fresh pair of eyes can't hurt."

"Sure. Thanks." He lopes off as if released from a starting gate, but I don't have any hope he will find it. It was in my rucksack, tucked safely into the bottom, and now it's not. It hasn't been merely mislaid. Somebody has deliberately taken

199

it. I look at James, at the scorn for me, for all of us, that hides in the twist of his mouth. He could be lying. He could have somehow secreted it away, in whatever kerfuffle took place upstairs with Mike, but if he has hidden it somewhere, that somewhere isn't in my room; he's not at all concerned about Peter going off to search.

"Could it have fallen out of the bag during your tumble?" asks Jana.

"Unlikely. It was right at the bottom, under my fleece, and my fleece didn't fall out." I think about it. Could I have pulled it out by accident when I retrieved my fleece? It doesn't seem probable that I wouldn't have noticed—the diary is not a small object—but I suppose it's possible. I shrug. "I guess it's theoretically possible that it's out on the hillside somewhere." The weight of the clock's stare has become a physical presence on my shoulder; without conscious decision, I yield and turn to it. The clockface seems smoke tinged, the etching on the pendulum fire bright as it swoops back and forth, back and forth, beating and beating, pulling me in . . .

"Now, perhaps we can talk about what really matters?" I hear James ask, but his words are muffled, as if the atmosphere has thickened to dampen them. When I breathe in, the air catches peculiarly in the back of my throat, scratchy and hot. I feel Jana's hand on my arm, bringing me back to myself. Even so it's a fight to turn my head away from the clock; it's as if the pendulum has beaten the air into the consistency of treacle. When I finally wrest my gaze away to land on James, I see the young man's eyes are not on me or Robert or even Mike, but on the grandfather clock. His face is flushed, but not with anger; his eyes have become glassy, and he's sweaty and pale, except for the high spots in his cheeks, as if a fever has taken sudden hold of him.

"No," says Robert decisively. "James, we understand your concern for Sofi, but you've acted abysmally." His tone has become chiding, full of sorrowful disappointment. *He's speaking to him as if admonishing a favored child,* I realize. "You need to apologize to Emily for invading her privacy. James? Are you listening?" James visibly starts and turns to Robert. "And . . . and you must beg her permission to be allowed to continue your stay here."

"What? You're not serious—"

"Completely serious. I suggest you either find a way to convince her or start packing your rucksack." I look at Robert, surprised at such a stark ultimatum from him. Perhaps Robert cannot envisage a scenario in which James would choose not to comply, but it's clear to me that James' pride may not allow him to. His pride—and something else. *The clock. The clock may not allow him to.* I shake my head—what am I thinking? The clock is nothing more than an overly large timepiece that displays inadequate timekeeping. Perhaps I'm concussed after all, no matter Olive's opinion. "You are here at my pleasure as a guest, and your invitation can just as easily be rescinded."

"You wouldn't—you can't just throw me out." For the first time, James looks shocked, and a surge of vindictive satisfaction wells up inside me at finally seeing him off-balance. I knew I didn't like him, but still, the strength of that wave of emotion surprises me. It's almost . . . hate. *But I don't hate him.* I don't like him, certainly, but—hate? I feel my hand creeping up, one index finger rubbing the crease between my eyebrows. The room is too hot, the air too heavy, the implacable tock-tock of the clock too oppressive . . .

"No, of course not," says Robert, gently. "But we can escort you up to the Hotel Le Prarion; I'm sure, as a favor to us, the

201

proprietor can find a space for you to lay down your sleeping bag if all the rooms are already taken this evening." He raises his eyebrows, waiting for James to acquiesce; encouraging him, even.

I can see the war within James, his struggle to overcome his pride. I see his eyes slide toward the clock; I see his head turn, tugged round by the relentless sweep, to and fro, of the pendulum. I see the exact moment when he loses the battle. "I will *not* apologize to that woman," he seethes. *That woman.* How exactly does he manage to infect those words with so much scorn? Olive visibly bristles on my behalf. "Not when . . ." He pauses, trying to regain some self-control in the face of the shock Robert is displaying, but his fury is burning too fiercely. *Like the clock*, I think irrationally. *It's infecting him too.* I know what he's going to say; he's too angry to be calculating now. Now he's going to lash out. "Not when *she*"—he points a finger directly at me—"knows what happened to Sofi."

And there you have it. There's a collective gasp from the room, followed by a chorus of protests. My mind scrabbles through potential responses as I desperately try to ignore the thump of my heart. *This is not the time to give in to the insistent beat, to lose my grasp on myself.* Peter is back, standing in the doorway—empty-handed as expected. He glances round the room, frowning, then crosses to the external door, only meters from me, and opens it. The sudden sweep of cold air is as gasp inducing as the waterfall shower, bringing with it the same clarity as if I'm waking from a dream. I hold up my hand for quiet and am pleased to get it. "That's quite a statement," I say conversationally to James. "What is it you think I know?"

"I know you were sleeping with her. I saw the two of you outside together; you know I did."

I'm dimly aware of Robert's surprised face swinging round to me even as I shake my head, feigning weary disappointment when what I really feel is an echo of my earlier virulent loathing—and no small amount of fear. An accusation like that, even just rumors of an accusation like that, could kill an academic career. *But I've already realized that I don't much care anymore.* That thought somehow galvanizes me. *It's just a game, and one I can win if I play it right.* "James," I chide gently, layering the name with lashings of deliberately patronizing patience, "we've been very patient with you. We know you're upset about Sofi, but this really isn't acceptable. I'm not quite sure what you think you saw, but I certainly wasn't sleeping with Sofi. My husband— Well, it's only been a few months since his death." I look down and take a deep breath. I'm not exactly acting but nonetheless I have an audience, one that I'm intensely aware of. The cool night air licking through the room seems to be honing my awareness of the knife-edge I'm balanced on. "I'm not—I'm not ready for a relationship with anyone, and if I was, it certainly wouldn't be with a student."

"She's lying," he spits out angrily, circling to eye every member of the room. "I tell you, she's lying." He swings back to me. "I'm going to tell the police about you." But the glassiness in his eyes is receding; he has the air of a man who doesn't quite understand how he came to be where he's standing, but is determined to brazen it out.

"You should absolutely do what you feel is best," I say steadily. The effort required to retain this facade of serenity is beyond measure.

"You're such a fucking liar!" His anger is mixed with disbelief. This isn't how he saw this unfolding. I'm sure he doesn't truly believe I know anything about Sofi's death; the real cause of his disbelief is that he's failed to convince other people. And the anger is because I'm making him look stupid. *No, not just that: the anger is aimed at himself too. He can't believe he put himself in this position.* "The diary will prove it."

"The diary nobody can find?" I ask gently.

"I'll find it." His words are fierce, and in that moment, I realize he doesn't have it after all; he hasn't cleverly hidden it away somewhere. And now it seems to be dawning on him that he isn't carrying the room with him. *Perhaps he'd failed to factor in the grieving-widow sympathy vote,* I think with grim humor. Without the diary, though, he has no leverage to speak of. "I'll find it, and you'll all see. You all know Sofi liked to fuck the fellows. It was her thing. She wrote about it in her diary. I've seen it; she's bound to have written about this. All we need is her diary—"

"That's enough." Robert's words are clipped, his distaste and disappointment clear. "James, I can see you're not going to apologize." He glances incongruously at the door Peter has opened. "Shall we shut that?" But Peter doesn't move, and Robert's gaze has already turned back to James. "Please go and pack immediately. One of us will escort you up to the hotel."

"Fine by me. I'd rather stay there than under a roof with *her*. Sofi is dead, *she* has motive"—that accusatory finger finds me again—"and you're all—"

"I said, that's enough," snaps Robert. He's on the balls of his feet now, his head jutting forward and a frown lowering the eyebrows over his sharply attentive eyes. I'm suddenly put in mind of a bull. To my surprise, James does quiet down, his nostrils flaring as he sucks in oxygen.

"Perhaps we should let him stay tonight," Will says in a quiet aside to Robert. "We shouldn't risk another accident on the mountainside, especially when we're all exhausted and emotions are running high. He can leave first thing in the morning." He turns to me. "If that's okay with you, Ems?"

I nod. "We certainly shouldn't put anyone at risk." The moral high ground. I daresay standing on it makes me look wonderfully magnanimous, though I am itching to see him gone. He's too angry with me now; he won't be able to help himself from spreading poison. Though ought I be even more wary of him when he's isolated, carefully plotting? It's hard to tell. How far will he go? "But I confess I'd rather not be in his company."

Robert nods. "That's completely understandable. He can eat in his room." He glances around, his gaze alighting on Peter. "Peter, can you please escort James to his room? He can stay there tonight and leave in the morning."

For a minute I think James might resist—and then what? Are we really prepared to physically manhandle him upstairs? But he goes with Peter, throwing one savage glare around the room as he departs. I uncurl my hands, suddenly aware of pain where my fingernails have dug half-moon welts into my palms.

Mike yawns. I blink: a yawn! It's so wonderfully prosaic, so normal and unstressed. "Thank God for that. I shouldn't think any of us want to listen to any more of his crap."

Robert shakes his head, suddenly weary and, in contrast to Mike, visibly upset. "I'm so sorry, my dear Emily. It's so very out of character for him." He shakes his head again, still clearly unable to understand the scene he's witnessed. "I can only suggest that grief does strange things to people."

"Of course, of course," I say soothingly, still atop my great hill of magnanimity. Mike finds a glass of something red and

205

puts it in Robert's hand; he stares at it bleakly for a moment, then takes a sip. "Shall we shut that door?" he says again.

"No, leave it," Julie says sharply as Akash moves to do just that. "I mean, please," she says, reddening a little as she recognizes her own abrupt tone.

"Well done," murmurs Jana from beside me on the sofa, too quietly for anyone to hear. "You handled that beautifully."

I blow out a shaky breath. "Jesus, do you think so?"

"Look around." I do: Julie and Olive look somewhat shocked, though I presume that is at James' behavior, since there are no sideways glances in my direction; Caleb and Akash remain wide-eyed at the drama but don't seem particularly thrown by it; Robert and Will are now conversing quietly, with Will scrubbing a hand through his hair in exasperation, and Mike is looking out of the open door at the growing darkness beyond. I can't tell what he's thinking at all. "Nobody is giving him any credit at all. How on earth did he get the wrong end of the stick?"

"I'll tell you later." I'm sure she will agree to share my room tonight, which will afford plenty of time and privacy to relay that tale, though it will feel like a betrayal to tell it at all; I can't imagine that Sofi would have wanted that.

Olive stirs and drags Akash with her to lay out a buffet of cold meats, cheeses and salad in the dining room. It's not an evening for a formal dinner at the table; we take our plates and balance them on our laps, dotted around the dining room and the salon, and Peter takes a plate up to James. I'm surprised to find I'm starving, though it doesn't feel like an ordinary form of hunger. It's more intense: as if my very survival depends on eating, as if I may not get another chance before the next onslaught. I shake my head at my own melodramatic tendencies: *the next onslaught*. What on earth does my beleaguered psyche think has yet to come? The grandfather clock is no longer hovering in my peripheral vision, but I find myself turning to it from time to time regardless. The smokiness has gone from the clockface; there's no suggestion of a smoldering fire inside, but nevertheless I feel a continual urge to check.

After I've eaten my fill, I take a mug of coffee and limp outside, taking care not to spill, to join Will, whom I spotted slipping outside to drink his on the bench. He glances round at my approach, the faint light from the windows of the salon sliding across his face as he does so, like a thin silken shroud. "Ems. Hey you." He puts down his mug and shrugs out of his fleece to tuck it around my shoulders. "You scared us a little today," he says with a deliberate casualness that touches me all the more.

"I'd apologize, but it wasn't exactly intentional."

I hear his wry smile in his words. "I bet." Then: "Was it awful, finding her?"

"Yes, at first. Then . . ." I can't find the words. The light behind us is too weak to reach far, and there are no stars tonight. We are both of us staring out into the dark. "I got to say good-bye, I suppose."

He nods. "I'm sorry." *For what?* That I found her, or that she's dead, or for his affair with her? As if he's read my mind, he makes an awkward movement with his hand. "For all of it. But mostly for the future that she's lost."

I lean my shoulder into him and he puts an arm round me. I feel the solid presence of him next to me, the reassuring press of a warm body, breathing in and out. It feels like a shelter, a form of protection, but I know that's an illusion. Nick was warm and solid, until he wasn't. Sofi too. But still, we sit together and drink our coffee, staring into the black.

After a time, I sit up a little straighter and he drops his arm. "James is—"

"Occasionally vile," he says viciously but quietly.

"Yes, he is."

"He's certainly got the knife in for you."

"Yes, he does. Not quite sure what I did to deserve that." It *is* odd, his enmity. The strength of it . . . Surely it can't be born out of nothing? But I truly can't think of a time where I slighted him. "But all of that apart, he's read her diary." My voice is barely more than a murmur. "Not the last entry or two, I would think, or he'd have seen that she apologized to me."

He nods. "That didn't escape me."

"I wonder why he didn't accuse you too. Perhaps he didn't get to that part yet?"

"Yes, perhaps. Or . . ."

"What?"

"Or he wants something. In return for silence."

He had certainly been willing to threaten me. "Blackmail?"

"The thought had crossed my mind," he says bleakly. He takes a swig from his mug, then grimaces, and sets it aside. "Gone cold." Then: "You've read the diary." It's a statement, but I know there's a question he wants to ask.

"Not all of it, but enough."

"How . . . how bad is it?"

"You mean, how incriminating?"

"Yes, that. But also . . . how bad?"

"Incriminating enough. But it also makes it clear that you weren't a predator, that she targeted you rather than vice versa."

He nods, though I have the sense that I haven't given him the answer he's looking for. "Well, I suppose that's something."

"Not really." The biting edge of the night air is strong enough to lean into and sharp enough to pare away all artifice. A nagging thought follows unbidden: *Sharp enough to strip away the effects of the clock?* I shake my head fiercely as if the motion might dislodge this nonsense from it. "We don't have it, and even if we did, if you're ever in the kind of trouble from which you're reliant on that diary to save you, you're already irredeemably fucked in the court of public opinion."

He winces. "Ouch. I don't remember you ever being quite so direct."

"No," I say thoughtfully, "I don't think I was. It's a new thing I'm trying out."

"I'd say you're taking to it like a natural."

We sit in silence for a moment. "If it wasn't lost on the mountainside, then somebody has the diary," I say. "Presumably that somebody will read it shortly and find out about you and her."

He sighs, a long exhalation of quiet despair that diffuses into the cold, clear mountain air. "Yes, that hadn't escaped me either."

16

I search my bedroom when I retire to it that evening, even though I know the diary won't be there. And it isn't, of course, but it was an exercise I needed to undertake, and I will probably feel the need to do the same in the morning, given that torchlight isn't terribly satisfactory for a search. I sit on my bed, exhausted and suddenly acutely aware of the relentless ache in my ankle and shoulder, even though both have been with me all day. Then I remember that Jana will be joining me, and I have to lever myself up again. I'm slowly clearing my things off the other bed when a rap sounds on the door.

"Hey." I swing my torch over to the doorway and find Jana, dressed in pajama bottoms and a vest, her sleeping bag and torch in hand. She grimaces, turning away from the light. I can see that her face is already devoid of makeup, and without it, she seems smaller, somehow. More defenseless.

"Sorry," I say, unscrewing the top of the Maglite torch to switch it into candle mode, then balancing it precariously on the wooden floor between the two beds.

She pushes the door closed, shoving it hard to get it to catch. "Ours is warped too," she remarks. Then she plays her torch over the room and drops onto the bed I've just cleared, looking exactly how I feel—as if the day has drained her of every ounce of reserve. I suddenly remember that she was feeling unwell yesterday.

"Sorry, I should have asked—are you feeling better?"

She yawns and waves a hand from her prone position. "You're forgiven; there's been quite a lot going on," she says with wry understatement. "But no, I'm not really feeling any better. If I'm lucky, I won't."

It takes me a minute to understand. "Oh! You think you might be—"

"Don't say it!" she interrupts. "I'm not saying it either. I just feel . . . different . . . and a bit queasy at times, and generally quite shit . . . but it's probably nothing." She starts to shimmy into her sleeping bag, then stops as she watches me jam the door handle with the chair. "Ems, really—paranoid much? Not that I don't appreciate good security and everything, but is that completely necessary?"

"Probably not. But it makes me sleep better at night."

"O-kay. Have you . . ." Her words are uncharacteristically cautious, feeling their way across to me. "Have you been sleeping badly, then?"

"No," I say lightly, "because I've been practicing good security."

"Right." She rolls her eyes at me. "Well, it's on your head if I wake the entire chalet just trying to get out for a pee."

"Speaking of peeing, can you take a test? Or is it too early?"

"No, not too early. I thought it would be tempting fate to bring one with me, so I'll have to go to the pharmacy in Les Houches. I'll go tomorrow. Jesus, it's freezing in here. Did you leave the terrace door open all evening?"

"No." But she's right: it *is* colder than normal; I swivel on the bed to reach out a hand to the terrace door, rattling the handle to check it's properly secure. It is indeed locked, but on closer inspection there's no sign of the key that's usually sticking out from the lock. Has someone moved it?

"What are you looking for?" asks Jana sleepily.

"The key for this door. It was here earlier." I'm sure of it. I can even picture it: a rusty brown metal key with a hollow oval loop for its bow.

Jana rolls to lean over the edge of her bed, using her torch to look under both her bed and mine. "There—look." I follow her pointing finger and see the key on the floor, a few inches inside the overhang of my bed. The cold light of her torch distorts the perspective; the rusty iron key seems absurdly large, the shadow it casts impossibly black. I feel embarrassingly reluctant to shove my hand under the bed to grab it, but I scold myself into it. *What's the worst that can be hiding in that darkness? A spider or two?* Still, it's a relief when my scrabbling fingers close around the cold hard metal and I can pull my arm up again.

"What did the police ask you?" Jana asks as I try to fit the key back into the lock.

"Probably the same as they asked you. What happened that afternoon and evening; where I was, where everyone else was. What you'd expect, I suppose."

"Same." She yawns. "Though I can't say I had great replies; I couldn't remember where everyone was. Thank heavens the gendarme interviewed Will and me together; at least he had some answers."

"Did he interview the others in groups, then?" The key isn't fitting back into the lock for some reason. I pick up the Maglite and turn it back into a torch.

"No, I think it was just that Will and I were together pretty much all of that time, so it made sense—Ems, what on earth are you doing with that lock?"

"The key isn't fitting. I'm trying to see if there's something wrong."

"Is the door locked?"

"Yesh." My answer is muffled on account of holding the torch in my mouth to free both hands.

"Then for goodness' sake, leave it. We can look at it in the morning."

She's right. I put the key on the floor and turn back around, shuffling into my sleeping bag before I switch off the torch. We lie in the silent dark for a moment. "Mike thinks someone killed her," I say in not much more than a whisper.

Jana doesn't answer for so long that I wonder if she's already asleep. "Yes," she says at last. "I heard him talking to Will about it. Something about no sign of her trying to break her fall."

I think of those perfect painted fingernails, that smooth unbroken skin. "It's true. I didn't see any, whereas I'm a riot of cuts and bruises and in desperate need of a manicure." I will be wearing the evidence of my ordeal for quite some days to come. "But . . . *murder*."

"It sounds so unlikely. Like something you hear on the news that happens to other people, not to people you know. But . . . I suppose someone always knows them." Her words are quiet, thoughtful. This is the Jana that few people get to see.

"Who do you think could have done it? And why?"

I hear her sigh. "Maybe some psychopath out on the French equivalent of day release? I can only imagine she was in the wrong place at the wrong time." She pauses. "Wait." I hear a sudden movement as if she's sat up in bed. There's an urgency in her voice now. "You're not really thinking it was one of our group, are you? You know those questions from that policeman— God, I swear he was clinically depressed; I've never seen anyone so miserable. You know those questions were just routine?"

"Yes. I suppose. It's just— Well, it crossed my mind."

"Well, have it cross back," she orders grumpily. "I don't need a conspiracy theorist for a best friend." It sounds like she's lying down again with a great deal of flouncing. "After all, what on earth would anybody gain from it?"

I smile into the dark. "Thanks for sleeping in here, honey." *Best friend.* Would I describe Jana as such? In truth, Nick was my best friend for so long that I wouldn't have considered the question at all.

"Thanks for still being alive." Half of her words are blurred by a yawn. "You scared us a little today."

I smile again; it's word for word what Will said earlier. "I scared myself," I say wryly. "Night, hon."

"Sleep well."

I should sleep well—I'm exhausted in all possible ways: physically, emotionally, mentally—but I don't drift off immediately. My mind has been caught, like clothing snagged on a nail, by Jana's seemingly rhetorical question: *What on earth would anybody gain from it?* What would they? It's the right question, assuming the culprit was acting rationally. Except: *Are we all behaving rationally?* In the daylight hours, I wouldn't doubt it. But at night . . . I think uneasily of James, of the glassiness in his eyes. It was as if something was driving him down a road that he might otherwise only flirt with taking . . .

But that's patently ridiculous, I tell myself. And anyway, if the assumption is that the perpetrator is not acting rationally, then there's no good reason to presume it's a member of the chalet party rather than a random stranger. I try to relax— tugging at the question won't help—and Mike's words float back to me: *Maybe she saw someone doing something they shouldn't have been. Such as, well, snooping through your things. Or trying to get into your room.* I feel my breath hitch. James was snooping through my things. James was trying to get into my room. What if . . . what if he was trying to point the finger at me to cover up his own involvement in Sofi's death? What if he had never been looking for the diary at all? Could that have simply been a cover story when in reality he was searching for Nick's laptop? Or am I merely considering him because I'm already predisposed to violently dislike him? *Dislike*, I remind myself. Not hate. What I felt within me in the salon weren't my true feelings. It was just the oppressive atmosphere, the tension, the . . . *the clock.*

Stop it! I think fiercely, beyond irritated with myself at the circular motion of my thoughts. I think resolutely of the laptop instead: I brought it up with me; it's sitting on the floor beside my bed. I reach down and feel for it in the dark, my hand brushing against the iron key once again before finding the smooth, cold surface of the device. I lift it up to my chest, and then, inspired, I push it down inside my sleeping bag, right to the bottom, where my feet barely reach it. There's no way anybody could steal it tonight without waking me first.

But James . . . why would he want Nick's laptop? Why would anyone, for that matter? It would have to be connected to Nick's work, I suppose. I remember suddenly that the IP rights team should have called me back by now, but I haven't put my mobile into reach of reception all day. I will have to limp up to the hotel tomorrow.

Finally I do drift off, to dream of a single eye, the iris the color of ancient polished wood, the pupil a dark black abyss that expands and expands, implacable and relentless, until it begins to swallow all around it. As it grows, I see that deep within it is a fire, the same glowing banked red that I've seen in the clock, and suddenly I realize the abyss *is* the clock and I back away, terrified, then turn to run, but I know that it's futile—it's coming for me. It's coming for all of us.

How are you feeling?" Peter asks me solicitously when I join the breakfast table the next morning.

"Soooo stiff." I groan, settling gratefully into the chair that he's pulled out for me. "And bruised. Like I tumbled hundreds of meters down a rocky alpine mountainside— Oh, wait. I did."

"Coffee might help." Mike pushes a cup across to me.

"It could," says Olive, nodding earnestly. "There are studies that suggest that caffeine can relieve post-workout soreness." Mike's eyes meet mine, then dart away; I have the sense he's trying very hard not to laugh. "But probably better to try a short walk if your ankle is up to it," Olive continues. "It should help you loosen up and get some blood flowing."

"Thanks, both." I look around the table, tallying the attendance. We're short James, Jana, Julie and Caleb. And Sofi. We'll always be short Sofi.

"I could mainline coffee this morning," Akash says, yawning as if to prove his point.

"Couldn't sleep?" Peter asks sympathetically.

"No, I slept— Well, not at first, because I thought I smelled smoke, so we all went to check—but after that, I slept. But jeepers, the dreams . . ." He trails off, shaking his head. "I've heard that dreams at altitude are vivid, but this was something else." His mouth twists in a rueful grimace. "I suppose I shouldn't have read Bochert again last night. That clock story must have got in my head."

My head snaps up just as Will, casually buttering some toast, says, "The clock? Snap—I dreamed of it too last night."

"I— Me too," I say, just as Olive says, "Weird, so did I."

I look at Mike, and he nods reluctantly. "Yup," volunteers Peter tersely. His hand has halted in its stretch for the jam, and his eyes, when they meet mine, are wide and unexpectedly troubled.

We all look at Robert, who glances round the table, his sharp eyes taking us all in. "I'm afraid I never remember my dreams," he says breezily, but his eyes slide quickly to the coffee in his hand. *He did dream of it*, I think. *He did, and he doesn't want to admit it.*

"Well, that's strange," I say carefully into the silence. *I'm doing it again*, I think. *Trying to project calm lest I be taken for a hysterical female.* "Some sort of collective phenomena?"

"We had a very stressful day yesterday." Robert's words are gentle. "I daresay it's simply a reaction to that."

But Peter is not deterred. "What did you all dream? What specifically?" I can see his leg bouncing under the table.

"Peter, we had a stressful day," repeats Robert, some irritation creeping into his voice. "I wouldn't read too much into it." I start to open my mouth, but he cuts me off firmly. "Now, has anyone seen Julie or Caleb this morning?" Peter's lips form a thin mutinous line, but he chooses not to press his point.

"I saw Caleb much earlier, waiting for the loo," volunteers Akash. The one chemical toilet in the chalet can attract a queue. "He's back upstairs with Julie; he didn't want her to wake up alone." I suppose that answers the question as to where Julie slept. I wonder if she got any sleep at all and, if she did, what she dreamed of.

"I'm not going to be up to much on this ankle for a day or two; I could use the time to help you look through the diaries," I say to Akash under the cover of the general hubbub of conversation that has broken out once again around the table. My words are casual, dancing lightly across the surface as if that way I can convince myself I'm simply being helpful: *No obsession here, nothing to see; move along!* But Akash doesn't question my interest; perhaps he's not one to look a gift horse in the mouth. "Great." His enthusiasm is palpable. "I'll give you a pile. Any particular era?"

"Whatever you like."

He reaches out and grabs a handful, scanning the spines quickly. "Here you go. Looks like . . . yep, 1956 to 1962. I'm between wars at the moment, in the early thirties, but I'll soon catch up to where you're starting: after World War Two broke out, there wasn't a trip until 1952. You should absolutely feel free to come back for more when you're done." He looks around the table at the deceasing pile of pastries. "You know, I should take some breakfast up to James," he says, as much a question as a statement.

Mike looks up. "Good man," he says, passing Akash a plate to load with a croissant and jam and a mug of coffee. I watch him leave the room, his thin shoulders already braced as if he's readying himself for an uncomfortable ordeal. "Thank you, Akash," I call after him.

"Is Jana still out for the count?" Will asks me.

"Absolutely dead to the world." I wince at my own phrasing, but Will doesn't react, so I forge onward. "I didn't think there was any reason to wake her just yet."

"Yes, that's fair." Robert nods as he butters a piece of croissant. "I don't suppose any of us will be going far today. The police may still want to speak with us, in any case."

"Are Sofi's parents flying in?" asks Mike. Just the mention of her name conjures up that awful expanding circle of sickly devastation. *It's the netherworld again,* I think. *What I saw was the netherworld flowing out of her, tainting all it touched.* Except I didn't, of course; it was just a hallucination. *What if that means the netherworld is inside me, infecting me too?* I feel the rising beat again and try to breathe steadily without alarming anyone. *Calm down. What you saw was just the result of a concussion, or shock, or the stress of the sheer awfulness of finding her.*

"Just her mother; she'll be arriving this evening," Robert is saying. I can feel the hammer of my pulse returning to normal as I concentrate on calming myself. "I'm not entirely sure of the home situation but it sounds like the father was never part of the equation. She grew up with her mother and late grandmother." *Mimi.*

"I suppose Tanner's not coming out now?" Peter asks, and Robert shakes his head just as Akash appears back at the door of the dining room, the plate and mug still in his hands.

"He's not here," Akash says.

Peter twists in his chair. "What do you mean, he's not here?" he demands.

"Exactly what I said," Akash replies with commendable patience. "He's not in his room, and his stuff is gone too."

"Jesus Christ," says Peter, turning back to the table and throwing his hands up in disbelief. "This is like fucking *Groundhog Day.*"

"Do we have to go searching for someone we're kicking out?" asks Olive of nobody in particular with no apparent intention of irony.

"If we do, forgive me if I don't join the search party this time." I don't bother to hide the acid in my tone.

219

"We do," says Robert firmly. Then he adds in a softer tone, "But if a search party is required, you're excused, Emily."

"I doubt it will come to that. But we have a duty of care to make sure he's safe, at least," says Mike. "He must have gone at first light, either up to the hotel or down to Saint Gervais. Did anyone hear anything?"

"Hear what?" asks Julie. She and Caleb have joined Akash in the doorway; he shuffles along to let them into the room.

"James is gone," Akash tells her.

"Gone where?" she asks.

"That's precisely the question," says Will.

"Typical James," says Caleb, his mouth twisting. "He'd rather leave on his own terms than be kicked out, and he couldn't give a toss if he inconveniences anyone with worry in the process." He looks at Akash. "Is that going spare?" he asks, gesturing to the plate in Akash's hands. Akash looks as if he's about to say no, but then shrugs and hands it over. Caleb pulls out a chair and reaches for more jam.

"But did anyone hear him leave?" persists Mike. Nobody pipes up.

"Who was sharing with him?" I ask.

"He was in with us—Caleb and me—originally, but then . . ." Akash trails off. I'm pleased to see that Julie doesn't blush. She shouldn't have to feel embarrassed for seeking comfort.

"Nobody wanted to share with him after yesterday," Will says almost apologetically; I can see he's uncomfortable speaking ill of a student in front of their peers. "Since Jana was with you, Mike and Akash came into my room—it has three beds—and James took Mike's room." So last night was a veritable case of musical beds.

"Right, then." Mike sighs, putting down his coffee mug decisively. "I'll have to go back up to the hotel to see Pierre; maybe James stopped in there—"

"He's going to think we've entirely lost control of our students," remarks Peter sourly.

"—or maybe the *télécabine* operator will remember him going down the mountain," continues Mike, ignoring Peter. "And I can ring him from there. Does anyone have his mobile number to hand?"

"I do," says Julie, fishing her mobile out of her pocket. She finds the contact details quickly and reels off the number to Mike, who reads it back to her. I can't help noticing that she has stubble rash on her chin. "You know," she says hesitantly, "James was really intent on finding that diary. You don't suppose he might have gone off to search where Emily fell? Just in case it came out of her bag like Jana suggested?"

The room is quiet, the silence broken only by the clink of Caleb laying his knife down on the plate. I look around. The prospect of another search, another disastrous outcome, hangs in the air amongst us all, though none of us wants to acknowledge it. Robert, seated at the head of the table, takes off his glasses and massages the bridge of his nose. "Well," he says at last, "let's hope he hasn't been quite that stupid."

"Jesus," Peter mutters. "*Groundhog Day* it is."

17

I'm keen to go up to the hotel, but I know I will hold Mike up, so I don't try to tag along with him; instead Julie and I decide to follow on together later. The dining room gradually empties until I'm left nursing a cold coffee alone, the chalet diaries I've been allocated sitting in an accusing pile before me. I sigh and reach for one, flicking through it. Scanning the text is harder than I'd anticipated: some of the diarists' handwriting is frankly borderline illegible, and just when I get used to each script, the trip ends and a new one begins with a new diarist's hand to become accustomed to. Still, I find a rhythm within the research. The record of each trip follows the same format: a list of attendees and respective roles, then a day-by-day account of the activities, as brief or as lengthy as suited the whim of that particular diarist. The repetitive nature is somewhat reassuring: the same walks, the same games, the same pattern of chalet life over half a century ago. I'm almost lulled into forgetting how different this particular chalet experience is panning out to be—but then Julie reappears, her grief weighing heavily in her wan smile and the dark smudges under her eyes, and I'm jolted back into the hopelessly bleak reality of *this* trip with nothing to show for my thirty minutes of research.

We head off together to the hotel, and initially I find I'm gritting my teeth with every step, despite the high-tech adjustable contraption that Peter has lent me to help take the pressure off my ankle—*Don't think of it as a walking stick*, he'd advised rather sweetly. *It's a hiking pole.*—but I gradually start to feel a little better. Perhaps it's the endorphins from exercise, or perhaps Olive is right and the activity is loosening my knotted muscles, but either way I'm surprisingly glad to be making this trek.

"How are you holding up?" I ask Julie.

She shrugs. "Okay, I guess. I don't know." Then, after a beat: "Nobody I knew ever died before. Nobody I was close to, I mean. I don't know . . . I don't know how to *be*."

"There's no rule book to follow. Just . . . try to be kind to yourself, and let others be kind to you." My natural honesty gets the better of me, and I add wryly, "Not that I did a very good job of that after Nick died, I have to admit." I'd lost myself for a while, oblivious to everything but that abyss of grief. And when I pulled myself out of it, I found that the abyss had stolen things from me. Time, for one: so much time spent grieving. And also pieces of me—important pieces, the pieces containing the ability to trust in myself and to have faith in the future. I don't know if I will ever get them back.

We go on in silence for a while, though it doesn't feel awkward. *If Julie was my age, we would be friends*, I think. I wonder if I would have worked that out without this bloody awful experience. It's going to be another beautiful day; once again there's not a cloud to be seen. *There should be rain*, I think. *Nothing so dramatic as a storm: there should be relentless gray drizzle, dreary and cold*. It was the same when Nick died. We had a period of unexpectedly beautiful spring weather, and I wanted to scream: *How dare the world shine like this, putting smiles on strangers' faces in the street, when Nick is dead?*

"I keep wondering, though," Julie says hesitantly, then stops. I wait for her to go on, the hiking pole marking out time with a *tak* sound every second step, but she stays silent. We're approaching the hotel now; I can see Mike pacing on the relatively empty terrace as he talks on the phone, his free hand occasionally gesticulating. "Yes?" I prod gently after a few seconds.

"It's just . . . I feel guilty. I feel like it's somehow my fault, like there was something I should have done." Now that the words have broken through, they come in a torrent. "Why wasn't I with her that afternoon? I should have been there, rather than playing bloody cricket—cricket! I hate cricket!—at the chalet—"

"Hey, hey, hey." I lay a hand on her arm and she turns to me, her eyes shining with unshed tears. Both of us stop walking. "It's not your fault. It's really not." She looks up at the cloudless sky, her throat working; then her eyes meet mine again, and she nods once jerkily. "I saw a therapist after Nick died. He told me that it's human instinct to try to make order out of everything. We tell ourselves there *must* have been a reason—and when we can't find one, we blame ourselves. But it's simply not true. None of us are to blame."

She nods, blowing out a shaky breath. "You're right. Thank you. I needed to hear it." Then she adds darkly, "Except someone might be to blame. If she was killed."

It's my turn to release a long exhalation. "Well, yes, there is that." I wonder if she came to that conclusion herself or if Caleb suggested it. We resume our walk to the hotel, the hiking pole making a more strident noise on the rockier ground here.

224

"You know, James won't be blaming himself," she says with distinct bite. "He couldn't bring himself to, even if he killed her himself. He'll be busy blaming everyone else."

"True. He's already tried blaming me." We're climbing the last few steps to the terrace. Julie picks a table for four and pulls out a chair as I struggle to fold down the pole. Mike is over by the barrier, still on the phone; he raises a hand in acknowledgment and mouths, *Be right with you.* "Julie, last night James seemed to suggest he'd read Sofi's diary before—did she know about that?"

"Oh, yes," she says emphatically. "They had a massive bust-up about it. When I think about it now, I can't believe I didn't see what he was like right then." She blinks, as if her former self has appeared in front of her and she can't quite comprehend what she's seeing. She'd held a torch for him, I realize with surprise. Caleb is without doubt an enormous improvement. "It wasn't a recent thing—it was last year. We were all living in college, and her room was right beside his; they were always in and out of each other's space." *Like Will and me in our final year,* I think. "But then she found out he'd read her diary—not only read it, but taken photographs of certain pages—and she was utterly furious. On the face of it, she forgave him, but I'm not sure she did really; I think maybe she just pretended for the sake of the wider friendship group. And this year we've been living out of college, on Iffley Road—not with James—so he wouldn't have had much chance to see her diary, I wouldn't think, even if he was dumb enough to do the same thing again."

"I see." *Last year.* Will said their affair started around Easter; James wouldn't have read anything about it, then. A waitress comes to the table, and we order coffee for ourselves and for

Mike, who mouths across his order. "But the photographs," I persist. "Does he still have them?"

Julie shakes her head. "She made him delete them." Then, as if hearing what she's said: "Though I suppose that's not foolproof. He could have copied them first. Or sent them to someone. Why? Do you think the police might be interested in them?"

"They might." Though that's not why I was asking. "Why on earth did he want photographs of her diary anyway?"

Julie reddens a little. "She, uh, she has—had—an interesting sex life." She adds, a little defiantly, "As she had every right to."

"Of course. Nothing wrong with that, so long as nobody gets hurt." I almost cringe: Could I sound more awkward and out of touch?

"Yes," Julie says, though that single word somehow passes from defiance into uncertainty, and her brow knits briefly. *Her thoughts may as well be written in the freckles on her skin,* I think.

"But still," I press, "why would he want photographs?"

Julie looks nonplussed as if she's never actually considered the question before, and is now wondering why not. "I . . . I don't know," she says slowly. "He's always been a bit like that— I mean, he likes to know things about people; knowledge is power and all that. He always seems to know the latest gossip before anyone else does."

"Hey." It's Mike joining us from his phone call.

"Any news on James' whereabouts?" I ask as he sinks into a chair.

"Some. He was at the hotel bright and early, asking for breakfast before they were ready to serve it; Pierre took pity on him and gave him a cup of tea and a stale croissant. After that, I don't know. He may have taken the *télécabine* down, but the lift operator couldn't swear to it."

226

"Does it matter?" asks Julie. "He's not a child, and now we know he was safe and well after he left the chalet, can't we just ignore him?"

"I'd love to, but there's a complication," Mike says. "The police want to interview all of us again this afternoon, and they'd prefer we stay in the country. I need to at least pass that message on to him, but he's not answering his phone."

"Stay in the country?" Julie says, startled. "Is that an order?"

Mike shrugs. "I'm not clear on whether it's a strict instruction or a polite request, but either way, I expect it's best to obey."

"Text James," I suggest. "Then you've done all you can."

"I have. I suppose it will have to do." He shrugs; clearly it feels inadequate to him. I watch him for a moment. Something is bothering him about this; the lines round his mouth are a little deeper. He feels the weight of my eyes on him and looks up quizzically. I half shrug and pick up my coffee.

"Why do they want to talk to us again?" asks Julie, but Mike is prevented from answering by the arrival of our drinks. He takes a moment to stir some brown sugar into his coffee, something I haven't seen him do before, and suddenly I'm filled with dread as to what he's about to say. "Sofi," I say, unable to wait for him to say it, "they think she was killed. That's it, right?"

He looks across at me, his gray eyes steady and direct as he delivers what I already know is coming. "Yes, they're treating her death as homicide."

Julie takes in a sharp breath, and I turn to her. It's midmorning now, and the sun is beating down strongly. She closes her eyes briefly and tips her head up. She might simply be enjoying the warmth on her face, were it not for the convulsive working of her throat. Then she brings her head back down and opens her cornflower eyes.

227

"Caleb said they would," she says. *Bless him for preparing her*, I think, but nonetheless, her composure is startling. "We've been trying to work out who might have done it. They deserve to rot in jail for the rest of their fucking life." I see it then in the set of her jaw, in the taut line of her shoulders, in the balled fists: it's not tears that her throat works so hard to lock in. It's anger. She's a hair's breadth from erupting in an outpouring of primal rage.

"Yes, they do," I say quietly.

"So," says Julie, sitting forward on her chair and barreling past my words, "the key period of time must be the afternoon, after we all came back from the walk. As far as I can figure it, Caleb, Akash and myself were together all of that time. Apart from going to the bathroom, which I would think we can all agree is too short a time to be suspicious—yes?" Mike and I hurriedly nod. "Okay. Where were you two? Is there anyone else we can rule out?"

"Julie," Mike says gently, "we'd do better to leave this to the police."

"Leave what to the police?" asks a voice behind me. I turn to find Will there, with Jana just behind him.

"Oh, hi," I say, grateful for the distraction; perhaps it will help derail Julie. It surely can't be good for her to develop an obsession with this, though it's all too easy to empathize. If Nick's death had been murder, would I have behaved any differently? "Join us, please." Mike gets up to drag across another table to add to ours as Will finds two more chairs.

"What are we leaving to the police?" Will persists as he and Jana lower themselves into the seats.

"The investigation," Mike says calmly.

"The police are treating it as homicide." Julie's words are tight, with staccato delivery.

"Julie suggested trying to figure out where everyone was on the afternoon that Sofi went missing," says Mike, unruffled.

"Jesus," says Jana, visibly unsettled. "Not another conspiracy theorist." I feel myself stiffen as Will lays a warning hand on her arm. "Homicide," he says, blowing out a long breath. "Not a surprise, really. Go on, then, where were we all? Who has an alibi and who doesn't?"

"James doesn't," Julie says flatly.

An awkward silence blankets the group. I glance around, wondering who is going to go into bat on this. It certainly won't be me. "Well—," starts Will cautiously, but Julie cuts him off.

"Nobody saw him after we came back from the walk."

"I saw him," Jana volunteers.

Will blinks. "Where?"

"When you did your calls, I had a little wander, just across to the *télécabine* and back—remember? I saw him walking up the path toward the hotel, but I don't think he went in."

"You didn't see him, Will?" I ask.

Will shakes his head. "No. I would have thought I would have if he'd come into the hotel proper—actually, from where I was sitting, I'd probably have seen him even if he stayed out on the terrace."

"You saw Sofi, though, right?" Mike asks Will.

"Yes, and we had a brief chat. She left before I did."

"Yes, that's right." Jana nods. "She'd gone by the time I rejoined you to walk back down." Will looks across at Jana involuntarily as if to check if she suspects anything untoward about his tête-a-tête with Sofi. *He will have to be careful of that,* I think. *He will give himself away.* Or maybe not; maybe I'm only reading something into his reaction because of what I already know. "I suppose the police are speaking with the staff here?"

Jana says. "They can confirm who was here when, who left together, et cetera."

"I expect so," Mike says. He turns to Will. "Sounds like you were the last person to see Sofi alive."

Will grimaces. "What an awful thought. I wish I'd said something—I don't know—something important."

"Me too," murmurs Julie.

"I think we all wish that," I say. That single iris gazes at me with infinite patience. What more do I have to say? There must be something, surely; otherwise what is it waiting for?

"I bet James doesn't," says Julie savagely. "And despite Jana having seen him, he's still unaccounted for during most of the afternoon."

There's a general exchange of glances around the group. Once again it's Will who sets his shoulders and tries to wade in. "Julie," he says gently, "you have to be careful what you—"

"Oh, for God's sake, Will, why shouldn't she say it?" says Jana with unexpected vehemence. "As I've told anyone who would listen, I personally think some local French nutcase—probably driven mad by all this wholesome mountain air—is to blame, but if you're going to indulge in these conspiracy theories, then at least have the honesty to face up to what you find." She turns to Julie. "If you think James might have killed Sofi, then by all means say so."

"All right then. I do think that." There's a blunt heaviness to Julie's words, like the thud of an ax in a block of wood: they can't be discounted; they can't be unsaid. The ax slices through, forcing each of us to consider which side we will fall on. "I think he killed her and that's why he's run off. I think he'll resurface back in the UK, safely under the protection of his father's no doubt reassuringly expensive lawyer. And I think

230

that if we don't get our act together and help the police, he'll get away with it."

"Um. Right. Well, okay," says Will. I can see he's attempting to regroup, looking around for support, but we're all teetering; we haven't yet picked a side. Even I, with more cause perhaps than anyone else to have animosity toward James, haven't yet thumped down. "Then tell me why. Why would he have killed her?"

"I haven't worked that out yet," Julie says thoughtfully. "But I will."

Later, I sit out on the terrace under the shade of a parasol, and work through my emails and voice messages. Will and Mike are doing the same, spread out over separate tables for a little privacy, but Jana and Julie left together to walk back to the chalet. One of my voice mails is from the IP office; I manage to get through to them but the person I need isn't available— would I like to leave a message? I grit my teeth and do indeed leave a message, wondering if I'll be back in the UK before I actually make any headway on this.

"All okay?" asks Will. I hadn't noticed him moving toward my table.

I shrug. "This lack-of-reception thing is really losing its shine for me."

He drops into a chair, sinking into it so deeply that his head rests on the back and his arms dangle over the armrests. "We could be here for a while if the police don't allow us to travel."

"You think they'll keep us here past our intended departure date?"

"I don't know. I've never been this close to a murder investigation before. I hope Julie doesn't derail them into wasting too much time looking into James; I'm sure that's a red herring. It's probably just easier for her, psychologically speaking, to pin it on someone who isn't with us right now, sleeping under the same roof."

Sleeping under the same roof. A deep, cold unease takes hold of my insides. "Christ, that's a terrifying thought."

"Sorry. I didn't mean to scare the living daylights out of you. I'm with Jana: I'm sure a local nutcase is to blame. After all, why would any of us want to kill Sofi?"

Why indeed? It bears thinking about. I haven't been nearly systematic enough in attempting to answer that question. He cocks his head. "Are you going to tell the police about . . . ?" He lifts one of his hands and spreads the fingers briefly before letting it flop back down toward the ground; the gesture could mean anything, except for the fact that he and I both know it means only one thing.

"I won't lie."

"Of course not. I wouldn't ask you to." He pauses. "But that's different from volunteering the information."

I don't say anything. I don't want to be in this position, to have this weight of responsibility. I think it over, looking out at the magnificent mountain view, the snowy whites, forest greens and granite grays as clean and sharp as cut glass in the brilliance of the sunlight. But it's an illusion: up close, the reality is muddled, messy detail. *Like physics,* I think, surprising myself. When I first learned mathematics and physics as a child, I adored the elegant exactness, but that was an illusion too. When you get right down to it, when you get close enough, I've come to understand that the truth consists of messy uncertainties and entanglements that we don't fully understand. *Perhaps we're not meant to look so closely.* Perhaps a certain distance is always best.

He sighs, taking my silence as a statement. "Yes, I know. A sin of omission is as good as a lie. I know. So . . ." I look across at him, but his head is tipped to the sky, his sunglasses concealing his eyes. "I think I have to tell Jana," he murmurs. "There's too great a chance that it comes out anyway, and I'd much rather it came from me." Now he looks at me, but all I see is the bright reflection in his lenses of myself and the terrace tables with their colorful umbrellas. "So if you could possibly just keep quiet until I've done that . . ."

I nod, but my heart is aching for Jana. Why does it feel like there is no right course of action in this situation?

"Thank you."

I clear my throat. "When will you tell her?"

"As soon as I get a chance." His mouth twists. "I daresay she'll come straight to you afterward, so you'll know as soon as I have."

"Will you tell her I knew?"

"Up to you."

I look out again at the perfect panorama, at the pretense it displays to me, to all of us. "Tell her," I say at last. "I don't want to lie." Then, after a beat, in as conversational a tone as I can manage: "Sofi had Nick's number. In her diary."

"She did?" He frowns, and then suddenly, unexpectedly, his face clears. "The IP office. She was doing some work with the IP office. It looked good on her law course application, and to be fair, she really enjoyed it. It must be that." The IP office. Could that really be it? Could the explanation be so simple and innocent? I feel the hope leap inside me, along with the guilt of having suspected him even for a millisecond. Will cocks his head toward me. "Did Nick have any patents in the works? I can't quite remember what he was working on."

"I don't know."

"I bet that's it." He rests his head back down again. "I can't think of any other reason. No offense to Nick, you know I'd have walked through fire for him, but I really doubt he would be Sofi's type."

A sweetly enthusiastic giraffe-sized nerd. "None taken," I say dryly. "Did you ever tell Nick about her?"

"No," he admits. "But then, nothing much had happened before he died."

"Would you have?"

He takes a moment to think about it. "Probably not. He certainly wouldn't have approved, and I would have . . . disliked feeling his disapproval." He grimaces ruefully. *Yes,* I think with a sudden rush of certainty. *Yes, he would have disapproved, and he would have been incapable of not showing it.* I know that. And I also know he would not have allowed himself to do anything he disapproved of. *So why on earth did I even consider that he might have been involved with Sofi? Was it because of the impact she'd had on me?* Dear Lord, a therapist would have quite the job unpacking that . . . "Sometimes," Will says quietly, almost musingly, "I wonder if part of the reason I was more . . . susceptible . . . was because of Nick's death."

I round on him instantly. "Don't you dare blame—"

"No, God, I'm not. I'm really not." My tone yanks him upright, palms raised toward me. "I'm sorry. That came out wrong. I just meant— Well, I was grieving. I don't know that you make the best choices when you're hurting like that. It's not an excuse; it's just a factor."

I look at him, and suddenly I recognize what he's doing: he's rehearsing, feeling out the strengths and weaknesses in his case. He's rehearsing for Jana. I push my chair back, suddenly queasy, sick of people and complications and intrigue and quite desperate to be alone. "I'm going to walk back," I say shortly.

"Oh. Okay. Well, I need to send a few more emails, so I'll follow in a bit."

My mobile starts to ring as I step off the wooden boards of the terrace: an Oxford number. The IP office, most likely. I take the call leaning against the barrier, aware of my head thumping as I try to understand what I'm being told.

"No patents in process at all?" I ask for the second time.

"That's right," says the (very patient) voice at the other end. I've already forgotten his name—Matthew, Mark, John? Something biblical.

"Then I don't quite understand," I say carefully. "You had a Miss Sofi Jenners working with you. She was in contact with my husband."

"Oh, Sofi. Yes, she's certainly done quite a bit with us. Well, if it wasn't in connection with a patent your husband was applying for, I suppose it could have been in connection to another patent application by someone else. A prior art search or something like that."

"Prior art?" I've heard Nick mention the term before, but I can't quite remember what it signifies.

"Yes, it means anything that's been made available to the public before the patent claim—anything relevant to the patent claim, I mean. If an invention has been described in prior art, then the patent application wouldn't be valid. Look, shall I have a word with her and get her to call you? She's a student; she's not actually working with us right now, but I'm sure she wouldn't mind."

He doesn't know yet. Of course he doesn't; it will take some time for the news to be disseminated around the university. I hadn't anticipated being the bearer of bad tidings. "Ah. That's going to be difficult, I'm afraid. She's—she died very recently."

There's silence down the phone. "Right," he says uncertainly. I wonder if he quite thinks I'm entirely stable. "I . . . Sofi? Really? Are you sure?"

Quite sure. I couldn't possibly have invented that single staring eye. "Yes, I'm afraid so." I can see Mike gathering up his stuff as I talk. I rather doubt I'm going to get my solo walk after all.

"How—"

"I'm not sure it's my place to discuss that." I'm aiming for gentle but firm, but it's possible I'm coming across as tearfully deranged. I clear my throat quickly. "Surely she must have been working under the supervision of another staff member?"

"Well, yes." He sounds relieved to be on firmer ground. "Of course."

"Perhaps you could get in contact with them and ask them to ring me? I'm keen to know what was being discussed. My lawyers tell me it might be important for Nick's estate," I add, hoping that the mention of lawyers might add some weight.

"Oh. Yes. Yes, of course. We'll come back to you as soon as we can."

"Thank you." I disconnect and start to unfurl the hiking pole as Mike approaches.

"The IP office?" he asks. I nod. "So? Did Nick have anything in process?"

I shake my head, still struggling with the pole.

"Really? That's a surprise. I would have put money on there being something in the works, either solo or with collaborators."

"No. I think that's why Sofi had Nick's number, though—she was working at the IP office."

"Right. That makes sense." We start to walk. It doesn't take many steps for me to realize that descending is going to be more jarring than ascending. "No patents at all," he muses. "Well, that's kind of a relief."

He almost has a smile on his lips. I can't imagine why. "A relief?"

"Now I don't have to worry that you killed Sofi."

"I . . . What?" I stop and stare at him.

He shrugs. "If her death was somehow in connection to the IP stuff, then you'd have the most to gain. I had to consider that you might have been playing dumb about not knowing about it."

"But . . ." I'm still staring at him. "I was in the salon all that afternoon. I have an alibi."

"True. But Peter doesn't, not for the whole time. You might not have been working alone."

"Jesus." I've been knocked so comprehensively off-balance that I almost can't process. "You've really been looking at all the angles."

"Yes." He's surveying me. I can feel his amusement even if I can't see any trace of it. "I'm not saying I thought it was very likely, but yes, I've considered it. Are you offended?"

"I ought to be."

"Really? You're a very smart, capable individual. If you wanted to commit murder, I'm sure you could get it done." He's examining my face with that unshakable gaze. "Would you prefer I thought you incapable?"

"You're saying I should see it as a compliment?"

"Exactly." Now I can see the crinkling by his eyes. "Surely you've considered me?"

"I . . ." *Have I?* Not with anything like the rigor he has clearly applied. *Call yourself a scientist?* I admonish myself. Twice in as many conversations, I'm being reminded that I haven't approached this systematically at all. I need to rectify that.

"I'm offended. You should consider me: nobody gets a free pass. I'll have you know I could do a very fine murder if I turned my hand to it."

"I'll bear that in mind." Then, after a beat or two, I ask, "Were the kind of things that Nick was working on really worth killing over? Isn't it just a myth that universities are making a fortune on patents?"

"You're right; most universities don't even make enough to cover the costs of their own intellectual property departments. But there's been a real push, at least in the engineering department, to try to address that. Peter's been a big proponent, to his credit. We've been collaborating early with the private sector to try to make sure that what is developed not only pushes knowledge forward, but also has real-world applications that can be monetized."

"I know. Nick used to moan endlessly about the NDAs."

Mike chuckles. "Well, he was kind of a genius; literally everything he dreamed up seemed to have potential. He had more collaborations—and consequently, more NDAs to deal with—than pretty much the whole of the rest of the department put together. I bet you now hold stock in quite a number of spin-off companies."

He's right; I do. I haven't quite got my head round it all yet; I'm still working through the finances. "But still—were these projects worth killing over?"

"That's quite a subjective question."

"Is it?" I wonder. "There must be an objective level at which most people might start to find themselves at least tempted. Ten times their annual salary, say. Or twenty times—I don't know.

There's probably a normal distribution around some kind of mean. Or maybe not a normal distribution; I wouldn't expect zero skewness . . ."

"Whatever the form of the distribution, your husband would have been way out on the tail."

"I know." I smile faintly. There is no amount of money that would have tempted Nick. He simply didn't work that way. "But we both know he wasn't exactly typical."

"Yes." Mike thinks. "Twenty times one's salary as a threshold for considering murder? I can sort of see that. And in that case, then yes, Nick's projects were worth killing over. I mean, his collaboration with Audi on the EV—electric vehicle—stuff . . . well, that alone could end up worth a very tidy sum of money. The sort of sum that's very much worth killing over."

Oh, I think blankly. *Worth killing over. And here we are with Sofi dead.*

Caleb

Aug 14th

Locations on the afternoon when Sofi went missing:

- *Me, Julie, Akash: always together, except for 5 mins here or there, which wouldn't be enough time—NO*

- *Mike: worked with Robert clearing the garden for most of the afternoon, but big stretches where he was elsewhere (said he was showering and then in his room, but unconfirmed)—POSSIBLE*

- *Robert: worked with Mike on garden clearance but also had a long nap (unconfirmed)—POSSIBLE*

- *Peter: stayed at the hotel to do emails after the walk, where he was seen by multiple people, but came down alone later—POSSIBLE*

- *Jana and Will: both were seen by multiple people up at the hotel and leaving together—NO. Wait: unless they killed her together? Which seems far-fetched, but all of this does.*

- *James: seen out walking on the main path by Jana,*
  but otherwise unaccounted for—POSSIBLE

- *Emily, Olive: both were working in the salon all*
  afternoon—NO

  So: Mike, Robert, Peter or James; or Jana and Will
  together. Or some random nutter, I suppose.

Motive? Tricky, that. If it was cold-bloodedly rational, then
the killer ought to have gained from it—and what on earth
could anyone gain from killing Sofi? She had no money or
power. A crime of passion, then? She wasn't sleeping with
James, and it seems highly unlikely that she'd have been
sleeping with Robert. If anything is or was going on with Mike
or Peter or Will, there's been no sign of it as far as Julie or I
could tell—though Julie did say that she thought Mike might
have been deliberately keeping out of Sofi's way, which is odd.
Could they have had a fling before? But—Mike? I just don't
believe it. I'd much rather think it was James, though there's
no reason to, and I doubt he'd have the balls. (To be fair, I
wouldn't either, not unless it was self-defense.) Mike would
have the balls, but I can't imagine him taking a single action
that wasn't well reasoned, so that rules him out of a crime of
passion. And he's such a good bloke—which shouldn't count
for anything, but he is.

Maybe I should try going at it from the other direction: What
do those six want? Robert wants everybody to get along
and learn something whilst they're at it—hardly the stuff
of murders. Mike, Peter and Will are rivals for that deputy
job. Peter is the most overtly competitive about it; for him
it's all about money and prestige. For Mike it's about being

thought of as a scientist first and foremost rather than as an ex–international rugby player (though if I'd played at his level, I'd happily rest on my laurels till the day I died). Will seems to be genuinely focused on advancing science, and Jana told Julie she'd like to start a family with Will. James wants to pull the strings on the whole fucking world. And none of that sheds a single ray of light on what happened to Sofi.

Fuck. What if we never find out?

18

You fucking prick!"

I look up from the 1957 chalet diary, on which I've made considerable progress since I've sat down on this sofa—the same sofa as before, with the grandfather clock ticking relentlessly behind me. We're all in the salon predinner, except for Robert, who is staying in Saint Gervais tonight to support Sofi's mother and aunt, and all heads swivel in unison toward the kitchen, from which the sounds of an argument are emanating—or at least one side of an argument: we can hear Jana's raised voice, but not much from Will in response. Judging from that scream of rage, I'd say that he has just confessed and is reaping her ire.

The next shout is a little less distinct. ". . . fucking kidding . . . ?"

I wince. *Really, Will, couldn't you have opted for a more private venue, like a bedroom? Ideally one in a different town?* Or was he counting on the close proximity of the rest of the chalet party to keep Jana's fury in check? A foolish error, if so: if Jana has something to say, nobody and nothing will keep her from saying it. I hear Will's voice in response, a low, indistinct rumble that nonetheless conveys a certain desperate urgency.

"Has something happen—," starts Akash.

"Does anyone have a speaker?" I hurriedly speak over him. "Some music perhaps?"

"I do," says Caleb. He unfolds himself from the sofa and scoots upstairs, taking the stairs two at a time.

Peter edges toward me on the sofa, his half-done *Times* crossword in one hand. I wonder where he picked up the paper—perhaps in Saint Gervais when he got the croissants? "What's that all about?" he asks me in a low voice, gesturing toward the kitchen wide-eyed. I shrug noncommittally. "Jana sounds like she's flipped her lid."

"Perhaps she has good reason," I say tartly, nettled by the implication, more in his tone than his actual words, that Jana is somehow to blame. *He probably thinks she's being hysterical.* It still rankles that he seemed to be automatically on James' side during that altercation out on the path. *Next he'll say she's just hormonal, and then I'll punch him and claim I'm hormonal too.*

"Really? Did something happen?"

I shrug. "I don't see that it's any of our business."

"True." He shudders. "But whatever it is, I wouldn't want to be Will right now." Caleb is back with the speaker, and soon we're folded into the embrace of the Rolling Stones, with only the occasional raised voice breaking through the sound of the time that Mick Jagger has on his side. I can't hear the ticking of the clock above the music from Caleb's speaker, but I know it's there. It's always there.

As if he can hear my thoughts, Peter says, "That was weird with the dreams and the clock this morning. Do you remember what exactly you dreamed?"

"Yes, I . . ." But I realize I don't anymore. Somehow the memory has dissolved during the day. "Actually, I'm not sure now. The clock—maybe fire? I'm not sure. You?"

"It's gone a little fuzzy for me too." He pauses, then goes on in the same low tone. "We could move it, you know."

"What?"

"The clock. We could move it while Robert is gone."

My head swings round to him. *He's disturbed by it too*, I realize. Somehow that is less reassuring rather than more. "But he'd notice."

"Yes." He taps his teeth with his thumbnail, his brow furrowed; then he shakes his head as if he's found himself in a dead end. "Yes, you're right; he would." I'm still staring at him: he gives a quick self-deprecating grimace as if to shake off the weight of my gaze. "I know it's nuts, but somehow it just feels like—I don't know—like a bad influence or something." He shrugs defensively. "I can't explain it. You must think I've suddenly gone alarmingly new age. Or insane."

I shake my head. "No. To be honest, I don't love it myself." But my choice of words irritates me. I think of Sofi's diary: *the power of understatement*. I think of Robert's litotes. I want to call a spade a spade, but in truth I don't have the language for whatever we're facing.

"It's nice to know I'm not the only one." The relief in his eyes is unmistakable; he really must have worried that I might think him nuts. "Maybe whoever shoved it in the attic was onto something." He gestures to the diary. "Any progress?"

"Yes, actually. It was definitely here in 1957. One of the diarists complains that it had begun striking single chimes at random in the middle of the night." I'm conscious of the clock over my shoulder listening to everything we're saying; my words have unintentionally dropped to barely more than a whisper.

"That sounds familiar." He grimaces. "Did you hear it last night? I think it was first at around two thirty a.m. and then

246

again at quarter past four." *Did I hear it?* I'm not quite sure. He drops back into silence and his thumb takes up the tooth tapping once more. A staccato burst of indistinct irate shouting rises above the speaker and we both wince.

"I wonder if the police asked some leading questions," muses Peter.

"What do you mean?" His sudden change of direction throws me; for a moment I wonder what the police have to do with the clock. But then I catch on: the police interviewed us all again this afternoon. In my case, the questions were almost identical to before, asked by the same lugubrious detective, with perhaps a little more focus on where everyone was and exactly when—right up until he asked about Sofi's sex life and the diary. It was clear James had already spoken with him.

Did you read Sofi's diary? Yes, the most recent entries of it, after Julie and Caleb asked me to.

Do you have the diary now? No, it's gone missing.

Were you engaged in a sexual relationship with Sofi? Absolutely not, and you can only have got that piece of misinformation from James.

No? But you were seen kissing her outside the chalet. No, James saw her *try* to kiss me and I rejected her advances. She fled immediately, then apologized the next day for misreading the situation.

Was Sofi involved in a sexual relationship with anyone else here at the chalet? Ah. Well . . .

I had told Will that I wouldn't lie, and I didn't. Faced with a direct question from law enforcement, I couldn't do anything other than admit that the diary suggested a relationship between them and that I'd seen evidence of it myself, marveling at the lose-lose of my situation: I would have felt awful keeping this from the police, and yet I don't feel any better for having come clean. I couldn't help noticing that the policeman, who spoke with both Jana and Will after my little revelations, did so separately this time. Perhaps Jana genuinely is hearing this from Will first. I wonder if that really makes a difference when it's clear he's telling her only because he has to. And then I wonder at myself for such a mean-spirited interpretation. *Jesus, I'm suspecting everybody of every possible transgression.*

"What do you mean?" I ask Peter again, rubbing my temples with both forefingers. I can feel a headache coming on, the sort that's caused by dehydration, though goodness knows I'm drinking enough water to hydrate an army. Perhaps the room is too stuffy for me. The air seems thick and heavy; I fancy it will drag at the pendulum, slowing the timekeeping.

Peter glances round the room, but nobody is paying us any attention: Caleb, Mike, Julie and Olive are playing cards, and Akash is once again working his way through the diaries. Peter surveys them all, then fixes me with a deliberate look, his mouth barely moving as he says, "You must have heard of Sofi's reputation. Her charms were apparently . . . much enjoyed."

"Yes." I can hardly deny that I've heard the same.

Peter nods, then raises his eyebrows slightly and tips his head toward the kitchen in a quick motion. Toward Will. "What?" I say, deliberately playing dumb. He has to say it out loud; I'm not going to bridge any gaps for him.

"I think that he might have been one of her victims. Or beneficiaries, depending on your point of view. Not the only one here either. Anyway, I imagine the police might have asked about that."

I find I'm gritting my teeth: I can't imagine him speaking in the same derogatory tone if the gender roles were reversed.

But I'm too curious as to why he has come to suspect Will to take up that fight. I carefully keep my voice even. "What makes you say that?"

"A couple of things. I mean, I don't know for sure." He chews his lip in a pretense of reluctance, but I can see he's itching to tell me. I raise my eyebrows queryingly, and that's all he needs. "Well, for one, I could swear I heard *cheating little shit* in Jana's tirade. Also, I saw them talking together on the street in Oxford once, which was kind of odd—Will and Sofi, I mean. And then they were having a very intense conversation up at the hotel the day Sofi disappeared." He pauses and looks around. "Isn't it a bit hot in here?"

"You saw them there?"

"Yes. I don't think Jana did; she'd gone off on a stroll. Will and Sofi were inside; I saw them when I went to the bathroom. I don't think they saw me. It looked like the kind of discussion that I shouldn't intrude on." What might he do with that information? I wonder. Is he capable of stopping himself from using it to his advantage? But his attention is not entirely on our conversation: there's a slight frown between his eyebrows and his eyes are still roaming the room as if searching for something. "It *is* hot, isn't it? Should I open the door?" He looks at my expression; I'm not entirely sure what it holds, but it obviously serves to chasten him a little. He leaps up and crosses the room to open the door. The cool evening air floods through the room instantly as if it had been pressing at the door, just waiting for the chance to enter. I see him take a deep breath, then another; I feel myself doing the same. The headache starts to drain away.

Peter crosses back to the sofa and drops into the seat beside me again, continuing on as if our conversation hadn't been interrupted. "Yes, I know, I know. I'm just guessing." There's a touch of contrition in his tone. "I'm not going to yell about it, and I certainly didn't say anything to the gendarmes." *No need. I did that for you.*

"Peter," I say quietly, and very deliberately, "don't you even think of suggesting any of this to Robert or Tanner." I lean toward him, trying to convey the utmost intensity despite my hushed tone. "Will is your *friend*."

He flushes with mortification. "I wouldn't dream of it; of course I wouldn't." But he doesn't quite meet my eye. He had been thinking of it. Of course he had, that active mind of his always searching for an angle. He tries for a laugh, but it emerges shakily. "You have a woundingly poor opinion of me, Ems."

I ignore his words; my mind is snagged on something he'd said. "You said *not the only one here*—who else?"

He raises an eyebrow. "You've just finished taking me to task, and now you *want* me to gossip?" I grit my teeth, and my expression causes him to quickly yield. "Oh, come on, I'm sure you can figure it out." My head swivels to Mike; then I look back at Peter questioningly. He returns my gaze steadily, as good an admission as I'm going to get. "Ask Jana," he says quietly, barely audible above Mick Jagger's repeated insistence on time, time, time . . .

"You might have noticed she's a little tied up right now."

"Ask her later, then. I'm following your advice and keeping my mouth firmly shut."

Suddenly Akash speaks up to the room at large. "Do you think I should check on dinner?" he asks. "Only I was on duty with Will . . ."

"I'd stay here if I were you, mate," advises Mike without looking up from his cards.

"The wine is in the dining room." This is Peter. He's already getting to his feet; to escape my questioning, I would guess. "We can make a start on that, at least."

"Yes, but the bottle opener is in the kitchen," Olive points out.

"Ah, but I have one on my Swiss Army knife." Peter shoves his hand into a pocket of his cargo trousers, producing a red enamel-adorned block of metal with a self-satisfied flourish.

"A proper Boy Scout." There's a sour taste in my mouth; the words that come out are coated in the same bitterness. Mike glances at me; I can see he's picked up on it. I feel myself flush a little. Surely I'm above shooting the messenger? Only I'm not quite sure what the message is yet.

"Never was a Boy Scout," Peter replies breezily. "But I'm a sucker for anything with twenty-two functions." He flicks various tools out of, and then back into, the block. "Even if I don't know what ten of them are for . . . No, no, not that one—and what on earth is that? . . . Ah, got it!"

"I'm out," says Caleb, tossing his last card down. I can't tell if he's won or lost; it's clear his heart isn't in the game either way. "Mike, I meant to ask: any news on James?"

"Oh. Yes. Sorry, I should have said. He's in Saint Gervais. Robert said he saw him and is going to talk some sense into him."

"Good luck with that," says Caleb caustically. "Peter, I'll come and help you with the wineglasses. How long do we hold off before braving the battlefield? I'm starving."

"A bit longer," says Mike firmly. He glances across at me again, over the top of his hand of cards. I know what he's thinking: sooner or later one of us is going to have to go in there, and I'm certain that he, along with everyone else in this room, will nominate me for that job. I can't argue with the logic, given I'm closest to both of the warring parties, but nonetheless I have absolutely no desire to walk into that kitchen. *We shouldn't see inside other people's relationships*, I think. *At least, not at times like these.*

I take the wineglass Peter offers me and return to the diary, but I'm not really reading it; I'm just periodically turning pages that I've already read. In truth it's a cover to allow me to do the thinking that I should have done before. The *why* is the thing I can't work out. The only person that I can imagine having grounds to hold a grudge against Sofi is Jana, and quite apart from being fully accounted for, until approximately twenty minutes ago she didn't even know about Will's affair. I suppose one could construct a premise whereby Will killed Sofi to cover up their affair, but then he'd have to have planned to kill me too—I just can't see it. And in any case, he's also fully accounted for. I suppose since Jana and Will walked down together, they could have killed her together—but to what end? It just doesn't make sense. Any one of Peter or Robert or James could have killed her too, but why? What do any of them have to gain?

Mike. I've missed out Mike. *What did Peter mean?* Surely he wasn't suggesting that Mike and Sofi . . . But he was. I know that he was; and whenever I manage to talk to Jana about it, she will tell me a story that I really don't want to hear. And one that probably isn't true, I reason: after all, Mike told me— Actually, what exactly did Mike tell me? *I've been privy to certain corroborating events, shall we say.* And *I for one am determined to steer well clear.* The implication was that he'd never been involved with Sofi, but he didn't exactly say that. And in any case, why should I expect that he would tell me the truth? If he had slept with her, surely he would never confess it to me. And why on earth do I care anyway? It's his own career, his own reputation that he's risking. It shouldn't matter to me at all.

But it does. I can feel that it does. Somehow I'm willing to forgive Will—who is in a relationship with one of my closest friends, for Christ's sake!—for his affair but I won't forgive Mike, who, as far as I know, is single, if indeed there is anything to forgive. I know why I won't forgive him. I've been avoiding thinking about it: my mind has literally skittered away at every opportunity. It's too complicated and too soon for me. But I can't ignore it now. And I can't afford for it to cloud my judgment. Mike could have killed Sofi, but why would he? To cover up an affair that there's no concrete evidence of? It doesn't make sense.

Mike's words return to me once again: *Maybe she saw someone doing something they shouldn't have been.* Maybe Sofi's sex life has nothing to do with it. If what happened to her is linked to the break-ins, and the searches on Nick's computer, then perhaps what set it all in motion was Nick's death, which was an accident, without doubt—a commercial truck turned left, unaware of the cyclist alongside; Nick was knocked off and crushed instantly—but nonetheless, in that scenario, Nick's work must be the vital link. The IP office and his computer are the only routes I can think of to investigate. Or . . . A sudden thought occurs to me. Nick had a private Gmail address too. Might I find something on there? And the follow-up thought, that I've repeatedly tried to squirm away from, can't be ignored: *If Nick is the link, then the only possible suspects are people from his own department: Peter, Will and Mike.* The logic is inescapable, and yet I can't truly believe it could be any of them.

A loud chime rings out suddenly; I jump, then turn involuntarily to the clock. The dying light outside is somehow flaring in the clockface, turning it a molten gold that's almost too bright to look at. The reverberations of the single strike continue in the silence; the chime has come precisely in the short gap between songs. The others are looking over too; we are collectively holding our breath. Then the speaker starts with the opening bars of "Play with Fire."

Julie makes a sudden movement with her hand. "I bloody hate that thing," she says unexpectedly. "I don't know why but it really freaks me out."

"You're not alone," I say, unable to control a shudder. Mick Jagger continues to croon menacingly from the speaker.

"Caleb, do you have anything more uplifting you can play?" Mike asks. "Like—I don't know—S Club 7?"

"'Reach for the stars,'" sings Peter with much gusto, adding jazzy hands and getting the laugh he was looking for. He's a little too eager to lighten the mood; I wonder if he is overcompensating to fight against his unease. I find my eyes sliding toward the clock again. The beat is building inside me, matching the tattoo inside my brain: *Peter, Will, Mike; Peter, Will, Mike . . .* The headache has resurfaced and I'm suddenly aware that the room is hot and stuffy once again; when I breathe, I feel the same catch in the back of my throat as the other night, as if someone has tossed a damp log on the stove, but we haven't even lit it this evening. I turn to look at the door Peter opened only fifteen minutes ago; it's closed, though I don't remember anyone closing it. *Peter, Will, Mike; Peter, Will, Mike . . .* I know, with complete certainty and complete irrationality, that the clock is somehow to blame for this wave of panic and dread. I need to get out of this room right now. Anywhere, even the battlefield in the kitchen, is better than here; I push myself out of the embrace of the sofa, saying, "I don't know about the stars, but maybe it's time I braved the war zone."

"Good luck," offers Akash only semi-ironically.

The kitchen door is ajar when I approach; it swings silently when I push it, and I breathe a quiet sigh of relief at the cooler, cleaner feel of the air inside the room. It's dark outside now; the only light in the kitchen is from the candles on the checkered table, the pool of which encompasses Jana standing with her back to the room, just in front of the rear door. Will is leaning against the range cooker, his shoulders slumped, almost entirely in shadow.

"Sorry to intrude." Will lifts his head and Jana swivels on her heel. Her eyes are red, one arm is wrapped across her rib cage and the fist of the other is balled against her mouth. "Sorry," I say again. "It's just that everyone is starving, and there's only so long we can placate them with wine before it's going to get very, very messy. Do you think you could maybe . . . fight somewhere else?"

Jana releases a mirthless laugh, then rubs both thumbs carefully under each eye to wipe away smeared makeup.

"Yes. Of course. Sorry," says Will. My eyes are adjusting; I can see him more clearly now. He scrubs both hands over his face, every movement drenched in weariness. "I'm on dinner duty—I promise I haven't let it burn."

"I can take over for you," I offer.

He looks at Jana. "Shall we . . . shall we go upstairs?" he asks cautiously.

Jana shakes her head decisively. "I'm done with talking. Unless you need to tell me about someone else you fucked?" Will winces. She adds something in Estonian that I'm certain is a very uncomplimentary description of Will, before demanding, "No? Anything?" He shakes his head silently. "Then I'm done. And I'm hungry. I want to eat." She sails imperiously toward the door, then stops suddenly and turns to me. "Do I have mascara everywhere?" she demands fiercely.

I want to cheer her magnificence. I want to hug her, but she will cry if I touch her; even the slightest contact will crack the fragile shell she's maintaining. "No. Your eyes are red but otherwise you look gorgeous."

"You'd better believe it." She continues out of the door, but not without tossing over her shoulder at Will, "Fucking prick."

I look at Will. His focus is directed at his shoes, but eventually he lifts his head to connect his gaze with mine. "So," he says bleakly with a small ironic shrug. "That went well."

19

Did you take the test?" I ask Jana.

She's sitting cross-legged in her pajamas on the other bed in my bedroom, applying face cream; she marched straight up here after dinner and Will didn't bother trying to argue. It's too early, really, to be in bed, but it's too awful to sit together and pretend that all is fine: that Sofi didn't die, that the police aren't investigating us, that the implicit trust of the first days of the chalet party hasn't been entirely shattered.

"Not yet. It's best to do it in the morning when the hormones are strongest." She reaches down and scratches her ankle absentmindedly but viciously, then starts to shrug herself into the sleeping bag. I do the same, then reach out to switch off the torch.

"What will you do if you are?" I ask into the darkness.

"Have it, of course. Oh—you meant about Will." There's a slight chill in her tone.

She's annoyed with me, and she wants me to feel it. Because I didn't tell her about Will? She's silent for a moment, then: "He's not perfect," she says quietly. "And obviously this is hurtful—very hurtful—and it may end up horribly public too; it will hurt his career more if it comes out later and it looks like he's tried to brush it under the carpet." She takes a deep breath. "And—and it makes me look like an idiot and I hate that," she bursts out.

"It makes Will look like an idiot," I say quietly. "Not you."

"Hmmph. Him, yes; but me too. And on top of that I don't even get to be mad at her because she's, you know, *dead*, and that would make me look like a really terrible person—" I start to protest, but she cuts me off. "Whatever. The point is, I didn't come this far to only make it to *here*. We have a life ahead of us, with everything we wanted—I've worked bloody hard to get us here. We have money and security and . . . I come from somewhere different to you, Emily. All of that matters to me. I know what it's like to be without it."

Okay, so I didn't grow up in Soviet-controlled Estonia with two alcoholic parents, but I was hardly born with a silver spoon in my mouth, I think wryly. My mother died in my early teens and my father was largely emotionally absent, and I couldn't have accessed the private school I attended were it not for a scholarship—but I don't say any of that; this is clearly not the time. Instead I say, "But do you think you can trust him again?"

She laughs, an odd bitter laugh that doesn't sound at all like Jana. "That presumes I trusted him in the first place."

"Didn't you?" I can't hide my surprise.

"Ignore me," she says, flapping a hand. "Of course I did. I'm just—I'm all over the place. But yes, if we're having a baby together, I can trust him." She makes it sound like a winning hand: a royal flush in poker. I want to cry out, *No, no, this isn't how it should be*, but who am I to say? Perhaps all of life is a series of calculations, whether we're aware of it or not. "It's all he wants. He wouldn't jeopardize that." She falls silent for a moment, then asks, "Well, you've known him longer. Do you think I should trust him?"

There's something antagonistic about the way she asks the question, born, no doubt, out of that resentment she's nursing toward me. But I give the question proper thought regardless. *Do I?*

"Yes," I say at last. "I think whatever happened came about under a specific set of circumstances. I can't see those ever being repeated." There will never be another Sofi for Will; there couldn't be. She might not have been his first love, but she was some other kind of first, one that I'm not quite sure how to describe. He won't be blindsided again.

"Yes, I think you're right, though I'm not feeling in any particular hurry to tell him that," she adds caustically. *She's still playing poker,* I think uneasily. But isn't that just Jana, always maneuvering, always pushing for a way forward? Why should I expect her approach to her relationship to be any different? "God, I'm flip-flopping between feeling like a kid on Christmas Eve and an inmate on death row."

At first I'm confused but then I catch her meaning: the pregnancy test. Even the revelations from Will can't displace it from the forefront of her mind. I can't think of what to say. *Whatever will be, will be? No point worrying; put it out of your mind?* Any platitude sounds like exactly what it is: meaningless words, cruel in their generalities. Instead I say, "Do you think you'll be able to sleep?"

"No. Except I'm soooo tired. So maybe yes. So long as that fucking clock keeps silent."

I lie in the darkness, listening to the sounds of others moving around the chalet, a comforting blanket of background domesticity. *The chalet is at its most content now,* I think whimsically, and almost immediately the corollary strikes me. *It's at its least content when we're all in the salon. Because of the clock*. That doesn't make any sense, but nonetheless I believe it. And after this evening, I would guess that Peter believes it too.

I hear Jana moving restlessly in her bed. Neither of us are sleeping. Perhaps I should attack her winter chill now rather than leave it to harden overnight—and in any case, I don't feel it's at all fair to consign me to the doghouse over it. "Are you angry that I didn't tell you immediately? You must see I was in a truly awful position."

"Must I?" she says acidly. I bite my tongue as she lies silent for a moment. Eventually she relents. "I suppose." Then, more quietly, "I really wish you'd told me." There's an unexpected note of desperation in her tone. "It would have—" She breaks off. Still I don't say anything. I won't apologize: I did the best I could in an untenable situation. "Anyway, yes, I am a little angry. Because it feels like you chose Will over me."

"Oh, honey, that wasn't it," I exclaim. *Would I, though? Which would I choose, if I had to?*

"Then what was it?"

"I . . . I didn't think I would have wanted to know. If I was you, I mean. If I didn't have to, if it stopped and it didn't mean anything."

"Oh. I see." She considers that for a minute. "I can sort of understand that—but you thought wrong. We're quite different, Ems: I would always want to know."

"Oh. I guess I really did get that wrong, then." A small bark of laughter escapes her. Perhaps a thaw is underway. I decide to push my luck. "Can I ask you something? Or are you still cross with me?"

"I'm considering my position," she says archly, but I can hear she's almost smiling.

"Well, can you consider quicker? Because I really need to ask you something. Two things, actually."

"Oh, all right, then. But only because I can't sleep and I'm curious."

"First thing—an easy one. Peter was throwing out hints that Mike had a fling with Sofi. He would only say, *Ask Jana*, when I pressed him on it."

"Ah. Well, he probably should have said, *Ask Will*; he was the one who told me. Wait— Oh, fuck. Now I come to think about it, that was probably a lie from Will to cover up why he was talking to her."

"What was?"

"I came to meet him at the department one evening and found him having an intense conversation with Sofi— though I didn't know who she was then. He said it was really awkward; he said she'd been involved with Mike and hadn't taken the breakup well. He was trying to get her to calm down and leave him alone because rumors like that could jeopardize Mike's future." I hear a long exhalation. "It was probably all rubbish. I'll ask Will, whenever I decide I'm talking to him again."

Lying. Lying well enough to convince Jana, who is nobody's fool. I wouldn't have thought it in Will's repertoire. But then again, I wouldn't have thought infidelity was included either. No doubt infidelity breeds the ability to lie out of sheer necessity. *Infidelity as a personal-growth opportunity,* I think with black humor. Definitely not a joke to share with Jana right now. "And you told Peter?"

"In my defense, it was the other night when I'd had a glass or three of wine, but . . . yes. Bad Jana: oops. Unless . . . unless it really was true and that's how Will got to know Sofi in the first place." She considers that for a moment. "Anyway, why do you ask? Oh! You're interested in Mike!"

"No, I just—" I can feel the heat in my face and I'm grateful for the darkness. *A door opened.* Apparently it's not just dangerous, but bloody obvious too.

"You are! I can tell you are! I even wondered about it the other day—Jesus, he's about as different from Nick as you can get."

How very like Jana to vocalize the comparison nobody is supposed to make. "Not really. Mike's an engineer too." I'm not sure why I'm being contrary.

"I meant physically. He's so . . . prehistoric! He could quite literally throw you over his shoulder and drag you off to his cave."

"I daresay Will could do that to you if it tickles your fancy," I say, amused.

"I doubt it at the moment. I probably weigh more than he does after all those drugs." She yawns loudly. "What's the second thing?"

"Someone's tried to get into Nick's laptop. Since we've been here, I mean." I explain quickly, and I include my sense of being hunted during the search for Sofi; she listens without asking any questions. "On top of the home invasion and the department break-in, well—"

"You think they're all connected," she finishes for me.

"I don't know. Maybe." *Peter, Will, Mike.* It must be one of them. It must be.

"And Sofi too?"

"I don't know. She was in contact with Nick through her work at the IP office."

"Mmmm." I can almost hear her thinking. "Peter or Mike, then," she says decisively.

"Peter or Mike what?"

"Who tried to get into the laptop. It would have to be Peter or Mike. You know as well as I do that Nick and Will hadn't collaborated on anything in, like, forever."

"Yes." She's right, actually. Now that she's highlighted it, I remember Nick, knife in hand as he chopped peppers for a salad, making a rather scathing remark about Will's research. *The telly stuff,* he'd said, stopping to pontificate in an alarmingly erratic fashion, given he was holding a very sharp knife, *is taking him away from serious work; he hasn't looked at anything worthwhile in absolutely ages.* "And to be honest, surely Will would just ask me if he needed something out of Nick's private files."

"Wouldn't Peter?"

"Before I started suspecting all my friends, I would have said yes." *What a bleak statement.* Does it say more about me or my friends?

"But now you're unsure." I can't deny it. *But you like Peter,* I remind myself. For all he's irritating me a little at present, I know it's nothing more than the result of enforced overexposure, given that we're all thrust together here under one roof—that and my current level of anxiety and paranoia. I can easily imagine what Nick would say: *Don't let a temporary lack of perspective destroy all your relationships.* But still, I can't refute Jana's statement. We lie silently in the blanket of darkness. There's an intimacy, a trust, in lying down to sleep in an unlit room with another person. I haven't done it in so very long with anyone except Nick. "Would it have to be a patent thing?" Jana asks.

"I can't think of anything else that somebody might want." *Want.* I didn't actively want anything at all at the start of this week. *Could I say the same now?* "A patent is the only thing I could think of that has tangible value."

"There are other, less tangible things of value. Reputation. Prestige. Will always said Nick's work was something special. Even if it wasn't at patent stage, that could be worth something. Somebody else could work up a paper out of it, gain themselves a rung or two on the academic ladder."

"Somebody else: Peter or Mike, you mean?"

"I guess. I don't know Mike well enough to judge, but Peter . . ." She's quiet for a moment. "You know I love him, but it would depend on what's at stake," she says at last.

What was it he said on that walk? *Everyone wants something for themselves, right?* "You're saying his integrity has a price?"

"Honey, everyone's integrity has a price. I'm saying his price is lower than others."

"You are quite possibly the most cynical person I know."

"Yep. It's one of my most charming qualities."

I smile into the darkness; it's so nice to hear she's reverted to her normal self with me. "But . . . murder? Really?"

"I know. That's a different thing altogether; I can't really see it." She yawns again. "And I can't believe Peter would want to hurt you either," she adds thoughtfully. "Maybe the chasing on the mountainside isn't connected at all."

"I'm willing to admit I could have imagined that." I'm yawning too now. "Night, night— Actually, wait, one more question. Last one, I promise," I add when she groans. "Have you ever dreamed of the clock?"

"The one in the salon?"

Is there another? "Yes."

"I'm not . . . I'm not sure." She sounds surprised, as if she's reached for something familiar and found it missing. "That's a weird question, and rather off topic. I mean, the clock can't possibly be connected to Sofi's death."

264

"I know. I didn't mean to imply a connection." *Except* . . . I had, sort of. My rational mind knows that the clock cannot be involved in any way, and yet the idea of it sits in some other, more primal part of my brain, just beyond reason . . . "Anyway, maybe none of it is connected."

"True. But somebody killed Sofi, or so say the gendarmes." Another yawn muffles the end of her sentence. "And on that cheery note, night, night."

"Night, honey." I close my eyes. Within minutes I can hear her rhythmic breathing. The chalet is still full of comforting creaks and soft murmurs. *But somebody killed Sofi,* I think. And if it is connected, I'm now down to two names, neither of whom possess a solid alibi.

Peter and Mike.

Let's walk today."

It's the next morning, and we're all at the table, having come down to breakfast in dribs and drabs. I look up from my croissant at Peter's pronouncement, taking in the expressions on the faces around the table: some hopeful, some uncertain. Peter tries again. "Doesn't anyone fancy some exercise? There's no reason why we can't, right?"

We've been in limbo, I realize, stuck here at the chalet with only trips to the hotel to liven things up. But life, a relentless, hurtling river, goes on; even grief can't hold you on the banks forever. Sooner or later the current tugs you back in and sweeps you along.

"I suppose." Olive is the first to respond, sounding a trifle doubtful. "As long as we stay in France, I don't suppose the police can complain."

"I wasn't suggesting we walk to Switzerland." Peter has the

bit between his teeth. I can see that he's been struggling with the lack of activity most of all; he will bound over any objections now that he's tasted the promise of an escape.

"Though walking to Switzerland is easier than you might think from here," puts in Akash.

"I'll pass, on Switzerland or otherwise," I say. "I don't think my ankle is up to it yet." It's true, but I'd also like to spend some time looking through Nick's emails and hassling the IP office for a response.

"I'll keep you company," Julie says to me. Caleb looks at her and opens his mouth to speak, but she preempts him. "You go, Cay. I know you're dying for some exercise."

"You're sure?" he asks her softly.

She smiles at him. "I'm sure." The smile drops. "I'm going to go down to Saint Gervais anyway. I ought to see Sofi's mum."

"That's good of you," I say quietly. I can't imagine how hard that's going to be.

"Didn't Pierre say the weather is going to change?" asks Olive.

"Not till tomorrow at the earliest," replies Akash. "At least, that's what the last forecast suggested; it's supposed to change on the sixteenth— Wait. The sixteenth . . ." He trails off, his mind evidently working. "Today is the anniversary."

"Anniversary of what?"

"The fire. The centenary. We were going to do a special dinner." He looks around the table. "Yeah, I suppose not, given . . . given everything." He pauses, then goes on diffidently. "Did anyone dream of the clock again last night?" Until he asked, I was completely unaware that I had, but his words drag fractured, ever-shifting images to the surface of my mind, too insubstantial to grab hold of: the clock, a red glow within it, the single staring, ever-expanding iris and the overriding sense that I have lost something and it's all my fault . . .

"The clock?" It's Caleb, his head swiveling toward Akash. "I did." His eyes are wide; they widen farther when he sees the collective nods that greet Akash's question. *All of us,* I think. *All of us are dreaming of it. Or think we are—did I really dream of it again, or am I remembering previous dreams?* "How did you know to ask? Wait—you said again? What's going on?" I remember Caleb and Julie weren't yet down for breakfast when horological dreams were discussed yesterday.

"Some sort of group phenomenon. A collective response to the stress of recent events combined with the effect of altitude, I would imagine," Olive tells him. "Though of course we can never be sure what we really have dreamed versus what we thought about when we first woke up and our brains were a little woolly."

"Or what our brains have reconstructed right now upon hearing the question," puts in Mike.

"It could be the random chimes," I put in. "Maybe we're hearing them subconsciously and incorporating the clock into our dreams because of that." I glance through to the salon, even though I can't see the clock itself. *What time is it keeping now?*

"Maybe that's why the clock ended up in the attic." This is Peter.

"Personally, I'd be okay with it ending up as firewood," says Caleb sourly. "If it chimes in the middle of the night once more, I'll set a match to it myself."

"There were complaints of the same in 1957, and in 1958," I say, reaching for the 1958 journal; I was reading it before breakfast.

"1958: didn't something happen then?" Will asks. "The prof mentioned that date, didn't he?"

"Yes, he did." Akash is nodding. "There was a small fire, but it was put out before it could do any damage."

"I haven't got that far yet," I say. "There were four 1958 trips; I'm on the second one." The first, in July, was reported in a wonderfully legible hand and appeared uneventful, with only one mention of strange chiming, but the writer described the phenomenon in affectionate terms, as if the clock was just another quirk of the chalet experience. *Which is how we should feel about it,* I think. *But we don't. None of us do.* The report of the second trip was much harder to decipher, and the diarist clearly didn't appreciate the value of brevity: one very dry account of a walk to the Bossons Glacier took five pages. I almost missed the single clock reference, squashed in among the excessively detailed commentary on the Tramway du Mont Blanc. I flick through the journal to find the page. "Here we are—God, this handwriting is genuinely terrible. Listen to this: *Tempers are considerably frayed today, perhaps due to broken sleep as a result of the malfunctioning clock. Edward even tried to still the pendulum in the middle of the night, but it was too hot to touch. Giles said that couldn't be; he must have dreamed it, which was not well received.*"

"*Not well received,*" echoes Mike, his lips quirking almost imperceptibly. "That sounds like a stiff-upper-lip English understatement for pistols at dawn."

"Indeed," I say. "So the clock was definitely in situ that year, and bugging the hell out of the chaletites. The fire must have happened in the third or fourth trip."

"Well, I don't think the fire was anything to do with the clock," Akash says. "I mean, not that the clock could be to do with anything anyway . . ." Around the table an uneasy silence falls. *I should read the rest of the 1958 diary,* I think. Or is that simply pandering to this ridiculous obsession we've all developed?

Mike glances around at the subdued faces and then clears his throat. "Did you have a route in mind, Peter? I know I'd really like to see the Mer de Glace." And with that, as if released, the conversation takes off, darting through the relative merits of the possible rambles with an energy that hasn't been present since . . . well, since before Sofi. Even Julie, who won't be going, looks more animated as she listens in. Only Will, sitting on my left, seems oblivious, working his way mechanically through a croissant as if he can't taste it at all, as if it's merely a task to be completed.

"Are you okay?" I ask quietly.

"Sure," he starts to say automatically, and then he stops and actually looks at me as if he's only just realized who asked the question. "Sorry. Not really, if I'm honest. It's hard to be fine when I've fucked things up so royally." He surveys the piece of croissant in his hand dismally, then puts it on his plate, uneaten. "I haven't exactly behaved like the person I thought I was."

Once again, his stark, objective assessment of his own self takes my breath away. "Does the university know yet?" I ask. He knows I mean about his affair with Sofi. "Will the gendarmes tell them?"

He shakes his head. "The French view these things differently: consenting adults and so on—they won't tell the Oxford powers that be. But I'm going to anyway. I don't want to live constantly worrying that it will come and bite me; I'd rather face the music." He looks at my surprised face. "It was Jana's idea. Like most things are. And she's right—again, like she usually is." He sighs. "Even in the face of everything I dumped on her last night, she could still think clearly enough

269

to say that. She reckons it will pass much more quickly if I own to it immediately." He picks up the piece of croissant again, but then puts it down without taking a bite. "Is she—is she up?"

"She was only just waking when I came down. She may have gone back to sleep."

"She was planning to test this morning."

"I know. I don't think she has yet."

He absorbs that, his eyes flicking upward as if he can see through the wooden ceiling, all the way to Jana in her bed. "I wonder if she'll tell me what the result is," he says bleakly. *At least he doesn't say he has a right to know.* "I doubt she'll want to walk. I could stay, but I doubt she'll want to talk either." He thinks for a moment, then looks at me questioningly. "But I suppose I could at least go up to tell her about the walk?"

I grimace. "I'd take her coffee if you're planning to do that." Jana in the morning, before caffeine has touched her lips, is a terrifying creature under normal circumstances, let alone under duress.

"Yes. Good thinking." He stands and reaches for an empty mug. It's only after he's left the room that I remember I meant to ask him about Mike and Sofi, though I suppose this wouldn't have been the place to do it anyway with Mike sitting across the table.

Mike. I can't imagine I will be anything but awkward around him now. I'm ridiculously, embarrassingly aware of him: of where he is in the room, of the inch of bare torso revealed beneath his T-shirt when he reaches out with a tanned arm to snag a second croissant. There's the oddest overlay too, as if two different tableaus are present within what I see. In one, I can imagine laying a hand on that tanned skin; I can imagine that forearm turning over and his fingers clasping mine, enveloping

270

them completely. In the other, that long arm reaches out and gives Sofi a brutal shove from behind; she turns halfway as she falls, that beautiful brown eye opening wide in shock . . .

I push my chair back abruptly and take my coffee outside.

20

Later, when everyone else has left, Jana, Julie and I climb the now familiar path up to the hotel. I'm itching to ask Jana the result of the test, but I haven't had a chance; Julie has been with me since Jana came downstairs. We choose to sit inside, despite the continuing glorious weather, as we all have devices to charge. The waitress welcomes us with a friendly smile—our faces have become familiar over the week—and takes our order; then Julie nips off to the bathroom.

I turn to Jana immediately. "So?"

She knows exactly what I'm asking and immediately shakes her head. "No. But I haven't had my period either, so it could be too early to tell. I bought a couple of twin packs; I'll try again tomorrow morning." She yawns. "More waiting: my favorite. It's so weird to feel like your whole life hinges on peeing on a fucking stick."

"And Will?"

"Truly apologetic. Can't do enough for me. He's actually very sweet when he's ashamed of himself; he has these soft, morose puppy dog eyes. Does it make me a bad person to admit that I'm really enjoying it?"

"Yes," I say dryly, pulling the laptop out of my rucksack and opening it up.

"Oh, well, then I'm a bad person; I may as well embrace it."

I shake my head at her, smiling, then look at the laptop. It doesn't seem to be firing up at all, which is odd because I could swear it still had at least a thirty percent charge the last time I used it. I'm bent over, scrabbling under the table to plug the cable into a wall socket when Julie joins us again.

"Emily—this is wet," Julie says, her voice alarmed.

I straighten, bashing my head on the underside of the table. "Ouch. What is?"

"Your computer." I look at it whilst rubbing my head: she's right. There's a thin sheen of condensation on the empty dark rectangle of the screen.

"Did you have a water bottle in your bag with it?" Jana asks.

"No." I look in my rucksack anyway, even though I know I didn't put one in. Suddenly I twig. "Oh, my God. Someone has fried it. That's why it won't wake."

"What do you mean?" Julie asks.

"If you had to quickly incapacitate a laptop, I'm guessing turning it on and shoving it in water would do a pretty good job." My words are tight with fury.

"But how did—," starts Jana, but she stops as Julie reaches past her to yank out the power cord. "You don't want to charge it after water damage," the younger woman explains. "There's a chance it can still be salvaged, if you let it dry out. Can the battery be taken out or is it one integrated unit?"

I shrug and push it toward her; she wipes off the screen with a paper napkin, then closes it and turns it over. "No, it's integrated. All you can do is keep it somewhere moderately warm and wait. You might be lucky; you might not."

"Never mind that," says Jana impatiently. "How did they get hold of it?"

"I don't know." It's almost a moan of despair. "I've been so careful with it; it's always been with me."

"When did you last use it?" Julie asks.

"Yesterday. Up here at the hotel. And it's been with me ever since."

"Why would anyone want to fry it anyway?" the younger woman asks, looking at Jana and myself in turn as if she might divine what she's missing from our expressions.

"You may as well tell her," Jana advises me. "A problem shared is light work— No, that's not it." She mutters in Estonian. "How does that go again?"

"A problem shared is a problem halved, and many hands make light work," Julie rattles off with impressive speed, then turns to me. "What is it you may as well tell me?"

I canter through the explanation. She listens carefully without saying anything until I'm done. "That's everything?" she asks.

"Yes."

"So at some point between when you were up at the hotel yesterday and now, someone deliberately sabotaged your laptop," Julie says thoughtfully. I can see she's not really looking for an answer: she's assimilating the information, filing and sorting and cross-referencing. "Which means . . ." She stops as if pausing to check her conclusion, then goes on. "Which means, whoever it is, they're not looking for information. They're looking to destroy information. They know what your husband had and they need it to disappear."

"Yes, I suppose so."

"So not a research idea or a formula or something that could advance a project, then," Jana says.

"No, it could still be that—the point would be to destroy

274

the evidence that Nick originated the idea." I rub my forehead: intellectual property. It keeps coming back to that.

"Who, though?" muses Julie. "Who could have had access?"

"Nobody. The laptop was with me the whole time. I even took to putting it inside my sleeping bag at night—" I stop; the waitress has brought our drinks. *"Merci."* I take a sip of my coffee. It's not the taste I've been yearning for. *I've been institutionalized,* I think. *When I want a coffee, what I really want is Costa or Pret a Manger coffee.* "Last night, though," I say slowly. Jana and Julie look up from their own drinks. "Last night I didn't put it inside my sleeping bag."

"But that would mean," Jana says, "that either it was me—and I didn't come to bed with a bucketful of water or even so much as a water bottle, though I wish I had. I was sooοo thirsty last night. Anyway, my point is, if it wasn't me, then someone must have got inside our room, which is kind of unlikely given how you like to barricade the door." She considers. "On reflection, I ought to apologize for giving you a hard time about that."

"Indeed," I say with mock severity. "So they didn't come in that way, which leaves the terrace door."

"But it was locked and the key was inside," Jana points out.

Julie wipes a mustache of hot chocolate off her top lip with a finger. "But all those terrace doors unlock with the same key."

"What? Really?" I ask, alarmed.

"Really. James showed Sofi and me. Apparently it was one of the things he learned to look out for when he was staying in dodgy hostels when traveling on his gap year. It's not unusual if the property used to be a house before it became a hostel—I mean, who wants to have a house with a different set of keys for every single window or French door?

If it's your own house you're really more concerned with keeping strangers out than keeping each individual room secure from the others."

"Oh," I say faintly.

"Was your key actually in the lock?" Julie asks. "That might have prevented someone unlocking it from the outside."

"No. No, I couldn't get it to fit." I remember fumbling in the darkness with the weight of the cool iron in my hand and the torch held awkwardly in my mouth. If only I had remembered to follow up the next day. *If only.*

"Probably because someone had put a key in from the outside," Jana says.

"Yes." We look at each other despondently. "James showed you this?" I ask Julie.

She nods. "And much as I'd like to blame him for drowning your laptop, I think that's a stretch, given he wasn't actually in the chalet last night."

"That we know of," points out Jana.

"I can't really see him trekking two hours up a mountainside in darkness just to sabotage a laptop," Julie counters.

"Fair," Jana concedes. She pauses, then asks Julie gently, "Do you still think James killed Sofi?"

Julie frowns thoughtfully. "I've been going over it a lot," she admits. "I can totally believe that he could—I mean, that he would, under the right circumstances. And it sounds bad, but I sort of want it to be him. I suppose because then it's done and dusted, neatly tied up . . ." She looks away, through the window toward the snowcapped mountaintops. It will be awful for her if the killer is never found, I realize. It will feel like it's never over. "But any way I look at it, I can't see how he gains. I was so sure it was him, that I would figure it out, but I just . . . *can't*. Nor Caleb or Akash either. We've been putting our heads together and getting nowhere."

"A crime of passion?" suggest Jana.

Julie shakes her head. "That's just it. Everyone fancied Sofi, literally everyone—but not James. I mean, yeah, sure, he'd probably have slept with her given half a chance, but he didn't have any particular yen for her. I never saw him really taken with anyone, to be honest."

"He wouldn't have wanted to lose control," I say. *He thinks of himself as the puppet master*. Even as I think it, I realize it's true. All those little secrets tucked away to use whenever benefits him most. He probably read *The Talented Mr. Ripley* as a teenager and has been modeling himself on Tom Ripley ever since. Then I remember Will's expression when he spoke of James' father. Perhaps the person James is modeling himself on is a little closer to home.

"Oh." Julie blinks. "Yes. Yes, that's probably right."

"Not James, then," says Jana. "So we're back to the same two names."

"Jana," I say warningly, "we can't go throwing accusations around." It's one thing to discuss this late at night with one of my closest friends; it's quite another to discuss it with a student.

Jana opens her eyes wide in a mockery of innocence. "I'm not throwing accusations around. This is a purely hypothetical discussion." She shrugs, dropping the innocent act. "You all know I think it was a local nutcase anyway."

"Which same two names?" presses Julie.

Jana looks at me for permission. I move my head equivocally, unable to commit either way, but that's enough for Jana. "If we're looking for an overlap between those who could have killed Sofi and also had some kind of professional link with Nick, then it has to be either Peter or Mike."

"Not Mike," says Julie without a moment's hesitation. Then she adds quickly, "Not that I'm damning Peter by saying that." Though she is, of course. "I mean, I really don't know him particularly—"

"Why did you say, *Not Mike*?" Jana gives me a pointed look as my curiosity gets the better of me. But even as the question exits my mouth, I see the same overlay as before: that tanned arm turning over to clasp my fingers; that same arm reaching out to give Sofi a violent shove . . . And now I see Sofi land on a bed of green that almost immediately begins to char into gray black as if a dreadful sickness is spreading from her body, contaminating everything in a widening circle—

"I simply can't believe it of him. Not of Mike." Julie's words bring me back to myself; she is looking at each of us in turn. "Can you?" she challenges.

"Sweetie, these days I can believe anything of anyone," Jana says. The jaded weariness on her face catches at my heart. "It's my special gift."

Still, like a broken record, we're stuck on the same two names, I think. Peter or Mike.

Later, once my phone has charged, I move to the terrace, more for a change of scene than anything else. Julie has left to meet Sofi's mum, the weight of the upcoming emotional ordeal already showing itself in her shoulders, which are creeping up toward her ears, and in the dragging of her steps. Jana has headed back to the chalet with every intention of taking a nap. I don't know if it's wishful thinking on my part, but I wonder if she looks different—though I couldn't say how exactly. Her hair? Her skin? Though any of that could just be the impact of the sun and the fresh mountain air.

It's already extraordinarily hot today, with barely a breath of wind. I sit under the shade of an umbrella with nary a glance for the spectacular scenery, and contemplate what to do next. I've come here specifically to investigate Nick's Gmail account, but I have the 1958 journal with me too. Reading that first feels like surrendering to this strange obsession, and yet I can't shake the sense that *not* reading it is like facing down danger by employing the defense of closing your eyes. I sigh: even though I can't name the threat, I can't ignore that I feel it. The journal and the phone lie on the table in front of me; my hand hovers between them, and then, almost without a decision on my part, swoops down on the journal. I yield and start reading.

The third trip appears even more ill-tempered than the second. Warned by the previous chalet party, the diarist is aware from the outset of the clock's quirks, which, he rather dismissively writes, *"might alarm those of a sensitive nature, but this chalet party is made of sterner stuff!"* However, within a couple of days, it's apparent that a rift has formed within the group: *"Owing to an unfortunate disagreement over dinner last night, after spending the morning reading, the group split to conduct two separate afternoon walks."* And later, I find an oblique reference to the nature of the disagreement: *"It is not possible to remain neutral in the face of the continuing hostilities between Dr. Ross and Professor Fischer. I confess I find it unlikely that a man of the professor's standing would have any need to unnecessarily discredit a colleague."* Later still: *"Dr. Ross and his supporters have taken to avoiding the salon entirely, though it is unclear whether that is to avoid Professor Fischer or the wretched clock. Perhaps it would be better if Ross had not found Bochert on the bookshelf; for a man of science, he is entirely too taken with the author's ludicrous Gothic leanings and insists on influencing others to be so too. Whilst the incessant thirst we're suffering and the occasional smell of smoke within the chalet are both indeed curious phenomena, I fail to see how they can be linked to a timepiece."*

A sudden, unexpectedly strong gust of wind flutters the check that the waitress has left under my saucer, causing me to look up from the journal. There's still not a cloud in the sky that I can see, but while I've been out here, a wind has undoubtedly developed out of seemingly nothing. The red-and-white parasols are vibrating a little in their attempts to stand firm; when I look at the mountainside, I see the long grasses being flattened and released in waves by the invisible gusts. A tourist at the next table gives a cry as her cap is twitched from her head; she reaches in vain for it, but her young son gives chase and manages to grab it before it disappears over the side of the terrace. I dig in my bag and find a scrunchie with which to tie up my hair; otherwise it will whip itself into a tangled mess.

I turn back to my reading, disquieted by the parallels with the current trip—the chimes, the mentions of strange thirst and phantom whiffs of smoke—and find this in the last entry of that trip: *"Yesterday Dr. Ross and six others made the regrettable decision to leave three days earlier than planned. This follows a frankly inexplicable episode in which Ross left the chalet during the night to conduct ablutions and was somehow unable to find his way back, spending a no doubt extremely cold, uncomfortable night without shelter. Quite how that is Fischer's fault is unclear; nonetheless, the seven have now left, claiming concerns over their personal safety."*

A clatter yanks my attention from the journal. One of the umbrellas has tipped, despite its solid weighted base. A couple of staff members are now moving through the terrace, removing pins from the upright umbrella poles to fold down the red-and-white canopies. "It's the Foehn wind," explains the waitress as she deals with the parasol nearest me. "A hot wind. It's unusual to have it in August. If you're going down in the *télécabine*, you should go quickly."

"I'm not."

"Ah, good. I expect they will stop it running very soon."

I'd better warn Julie, I think. I fire off a message to her and get a response almost immediately:

I know. I heard the same at the bottom. I'm coming back up. I've sent Caleb a message about it.

Okay. See you back at the chalet, I message back.

The wind is getting strong enough to bring tears to my eyes; I'm going to have to move inside to get anything done. I'm not the only one taking shelter: a number of us share rueful smiles as we settle our windswept selves at the interior tables. Glancing at my watch, I find an alarming amount of time has passed. I really must focus on accessing Nick's Gmail now, or I will have squandered this opportunity; therefore I carefully place the diary in a plastic bag that was lurking at the bottom of my rucksack, wrapping it up fastidiously to prevent any residual damp within the laptop from damaging the fifty-year-old book. Then I use my mobile to access Nick's Gmail account through the Internet, feeling my stomach twist uneasily as I do it. Private diaries, private email accounts: in recent days, I've become quite the accomplished sneak, but it doesn't sit comfortably with me. In this case, what am I frightened of seeing? *Anything that might jeopardize how I believe he thought of me*, I realize. *What I said to Jana was true*: *if I don't need to know, I don't want to*. But if there is something in Nick's messages that explains at least some of what's been happening, then for the safety of all, I have to know it.

I start with a search for emails from the IP office and find several, but none more recent than twelve months ago. I go through them anyway, but if there's a smoking gun among them, it's certainly not obvious to me. So I change tack, instead scanning all the emails Nick received in the three weeks before he died, but again nothing jumps out at me, unless one counts the unexpected discovery of quite how shockingly expensive Nick's golf club membership was. *I will have to cancel that quick smart,* I think grimly; that one had somehow slipped the net of the horrendous administrative burden that the death of a loved one brings—as if it wasn't all awful enough already. I tap the table in frustration: *What else can I try?* In a last vain hope, I look at Nick's sent messages. Most of them are addressed to me, of course, or to friends whose names I recognize—after all, this is his personal account, not his professional one. *Peter or Mike,* I think, and focus on emails to Mike. There are many, as it turns out, spanning months, on a continuous thread titled *Squash game??* and they are all, as far as I can tell, about exactly that: when to meet, where to meet, whether they'll have time for a beer afterward. With Peter, there are far fewer, which makes sense, as I imagine they mainly used their professional accounts, given their frequent professional collaborations—and that makes it far easier to home in on the email Nick sent Peter just ten days before he died, in response to one Peter had sent. An email titled *Re: Sorry.*

Peter,

I appreciate the email but I still do not understand why you chose to do this without even speaking to

me first and I have to say that I still find it very hurtful.
It will take some time to get past this. I will not share
this incident with anyone, as I would not want your
career to be impacted by such a lapse of judgment,
but equally I'm glad you have withdrawn the claim.
You must know I would never allow it to stand.

Nick

Peter, you idiot, what did you do? I lament. I can't tell whether
I'm more frustrated, disappointed or annoyed with him as I
scroll down, expecting to find the original email below Nick's
reply, but it's not there; nor can I find it on a general search. I
reread the email that I do have. There's nowhere near enough
detail for me to divine exactly what transpired between the
two, but there's enough to guess at the general thrust: Peter,
with his perpetual vaulting ambition, attempted to overreach in
some way, and Nick, with his obdurate (and admittedly slightly
pompous) integrity, blocked him. *It's like a bloody Shakespearean
play with character as destiny,* I think in despair. I'm sure neither
could have possibly behaved in any other way; it simply wasn't
within them. But still, it's hardly the smoking gun I was looking
for.

Or is it? I consider again. *I'm glad you have withdrawn the
claim* . . . Presumably a patent claim. Did Peter really withdraw
it, though? And even if he had, perhaps he resubmitted after
Nick's death? After all, if Nick was the only obstacle, why not
revert to the original plan? If the expected payoff was great
enough, I imagine he could have reasoned his way to it.

There's only one way to find out. I pick up my phone and
dial the IP office again, but without any luck—the patient chap I
talked to before is not at his desk. Outside, the wind hasn't abated,

but there's no reason to assume it will and therefore no reason to delay my return to the chalet. I call *au revoir* to the staff as I leave, and as soon as I'm outside, I find that I need to put on my sunglasses—not only as protection against the sun, which is indeed still blazing, but against the fine grit that the wind is peppering me with. Perhaps when I descend a little, it will subside.

Peter, I lament again as I walk, *what have you done?* I remember him on the plane ride: *We argued. Properly argued,* he'd said. *Did he tell you about it?* His face cleared when I said Nick hadn't told me—I'd thought at the time that he took that to mean it hadn't been significant for Nick; perhaps instead he was relieved that I wouldn't know what was at stake. The home intrusion—could that have been Peter? I think about the height, the size, the athleticism. The first two, certainly, and though I wouldn't have put Peter into the category of being particularly athletic, I remember my surprise when I saw his unexpectedly effective bowling. *Yes,* I think, *the athleticism could fit too.* And he's been in our house often enough to know that Nick worked in the little study niche off the living room and that there's an access lane at the bottom of the back garden. He'd also have been expecting me to be at the airport, so he wouldn't have been concerned about anyone being home.

The department break-in? That could have been him looking for Nick's laptop, or it could have been a coincidence. But Sofi . . . Sofi is a different matter. Surely he wouldn't have gone so far as to actually kill a young woman? What was it Will had said? *I'm now imagining Peter stomping on the heads of all the obedient souls standing on the escalator as he makes a mad dash for the exit.* We had all laughed, because we could all imagine him doing exactly that in a cartoonish sort of way. But—killing? Surely that's a step too far for anyone?

Yes, I think. *And yet . . .* In truth, how well do we really know anyone? Before, I would never have said Will was capable of cheating on Jana. That glimpse I saw of Will, of something *underneath* the Will I've always known, continues to cast an uneasy shadow on me. What might be underneath Peter too? And then I think uneasily of the glassy look in James' eyes, of the way he couldn't tear his gaze from the sweeping pendulum. I think too of the ill-tempered chalet parties of 1958; of how, reading quite literally between the lines, it seems that small jealousies and petty rivalries were somehow being fanned in the febrile chalet atmosphere. *It's happening to us too*, I think. Whatever darkness is within each of us is coming to the fore. I'm certainly not immune: all my terrible, uncharitable doubts and suspicions, which I might ordinarily be able to move past, refuse to be dismissed. They sit inside me, deep down in the dark, twisting and bubbling in my gut, where I can't quite see the poison they're brewing but I feel it nonetheless. *It's not healthy to live like this. I should go home*, I think miserably, and then immediately I think the opposite: *No, I should stay: I'm safer here than alone in a terraced house. At least here I can ask Peter about that email and gauge his reaction with the benefit of the safety that comes with numbers.* Though if I were to go home, I'd be beyond the reach of that clock . . .

I'm perhaps two hundred meters from the little track to the chalet, and still suffering the pricks and stings of the gravel swept up by the blustering winds, when I notice a figure climbing the path toward me, blond head down, intent on making good time. *Peter*, I think, and feel a thread of genuine unease run through me. But as the figure approaches, I realize the blond hair is too short, the shoulders too broad: it's not Peter.

It's James.

21

James. What is James doing here?

By sheer instinct, without any conscious thought, I find myself ducking off the path. There's an outcrop of boulders in the long grasses off to the right some twenty meters away; I veer quickly toward them, stumbling on the uneven ground of tufts and hillocks and glancing back toward James on the path, but his gaze is fixed on the rock-strewn ground as he walks, pushing his hands against his knees on every step to help him ascend—clearly he's in a hurry. I hunker down against the boulders on the uphill side; the boulders impede my view downhill and therefore ought to also hide me from him. Unless he turns around when he gets a bit higher in order to survey the route he's just taken, he won't see I'm here.

What is he doing here anyway? Presumably he's on his way to the hotel or the *télécabine*, but has he already visited the chalet? Is he planning to rejoin us there? I suppose he might if Robert had convinced him to. Or if his father ordered him to. Despite the fact that James has no solid alibi, Julie is right: it makes no sense that he would have killed Sofi. If he returns to the chalet, it will be unpleasant to have to put up with him, but that's all. I sit, looking across to the path, waiting for him to climb past and wondering what exactly has come over me. Am I truly so uncomfortable at the idea of speaking to James that I'm willing to dive off into long grasses and scrubland? *Evidently so*, I think wryly. He's passing me now, his long legs covering the distance efficiently; in mere seconds he's far enough away to be nothing more than a splash of color. James is not the problem, though, I realize. It's anyone—and everyone. Probably Jana, Will and Julie are truly the only people I'd be comfortable being alone with right now.

I wait until James is out of view, then get to my feet to start the laborious process of returning to the path. I'm wearing shorts and, with this wind, the exposed skin on my legs is being uncomfortably whipped by the long grasses. But when I reach the path, it provides no comfort, as instead my skin is abraded once again by fine grit. Even with the sunglasses as a barrier, my eyes are irritated by the wind and the debris it carries and have begun to stream; I have to concentrate very hard on where I put my feet so as not to turn an ankle on an unseen rock.

Suddenly I feel someone grab me. I spin quickly, pulling away, ready to run—

"Emily! It's me." Peter's face, with evident surprise at my reaction writ large upon it, looms in my field of vision. "God, sorry—did I scare you?"

"I . . . Yes. I didn't hear you come up behind me." *Peter.* I've avoided James only to find myself alone with Peter. It feels like jumping from the frying pan into the fire.

"Yeah, I was calling your name, but with this wind . . . It's called the Foehn, you know."

"Yes, I know." My words are as dry as the hot wind itself.

"I caught sight of you off by the boulders." He takes off his sunglasses to try to clear some grit from his eyes but just as quickly replaces them, as if realizing the futility of it. "What on earth were you doing?"

"Oh. Well. Hiding, if you must know," I admit a little ungraciously. "I didn't want to have to speak to James." *And I don't want to have to speak to you either. Not alone.*

"Ah. I saw him; he just went past me."

"What did he say?"

"Nothing really. I couldn't get out of him what he was doing here." He looks up the path thoughtfully as if the answer might be written there. "There are plenty of other places to go for a walk if that's what he was after."

"Where are the others?"

"They stayed down in Les Houches, grabbing a bite to eat, but I wanted to get on with the paper I'm writing. Unlucky for them, as it turns out; they'll have to walk up now that the *télécabine*'s shut down. Were you up at the hotel?"

"Yes. Doing emails and so on."

"Are you heading to the chalet? I'll walk you back."

"I . . . uh . . ." I look around. If we walk together to the chalet, we shall have to leave the main path. We shall have to cross the grasses and the little bridge and enter the tree line, and at that point, we'll be completely hidden from view. And whether there's any substance to my fears or not, I know that I do not want to be hidden from view in the company of Peter. Even when we get to the chalet, there will only be Jana there, and she'll likely be sleeping. "I . . . um . . . I don't think so."

He looks understandably confused. "You don't think you're headed to the chalet?"

"I am. I think I might just wait for Julie, though." I look down the mountainside. There are a couple of trail runners perhaps three hundred meters below. The landscape between

288

us is very exposed; they would see if Peter were to attack me. *Don't be ridiculous; he's not going to attack you,* I scold myself. But still, it's a relief to know the trail runners are there.

"Right." He frowns and puts a hand to his forehead, simultaneously pushing back his sandy hair and shielding his eyes from the bright sun. "Emily, did I do something to offend you?"

I look at the trail runners, at the bright red and blue of their athletic gear, sharp against the mountainside. I'm not dressed nearly so colorfully, but still, they must be able to see me clearly. *I'm safe. This is as good a time as any.* "I don't know. I'm trying to figure it out."

"I don't understand."

"No?" I turn to him. "I found an email from Nick to you." He stills, his only movement the whipping of his hair in the wind. "I expect you remember it. He mentions a career-ending lapse of judgment and a claim you're supposed to have withdrawn." I shrug. "Ring any bells?"

"Emily, you've got the wrong end of the stick." His voice is tight.

"Have I?" I glance down the mountain. The trail runners are still on the path, making impressive progress toward us. "Because from where I'm standing, it looks like you've stolen my husband's work, passed it off as your own and are busy trying to eradicate all evidence."

"That's patently ridiculous," he says stiffly. His eyes are obscured by his sunglasses, but I can see the tension in his jaw.

"Patently. Interesting choice of words."

"What? Have you been speaking to the IP office? What did they say?"

I ignore his questions. "What was your argument with Nick about?"

"It was about—" He breaks off. "Look, it doesn't matter. It's too late anyway; he's gone." He moves a hand impatiently as if to dismiss my words—as if to dismiss me. "Do you have any proof of these ridiculous allegations?"

"Proof? If I had proof, I'd be calling the police to have you arrested. You broke into my house, Peter—*my house*—"

"What? I . . . I did not."

"And my office and Nick's laptop."

"No, I didn't. This is ridiculous."

"I don't believe you." As I say it, I'm stunned to realize it's true. I really don't believe him. I'm not sure what I thought before I started flinging out these accusations, but looking at him now, I'm suddenly, chillingly, certain that I'm right. There's no burning righteous indignation in his responses; instead, I think he's squirming inside. He's done something for sure, but what? Exactly how far has he gone?

"*Bonjour,*" calls one of the approaching trail runners. He is lean and wiry and walnut brown, his straining tendons alarmingly visible. The man following him is a slightly taller carbon copy.

"*Bonjour,*" Peter and I chorus in response, stepping farther apart to allow them to run between us. Peter looks away, his hand reaching up to push away the hair that's streaming across his face. I smile overbrightly at the runners. *How very British of me to put on a show of normality for complete strangers.*

"Peter," I say quietly, almost pleadingly, when they've passed. Their interruption has lowered the temperature a little between us. "You may as well tell me. I'm going to find out anyway. What have you done?"

"Nothing," he says tersely. "And I resent your accusations," he bursts out. I've misread this: the temperature hasn't been lowered; instead he's building up a head of indignant steam. "I've been nothing but a friend to you, Emily—"

"And what about to Nick?" I challenge, equally hotly. "Were you nothing but a friend to him? It didn't look like it in that email."

He takes a step closer, his finger pointed at my chest. "You don't know what you're talking about and I suggest you are extremely careful about what you say and to whom—"

"Are you *threatening* me?"

"Is everything all right?" a voice asks, though I hadn't heard anyone approach. Peter and I turn our heads in unison, and I almost laugh. It's James. My savior from this situation is James.

"Yes, thank you." My voice sounds remarkably steady. "Though obviously we've just been having a disagreement." Peter scoffs and turns away.

James looks from me to Peter's half-turned shoulders and then back again. "Oh. Right. Well, I'm having to walk back down; the *télécabine* isn't working."

"Yes, we know," says Peter shortly.

"Really? You might have told me when I saw you earlier."

"Yes, I suppose I might have." Peter's tone is savage.

James' eyebrows lift in surprise. "Well, thanks for that," he says. He looks at me, a little nonplussed.

"James, shall I walk you down as far as the chalet?" I say. "I think perhaps you and I should talk." James' eyes shoot to mine, then quickly away, the apprehension on his face swiftly replaced by belligerence. But before he can say anything, Peter steams in. "Right," he says, his voice curdling with sarcasm. "So you're comfortable in the company of a student who actively accused you of being involved with Sofi's death, but not with me?"

"Oh, but James doesn't think I killed Sofi. Do you, James?" James pauses, then shakes his head—with a little surliness, it's true, but still, it's a shake.

Peter throws up his hands. "Fine. I'm going back to the hotel. I need a drink."

No, I think, watching him stomp off with narrowed eyes. *You're going back to the hotel so that you'll have reception to call the IP office and find out what they've been telling me.*

"What were you arguing about?" James asks as he too watches Peter go.

"Something work related."

"I heard him threaten you."

His hypocrisy would be amusing if it weren't for the fact that I'm on the receiving end. "You did too, once."

"That's not the same at all," he says, bristling.

"Really? The finer points of that distinction escape me." He's moved round such that he's below me on the path. I look down at him from my higher vantage point, considering. "Did Robert suggest you come back to the chalet?"

"No. I mean, yes, he did, but that's not why I'm here."

Of course not, I think, hiding a smile. *God forbid you should do anything to please others.* "No? Why did you come, then?"

"Why do you care?" He kicks at a rock, inspects it and then kicks it again.

"I don't much. But I expect you came to look for Sofi's diary."

He looks up sharply, then away. "Yes, I did."

"Did you find it?"

His head swings up to me. "Of course I bloody didn't—you burned it!"

"Not guilty, I'm afraid."

"You would say that."

"Hardly the most compelling argument. Do you have any evidence it's been burned?"

He shoves his hand in his pocket and pulls out a handful of mangled, curled wire. "It's the spiral binding."

"Oh," I say, surprised, coming closer to inspect it. It looks exactly like one might imagine the binding would look if someone tried to burn the journal. "Yes, I think you're right. Where did you find it?"

"You know where I found it," he challenges.

"I'm afraid not," I say with as much patience as I can muster. "That's why I'm asking."

He narrows his eyes. "Where have you come from?"

"The hotel."

"How long have you been up there?"

"A good couple of hours."

"Can you prove it? People saw you there?"

"Yes, plenty of people saw me there. Why?"

"Then you didn't do it," he says, clearly surprising himself. "I found it out the back of the chalet," he says slowly. "You know where that firepit is? Not the one out front; the old one at the rear. It was still warm, and I don't think it was just from the sun." That doesn't sound conclusive to me: the sun is so very strong, it could have warmed the metal. And the wind is so hot that I don't think it would materially cool it; I really don't see how he can tell. "I dug around a bit to see if there was anything left that hadn't burned, but no. But I don't know who lit it; there was nobody at the chalet."

"Really? Jana should have been there. And maybe Julie." Maybe Jana was using the waterfall shower?

"I didn't see either there. And I checked every room."

"Of course you did, looking for the diary," I say dryly. He doesn't even have the grace to look ashamed. "You should take that to the police, you know. It might be relevant to their investigation that the diary has been destroyed."

He looks back at the mangled wire in his hand thoughtfully, then starts to pocket it again. "How's Julie doing?" he asks stiffly.

"She's holding up, though she thinks you might have killed Sofi."

"What?" He startles, genuinely shocked, his hand still shoving the wire into the pocket of his shorts. "No! Of course I didn't kill her. What would I have done that for?"

"I can't pretend to understand why you've done anything. That vile bet with Sofi. Taking photos of her diary—"

"That was *ages* ago; it was wrong of me and I apologized—"

"Being so antagonistic to me and blaming me for Sofi's death when I never did anything to you—"

"Yes, you did."

"What?" His lips thin and he turns his head away. "James, what have I ever done to you?"

"I heard you, talking to Will; I was up on the terrace. I heard you telling him not to hire me. I'd be perfect for that job and you—you ruined it."

Not squirrels, then, I think resignedly. Those noises on the terrace above Will and me: not squirrels. "You're kidding, right? Will is a grown man who makes his own decisions. He won't ever hire you because he thinks you're a sneaky, mean, entitled little shit without an ounce of compassion, not because I told him not to."

"He . . . he doesn't think that of me." His voice is faltering, though.

294

"Doesn't he? Do you really think you can go around being mean to people like Julie when the whim takes you, and nobody will notice?" *God, I'm on a roll. First Peter, now James . . . Is everyone destined to receive an uncensored piece of my mind today?*

He looks away. "Whatever. You shouldn't have said that."

"I shouldn't have an opinion that I expressed privately to one of my oldest friends?"

"It wasn't private. I heard you."

"That's true." He has a point. "I'm willing to concede that I should have been more careful about where I expressed it."

"Yes, you should," he says emphatically. Then he kicks the rock again as if recognizing the hollowness of his small victory. "I was—I suppose I was a bit . . . jealous," he admits at last. "Of Julie, I mean. It all got so—I don't know. It was like being in a pressure cooker. I couldn't seem to think about anything else. Will was so enthusiastic about every single thing that Julie said. He's been trying to entice her to come and work with him, and I . . . I just really want that job. Or thought I did . . . It seemed like time was running out for me. I didn't get a job offer from any of the interviews my dad set me up for; I didn't really want those jobs anyway, but my dad can be—Look, never mind. I just—I let my temper get the better of me." He actually looks ashamed. "You probably won't believe me, but I never, ever let that happen. It wasn't like me at all."

I do believe him. I think again of the altercation in the salon when he flung all those accusations at me; I remember the glassiness in his eyes. He truly wasn't himself. "How do you feel now that you've been out of the group dynamic?" I ask gently. *And away from that fucking clock.*

For a moment I think that he will dissemble, that his pride won't allow him to answer the question, but he surprises me.

"Pretty bloody stupid if I'm honest. There are other jobs. I don't really know how it all got so out of hand; I totally lost perspective."

I try to remember the rest of the conversation that James listened in on. It must have been the morning after I saw Will and Sofi in the store cupboard. Surely if he'd heard *that* part of the conversation, he'd have made it known by now? "What else did you overhear?"

"Nothing. Just that really." He cocks his head. "Why?"

"I was talking about my husband," I improvise. "It was personal."

"Oh. I didn't hear any of that." Then he adds awkwardly, "Sorry. About your husband, I mean."

I look across at him, mildly surprised. "Thank you." *There's hope for him yet,* I think. And he did intervene when he saw Peter trying to intimidate me. "Why did you come back for the diary?"

"To help find Sofi's killer, of course." But it doesn't quite ring true; he grimaces as if recognizing it himself. "And I thought, if I found it, it might back up what I said about you."

"You thought it might vindicate you in some way?" He was looking for a face-saving way back into the group. At my expense as it happens, but nonetheless, it's a baby step in the right direction.

He shrugged. "Then everybody would understand." He seems to belatedly remember to whom he's talking. "Um, no offense."

"None taken," I say dryly. "Why did you photograph the diary? Before, I mean."

He bristles. "Look, I apologized. I know it was wrong."

"I know. But why?"

"Oh. Well." He shifts uneasily, his feet turning away as if searching for escape. "There's always a benefit to having info."

"Blackmail." *Just when I was coming round on him.*

He flushes. "No, not blackmail, just . . ." He trails off. "I suppose it looks like that, but that wasn't . . ." He trails off again. "Look, it's just how the world works, okay? You have to take note of whatever edge you can find. You never know when it can play to your advantage."

Is that what he really thinks, or is that what his father tells him? I look at him again. Just like with Mike, I can see two possibilities: in one, the conniving, manipulative aspect of his personality wins and he becomes a bitter, twisted, dangerous human being. In the other, the entertaining, polite, considerate side of him wins and he finds a way to be happy. Perhaps the most likely result is somewhere between the two. "Find another worldview. That's not how my world works."

"Then you're sticking your head in the sand."

Maybe. I'd certainly prefer to. But regardless, I'd rather not live in his world. "What did you do on the day she died?"

"I told you, I never—"

"I know, I know. I don't think you killed her. It's just that some of us have been trying to figure out who was where and when. Jana saw you walking up toward the hotel."

"Did she? I didn't see her. I only saw her later, walking down."

"Did you see Peter at all?" He shakes his head. "Did you go into the hotel?"

He shakes his head again, then hesitates and admits, "I was going to, but I decided not to. I just sat out and messed around on my phone for a bit. I'd seen Sofi go in, you see, and I didn't want to speak to her; we'd had an argument that morning." He makes a gesture with his arm as if to cut off a question that

297

I haven't yet asked. "Not about anything relevant; she was just giving me a hard time about being nicer to Julie."

"As you should be," I say severely, then cringe: *Could I sound more like a schoolmarm, laboring the point?* And then I counter my own self: *He's a student; I'm supposed to teach him. We're supposed to teach them all, by example if nothing else.*

"Yeah, well, like I said, I wasn't myself." He ducks his head equivocally, then wipes at one eye. "Jesus, this wind. Bloody grit." He pauses. "I told the police I thought you were to blame." If I didn't know better, I'd almost think he was ashamed.

"And yet I'm one of the people with a cast-iron alibi."

"Yes. They said that. I didn't really think it; I don't know why I . . ." He trails off. "They said I was wasting their time." Now I'm sure that he's ashamed. "They told Robert and her mum . . . they told them she was smothered."

My breath catches. "Smothered?"

"Yes. Hit on the head first, behind her ear, which probably knocked her out, and then smothered. They found tiny blood bursts under her eyelids; apparently it's a telltale sign. It has a special name, begins with a P." He thinks, then shakes his head. "Nope, it's gone."

"Oh, Jesus." That single perfect staring iris wasn't so perfect after all. What would it have seen, had she been conscious to see it? Starbursts of light? Darkness creeping in from the edges? I close my eyes behind my sunglasses, feeling the ground swoop beneath me even as the wind buffets against me. *There is nothing solid here*, I think. The beat is rising inside me—the beat that seems somehow ridiculously to be linked to that awful clock. *There is nothing solid, and I will tip and fall . . .*

"I know," he says. Then, cautiously, "Are you . . . are you all right?"

"Yes." *No.* I open my eyes: *Breathe.* "Yes. Come back to the chalet," I say, surprising myself. "I'll put in a good word to Robert for you. Say you've apologized."

He looks at me, surprised too—and a little suspicious. "I haven't, though."

"Yes, I noticed," I say dryly. "I'm living in hope."

A short bark of laughter escapes him. "My stuff is in Saint Gervais. I'd be better off walking down and staying there again." He gestures down the mountain, and both of us start to walk, retracing the steps he's just taken. *I shouldn't have suggested that he come back,* I think, *not while the clock is still there. Otherwise we risk a relapse to the James of old. We'd have to move the clock, and I don't know how to square that with Robert.* I turn it over in my brain, looking for a solution that might be palatable to Robert; I don't know why I'm sure he'll resist, but I am. *Perhaps if we all voted to move it? Democracy in action? Still, Robert would be upset.*

After a minute or so, James says. "Maybe tomorrow I'll come back up with Robert. Sofi's mum is leaving then."

"Have you seen her?"

He nods. "She's pretty broken."

"Poor thing. I can't even imagine." We're at the path to the chalet now. "Be safe," I say lightly, turning to go.

"Emily—," he starts.

I turn. "Mmm?"

"I—" His mouth works but nothing comes out. I wonder if he is stumbling over an actual apology. "I— Nothing. You be safe too." It actually sounds like he means it. Another baby step.

I pick my way along the narrow, overgrown path to the chalet, the long grasses around me whipping in the wind and my mind full of what James told me. *Smothered.* How would one do that exactly? A jumper stuffed over the face? Or one hand closing the nose and the other shutting off the mouth? *Mike would need only one of his enormous hands to do both*, I think. *Peter would have needed two.* If she was already unconscious, would she have struggled at all? Would her eyes have been closed or open? I shake my head, trying to dislodge the awful thoughts. I don't want to have to live with them inside me like a cancerous shadow that will surely grow and grow, just as that blackened circle around Sofi grew and grew . . . *I'd always rather not know.*

Peter or Mike, though. I'm almost certain now that it was Peter inside my house in Oxford and that he is to blame for the laptop incidents. I still don't know why, but it can only be a matter of time before I work it out with the help of the IP office. But Sofi? Could he really have killed her? Any sense of perspective has been completely washed away by the nonstop tide of paranoia and unease I've been drowning under ever since I got here—in fact, before I got here. Ever since the break-in at home. *No, be honest*, I think. *It started before that. It's just that being here has exacerbated it. It started when Nick died.* Ever since then, I've been operating under a nagging sense of anxiety and an inability to trust my instincts. But recognizing it doesn't exactly help. I still don't know whom to trust. *I shouldn't have been telling James to come back to the chalet. I shouldn't be going there myself.* I could take a room at the Hotel Le Prarion, or down in Saint Gervais, until the police allow us to travel. I'd be alone then, though. Would that be better or worse than staying with others at the chalet, even if there's a threat among them? *Better*, I think. *Anywhere away from the chalet would be better.* And then: *I'll do it. I'll collect my stuff and walk down tonight.* Instantly I start to feel lighter. It's the right decision. Everyone will understand if I say I'm finding it difficult to remain at the chalet after the trauma of finding Sofi. *Yes, leaving is the right thing to do.*

I'm so preoccupied with planning my exit that I've almost reached the lawn of the chalet before I notice it: just the faintest hint of a smell of smoke. It takes a moment for the oddness of that to catch up to me. I don't remember ever seeing anyone barbecuing anywhere at all in the area—would it even be permitted? With the recent dry weather, surely any open flame would present a hazard? I stop and look around. Is there a faint haze of smoke in the air uphill of me? I can't quite tell—and then a sudden change in the direction of the buffeting wind leaves me in no doubt. I can absolutely smell smoke.

Jana, I think, and start to run toward the chalet, ignoring the stabbing pain that jabs through my left ankle on every step—it has recovered well enough for walking, but running is definitely ill-advised. I burst across the lawn, yelling her name. Ahead of me, the chalet is silhouetted as if against a liquid gold-red sunset, its metal roof glowing with reflected color—but no, that can't be right. It's not even late afternoon . . .

Fire. The forest behind the chalet is on fire.

22

_____

Jana! Jana!" I burst inside, skidding through the salon, halting only long enough to take in the fact that it's deserted, before racing through the dining room and the kitchen. Through the kitchen window, I see an angry red glow behind the trees nearest to the chalet. It seems to swell and subside with the gusts of wind as if it's a living beast and the wind is simply its breath. Brightly sparking orange embers are eddying upward as if dancing toward the heavens. The fire is close—too close. With this wind, it could make the leap across to the building any second. _There's no time,_ I think, my eyes full of fire and my head full of that awful, relentless beat, faster than it's ever been, pounding away at my very self. _No time left at all._

"Jana! Jana!"

I leave the kitchen, scaling the stairs two at a time to bash open each bedroom door in turn, yelling her name throughout, but surely she can't possibly be here; she couldn't be sleeping through the banging, crashing racket I'm making. But I have to check. I have to know she's not here before I leave myself. I thrust open each door in turn, with my own bedroom the last of all. The door sticks as it always does, and I almost lose my balance when it yields suddenly, but the room is deserted. I stand uncertainly for a second, the drumming inside me hammering at my lungs, my rib cage—hammering at everything that keeps me alive. The whole chalet is deserted. The only person here is me, and even I shouldn't be here any longer. It's time to go.

I look around my bedroom. *What do I need for safety? What do I need to take with me?* Water, surely. I realize I feel the same catch in the back of my throat as before, only this time there's a genuine reason for it: I'll need a wet cloth to cover my nose and mouth. I grab a long-sleeved cotton top, with the intention of using it a makeshift mask, and my sleeping bag; I'm pretty sure the latter is fire-retardant and I can douse it in water and wear it as a protective cape. Then I descend the stairs, retracing my steps to the kitchen. In the few short minutes that I've been upstairs, the red glow as glimpsed through the kitchen window has increased in intensity; its acceleration is frankly terrifying. There's a faint roar too: some combination of the fire itself and the vicious winds that are fanning it through the trees. The intensifying billowing smoke is obliterating the previously bright afternoon, laying a premature nightmarish twilight across the landscape in that direction, though the view I glimpsed through the salon window was still bright and carefree—but for how much longer?

There's no time. I should have been gone twenty minutes ago, I realize with dawning horror. *I should never have been here at all. It's always been too late.*

I flip up the tablecloth, looking for the bottled water, and find plenty of it. Four two-liter bottles go straight in my backpack—that's all I can fit, even after pulling out the laptop to make space, and I'm not sure I'd want to carry more weight anyway. I lay my sleeping bag and T-shirt on the floor and douse them, and then myself, with the contents of one of the half-empty five-gallon containers, uncaring of the mess I'm making of the floor, because it's time to go—in fact, it's long past time to go. When I'm finished with the container, everything is absolutely sopping wet, including my hair and everything I'm wearing. I tie the long sleeves of the T-shirt in a knot behind my head. The wet cotton plasters itself against my face; I have to deliberately position my mouth to avoid creating a seal with every breath in, but I'm ready now. Somewhere along the way, I must have put my sunglasses down without picking them up again, but it doesn't matter. It will soon be too murky outside to wear them.

I cross the salon, the sleeping bag draped and dripping over my shoulders, squelching awkwardly in my soaked climbing boots, to exit the chalet. I'm almost out of the door when something at my shoulder pulls me abruptly backward, forcing me to stumble and knock my head hard into the frame. I cry out, my head ringing and my vision temporarily blurred, and turn to find that one of the straps of my rucksack has caught on the grandfather clock. I tug—hard—but it won't release.

The clock is trying to trap me, I think, and somehow that panics me even more than the fire outside. *But no, no, I see it now. The clock is the fire and the fire is the clock and there's almost no time left; the beat is racing—time itself is racing, so fast that's it's nearly all used up . . .*

Stop! Breathe.

I take a step toward the clock and see that the rucksack strap has caught on the knob that opens the front panel. Behind that glass panel, the pendulum is swinging back and forth, hypnotically alive with fiery rivulets of red light running through its etchings. The clockface above is unexpectedly devoid of any tinge of red, which oddly makes me more uneasy, as if the fire that I glimpsed banked within it has been released. Something odd about the hands on the face ensnares my attention. I don't remember noticing it before, but the ironwork is not smooth; instead it's pitted and uneven and almost cracked in places as if the hands have been cobbled together from tiny molten pellets, each still retaining an echo of its shape. The light swoops along the tiny ridges, urging my eyes to follow, and I want to. I want to see where it's going; I'm suddenly completely certain that everything will make sense if only I follow the light. I'm dimly aware of a sudden *crack* from outside—a tree exploding in the heat?—but the thought passes through my brain without sticking, for all that matters is that I follow the light. I must follow the light. I must trace every ridge, consider every depression, understand every single demarcation. And then a searing pain slants through my head, causing me to cry out and stumble, and in the instant of slicing pain, I see that familiar rich brown iris pulsing at me as if moving in and out of focus, a desperate urgency to its beat, and I find myself calling out, "Sofi!"—and with that, the trance is broken.

I think with dawning understanding: *It's the clock. It won't let me go.* But I won't be held—Sofi won't let me be held. I shake myself and look again at the caught strap, careful to keep my eyes away from the pendulum or the clockface. It should be a simple matter to unhook it, but when I reach out, I find the knob is oddly searingly hot—far hotter than it should be, given the ambient temperature; I have to wrap my hand in the sleeping bag, which means I'm clumsy and I make heavy work of freeing the strap. The sleeping bag is nowhere near as damp as I expect it to be: how long have I been standing here? At last, I'm free to go, but as I pass the clock, I turn and pause. A savage, destructive urge is burgeoning in me, sweeping through me, and as it grows, I don't try to restrain myself. I simply give in to it, reaching out to squeeze the fingers of both my hands in between the grandfather clock and the wall, pulling as hard as I can until it falls forward, smashing to the floor, with a truly satisfying crunch of breaking glass among a metallic clanging, to lie inert facedown. The unpatterned and unmarked wood of its rear, darker than that of the front, which must have been bleached over time by natural light, is shuttered and blank, as if the clock has closed its eyes. I look down on it over my damp cotton mask, breathing unevenly. *Just like that poor father, I would take an ax to you if I had one*, I think. *I would chop you to splinters and snap your clock hands and melt down your metal parts.* And then I realize that the back is not entirely unmarked. There's a small metal plate, curiously clean and shiny, screwed into the wood right at the very bottom as if trying to escape notice. I lean over to read it, stumbling over the unfamiliar words, trying to decipher the French before I realize it's not French: *Tempus invenit re vera nos ipsos.* Latin. *Tempus*: something about weather? No, time. Time makes much more sense.

But it's long past time to go. I step through the door and out onto the lawn, crossing it swiftly, half jogging as I head toward the tiny trail. I'm feeling oddly woozy. Perhaps the T-shirt that's plastering my mouth is to blame or perhaps it's the smoke; whatever the reason, my breathing feels labored and my head oddly wobbly. There's a heavy haze of smoke now on this side of the chalet too; it could almost be sundown. The faint roar I heard before is louder now and I turn to glance back. The scene is truly, horrifyingly apocalyptic: it's like watching a hurricane but with billowing clouds of dense black smoke and fire embers instead of rain. Behind the chalet, the trees closest to me stand out, black and stark, against the red glow behind them, their upper branches violently bent over by the gale-force winds. One, not far from the chalet, is already on fire, the flames reaching up to impossible heights. I cannot imagine how the wooden chalet can possibly escape the hellish destruction that lies ahead of it. *Jana,* I think. *Please be safe.* And then, *Julie! How can I have forgotten about her?* But I didn't see her in my search for Jana, and James didn't see her either; I can only hope she's at a safe distance somewhere.

Survival, I think as I enter the trees on the far side of the lawn. *Do one thing. Then the next, and the next. First, I have to get to the main path.* I presume the grassland will burn quicker than the wooded areas; once the fire breaks through to that, it will spread very quickly, but the main path is dirt and rocks; at least I ought to be able to make quick progress there. But in which direction? Down must be better than up, but I will have to see what effect the wind is having on the direction of the fire. *No matter. Concentrate on the first thing: get to the main path.* The smoky haze seems less acute among the trees, but I'm not sure if that's just because the trunks help with depth perception. I quickly discard the sleeping bag: all it does is snag on branches and yank me back in a horrible echo of the clock. I'm moving at a fast jog, which is as fast as I dare on the tiny uneven trail; it's hard to place my feet safely, given that my eyes are streaming due to the acrid air and the gusting wind. The last thing I want to do is turn an ankle or lose my way. My breath is coming fast and it's an effort to control it, to stop myself yanking away the damp cotton that every instinct screams is depriving me of oxygen and causing this curious light-headedness.

"Emily! Emily! This way!"

I stutter to a halt and look up, squinting through the murky air and trying to get a sense of where the shout has come from. Someone—first I can see only a shapeless gray entity, and then a person, and then I can see that it's a man—emerges from the murky gloom ahead of me, waving energetically as he jogs in my direction, becoming sharper and more distinct with every step.

Peter. I feel myself tense. He has something pulled up over his mouth: some kind of athletic-looking neck warmer. He pulls it down to shout across to me. "Are you okay?"

"Yes," I call back, though it comes out more as a muffled croak through my makeshift mask. He's perhaps ten meters away now. "Have you seen Jana?"

"Come on! This way, quick!" He's gesturing uphill, off the tiny rabbit trail we're on.

"Have you seen Jana?" I repeat.

"No. This way, come on."

"Why? Isn't downhill better? Won't the fire spread faster uphill?"

"No, the wind is affecting it—come on. There's no time!"

I know there's no time; I've stopped the clock. But I don't move. He comes closer. "Jesus, what happened to your head? Are you okay?"

"My head?"

"You're bleeding."

Am I? I put my hand to my head where it knocked against the doorframe. When I look at my fingers, they're sticky and dark; in the odd crepuscular light, it appears as if they're covered with tar rather than blood. "Look, we have to go. This way." He gestures up the slope again, away from the rabbit trail, away from the only route I know for certain leads to the main path.

"No. Not that way." Every single fiber in my body tells me not to leave this trail. *And especially not with Peter.*

"What are you talking about? We have to get away from the fire."

308

"You go."

"Don't be ridiculous, Emily. I'm not leaving without you." He takes a step toward me and reaches out to grab my arm, and I find myself rearing back in alarm. "Emily—what the fuck?"

"I . . . I don't trust you." *He could hit me over the head and then the fire would do the work for him. He wouldn't even need to use both his hands to close off my nose and mouth.*

"What? Because of the patent thing? Jesus Christ. We're in the middle of a wildfire that might genuinely kill us—don't you think all that other stuff can wait?" He reaches for me again, and I back up a step, shaking my head, but I stop that very quickly.

"I don't trust you," I repeat. The skin on his bare arms is charcoal smeared, as are his clothes. I look down at myself, damp and blackened, and around at the murky air. It's as if all color is being obliterated from the world.

"Come on, Ems, it's me." He looks over my shoulder, and I turn to look too, but all I can see is a red glow through the trees; nothing is evidently on fire immediately around us. *At least not yet.* "Look, it's true. I may have overstepped on that patent stuff. I should have come clean to you, and I will when we get out of here, but you've got to know that I would never hurt you." *Do I?* I don't think so. *I don't think I know that at all.* "Not intentionally."

Not intentionally? I stare at him. "What did you do, Peter?"

"Nothing, I—"

"What did you do unintentionally?"

He looks away and I see his throat working before he says defiantly, "Nothing. I don't know what you're talking about."

"Sofi? Did you kill Sofi?"

He rears back. "Jesus. Of course not."

"Well, you did something." My mind flicks through the past week at the chalet, grabbing and discarding possibilities. I can't see his eyes but there's something odd lurking around his mouth: is it fear? "Was it you that chased me in the forest when I fell?"

"What? No—Ems, this is ridiculous."

"The glass," I say suddenly. "The shards of glass. You did that." He freezes. For once there's not even a flicker of movement on his normally dynamic face. I'm shocked beyond all measure. "Peter," I breathe.

"It was an accident," he says, his jaw set.

"An accident?" But to do it, he must have deliberately smashed something. He must have picked out the shards to drop into the wineglass, including that lethal isosceles triangle. I see it again sitting in the burgundy dregs of the wine, its razor-sharp edges just waiting for some vulnerable skin to slice open, for blood to well up in the hairline slashes . . . "I don't believe you."

A range of emotions crosses his quick mobile face, each flickering out quickly to be replaced by another; my vision is too blurred and my head too fuzzy to identify each one. I recognize the one that sticks, though: anger.

"Seriously, Ems? You really think I would try to hurt you? Thanks a lot," he spits out. "After all our years of friendship? You know I only came back down the mountain to look for you?"

To save me or silence me? I can't tell. I can see it both ways, just like with Mike: I can see the two tableaus overlaid on each other, like congruent tiles. They can't both be true, but it doesn't matter, because of the way that the colors seep through, staining all around. Just having thought of one automatically besmirches the other; I can't have unshakable belief in either.

He steps toward me again, and I step back quickly; his face twists and he turns away. "I'm going this way, uphill, away from the fire; the winds are pushing it across and down, toward the valley. I'd suggest you follow, but"—he shrugs—"it's your fune—your choice."

It's your funeral. That's what he was going to say. It almost robs me of breath. *Your funeral, your choice.* He starts to push his way through the woodland, moving quickly uphill. This one decision, whether to follow Peter or not, might be the most important in my life. I try to reach for Sofi, for the guidance of that single eye, but nothing comes. My eyes follow Peter as I remain standing, suddenly uncertain, suddenly terribly aware of the roar of the fire as loud as a freight train. The urge to follow him is strong, but is that simply the natural human instinct that prompts us to stay with the pack? *If I let him go on without me, I will be alone.* But safety in numbers doesn't necessarily work if that number is only two, and the other can't be trusted . . . He's climbing quickly. Before long he will be lost in the murk.

I find my feet are moving, but not uphill. I'm following the little trail, the one that I have faith in, that I know leads to the main path. *I've been alone before. I can survive that way again.* And then, defiantly, *It's my decision. It may be my funeral, ultimately, but at least I'm not drifting into it.* I concentrate on the trail, on moving as fast as I can—which is a jog that needles at my ankle on every impact—on controlling my breathing through the now merely damp mask. It's astonishing how disconcerting this odd half-light is: everything around me is sepia toned and unfamiliar. Tree trunks loom out at me suddenly from the smoke-filled gloom: not there at all at one moment, and then, in the next, so close that I can make out the texture of the bark. I'm increasingly unsure that I'm going the right way: I can't have veered off the trail when there is only one route to follow, but where are the little wooden bridge and the stream? Shouldn't I have reached them by now? Is the stretch of path through the woodland really this long? Do I recognize that outcrop of rocks, or am I just confirming my own bias, my desire to believe that I'm on the right track? Everything is a question and nothing provides an answer.

Then suddenly the little path bursts out of the trees onto the tiny wooden bridge and I feel a wave of relief and a burst of affection for the structure—nothing more than a couple of planks and two thin handrails on either side at waist height, without even any paneling to stop a child or a dog slipping under the rails into the water, but nonetheless a landmark that I can be certain of. *Though it will burn,* I think sadly as my boots stomp down on the wooden slats for what must be the last time. *It's inevitable.* I wonder how old it is, how many people have crossed it.

"Emily! Oh, thank God!" I stop in the middle of the bridge. It's Julie's voice, but I can't see her.

"Julie?" It's almost a cry of despair: she's not safe after all. I would give almost anything for her not to be on the mountain right now; the ferocity of that protective feeling is a surprise.

"I'm down here." I hold the handrail, looking for her downstream, and find her, standing calf deep in the water, only ten meters or so from the bridge.

"Did you see Jana?"

"I saw her earlier. She went down the mountain to meet Will; I'm sure she's fine."

I close my eyes briefly: *At least Jana is out of harm's way.* "Are you okay?"

"Mostly. I was just out of the waterfall shower when I realized what was happening. I didn't want to go back toward the chalet to pick up the trail, not with the fire so close to it, so I worked my way upstream along the banks to here." *Smart girl.* "The thing is"—she grimaces—"I slipped just now, which is how I'm actually *in* the stream. And now my knee isn't exactly working properly."

"How bad?"

"I don't think I can run." Her cornflower eyes are fixed on mine. She knows the implications of that; we both do. Running might very well be required.

"Okay," I say, trying to think. *Do one thing. And then the next, and then the next.* "You need a mask," I say, crossing the remainder of the bridge to the bank. She looks at me dumbly. I gesture toward the sky blue fleece that is tied around her waist, an unexpectedly clean burst of color in the gloom. "Maybe that? Soak it in the stream first. Soak all of you in the stream." I'm climbing down to her to do the same, given that I've dried off considerably since I first doused myself. The rocks are slippery underfoot and the icy-cold water is an assault on my feet; I feel it pouring over the top of my walking boots, invading the spaces within and making me gasp. The contrast of the hot, thick, murky air with the pure, clear glacial water on my calves and feet is stark: breathing this soup cannot be good for us. *Who knows what kind of particulates are getting into our lungs, even with these makeshift masks?* But there's nothing to be done about that, so I force myself to drop to my knees in the icy water and then to entirely submerge myself, lying down first on my front and then my back. Julie copies me, holding her phone out of the water as she does so. *I suppose, if we survive this, I will find out if mine truly is waterproof,* I think wryly.

"You're bleeding," says Julie in surprise once she clambers awkwardly back to her feet. Her words are muffled by the fleece she's tying across her face.

I shake my head. "It's old blood. I'm okay; I just bumped my head." My words are muffled too, but it feels like the fuzziness is on the inside. No matter. *What next?* "We'll have to see how bad your knee is. Can you climb out?" I scramble up the bank and turn to help her, holding out my hand to yank her up. She manages it in a strange crablike motion; it's clear that she can't put much weight on that leg. The stream acts as a border to the woodland; from here on, the path is through grassland. I look at the tiny trail. It's not wide enough for us both side by side. A dancing orange firefly catches my eye, but it's not a firefly—of course it's not. My eyes follow it as it writes squiggles in the air and then settles gently on the grasses. I look back toward the chalet, where I've just come from. There are more embers: tossed around in the air, settling on the ground beneath the trees or catching in branches. Sooner or later, one will succeed in setting everything around it alight. I turn back to Julie.

"Do you think you can walk behind me, hanging on to my rucksack for support?" She can't understand my words through my soaked cotton T-shirt; I have to pull it down and ask again. She nods, her eyes staunchly determined above the matching blue of the fleece that obscures most of her face. "Shout if I'm going too fast." We set off like a pantomime horse without the costume, Julie bent a little at the waist with her arms outstretched so as not to step on the back of my heels and her weight dragging on me through the straps of my rucksack on every second step. We can't have more than a hundred meters of grassland to cross, but in this terrible hellish twilight, it's impossible to have a sense of making progress: around us, nothing changes step by step. My aching, itching, weeping eyes keep switching from picking out the route right in front of me to scanning the landscape ahead of us in case the fire has already jumped and taken hold. It seems to be getting darker by the minute, which can't possibly be a good thing. I daren't look behind us, and yet I must. I have to know if the beast is about to swallow us up—

Suddenly I stop, Julie stumbling into my back with a small cry. She peers around me, both hands still on the rucksack. "What? Oh, fuck."

"Yes." Up ahead, the grasslands have ignited in a sea of transparent orange flame rippling in the fierce wind. For a second I consider that we might try to run through the flames to reach the main path, but I discard the idea just as quickly. I'm not exactly sure how far we are from the path but it must be tens of meters, and most of that through fire. And Julie clearly can't run.

"Fuck," says Julie again, but hopelessly this time.

"Yes." *Do one thing,* I think dejectedly. *And then the next. And then the next.* But I don't know what to do next. *That's the flaw in that survival plan.* I'm all out of nexts.

23

I look behind us, because where else do you look when the path ahead is blocked? The wind is whipping around in gusts; while it's mostly sweeping the fire uphill now—*so much for Peter's theory*—it blusters and wheels in all directions. Nowhere on this grassland will be safe for long. So I look behind us, steeling myself to see the fire beast with its jaws open, ready to snatch us. I can just make out the woodland through the gloom. The trees that line the stream aren't on fire, but those immediately behind them appear to be. The grassland on our side of the stream is starting to catch in places.

"You could maybe run through the fire to the main path," says Julie. "That can't be burning—it's dirt and rock. You could make it across."

I shake my head; it still feels wobbly when I do that. "I'm not sure that I could. And anyway, I'm not leaving you."

She looks at me mutely with a grim maturity; comprehension and resignation and sadness and pain are all mingled in her eyes. "You should."

"I won't," I say tightly. *She is too young for this to happen to her,* I think desperately. I feel the responsibility of her being here with me—that unexpected protectiveness—as an unwelcome shove; if I were here alone, I might be able to give up. But I cannot give up on her. *There must be a way. There must be a next.* I look around again, scanning a full three hundred sixty degrees around us. The only thing not at risk of catching fire at any moment is the stream. *The stream.*

"The water," I say, turning urgently to Julie. Her sky blue fleece is no longer bright and clean, but streaked with grime. She shakes her head, not comprehending. I pull down my T-shirt temporarily. "We should get back in the stream. Maybe make our way back to the waterfall pool where it's deeper?"

"The trees around it might already all be alight." She looks around quickly, cataloging and assessing. "But yes, all right; I can't think of a better idea." She looks ahead toward the main path, her eyes almost wistful. "And we definitely can't go that way."

"No. Let's go."

She nods. "I'll keep an eye out behind," I think she says; it's so hard to understand with the roar of the fire and the snatching wind and the muffling effect of our face coverings. Our naked pantomime horse turns, and we start back, retracing every step we've taken. It feels wrong, this: we're literally walking, as fast as Julie can manage, toward the danger—a danger that's growing right in front of our eyes, filling all our field of vision. The smoke streaming out of the forest is dense and black and ugly, as if what's burning is an oil field rather than a forest; the only colors I can see are the black of the silhouetted trees and the smoke and the blazing red-orange glow of the fire. We see a tree catch fire on the water's edge, the flames—initially transparent and weak, but increasingly intense as the conflagration takes hold—fanning like diabolical red foliage in the branches. The direction of the wind seems to change by the second; the embers dance gleefully, tossed this way and that, some climbing skyward to who knows where, some settling in other trees, where they might die out or, equally, take hold. The ones that journey across the stream worry me the most. There are already several small patches of grassland burning between us and the water. At any moment those little fires might join hands and barricade our way. We don't have far to go but we're not moving fast enough. I pick up the pace, feeling Julie dragging me back until she recognizes the acceleration for what it is and tries to adjust.

She calls, "I can't—"

"We have to; look ahead," I shout over my shoulder urgently. The gaps between the little fires are closing. In minutes, seconds even, there will be a swath of blazing grassland to cross to reach the stream.

"Oh, shit. Go, go! I'll hang on."

I go as fast as I can with her dragging awkwardly on my rucksack; it's not quite a sprint but it definitely qualifies as a run. I can hear Julie's breath rasping through her fleece; I can hear my own too. The face covering makes me feel oddly detached, or perhaps the bump on the head does that, but regardless, despite the physicality of what I'm doing—the burning in my lungs and leg muscles, the streaming gritty eyes, the stinging skin, the uncomfortable heat around me—I feel as if I'm operating separately to the world in some sort of enclosed suit. *Like scuba diving*, I think, recognizing the feeling. *How odd to be thinking of scuba diving in a wildfire.*

Up ahead, fifty meters from us, the bridge has caught fire, the flames licking up one handrail and reaching out into the void of air beside it with each gust of wind as if stretching out blindly in search of more fuel. I stumble on the uneven ground and Julie cannons into me; we right ourselves quickly and are off again, but now I can see what I feared: the little fires have united. A line of flame lies between us and the stream, burning right along the bank. We're going to have to barrel through it.

It's fine, I tell myself grimly. *It's only a meter or two wide, and the flames aren't intense. And then we'll be in the stream.*

"We're going to have to go through the flames," I shout to Julie, slowing down and turning to her. "There's water in my rucksack; we need to douse ourselves."

She nods, her hands quickly moving to my rucksack. She pulls out two of the two-liter water bottles and hands one to me. We both pour them directly over our heads, soaking our hair, our clothes, our skin. The water mixed with my own grime stings my eyes, but there's no time to wipe them; the protection won't last long in this heat. "Let's go," I yell. *Don't trip*, I think. *Do not fall.*

We go. In the time it took us to soak ourselves, the line of flame has moved toward us. I take as deep a breath as I can, given the mask, and run straight into the flames. I can feel them lick at the bare skin on my legs, but we're through in less than a second, then crossing a couple of meters of burned-out grasses—and then the bank of the stream is right there; we slip and slide down it to splash into the water, the cold of it a pleasant shock. Julie lies back and rolls over, soaking every part of her, and I do the same. The stream is not wide here, not even three meters across, and only knee-deep—but it's a blessed relief from the heat. My legs are stinging in places but it hardly matters. We're in the stream now.

No, I think. *That's not enough. What next?*

I tug on Julie's arm and gesture downstream; she nods and we start moving, shuffling on our bottoms with our feet ahead of us, occasionally leaning back to resoak our shoulders. The bottom of the stream is uneven, sometimes inches deep and sometimes a few feet deep. Behind me I can hear Julie coughing through her mask. *That can't be good.*

The banks of the stream could be scenes from two different movies. On our right is the forest, with its angry red glow as if a giant furnace has opened its yawning mouth just behind the trees. Not many of the trees that immediately flank the stream have caught fire yet, but the odd one or two have. The rest are simply solid black silhouettes patiently awaiting their fate. The left side of the stream is different. Where the fire has taken hold, the grass and occasional bushes are burning quicker, and the smoke that rises is white, not black.

Julie must be thinking the same as me. "The grass might burn out," she calls from behind me. "We might be able to walk down over the burned section."

I stop and wait for her to shuffle to me, pulling my T-shirt down to talk. "Yes. We probably shouldn't go much farther." Soon, the stream will dart right such that both banks will be heavily wooded. "We won't be visible to the mountain rescue teams if there's woodland on both banks."

"I saw a helicopter earlier. Just before we found each other. I don't think it saw me." Then, quieter, "Caleb will be so worried."

"There must be people looking for us." *There must be; surely there must be.* Eyes stretched wide in search of us—other than that still brown iris that simply stares rather than seeks. "They'll find us." *Please let them find us.* If Peter has made it somewhere safe, will he tell people that I'm still on the mountainside, or will he hope that the fire has done his work for him? Which one of those stained scenarios am I living in?

"Ouch!" An ember has just landed on my shoulder; I brush it off quickly. "Let's find a deep section to hunker down in for a bit and see if the fire burns out on our left."

We continue on and are rewarded by an outcrop of rocks that leads to a mini waterfall pool that's as deep as a bathtub, though not much larger. I flop over the rocks along with the unexpectedly fast-flowing water, and Julie follows in a rush, such that we end up in a tangle in the pool with her more or less on top of me.

"Oof! Sorry. Jesus Christ, this is freezing." She's gasping; the faster the water, the colder it seems. We rearrange ourselves until we are both on our sides, wedged against the rocks with the fall of the water by our feet rather than our heads. "We're going to be the first people in history to die of hypothermia in a bloody wildfire."

I can't help it; I start to laugh. After a second, she joins in; we clutch each other, giggling helplessly at the incongruity of it all, the water flowing around our necks and tugging at our face masks, plastering them ever more closely to our faces.

"Olive would tell you it's good for your knee," I say. "Like putting ice on it." That makes us laugh even harder.

We lie in the pool, our heads partially supported by rocks, looking up toward the sky, which we can't see because of the smoke. We can't see much to our left or right either, because the banks of the stream are much steeper here. I can feel welcome heat where the length of Julie's body lies against mine; I can feel the icy water trying to whisk that heat away as it flows relentlessly around us. "My phone is definitely fucked now. And I am weirdly really hungry," Julie says after a while. I'm not sure how long it's been since we've spoken. *I'm losing track of things. That's not a good sign.*

"Not me." I actually feel quite nauseous, but I don't want her to worry about me.

"Spaghetti Bolognese," she says longingly though her teeth are chattering, "with a bloody good red wine."

"I'll share the wine with you, at least." My teeth are chattering too, and yet my throat is increasingly hot and hoarse. *We can't stay in this water forever, getting colder and breathing in more of this toxic air.*

"The crime scene will have all burned up."

"I expect they got whatever they needed from it already." It's a platitude—I have no idea how long forensics take or any real idea of how the process works—but it seems enough for Julie. It catches at my throat that she's thinking of Sofi, of justice for her even now. And then I realize that I haven't been thinking of Nick. *Perhaps near death is an effective mechanism for aiding the grieving process*, I think with black humor, *though I'm not exactly sure how you could ethically test the theory.*

"I wonder what started this in the first place?" Julie muses. "The fire, I mean."

I'm silent. I've been trying not to wonder that; I've been trying not to think of that handful of twisted metal binding that James held out. *I found it out the back of the chalet,* he said. Was he right? Had someone just burned the diary? Something like that could have easily sparked this fire, given this wind and the remarkably dry conditions we've experienced—that the area has been experiencing all summer, in fact. It's an appallingly distressing thought, that all this destruction and devastation might be linked once again to Sofi. "Perhaps we'll never know," I murmur. Is it better to know or not? Until recently, my answer would have been clear: I'd rather not know. But perhaps ignorance is not bliss. Perhaps ignorance is just danger hiding away, waiting for the right opportunity to creep out and wreak the most havoc.

"We're going to be okay," Julie says quietly. I'm not sure if she's trying to reassure herself or me.

"Yes." I don't know if it's true or not, but either way, it occurs to me that if I had to choose, Julie is a pretty good person to be in this situation with: no dramatics, just clear, sensible thinking. I maneuver my arm round her shoulders and squeeze briefly. "Yes, we will. We got this far. One step at a time." I'm not sure I can feel my toes any longer.

"One step at a time," she murmurs. Then she says, "Déjà vu."

"Déjà vu?"

"I saw this. The fire, the trees alight. In the clockface. Or was it in my clock dreams? I don't know."

"You dreamed of the clock too?"

She doesn't answer. I don't know for how long. The water gurgles around us. The fire roars. Occasionally there's a loud crack, presumably from a branch exploding. *Nick will be worried too*, I think, but no, that's wrong, Nick can no longer worry about anything ever again. I'm losing track of time, and it's making me fret, even though I know I stopped the clock . . .

"What's next?"

My eyes open. I wasn't aware I had closed them. I'm not sure who spoke those words—was it me? I glance around. Julie is gazing upward. "Did you say something?" I ask her. She doesn't reply, but Sofi's iris is with me again, insistently unblinking still. *I'm here*, I tell it silently. *I'm still alive. I'm going to keep trying to stay that way.* I look around. I'm not sure that I'm cold anymore, and that can't be a good sign. "What's next?" I mutter to myself. *I need to cling to that question*, I think grimly. I can't let it slide away from me or me from it. It occurs to me that if we get through this, it will be because I learned how to survive after Nick's death, how to keep on plodding onward in the face of all hopelessness. And because Sofi won't let me do otherwise.

I start to move, unwrapping myself from Julie to try to get to my feet, and instantly find I'm struck by dizziness; I have to bend over for a few breaths before I can straighten up. But even when I'm finally upright, I can't see above the steeply banked side of dirt and rock to check the fire's progress, and I don't think I can climb out either. "Julie, I'm going back upstream to see better."

"Okay," she says dreamily.

I glance across: her eyes are closed. "Julie," I say sharply. They open, their brilliant blue an unexpected splash of color in this grotesque world of red and black and gray. "Sit up; get some heat into your body. I have to go upstream for a second. You can't sleep, okay?" She doesn't move; I lean across and grab an arm, yanking her half out of the water and that seems to rouse her. "Are you okay? I'm going upstream to check on the fire. You can't sleep. Will you be okay?"

She nods, suddenly much more awake, and heaves herself more upright in the water now that she has the space without me there too. "Okay. Yes. Right. I'll sing," she says with remarkable practicality. "What do you want to hear?"

"Your choice." I start to wade upstream, slipping and sliding, as my feet are so cold they barely feel like my own. She breaks into a slightly muffled "Amazing Grace" in a surprisingly good alto. The heat in the air feels good on my skin after the cold of the water.

"'I once was lost, but now I'm found,'" sings Julie. How apposite. *Please let us be found*, I think. *Please.*

Up ahead I spot the sad, charred remains of the bridge; we haven't moved downstream nearly as far as I thought. The angry red glow on the tree-lined side is just the same as before, but it seems to me that no new trees have caught alight—perhaps the wind has mainly been blowing into the woodland? I can't quite tell either if the wind is dying down; one might expect it to in the evening, but I've no sense of the time of day, and I don't appear to be wearing my watch. When did I lose that?

"'How precious did that grace appear . . .'"

To the right, now that the height of the bank is reducing, I see scorched gray-black ground as far as my eye can penetrate through the gloom, with burned-out stubby bushes dotted here and there. I feel a jolt of recognition. *This is what I saw flooding out of Sofi,* I think. *All the green turning to this.* But for Julie and me, it's not our ruination; it might just be our salvation. *Thank you, Sofi,* I say silently. *Bless you.* I stand, submerged up to midcalf level in the glacial water, the rest of me already almost dry in the hot, parched air, and think, *We can make it,* not with any exultation, but with a kind of relieved determination. There are still obstacles to overcome, but it's actually beginning to look like we have a chance.

We might just be okay.

24

Of all the things I've endured today, it is, oddly, the walk through the burned-out grasslands that haunts me later as I try to sleep. It takes some time to get Julie and myself up out of the stream; her injured knee, despite the lengthy impromptu ice treatment, is visibly swollen in comparison to the other and much stiffer and more difficult to use. But at least this time we don't have to travel one in front of the other along a tiny trail: the wildfire has cleared our route. We limp slowly across the blackened hillside, Julie's arm slung over my shoulders and mine anchored around her waist, struck silent by the apocalyptic scene around us and navigating more by instinct than intelligence. The wind has definitely dropped; smoke rises lazily from some of the stubby bushes, black and bare and seemingly utterly spent but somehow still smoldering, thrusting upright from the scorched ground like headstones in a cemetery, a silent accusation in the spread of their ravaged branches.

When we reach the main path, we stop for a moment, looking at each other with a sort of exhausted grim satisfaction at having reached that milestone, and mere seconds later a fire truck roars up, audible long before it's visible, given the smoke, only coming into view remarkably close to us and slewing to an ungainly halt on the gravel and dirt. The sheer joy in the grin of the grimy-faced French driver when he sees us makes my throat so hot and tight that for a moment I'm unable to give our names; I can only nod repeatedly when he asks, *"Êtes-vous du Chalet des Anglais?"*

Now we lie in the hospital in Chamonix, in a small room of four with the other two beds empty, where we're being treated for smoke inhalation and minor burns, mostly on our legs from leaping through the flames—the doctor said we would have been in real trouble had we not soaked ourselves first—and also, in my case, a suspected concussion, and in Julie's case, a torn anterior cruciate ligament. Mine seems the better deal: I may have a headache for a couple of days, but otherwise I'll be fine; Julie's future holds reconstructive surgery when she's back in the UK and at least six months on crutches. We asked for and were given beds right next to each other. There will only ever be one other person who understands the kind of day I've survived; somehow that has linked us.

Neither of our phones work after their violent overexposure to both heat and cold water, which means that it takes a clandestine visit from Caleb (well outside visiting hours, but smuggled in by a nurse with either a strong romantic bent or a fondness for very polite young Englishmen) for us to hear that everyone else is safe.

Even Sofi, I think. *Nothing can ever hurt her again.*

Peter apparently made it up to the Hotel Le Prarion and was airlifted out along with the hotel staff, though from the sound of it he was very lucky to outsprint the flames when the wind changed and they spread quickly uphill. Jana had already reached the rest of the party in Saint Gervais and James too was well below the line of the fire by the time it really took hold. The chalet, of course, is completely destroyed; Robert is beyond distraught and Caleb wonders if all the distress is making him physically unwell.

"Is there any news on what started the fire in the first place, or is it too soon to know?" I ask because I have to, though I'm afraid of the answer, afraid that what I hear will evoke images of flames curling up from an A5 jotter, contorting in the wind, watched over by a familiar face . . . It's such an awful thought that that single person might have to bear the responsibility for all the destruction. *Realizing that it's better to know the truth rather than hide in ignorance doesn't make it any easier to bear,* I think wryly.

"A power cable snapped in the wind, a mile or so from the chalet," Caleb says. "It might have been that; at least, that's the current theory. No pun intended." *A power cable.* The relief is overwhelming. So whoever burned the diary didn't cause the fire. "With the dry weather all summer, the landscape was pretty much a tinderbox. It's meant to rain tomorrow, though."

Rain. I suppose that's a good thing; there are areas that didn't burn that would be protected from another fire by a good drenching, but I can't help thinking, *Too little, too late.* Too late for those silent, reproachful burned-out bushes. Too late for the little bridge, and the trees, and the chalet. *Much too late.*

After Caleb leaves, promising Julie that he'll return tomorrow, I say, unable to help myself, "He really is a very sweet guy." *So this is what near-death experiences do for you,* I think with rueful amusement. *They turn you into an absolute mess of sentimentality.*

"I know." She pauses. "It sounds like an odd thing to say, but I really admired Sofi for how she went after the things she wanted. She had to work for everything; nothing was on a plate for her. In comparison, it's always been so much easier for me. It . . . it makes me confused as to what I really want."

I don't quite understand. "Are you confused about Caleb?" I ask cautiously. Surely not—they seem to fit together so perfectly. The romantic in me will be crushed if she doesn't feel the same as he evidently does. Caleb's heart is in his eyes every time he looks at her.

"No. That's my point actually. It's unexpected, but he's something that I know I really want."

I find I'm smiling. It hurts: my lips are blistered. "Hang on to that, then." *Wanting is good,* I think. *It's what living is about; we should want things. We must want things.* Perhaps those doors that are beginning to open for me shouldn't all be something to fear, though I can't stop the uneasy thought that follows: Might not all that wanting drag one off-kilter? Isn't that what the clock was doing—augmenting the worst of our instincts, throwing us off-balance? It must surely be ashes now, but even so, I'm still afraid of losing my footing. I feel like I'm only just regaining it.

Knock, knock." It's the next morning; I look up to see Peter at the door, brandishing a pink helium balloon with *Congratulations* scrawled on it above a cartoonish baby image. He's wearing a navy blue Patagonia T-shirt and hiking trousers that I haven't seen before; no doubt the local shops will do quite well out of our party, given all our belongings have combusted. "Sorry, but they didn't have any well-done-on-surviving-a-wildfire balloons in the shop."

"They're missing a trick. Is it raining?" The shoulders of his T-shirt are visibly damp.

"Yes, thank God; it started very early this morning." The firemen must be thrilled. I should be imagining those towering flames beaten into submission by the precipitation, but I find

I'm thinking of the burned-out grasses. By now the blackened ground must be a gray soup of wet ash and debris.

He's still hovering. "Can I come in?" he asks. I gesture to the chair by the bed that I'm on, though I'm fully dressed and on top of the covers rather than under. He enters, leaving the door ajar, and ties the balloon onto the chair's arm, where it sways gently in an invisible draft, before he sits down, leaning forward with his elbows on his knees and his hands clasped ahead of him. It should be a relaxed position, but he seems awkward and tense. Through the open door, I spy a nurse passing along the corridor, and there's a help button on the device that controls the position of my bed. I hate that these thoughts have crossed my mind; I hate that events have made it necessary to think that way. *Events*. I should call a spade a spade. It's Peter who has made it necessary to think that way. "I wanted to see for myself that you're all right," he's saying.

"I am. I'm getting out today, once they find someone to sign off on some meds."

"And Julie too?"

"Yes. She's just with the physio now, getting crutches. She'll have the surgery in a few weeks back in the UK."

"Good." He looks at his tightly clasped hands, unnaturally still and stiff for the man who usually lives with electric currents just below his skin. "That's good."

The silence lengthens. His gaze stays fixed on his hands. "You owe me some answers, Peter," I say.

His eyes flick to my face, then away. "Yes. We don't have to do it now—"

"Yes, we do."

"I . . ." It seems like he intends to argue, but then he abruptly yields. "Yes. Okay."

I wait, but he doesn't say anything. "Well, go on, then."

He finally looks at me properly. "What do you want to know?"

"Did you break into my house?"

He looks around. *He's checking whether anyone else can hear,* I realize. "Yes," he says quietly. "Believe me, I had no intention of scaring you. You weren't supposed to be there. But you missed the flight and . . ." He shrugs. "You used to keep a spare key out the front," he adds plaintively. *As if it's my fault he had to break in.* It's almost funny. But he brought a balaclava and something to force the back door. He was prepared for it.

"I took in the key after Nick died." Nick always had a very loose grasp on the location of his keys—of most of his possessions, in fact. If I hadn't taken the key in, if he hadn't had to force the back door, if I had caught that flight, would I have even known he'd been in the house? Somehow that seems even more chilling than having surprised him there. *The police officer was right: I should definitely get an alarm system.* "What were you looking for?"

"Nick's laptop."

"I know that. What specifically?" He doesn't say anything. His gaze is on his clasped hands again. The knuckles are white. I have an urge to strike at them, to break them apart and release him from his self-imposed constraints so the truth comes flooding out of him. "Peter, you promised me answers." There's a warning note in my tone that makes his gaze flicker to my face again, but he still doesn't say anything. "Give me answers or I will call the UK police and tell them that you were the intruder."

That gets his attention. "You wouldn't." *Yes, I would.* Whatever he sees in my eyes causes his own to skitter away. After a moment he says, "Anyway, you've got no proof."

"That will be up to the police forensics team to determine."
Who don't have any forensic evidence at all, but he doesn't know that.

He looks uncertain. "I didn't . . . It wasn't really like breaking in. I mean, we're *friends*."

This time I do laugh. "Oh, I see. It doesn't count as a crime if you do it to your friends."

"No, I . . . I didn't mean . . ." He shrugs his shoulders up and down, as if limbering up for an athletic event, and then looks at me. "Okay. So here's the thing. I filed a patent claim. On a thing I'm working on."

"The power-trains thing?"

"No, not that, though somewhat related. Still on EV technology, at least. You know that solid-state batteries, like Nick and I have been working on over the years, typically suffer from degradation because of the formation of lithium dendrites?"

"Sort of." It rings a bell, at least. It was impossible to live with Nick without picking up a little knowledge.

"Well, anyway, they do. The dendrites effectively drill through the damn thing and short-circuit it. I applied for a patent on a new structure, sort of interesplicing different electrolytes with varying properties for stability and dendrite penetration and— Well, anyway, it's game-changing for the electric vehicle industry. Range, charging time: massive improvements. Game-changing. And then Nick was apparently contacted through the prior art search, and . . ." He stops, flexes his fingers without separating his palms and then reinstates his grip as if bracing himself. "Well, he thought my work was, at least in part, based on an idea of his."

Oh, Peter. I take a second to work through what he's said, reading between the spoken words, checking whether it really is exactly what I'd feared. "So what you're saying is, you stole one of Nick's ideas and passed it off as your own?"

"No! No, of course not—I mean, not intentionally. You know how it is: you work with someone for so long, you start to forget which idea was yours or theirs." He tries for a self-deprecating grimace, but drops it quickly in favor of earnestness. "If I did, I didn't mean to. If it even *was* his idea first."

"And the prior art search was the first Nick heard of this project?"

"Yes." If he wasn't holding himself so rigidly, I swear he'd be squirming. *He can try to rewrite history by telling himself that he thought it was his own idea as often as he likes, but that won't make it true.*

"Usually you showed everything to Nick."

His jaw tightens. "Well, I didn't this time. It doesn't mean anything." *Yes, it does.* "I was just in a rush to get the application in."

In a rush. As he always is. In a rush to take charge, in a rush to get ahead. In a rush to take any advantage he can. He sees my expression and gives up trying to argue the point. "Whatever. Anyway, I apologized—repeatedly, if it even was my error, which I'm not at all sure of." He sees my face and hastily moves on. "And of course I immediately offered to put Nick's name on the claim too." A flicker of incomprehension crosses his face. "But he refused; he said he'd shown a poster of it at a conference when he was a postdoc years ago."

A poster, displayed publicly. *The very definition of prior art.* "Which would invalidate the patent claim."

"Yes. If it really was the same thing. And I suppose, if anyone actually read the poster or spoke to him about it; I mean, that would probably be hard to prove after all this time. I tried to tell him, but . . ." He trails off and shrugs.

Character as destiny. Peter, so keen to pursue the prize, and Nick, unable to take a route that wasn't exactly by the book. When I think about it, it's actually more surprising that it took as long as it did for a clash like this to develop between them. "So you withdrew the claim, like Nick asked?"

"Yes."

"And then Nick died and you started up the claims process again." He nods, a touch sheepishly. "Without putting his name on it."

"Yes, but I can absolutely add him if that's what you—" He stops when he sees the scorn that I make no attempt to hide. "No. Of course. Right."

"It's not about whose name is on it anyway. Just the existence of the poster would be enough to invalidate the claim."

"Well, yes, if—"

"Peter," I say, cutting him off. "It was the same concept. If Nick said that it was, then it was. You know that."

"I . . ." He stops. His lack of protest is as good as agreement.

"You were trying to remove any evidence of it. I suppose you think any hard copy of the poster will have been destroyed a long time ago. But Nick would have kept an electronic copy. You wanted to delete that file."

"I mean, that's not quite . . ." He trails off; even he can't think of a different way of putting it. There isn't one.

"So you tried to get into my room; in fact, you did get into my room, and you got on the laptop, but not for long enough to find what you wanted. And then I changed the password. So you gave up on deleting a single file and instead just fried the whole bloody thing." He looks away. He's not going to own up to it, but once again his silence is admission enough. "What if he had backed up the laptop?" I challenge.

334

"Come on, we both know Nick put anything important on the university network precisely so he never had to worry about backing up his home laptop."

It's true. "And I suppose you've already been through the network files."

"The department asked me to sort through them after he died."

"How wonderfully convenient for you." Even to my own ears, I don't sound like myself. His shoulders hitch a little as he flinches from the rain of acid in my words. "Speaking of departments, I suppose you're the one who broke into mine."

"I didn't break in—I didn't, truly." He sees the skepticism that I'm not bothering to hide. "I really didn't break in." He seems genuinely affronted; I almost believe him. And then he says, "I was in there legitimately, seeing Don." *Ah. So his protest is merely semantics about the form of access, not about whether he accessed my office at all.* Don is a professor who has worked on various cross-disciplinary projects with Peter and others. I'm sure Peter *was* there legitimately, though no doubt on a manufactured pretext. "And then I just . . . waited. Technically, I wasn't even trespassing." I can imagine him waiting, probably in a cubicle of the men's bathroom. Waiting until darkness fell outside, not moving lest he set off the sensor for the lights; waiting until the footfall and good night cries around the department had faded, until there was nothing but the low hum of the emergency lighting and, from time to time, the muffled sound of a passing car. "Anyway, nobody can prove anything," he says defiantly. "There wasn't even a crime: nothing went missing."

"Only because Nick's laptop was with me." He looks away again. I don't suppose he'd imagined I might have it with me. It must have been an unexpected stroke of luck for him, realizing that I'd brought the very thing he wanted to the chalet.

A nurse walks past the open door again. I have the bed controller with its call button held in my hand; I am not alone. I steel myself to ask the most important question. "And Sofi? Were you telling the truth?"

"Yes. Absolutely nothing to do with me." He sits up properly for the first time, raising both hands, the palms facing me. I look at him as if I might see under the surface, as if I might see to his very core. For the first time, he's properly holding my gaze, willing me to believe him. And actually, I think I do. There's a tightness in my chest that releases a little. I can understand ambition, how it might drive a little corner cutting; how it might drive a person to build a narrative to justify the actions they so badly want to take. I almost feel sorry for him, for that relentless compulsion: *wanting, always wanting*. But murder . . . that I can't understand. I see the moment when he realizes that I believe him, the slight relaxation of his shoulders. "If you ask me, Jana's on the right track with that one. Some local psychopath is most likely to blame." He puts his palms flat on his thighs and looks at me, accusation in his eyes. "You know, it really hurts that you would think that was me. I thought we were friends."

"So did I. And yet you broke into my home and my office and tried to destroy my property, all for your own material gain, while terrorizing me in the process— Oh, and you fed me cut glass." He opens his mouth to speak and then closes it again. "So I guess I was wrong about the friends thing."

"That's not fair. That's not how it is—"

"It is from where I'm standing." Were we ever really friends? I had thought so. We had always got on well; we'd always found our way to a sidebar conversation, just the two of us, in any gathering. I wonder if he would have done all these things if I'd been a perfect stranger? Somehow I don't think so. Weirdly, me being his friend gave him license to take liberties. He probably told himself, *She won't really mind*, and *She'll never know anyway*. And yet I do know, and I do mind. *And I'm rapidly revising my opinion of the what-you-don't-know-won't-hurt-you school of thought*, I think sardonically. "You should go now."

He stares at me, then makes a noise of exasperation and stands. "You can't prove anything."

"No. I know."

He turns back. "The glass thing really was an accident. I would never intentionally put you in harm's way."

"So who was it meant for, then?" He flushes, and I see I'm on the right track. I work it through. "Jana?" She'd brought her glass with her when she joined Will and me at the table. I must have picked it up by accident; I remember thinking that the wine tasted different . . .

Peter nods miserably, and then words start to tumble from his mouth. "It wasn't—I didn't—I didn't want to hurt her, not really; I just thought that if Jana got a minor injury and had to go home, Will would go too—"

"A minor injury? You could have killed her! Or me, as it happens."

"I didn't . . . I know. I don't know what I was thinking. I wasn't—Christ, I wasn't myself. It's so strange when I think about it. All I could think of was the deputy job, of how if Will wasn't there when Tanner came out to join us all, it would end up being mine. I mean, I wanted it before, but this was—this was different. And then when I saw how I'd nearly hurt you, it was a proper wake-up call; I saw how *obsessed* I'd become. I know I've been guilty of doing some things that I shouldn't have, but actually hurting someone? That just wasn't me." He stops, breathing hard and taking in my face. I don't know what expression is on it; I don't know how I feel. He starts speaking again, but more calmly: "You'll think I'm nuts, or you'll think I'm trying to off-load responsibility, but I sort of blame—"

"The clock," I say.

He cocks his head. "You felt it too," he says slowly. "I wasn't sure when I tried to talk to you about moving it."

"I saw its effect on James." *But yes, I felt it too.* I don't know why I'm not willing to admit it to him. "As if it—I don't know— amplified all his worst instincts." For me, that was anxiety and the paralysis of fear. And for Will and Sofi, presumably it was recklessness. Was everyone affected? I expect so. Then I think of Mike, of his granite inner strength; of Olive's complete lack of artifice. Perhaps some were less affected than others.

Peter is nodding energetically. "Yes! That's how it felt. I can't for the life of me understand it in a logical sense, but I'm willing to admit there are things that science hasn't got a handle on yet." His open-minded approach is a surprise to me, though I suppose it shouldn't be; Peter's intellectual curiosity has always stretched far and wide. "But anyway, after the glass thing, I was— Well, I guess I was more careful. Forewarned is forearmed. But at least the bloody thing must be burned to a crisp now."

"I hope so." My words are uneasy, though. *It did survive a fire once before . . .*

He turns to go, but stops in the doorway. "Are you going to tell anyone at the university? Not about the clock, I mean, but about the—the other stuff."

He means, am I going to tell anyone in authority? "I don't know." I consider. "I suppose you'll just deny it if I do." He nods, quick

338

and sharp, as if, if he does it fast enough, the agreement can't stick to him. *Nothing is sticking to him,* I think resentfully. *He's going to get out of this entirely unmarked and probably with a healthy money spinner of a patent to his name too.* "Will you withdraw the application?"

He pauses, then says exactly what I knew he would; the only thing he can say, because he's Peter and I was wrong: it's not electricity that runs beneath his skin, but a restless, yearning desire for *more, more, more.* "No." Then, with some urgency, "Look, you must know how this works by now: it's not really my name on the application; it's the spin-off company we've created. I can't just—I can't just yank it with no reason. I'd be a laughingstock."

"But you did before." My words are even.

"Well, ye-es."

"You said you did. You told Nick you did."

He's squirming again, his eyes flitting away from mine. "I, uh . . . Maybe it would be more accurate to say that I had it put on pause." He adds with a rush, "I thought I could convince Nick to join us. Some equity in the company maybe—"

"I see." I do see. I see that he never understood Nick.

"So are you going to tell anyone at the university?"

"I'll have to think about it."

He nods, but still doesn't leave. He has one hand on the doorframe, his expression earnest, his eyes fixed on mine. "I really am glad you're all right, you know," he says quietly. "I was so worried; I kept thinking I should have somehow made you come with me."

"If you had, I doubt Julie would be with us."

"True. But still, I'm glad you're all right." He breaks off eye contact and taps the doorframe twice with the flat of his hand.

"See you at the hotel." I watch him disappear through the open door. *He did at least try to come back for me*, I think. *That ought to count for something*. And then I catch myself. *Despite it all, there's a part of me that still likes him*, I marvel. As one might still like a naughty child who needs to have boundaries established. *A naughty child who committed a home intrusion and destruction of property, popped broken glass in a drink and is following all of that up by trying to enact fraud*, I remind myself. But what am I going to do about it? I genuinely have no idea.

Jana takes me shopping when I'm out of the hospital, which is not exactly the activity I'd have chosen, but nonetheless, I have to concede it's necessary: the clothes I walk out of the hospital in are not only filthy but ripped and scorched in places. It turns out that my wallet, tucked as it was in an inner pocket within my rucksack, survived the ordeal remarkably well, and my credit cards are all in working order. The rucksack itself now sports singed holes and is nowhere close to the color it once was, but deep within it, I found another unexpected item: the carefully wrapped plastic bag containing the 1958 journal, with only the slightest touch of water damage. Even with the clock surely a pile of cinders now, the diary provokes a curl of unease in my belly. I haven't been able to bring myself to read it yet.

Despite the wet—the much-appreciated rain is less a downpour now and more a steady drizzle that's unexpectedly effective at saturation—Chamonix is an appealing town: pedestrian friendly and just the right mix of traditional and modern. The Alps are lost in the low gray cloud, but I can imagine how stunning it must be to look along this street and see the backdrop of the mountains, with the Bossons Glacier tumbling down like a frozen waterfall.

"It's amazing, I found a clothes shop that actually *doesn't* sell running kit or mountaineering gear," enthuses Jana as we walk along what appears to be the main shopping drag of Chamonix. She has a point: I've never seen so many outdoor clothing brands in such close proximity. "The owner is my new best friend. Look, that one on the corner."

We enter a chic little boutique with jeans and shirts and knitwear and skirts and absolutely none of it meant to be worn during exercise. The shopkeeper, a frighteningly elegant Frenchwoman with an unexpectedly disarming manner, does indeed greet Jana like an old friend. Jana starts to peruse the hanging rails. "Shall we get this for Julie?" she asks, pulling out a printed skirt. "Better than trousers, given her knee brace, wouldn't you say?"

"Absolutely. I can see her in that."

"Good." She nods decisively. "Oh, and remember to keep the receipts. I expect you can get reimbursed on your insurance." She turns back to the rails, humming contentedly with the skirt slung over her arm, and I watch her for a moment, speculation forming in my mind. "Jana," I say slowly, "you are suspiciously happy." She turns to me, a wide free smile forming and I see immediately that I've guessed right. "You tested?"

"I did." Her mouth is stretched so wide that her face is nothing but smile.

"You are? You really are?" I gasp.

"I am." And then we're hugging, my face in her neck and her hair in my mouth and the metal hanger of the skirt on her arm digging into my side, but I don't care because I'm so very, very happy for her that everything else is mere detail.

"You tested this morning?" I ask when we break apart. I can see the shopkeeper looking on, smiling too, though she does seem a little mystified as to why there might be so much joy spilling over in her boutique.

"No. Yesterday afternoon. That's why I walked down: to tell Will. Who'd have thought peeing on a stick would have saved me from a wildfire?" She shakes her head in disbelief. "I don't even know what possessed me to test then rather than wait till the morning— Well, I do. I was just too impatient and couldn't wait. I tested again this morning just to be doubly, doubly sure."

"Will must be so thrilled."

"Totally thrilled. Off the charts. I keep telling him that it's early days, and we shouldn't be getting overexcited but . . ." She shrugs, and that smile blossoms again. And I forget about the question I meant to ask her, or maybe I intentionally tuck it away for another occasion, because nothing and nobody should be allowed to disrupt a day like today. *This is what the word* miracle *is reserved for,* I think. *We have to hold it dear for times like this.*

Official Chalet Chronicle

Aug 16th

*It has unfortunately been confirmed to us by the firefighters
that the Chalet des Anglais is no more. The wildfire yesterday
that destroyed much of the flora on the Prarion mountain took
hold of it and apparently very little is left of the structure—not
surprising, given it was constructed almost entirely of wood.
Those caught on the mountain are extremely fortunate to be
alive. I have, in clinical practice, seen firsthand the effects of
smoke inhalation, which can often be somewhat delayed, and
I'm pleased that Peter, Emily and Julie are showing no signs of
ARDS.*

*The date of this fire, coming one hundred years to the day
after the previous chalet structure burned down, has certainly
caught the public interest. The* Times *intends to run an article
on it in this weekend's supplement, which might help with
fundraising for a new build (preferably one constructed in a
more fire-resistant manner). A local woman, elderly, claiming
to be a relative of the poor woman who died in the previous
fire and her father—who had the sudden cardiac arrest—came*

to the hotel to ask the professor if the grandfather clock had been burned (which of course he couldn't answer, though one presumes so); it's interesting to note that their descendants are still living within the area.

Along with the chalet itself, we have also lost the diaries and historical records, which were on the shelves in the salon. There was a recent project to digitize them, but it was unfortunately not yet complete. Peter is keen to reach out to former visitors to the chalet to try to amass all we can through their own photos and records. It's an endeavor I would like to help him with.

With the truly awful death of Sofi, and the destruction of the chalet itself, this trip must be one of the low points in the history of this unique retreat. That does not feel like a hopeful note to end on; therefore I can only express my fervent wish that rebuilding gets underway quickly so that happy times can once again be enjoyed in the Chalet des Anglais.

Signing off as official chalet diarist,

Dr. Olive Mathers

25

That evening, at the hotel—a charming little place that has been remarkably hospitable to *les anglais sans-abri*, the homeless English, despite us all being the most unconventional of guests, without luggage or even the requisite passports for checking in (apart from Caleb and Peter, who it turns out rather sensibly always carry their passport on their person when traveling)—I find myself cornered on the terrace after dinner by Mike. He doesn't waste time with pleasantries.

"What's up with you?" he asks, putting his glass of red wine on the table and pulling up one of the metal chairs. Its legs shriek in protest as he drags it across the flagstones.

"Nothing." He's flustered me; I pick up my own glass of red wine as if it might offer some kind of defense. The lighting is dim and uneven; the liquid in his glass seems nearly black, yet mine is ruby red. "What do you mean?"

"Nothing?"

"Why would anything be up?" I take a sip of the wine, not looking at him and feeling the heat rising in my face. Perhaps I'm in a patch of the terrace that's too dimly lit for him to spot that, but I doubt I'm that lucky.

"Let me see. Because a woman we know died only a few days ago; because you barely survived a wildfire; and because every time I look at you, your eyes jump away like you're scared I might see what you're thinking. So I'm wondering: What's up?"

Now my cheeks must truly be the color of my wine. Or perhaps they seem dark like his. "I . . ." I glance around the terrace quickly. There's a French couple a few tables away, but we're the only ones from the chalet party out here at present. The rest are probably finishing their coffee inside; I had felt an urge to sit outside for a moment and look at the stars, visible now that the rain has let up after a solid day of drenching. *Sofi was right: they're worth looking at. I can see that now.* "I heard something. About you and Sofi."

"Me and Sofi?" He's genuinely surprised: I can see it in his ever-so-slightly raised eyebrows. If he's acting, then he is truly a master—both of the craft, and of knowing himself, of knowing that almost any expression at all would be too much on his granite features. "What?"

"That you were involved. With her."

"One hundred percent false." His reply comes back instantaneously. "Where did that come from?"

"A somewhat unreliable source."

"Completely unreliable, I'd say." He shrugs. His complete lack of concern is utterly convincing. "You read her diary. Did she even mention me?"

I try to remember. *Did she?* Now that I think about it, she did write something. That's right: something like *He's not in the slightest bit interested in me* . . . "Yes," I say at last. "But only to say that you acted like you'd been warned off her."

"Ha! Well, I wasn't aiming for subtlety." The amusement subsides and he grimaces minutely. "The thing is, I had a bit of an education on that sort of thing in my rugby days. You learn

346

to pick out who's going to land you in the papers and who's a bit more serious." He cocks his head. "So you wondered if Sofi and I had had a thing. And then you wondered if I killed her over it."

"I . . . yes."

"No and no." He pauses. "Does that clear it up for you? Can we go back to being able to hold a conversation?"

"Yes." Can we, though? His shirt is rolled back above the elbow; his bare forearm is laid along the arm of the chair, the hairs glowing golden in the light from a wall-mounted spot. I could turn that arm over and stroke along the soft skin on the underside; he would go still and then I would hear a sharp intake of breath. That's as clear and sharp in my mind as another scenario, where that same arm reaches out to shove Sofi . . . The first could still happen, and the second never did; yet they both live within me. Along with Sofi's beautiful staring iris, which still hasn't left me. *Why won't it leave me?* I wonder, not for the first time. *What does she need from me?*

I put down my glass. "*Somebody* killed Sofi, though. If it was one of our group, I had it narrowed down to you or Peter. And I don't believe it's Peter now. Nor you. Which means we might never know. It's so unfair and unjust and . . ." I can't find the right word. If we don't know, it will never be over. Her single iris will be with me forever.

"Yes. Not knowing is the worst thing." He looks around, checking that we still cannot be overheard. "Why not Peter? I'm not saying I think it's him, but what ruled him out?"

I too glance around the terrace—conscious of looking upward too this time; the incident with James has at least taught me that—and then explain about the patent fraud in not much more than a whisper. He drags his chair closer to mine,

347

such that we're sitting shoulder to shoulder, and tips his head toward me. I can't help but feel the intimacy of whispering to him on a secluded terrace on a summer's evening under the stars. *If there are enough occasions like this,* I think, *I will forget that I ever imagined that long arm reaching out and shoving. I will forget I ever pictured his large hand over her mouth and nose.* He whistles a low note when I describe Nick's innovative battery idea. "That really is game-changing, you know." Then he laughs out loud. "Only Nick could have been sitting on a concept like that."

"If I've got the timing right, I think he got funding on the power-trains thing around then; he probably meant to go back to it later."

"What are you planning to do?" he asks.

"I don't know. I have no evidence." I've been going round in circles on it and coming to absolutely no conclusion. "If I was smart, I'd demand that he put Nick's name on the application. He even offered it. Then at least I'd make something out of it, if there's anything to be made."

Mike nods slowly. "But you can't."

"No, I can't." We both know why. Nick, with his unbending opinion of right and wrong, wouldn't have approved: he'd made a poster and displayed that publicly, and therefore the work couldn't possibly be patented. Even if there was no proof that he'd done so, he'd have known he had; he would never, ever bend the rules, and there's not enough money in the world to entice me to do something with Nick's name that I know, categorically, he wouldn't have done himself. "And if I start shooting my mouth off, there's a risk that it's perceived as sour grapes; or worse, everyone might just say that Nick's widow is trying to cash in on what she's not entitled to. I could end up dragging his name through the mud by association." I haven't even told Jana or Julie, and neither has asked. In comparison with the wildfire and Sofi's death, the mystery of a sabotaged laptop ranks understandably low. Nor have I mentioned the glass shards to anyone; perhaps I'm being too forgiving, but I believed Peter when he said he wasn't himself. Many of us haven't quite been ourselves.

"Yes, I can see that," Mike says slowly. "It rankles, but you may well be best to leave it alone. For now."

"For now?"

He shrugs. "I have an extremely vague and unscientific belief in karma. Though usually I only own to an optimistic outlook."

"Your secret's safe with me," I say lightly.

"I have another secret," he says. He shifts diagonally in his chair so that he can look at me more easily. I feel the weight of his eyes as I gaze out across the small garden of the hotel. There are fairy lights in the trees and subtle lighting among the plant borders. Beyond, breaking the pitch-black, there are yellow lights dotted around, much higher than one might expect them to be—what can be up there, so high up these mountain Alps?—and still above that there are the twinkling stars. My eyes catalog all the little lights, near and infinitely far, so that I won't look to my right, to the giant who is sitting patiently beside me, all of his focus on my face as if he somehow might glean the secrets of the universe from what he sees. "So here's the thing," I hear him say in his gravelly rumble. "I've literally wanted to kiss you since the moment I first saw you out on the lawn at the chalet." I can't help it: my eyes fly to his. There is enough light to meet and hold them, but not to see their color. His gaze is as steady as ever. "I'm not sure if maybe you've figured that out by now; perhaps it's not a secret. I know it's too soon for you after Nick . . . I know that, but I just—" He breaks off uncharacteristically, looking at the glass in his hand and then shaking his head as if annoyed with himself before fixing me again with that steady clear gaze. "I just want you to know that, when you're ready, if you're interested"—he shrugs—"give me a call."

"I . . . I don't . . ." *I don't know what to say. Or even how to say it.*

"Yes. It's too soon, I know. I just . . . I just didn't want to miss a chance—later, I mean—because I didn't say anything now. So." He shrugs. "I'm just saying. I'm not expecting you to say anything." He lifts his free hand and rubs the stubble on his jaw with the heel of it, looking at his wineglass. "Unless it's to tell me that I'm on completely the wrong track and that I hold zero attraction for you; I suppose it would be better to know that right now."

I find that a smile is hovering by my mouth. "I can't tell you that."

"You can't?" His eyes leap to catch mine.

"No, I can't."

A smile starts to break out across his face: a genuine, honest-to-God smile that anyone would interpret as such. *That smile is for me*, I think. *Because of me.* It feels like an extraordinary gift. "Well, all right, then," he says, and we're both smiling.

Given the utterly grueling time we've experienced, I thought we would all fly back on earlier flights than originally planned, but the process to sort out replacement passports is neither smooth nor quick. The undergraduate students are particularly worried about the cost of the hotel, but Robert assures them that he is securing a subsidy from the college and that it will apply to all of us, though Mike, Will and I privately tell Robert to redistribute our subsidy among the rest of the group. I don't know if Peter makes the same instruction; I'm avoiding one-to-one conversations with him, aided on occasion by Mike's blocking tactics. It's not clear to me whether anybody else has noticed, and I also have no idea what I would say if they did notice and challenged me on it; the urge to tell everyone of his sins nags insistently at me whenever I see him. Perhaps all it would take would be one pertinent question and my resistance would crumble.

One morning at breakfast, I hand Akash the 1958 journal. "My God," he marvels. "You saved it."

"Not intentionally, but yes."

"This might be the only chalet journal left now. Have you read it all?"

"Not the last trip. The third one is quite disturbing, though. I imagine the last one is worse."

"Disturbing?" He looks at me doubtfully.

"You'll see. Read the first three and then we can read the last one together."

He opens the journal and starts reading then and there, his jam-laden croissant forgotten. I take my coffee and pain au chocolat out onto the terrace, where he finds me some twenty minutes later, his face pinched in its earnestness as he stands before me, waving the leather-bound journal in one hand. "The similarities. . ." he says, then trails off.

"I know."

"Even Dr. Ross' obsession."

Like his own, he must be thinking. "I know."

"It couldn't have been causing anything," he bursts out. *It.* The clock. "It *couldn't*."

I don't say anything. It's too hard to say the words, to voice what we both feel is true, even though it can't possibly be. He puts the diary on the table and flops wretchedly into the chair beside me, the heels of his hands in his eye sockets. "We should read the last trip," he says, reluctance soaking his words.

"Yes."

He pulls himself upright in the chair with visible effort. "Together?"

"Together." I reach for the journal and leaf through to the right place, skimming through the unusually small list of party members—only eight—and waiting for Akash to nod before I turn each page. The clock looms large in the commentary from the start: once again, the diarist has been warned of its peculiarities, and the group appears determined to remain unruffled. Akash starts to read aloud: *"Margaret is finding the proximity of her room—* Wait. Who's Margaret?"

I flick back to the list of participants. "Um, let's see— Ah, she must be Mrs. Boswell. Dr. Martin Boswell's wife. Look: it says here that they're newlyweds."

"Right." He resumes reading aloud. *"Margaret is finding the proximity of her room to the grandfather clock most disturbing for her beauty sleep. Despite reassurances that the chimes are quite capable of penetrating the sleep of those in the farthest-flung chambers too, an elaborate series of room swaps has nonetheless taken place."* He looks at me. "Either she's a real pain in the butt or this writer is verging on misogyny."

"I daresay both could be true." We both scan through a (thankfully brief) account of a long walk, followed by a much longer account of dinner; the diarist seems to be something of an epicurean. All appears calm until the following day. "Listen: *Margaret has refused to cater today, and we do not, as on prewar trips, have a maid; Martin is the model of forbearance and does not insist but I cannot understand her intransigence."* I look at Akash. "I can.

Why can't he do the cooking, since he cares so bloody much about the food?"

"Too right; I'm definitely leaning toward misogyny now. Oh, look—here and here—they're all getting thirsty and complaining about smoke. *There was an acrid taste in the back of the throat all evening, as if something ill-suited for it had been burned on the stove, though Margaret insisted she had not touched it at all.*"

"And they're dreaming of the clock," I say. "Here: *A rather curious phenomena has emerged, where we all appear to be participating in the same dream, or at least similar dreams, all involving the clock. A coincidence, of course, but the timepiece is a rather oppressive presence, I must say, and with the disturbed sleep from the chiming, I expect we are all rather more susceptible to superstition and fancy.*"

"Oh! Look here," says Akash. "*I do feel the balance of the party would be somewhat improved if she had not come; it is difficult to have a proper conversation with Martin without her inserting her presence, which is an unfortunate curb on our strong friendship.*" He looks across at me, his nose wrinkling. "I really do not like this guy."

"Me neither. He's really got it in for Margaret, hasn't he?" I say thoughtfully.

"Jealousy?" suggests Akash. "Maybe he feels pushed out by Martin's new wife?"

"Could be." The unease that's roiling turgidly in my belly is reflected in Akash's tone. *Jealousy. The clock will surely have a field day exploiting that . . .*

We skim over more walks and dinners and reading mornings, and then I start to read aloud: "*By a stroke of fortune, Martin and I were downstairs at the time, both having had trouble sleeping; thus, when alerted by Margaret to the strong smell of smoke, we were able to put out the fire in the kitchen very quickly with blankets and what small amount of water was readily available. Margaret is quite unnecessarily furious*

353

and has demanded that she and Martin leave tomorrow, though her burns are not serious and I have apologized many times for the accident that caused her to trip into the flames. Her accusations of my behavior in regard to her husband are most indecorous, but I will not of course dignify them with any response. The kitchen is usable, although the smoke damage is considerable and the pantry would benefit from extensive repairs."

"Jesus." Akash looks at me, horrified and confused in equal measure. "I don't understand. What just happened?"

"At a guess, I'd say the smoke woke Margaret and she came downstairs to find her husband in flagrante with the diarist," I say grimly. "And then when all three tried to put the fire out, the diarist contrived to shove her in the flames."

His eyes widen. "Oh!" He looks down at the journal, considering. "Yes, I think you're right. Interesting that Margaret detected the smoke rather than the two that were already downstairs." *But they were under the influence of the clock,* I think. Enthralled by it or by each other, but in any case, oblivious to their senses. *Like I was, for a time.* They would have burned without Margaret. *Sofi was my Margaret, even though she was already dead; without her I would have been burned, all while lost in reverie in front of the clock.* And before that, there was the maid in the fire one hundred years ago. Always the women doing the saving; always the women paying the price. But Margaret seems to have survived in this case—though I doubt her marriage did. I belatedly realize Akash is speaking: "Does it say exactly what caused the fire in the first place?" We look through together, but that detail is missing. "Did the Boswells leave after all?" he asks. We put our heads together over the journal, and then he answers his own question: "Yes—here. They left the next day."

I'm reading ahead and suddenly I feel a jolt of excitement. "Akash—look, this is what you've been looking for. *I'm afraid*

I was outnumbered by the remaining members of the party, who determined that they wished to spend their last days at the chalet uninterrupted by chimes, and who have thus consigned the clock to the attic. I do hope the mechanism, somewhat eccentric as it already is, is not damaged by such treatment."

"Yes!" He punches the air in satisfaction, bringing an involuntary smile to my face. "Mystery solved! What date was that?"

"Erm, August sixteenth."

"Sixteenth? When was the fire, then?"

"The fifteenth."

"Really? You're sure?" He pulls across the journal to see for himself. "Every fire," he says, half under his breath. "Every fire, August fifteenth." He looks at me and says more strongly, "The same date, every time."

I nod.

"It's not . . . It can't be . . ."

"I know," I say quietly. "And yet . . ." We look at each other. His eyes are pools of dark worry. *We cannot say it,* I think. *We are conditioned to be rational thinkers; we cannot allow ourselves to be seen stepping outside that framework. Would it help if we could? Is there truly a benefit to naming the beast?* "I've been thinking," I say carefully. "I'd like to go up to see the site of the chalet."

He catches on immediately, nodding. "Just to check that . . . Well, just to check." I nod. "I'll suggest it to the others," he says, immediately switching to planning mode. "Drum up support. We can all make a trip of it."

"Yes." A trip. Just to check. I cannot see how the clock can be anything but cinders and ash, but we owe it to anyone who has ever been blighted by its presence to check.

*

The next day we do indeed make an odd sort of pilgrimage up to the remains of the Chalet des Anglais: all except Robert, who does look rather unwell—even James is with us. The *télécabine* infrastructure remained thankfully undamaged through the fire, and thus is still operating, with higher-than-average traffic, as some people have come to gawk at the fire's aftermath from a bird's-eye view, crowding the side of each cabin that gives the best view and no doubt giving the operator a headache with such a weight imbalance. We can't see the chalet or where the chalet was, but the line of destruction across what once was grass is stark: on one side of it, there is the blackened, charred earth, and on the other, the verdant landscape we walked through all week. The weather is mixed today: from our elevated vantage point, we can see shadows racing across the ground, cast by the clouds that scurry in front of the sun from time to time. The forested areas where the fire touched are more of a surprise to me. Many of the trees still have some green leaves in their upper reaches, though the undergrowth is entirely burned out, and it looks as if a smattering of snow has fallen on the ground. *Ash*, I realize. I wonder how many of those trees will ultimately survive.

"Peter says it will recover remarkably quickly," says Julie, peering through the glass alongside me. Despite her knee and the crutches that she is using, she was adamant that she wanted to come. "Life is resilient. It finds a way to survive."

"Yes, I suppose we could come back and see."

"Would you, though? Would you come back?" I know she's not just thinking of the fire, but of Sofi too. The fire has not stopped that investigation, of course, but there's been no progress. Robert has privately expressed the view, more than once, that it will remain unsolved. There was apparently a woman killed not far away, over the border in Verbier, in a similar manner last summer. The police are considering that there may be a link. It's entirely unsatisfactory, but I don't know to whom or what to direct my wordless, white-faced fury.

I realize I haven't answered Julie, and in truth I don't have much of an answer. "I don't know."

"No," says Julie thoughtfully. "Me neither."

We stop at the Hotel Le Prarion, which was ultimately spared, and Pierre gives us drinks on the house, bemoaning the terrible events.

"Do they still think it was a snapped power cable that caused it?" I ask him as he unloads the tray he has brought out to our table on the terrace.

"Ah, no," he says. "Now they are blaming hikers. They say they must have thrown away a glass bottle that acted as a magnifying glass. But it stinks: Who hikes with a glass bottle? Maybe the power company is pressuring them to say that." He descends into a diatribe on the failings of the power company in a combination of French and English and I nod back, while considering the fact that I still haven't asked Jana the question I meant to ask her. It's not that I keep forgetting exactly. Nor have I deviated from my newfound faith in facing the truth. But a little reluctance in facing painful things is understandable, surely?

When we finally reach the chalet itself, it's to find that barely any of the structure is intact, except for the metal roof and some of its supporting struts, which have collapsed backward as if a mythical god swiped them off with a single blow.

"Jesus Christ," says Jana, sounding dazed. "I actually can't believe you and Julie and Peter survived this." She throws her arms around my middle and hugs me tightly, her head down and her shoulders under my arms, like a child might hug.

"Christ, we were lucky," agrees Peter somberly.

"And smart," says Will, coming to join us as we stand in a little band on the forlorn gray-black remnants of the lawn. He puts his arms around both Jana and me, still wrapped in our hug. "None of you would have survived if you hadn't used your heads."

"I think there was more luck in the outcome than judgment," I confess. *And a little helping hand from Sofi.*

Jana and Will wander off together, hand in hand, and I watch them go, wondering if it really can be the case that a positive result from peeing on a stick has solved everything. I can't imagine that it would be enough for me. But then, we're all fueled by different desires and needs. Nick had been keener to get on with having children than I was. When our friends started having children, it was as if we could see them passing into another country, one for which we hadn't been issued a visa. But the prospect seemed so terribly *definitive* to me. Once you've entered that country, they don't let you out.

I turn at a small sound; it's Peter. I hadn't realized he was still beside me. We survey the wreckage in silence until something occurs to me. "What did you break for the shards?"

"A wineglass," he answers reluctantly. "Why?"

"What did you do with the rest of it?"

"I buried it."

"Out the back? By the firepit?"

"Yes." Suddenly he catches on, shaking his head. "No, no, I buried it very carefully. And anyway, nothing would have dug it up; no animal would be interested in glass."

"True." But still, somehow the clock has had its way. What did Julie say? She saw the fire in the clock; I saw it too. All of this destruction: it drove Peter into smashing the glass. It drove . . . *James,* I think. What did he say? *I dug around a bit.* He could easily have disturbed the buried fragments. I imagine the sun rays, focused through the curve of a fragment of wineglass, boring into a dry leaf until it caught alight, the wind feeding the small orange flicker of flame to run greedily, gleefully, across the dry ground—

"Are you ever going to talk to me properly again?" I look at Peter and see an uncharacteristic droop in his shoulders.

"That depends. Are you going to withdraw the application?"

"I . . ." He stops. There's barely any evidence of his usual crackling energy, and there's a sadness in his eyes; despite everything, it catches at me.

"Don't worry," I say with only a touch of derision. "I won't be staying in Oxford long term. Soon you won't have to see me at all."

"You're leaving?" His eyebrows, bleached almost white by the sun during this week, quirk upward to hide in his mop of sandy hair.

"I think I need to." If nothing else, this terrible, terrible week has shown me that.

He nods, and then says with unexpected self-awareness, "I'll still know that you're not talking to me, though, wherever you happen to be."

"Yes. You will." I leave him then, hearing his long sigh blow out behind me as I walk over to the bones of the chalet. *He's a child who needs boundaries,* I think. I wonder how often Nick was his reins. He will need to find someone else with similar integrity to work with. Or, better yet, develop some himself; I'd like to think people can change. Myself included.

26

I stop near where I judge the entrance to the chalet to have been, and poke around with the toe of my (new) trainers, pretending that I'm not looking for anything, not for anything at all, but I'm certain if it's there, I will find it—and I do. It's the jumble of cogs among a pile of ash that first catches my eye. Apart from the discoloration, they could be utterly undamaged, though other unidentifiable parts lie twisted and misshapen around them.

"What's that?" asks Julie. I hadn't heard her approach, even with the crutches.

"The grandfather clock."

"Well, I'm not in the least bit sorry about that." She comes to stand beside me and together we survey the twisted, blackened metal among the burned wood and ash. She pokes at it with one crutch. Her pale eyebrows draw together. "You know, the mechanism doesn't look as damaged as I would have expected."

"No," I say thoughtfully. "It really doesn't, does it?" I reach down and pick up what seems to be the pendulum rod, which has become separated from the pendulum itself; I can't bring myself to touch that part. The rod, though, is surprisingly heavy. I look at Julie. "I wonder what we can do about that."

She grins, catching on. "Look, I think those are the hands of the clockface." She hunkers down, hampered a little by her bad leg, to pick them out from the detritus. They lie on the open palm of her hand. She pokes them with the forefinger of her other hand; her skin becomes blackened wherever they touch. "You know, even if we bent them into something truly twisted, someone could remold them."

"Yes." I was thinking just the same thing. "Perhaps we should separate the parts."

"Like hanging, drawing and quartering. Only for clocks."

"Exactly." I take off my rucksack and slide the pendulum rod into it. It's too long: it pokes out of the zip to one side. Then I take the fleece that's wrapped around my waist and use it to gingerly pick up the pendulum. It's so blackened by the fire that it's impossible to see whether the etchings on the surface are still there, and I purposely don't try.

"What are we doing here?" asks Mike, coming to join us with Akash trailing after him.

"Disarticulating the clock," I say.

"It survived?" asks Akash, unable to hide his alarm.

"Bits of it did." I hand Mike the fleece-wrapped pendulum. "Here's your bit. We'll dispose of the pieces in separate bins, well away from one another."

Mike takes it, looking down at the bundle and then at Julie, Akash and me. "Completely unnecessary vandalism. Bold move."

"This is actually completely necessary," Julie tells him firmly with Akash nodding vigorously beside her. "Can you hand me those cogs, Mike? I'll take them with the clock hands. I'm not superstitious at all, but this clock really freaked me out, and from what Akash tells me of that 1958 journal, I'm not the first to feel that way."

"Don't tell Robert," Akash warns. "He's very fond of the thing."

"I don't understand why." This is Julie.

"I asked him once actually," Akash says, surprising me. "He said he found it soothing. That there was a peace in its hypnotic effect—it eased his aches and pains." I think of how tired and unwell Robert has looked on occasion, and feel a twinge of concern. Akash goes on: "I liked the history of it, but I can't say I'm sorry it's burned." There's a defiance in his words, as if his matter-of-fact approach might wipe away all his unease. He leans down to pick something up. "Is this part of it?"

"Yes," I exclaim. It's the silver plate, though it's much less shiny and clean than when I last saw it. "That was on the back of it."

"The back?" asks Akash, puzzled, but I brush past his words. "Anyone know Latin?" I ask.

" '*Tempus invenit re vera nos ipsos,*' " Akash reads. "I did it at A-level. It's been a while, but I think . . . um . . . Time finds the truth? No, wait: time finds our true selves. Yes, that's it. I mean, I think so." His eyes, wary and concerned, jump to mine.

Time finds our true selves. I shiver. Were we our true selves in the chalet? No: I think some of us were our worst selves. "Take it and toss it," I tell Akash, and he nods. I feel Mike's eyes on me for a moment, but after a pause he simply says, "I'll take this too," and bends forward to pick up a misshapen black annulus that I realize is the ironwork of the face, with the roman numerals. I start to lean toward it, then catch myself; I have no need to inspect the damaged remains.

The group splits up on the way back, as we cannot all fit in one cabin of the *télécabine*; Julie, Caleb, Mike and I ride down together. The pendulum rod burns at my consciousness from my backpack until I find a bin to leave it in near the bottom of the *télécabine*, Julie and Akash having disposed of their pieces in two separate waste bins at the top. Mike hangs on to his until near the hotel; Julie and I, with a bemused Caleb hovering nearby, watch him lift the lid on one of the giant communal waste bins and toss it in. It clanks loudly against something inside, in a hideous parody of a chime. I stand for a moment, waiting to feel— What? A sense of release perhaps or a kind of finality; something, anything, akin to closure. Nothing manifests.

"Right, then," says Mike, handing me my now dirty fleece. "Shall we have a drink to celebrate this clock-massacre ritual?" He gestures to the small bar that's opposite our hotel, with comically tiny round tables spilling over the pavement.

"Most definitely," says Julie. "Though I promised I'd call home around now, so I'll join you in a bit." She and Caleb move at the slow pace she can comfortably manage toward the hotel, while Mike nabs a table for us. The waiter comes almost immediately to take our order. I shouldn't have a glass of wine, but I order one anyway; there aren't too many days left in which to be mildly decadent in a beautiful French town with the Alps soaring around us. The clouds have scurried entirely away; it's a beautiful afternoon now, though much cooler than before the rain came. I tip my head up to watch the paragliders coming down from Le Brévent, their colorful canopies swooping and wheeling against a backdrop of blue sky and snowcapped mountains.

"Christ, this wasn't designed to hold much more than an ashtray," Mike says, eyeing the table.

I shiver involuntarily, my eyes still on the paragliders. "I've had enough of ash today."

"Sorry to continue the theme, then, but I've been meaning to ask: I've heard you question a couple of times how the fire started. What's driving that?"

He really doesn't miss a thing. I bring my gaze back down to earth reluctantly. "Well, I've been wondering if it started at the chalet. At the firepit." The drinks have arrived. *"Merci,"* I say, taking mine hastily in hand; the tiny table is none too stable.

"Why the firepit?" he presses.

"Initially it was because of James." I explain about what James found and wonder if I should also tell him that I now believe the broken, buried glass was to blame. But if I do, he will literally never forgive Peter, and he has to work with him . . . "Anyway, I thought maybe it was from Sofi's diary, that someone had burned it and accidentally started the fire—"

He's already shaking his head. "No, I know what you mean—that twisted spiral of metal, right? It was there when we got to the chalet. I know because I checked both firepits every night and morning to make sure nobody had felt like a midnight bonfire and left something smoldering; Robert had me absolutely paranoid about fire." He tips his head briefly sideways and back. "Which now seems entirely fair. Anyway, whatever that binding once held together, it wasn't Sofi's diary."

"Oh." *Not Sofi's diary.* Something inside me lifts. I don't have to ask Jana if she stole it from me and then burned it. I don't have to think through what it would have meant if she had. It wasn't Sofi's diary. "Well," I say faintly, "that's a relief." He tips his head to look at me. "Though we still don't know where the diary is," I reflect. "I suppose it most likely burned up in the wildfire, either somewhere in the chalet or out in the forest."

He shakes his head. "Nope."

"Nope?" My eyes narrow. "What do you know?"

"The diary is just fine. The gendarmes have it. I gave it to them."

"You— What?"

"I took it from your bag without James realizing when I was escorting him, shall we say, downstairs." The humor in his eyes as he says *escorting* is unmistakable. "It was safely tucked in my trousers during that whole episode."

"But . . . why?"

"It seemed to me that the best way to protect it until I could get it to the police was for everyone to think it had disappeared."

"Oh." There's a certain amount of logic to what he's saying, but I'm still rather surprised. "How does that make you any better than James?" It's not an accusation: I'm genuinely interested in his thought process.

"I suppose it doesn't, except for the fact that my intentions were pure. The police needed to have the diary; at least one person was trying to get their own hands on it for reasons unknown; and I just thought it best that it disappeared. I definitely didn't want it to remain with you and turn you into a target."

"Oh." The utterly matter-of-fact way in which he owns to his protective instinct is somewhat disarming. It also proves that my hunch not to tell him about the broken glass was right. Maybe one day, but not just yet. "Did you read it before you handed it over?"

"Yes."

"All of it? I read only the last few entries."

"Yes, all of it, which, again, you could say is indefensible, but I really was doing it in case it held something pertinent." I raise my eyebrows: he knows what I'm fishing for. "On the whole, Will comes out remarkably well from it."

I wince. "Did you know already?"

"Nope. Absolutely no clue." Peter didn't know either. Will seems to at least have kept it from being an open secret. "There's another fellow besides Will who ought to be rather unnerved about the existence of it; he doesn't come out nearly as well. And I expect there are others who ought to be unnerved by the existence of earlier volumes."

Earlier volumes. They would go to Sofi's mother, I suppose. Should mothers read that sort of thing? I can't think how I might feel if I were Sofi's mother. "What will the French police do with it?"

"Keep it in an evidence locker, I would think. I don't expect it to see the light of day in the UK for a long, long time, if ever." He shifts in his seat, surveying me. "Who did you think was burning it that afternoon?"

I squirm. "Well, Jana, I suppose." His eyebrows lift: a rare show of surprise from him. "I know, I know: that makes me sound awful—"

"No, no, I'm impressed. You actually took my advice: consider everyone."

"I did, though it didn't exactly make sense that she would have burned it anyway."

"How so?"

"Well, why would she have gone to the trouble of stealing the diary from me? She didn't know about Will and Sofi until much later. I mean, we all heard the fallout when she found out—"

"Ah, that's what they were fighting about in the kitchen?"

"Yes, Will came clean to her that evening." He nods, absentmindedly cleaning his sunglasses with a lens cloth, though we are shaded here and neither of us are wearing them. He likes to have something in his hands, I'm learning. I ask curiously, "Do you think less of him?"

I see his lips purse by the tiniest amount as he considers it. "Well, I certainly don't think *more* of him."

I can't help but try to defend Will. "He didn't have your rugby education on dealing with approaches from beautiful, bright young things."

He produces his low rumble of a laugh. "I expect not. I do understand how it happens. It doesn't make him a bad person, but he's still—at the risk of sounding überjudgmental—weak. Or at the very least, an idiot." I can't exactly argue with that. After all, isn't that where I landed myself? Will's voice rings in my head: *I'm a fucking idiot and you love me*. He is, and I do.

"We may never know who killed her," I murmur, as if saying it out loud might become a form of acceptance. I try it again: "We may never know." It doesn't work any better the second time. I tip up my chin to look at the paragliders again. They could be exotic birds with their bright plumage, dancing and whirling and swooping as the whim and the wind takes them, taking pride in their own skill and caring not a whit for what might befall those bound to cling on to the earth below.

At dinner that evening, I find myself sitting next to James, and I actually don't mind. He makes a real effort: he's funny and self-deprecating, and for the first time, I can see why Robert became so taken with him. I can't trust him, of course, but that doesn't mean I can't enjoy his company. *Perhaps I should expect less of people*, I think. *Perhaps that would make it easier to enjoy the simple things in life, such as a meal with good conversation*. And then I catch sight of Peter and feel anew the bite of what he did, what he continues to do, and I see that something within me *can't* expect less of the people in my life—at least, not of the ones who matter.

"I've been wondering something," I say in a lull in our conversation. James tips his head quizzically. "I've been wondering if it was you who chased me on the hillside."

His eyes jump to my face and then just as quickly slide away. I can see him casting through all possible responses, though at this point he must realize it's too late: the truth really is out there. Once I realized it wasn't Peter, then the answer was obvious: James was part of the search party that swept the bottom third of the circle. They were working clockwise while Peter, Akash and I were working anticlockwise; in a perfect world we'd have met at the boundary of our respective areas—but this is not a perfect world. I wait for James to answer me, not at all sure what tack he will choose. "Yes," he says eventually, looking at his plate. And then he lifts his chin and turns to me. "I'm sorry."

"You weren't at the time."

"No, but I truly am now." Now that he has admitted it, he's keen to explain himself. "I didn't plan it or anything; Jana was moving really slowly, and I got ahead of her and Will, and I guess I overshot our search area—and there you were. You were already a little disoriented. I just wanted to scare you a little, because I was angry at you . . ." He trails off and his brow knits. "I genuinely don't know what came over me. But I am sorry." He looks at his plate again. "I don't expect you'll forgive me."

"I might," I say judiciously. He looks at me, perplexed and a little uncertain. I shrug. "I believe in second chances," I say lightly. I'm not about to tell him that I'm forgiving him because of my odd belief—though belief it is—that there was something at work amplifying his worst character flaws; he doesn't need to be let off the hook quite *that* thoroughly. *Time finds our true selves*: once again I think the inscription was wrong. I don't imagine the Clockmaker was looking for truth when he created the timepiece; he was looking to punish. "Though two's the limit," I add severely, "and some transgressions don't qualify."

"Sofi's killer doesn't deserve a second chance, that's for sure." He says vehemently. "You know, I keep thinking about the day she died. If it was just a random psycho, it could have been any of us—well, any of us who were walking alone down that path that afternoon. Me, Peter, Jana. It's . . ." He takes a deep breath. "It's terrifying how much luck plays a part in life." He moves a hand sharply. "Well: death, I suppose."

"Yes," I say gently. "It's a sobering realization." Perhaps it takes the death of a loved one to really drive it home. *Had Nick been cycling one minute earlier or one minute later; had the driver checked his mirrors more frequently, then . . .* I shake my head: I don't want to get stuck in that loop again; I spent enough time there in the weeks after he died. Instead, I concentrate on replaying what James just said: something about it is nagging at me . . .

"Did you say Jana?" I ask, puzzled.

"What?"

"Walking alone. Jana?"

"Yes, I saw her walking down the path."

"On her own?" *On her own? Without—without Will? Where was Will, then?* But no, that can't be: Jana and Will walked down together. I remember Jana saying so: *She'd gone by the time I rejoined you to walk back down,* she said of Sofi. And Will's gaze jumped across to her; I saw it and noted it, but I ascribed the wrong reason for it . . .

"Yes."

"But—" I stop; one of the waitstaff is clearing my plate. It gives me a second to regroup. "Ah, dessert time," I say brightly to James. "Will you have some? I hear the tarte tatin is very good." And the dinner and the conversation continue as if nothing at all has happened, which I suppose it hasn't, for everyone except me. I know what I should do, what Nick always counseled me to do: take a breath, think it through, sleep on it. But I can't: my mind is tumbling through everything I know, or thought I knew, arranging and rearranging, under the gaze of that single brown iris, pressing into me, boring through me . . . I can't sleep on it. I have to act; I have to know *now*.

In the melee after dinner—some taking coffee, some going on up to bed—I find Mike quickly. Then I leave him chatting and search instead for Jana, dragging on her arm to pull her out of a conversation with Akash and Olive.

"I have to talk to you," I say quietly.

"Is everything all right?" Her whisky-colored eyes reflect the soft, warm lighting of the room.

"Come outside."

"What? Okay." She follows me out to the far end of the terrace, confusion mixed with anxiety in the lines around her eyes and mouth, wrapping her arms across herself, each rubbing the other. "Jesus, it's cold out here at night. What is it? Are you okay?"

"I'm fine." I put my fingers to my temples. I don't know where to start. There are fairy lights in the trees and stars up above; the setting is in no way fitting for the conversation I'm about to have—the conversation I *need* to have. "Jana—Jana, I know you and Will didn't walk down to the chalet together on the day Sofi died."

"What?" Now there's only confusion to be read on her face. "I walked down with Will. I'm sure the staff members at the hotel have confirmed it to the police."

"I doubt the staff can confirm either way." I waited tables in my teens: once the check was settled, I paid almost zero attention to exiting customers. And in this case, we were in and out of the hotel continuously all week. If anyone did have a memory of either Jana or Will leaving alone, I doubt they could be sure which particular day it was from. Jana must have been banking on exactly that confusion. "James saw you walking down alone."

She's utterly still for a heartbeat; for two, three. Then she says desperately, in a fierce whisper, "It's not conclusive. It doesn't mean he did it." For a moment I'm completely thrown. "He'd broken up with her anyway; he had no reason to kill her." Then, "Will you tell the police?"

"I . . . I don't know if James already has."

"It wasn't him. It wasn't Will." Her words are all the more fierce for barely being above a whisper; her hand clutches my forearm. "I only said we walked down together because it was simpler; it cut off any chance of anyone doubting him. But it wasn't Will. I know it. It wasn't him. You can't think that it was."

I look at her, marveling at the fierce conviction in her face, her body—her very essence, in fact. Everything she does, she does at full tilt. "Jana, I didn't—I don't," I say gently. "I think it was you."

27

I think it was you.

There. I've said it. I see her lips part as if to breathe in the words I've just spoken. There's that moment of stillness again, but I'm sure it's a facade. Underneath she's paddling furiously.

"That's . . . that's completely ridiculous, Ems. Why on earth would I have wanted to kill her? I didn't even know about her and Will until after she was dead."

"You knew," I say, shaking my head. "The idea of Will lying—lying well enough to fool *you*—is frankly laughable. I bet you've known about it almost from the beginning. You had no intention of coming here originally; I imagine that changed when you learned who was on the invitation list. You weren't going to leave Will alone with Sofi for a week."

"I see," she says carefully, releasing my forearm. She's projecting a mixture of hurt and anger now. It's so well done, I almost want to cheer her. "So you think I'm the sort of person who would kill someone purely out of jealousy?"

"No. Not jealousy." *Not purely.* But there must have been some of that in there too. *Time finds our true selves.* Was it jealousy that compelled her to think of it, and then she rationalized her actions as being the best for her and Will? I can't tell. Jana's instinct for pragmatism is so strong that that truly may have been the driving force: simply a case of identifying and eliminating the threat.

"What, then?"

"To protect Will's career. To protect everything you want for the pair of you, to make sure nobody ever knew."

"She wrote a bloody diary, Ems! What would be the point of killing her without disposing of that?"

"Ah, but you didn't know about her diary. Not till afterward." Nor did she know that I saw Will and Sofi in the kitchen cupboard. *How very long ago that seems* . . . Jana is nothing if not purposeful, driven: Jana gets things done. Even without the influence of a nefarious timepiece fueling her worst instincts, Jana gets things done. What was it Will had said? *She bulldozes through every obstacle.* In this case, she'd thought she had all the information, but she was missing some crucial details. "I expect you just led her along the wrong trail and then . . ." Had she planned it like that or was it opportune or a little of both? I don't want to think about it. I don't want to think about it being Jana's hands that covered Sofi's nose and mouth. She must have hit her with something first to knock her out—what? A tree branch? A rock? After which she presumably tipped Sofi over the edge into the canyon—*I don't want to know.* Facing the truth is one thing; wallowing in it is quite another. "But after you learned about the diary, you must have realized you'd miscalculated: their affair would come out anyway; you needn't have killed her after all. So you moved into damage control. I mean, we all heard your fight: everyone there would say, in retrospect, that that was the moment you learned of the affair."

"You've really been thinking this through."

"Yes." Finally but only recently. It was only when I started wondering if Jana had burned the diary that I started to consider that the fight may have been staged, at least on her side. *How odd that something I was wrong about actually led to the right conclusion.* For I *am* right. Her face has changed. She's given up on desperate earnestness; the calculations that she's making are plain to see now.

"Where's your phone?" she challenges suddenly, looking at my hands and suddenly reaching out to pat my pockets.

I blink and let her. "It's in my room. It doesn't work anyway after being dunked in the water for so long."

She draws back and nods sharply. "So have you thought this *all* the way through?" Her eyes are narrowed.

"What do you mean?

"Well, what are your options now? You could go to the police. Tell them what you believe. They might agree. Or they might think that Sofi tried to end the affair, and Will became distraught, unhinged . . . I suppose I could always break down and tell them that he'd been violent before. You've got to consider it from both sides. If I don't have Will for an alibi, then he doesn't have me either."

I stare at her, stunned. *Will? Violent? She'd really say that?* I can't even excuse her response in any way: the clock is no more. "You'd put the blame on him?"

"If the alternative is that the blame would land on me?" She raises an eyebrow. "What do you think?"

It's intended as a rhetorical question, but I don't take it as such. "You might," I say at last, shocking myself even as I say it. *Could Jana really blame an innocent man—not just an innocent man, the father of the child growing inside her—just to escape punishment herself?* "Yes, you really might. Does he know?"

She tips her head, a knowing look on her face. "Of course not. He won't let himself know. He wants us—the baby, me,

374

everything—too much." She pauses. "I just wanted to speak to her," she says quietly. "To get a measure of whether she was going to be a problem. But she was so very *sorry*. So incredibly fucking *apologetic*. Can you imagine?" She shakes her head viciously, and suddenly I see what Sofi did that was so very unacceptable. It wasn't that she had slept with Will. It wasn't even that she threatened the future Jana had planned. It was that she had made Jana feel like a victim, and that could *never* be allowed. I close my eyes briefly. *How horribly ironic: if Sofi had been more brazen, less aware of the impact of her own misdeeds, perhaps she'd still be alive.* It wasn't rational, what Jana had done, for all she might pretend it was. *How much did the clock have to do with that?* But as I told James, some transgressions don't qualify for a second chance. "Well, sooner or later, she was obviously going to tell someone; she'd be looking for someone to absolve her of her guilt." Jana shakes her head again, then tosses her hair imperiously. "You know, this is all your fault too."

What? The sudden change of pace catches me off guard. "How do you figure that?"

"If you'd told me immediately that you'd seen Will and Sofi together that night, then things would have turned out differently."

I catch my breath sharply. "No, that's not—that's not fair—"

"Isn't it?" She raises an eyebrow. "You made a decision to protect Will and look what it led to. Now you have another decision to make. I doubt the police will set much store by anything James says; they're rather miffed with all his misdirection, as I understand it. And there's no DNA evidence or they'd be swabbing us all like crazy and confiscating the clothes we were wearing—clothes that literally just went up in smoke. Either way, she's still dead. You can ruin Will's life.

Or not." She surveys me, taking in my shallow breaths. My heart is thumping and the hairs on my neck are standing on end with the sweep of adrenaline that the threat in her words has brought on, but it's not like previous episodes: the beat doesn't threaten to drag me under. Time is steady, reliable, endless. I only need to keep breathing.

She takes a step away, rubbing her arms again for warmth. "Well, you think about it," she says over her shoulder as she heads back in. "Think about it all."

28

When I return, Oxford is not the place it once was for me. Or perhaps it's that the people within it are not quite the same, myself included. My failures face me at every turn here; I cannot step away from them. I am so bitterly disappointed with myself and with what I've done, or haven't done, and yet I don't truly believe any other action would be any better.

What I haven't done . . . Well, I haven't told the French police who I believe killed Sofi. I owe it to Sofi to do what I can to expose the truth, but at the expense of Will? Even with all the physical evidence in the world—and I certainly don't have that—Jana is not somebody I'd want to get into a dogfight with. It isn't that I've made an active decision not to; instead, it's that I can't decide at all, and that indecision seeps into everything I do and see. Sometimes it's a physical weight sitting inside my chest and dragging me down to the floor—through the floor even, to the very core of the earth. Sometimes it's a blanket of fog obscuring everything I look at and everything I touch. And through it all, that beautiful staring iris stays with me, trained unblinkingly on me. Perhaps I'm wrong to believe that there is something I can do to allow it to leave. Perhaps it will be with me forever.

I haven't found a way to stymie Peter either, and if Mike's karma theory holds true, it's playing out over a much longer timescale than I would like. I searched the house when I got back, looking for a printed copy of the poster—and I found several conference posters in fact (all badly punctuated), but none of them mentioned dendrites or solid-state batteries.

It is easy, then, to maintain my resolve to leave the city, but harder than I might have expected to extract myself. There are courses that I promised to teach, people I don't want to let down. There's the question of what to do with the house. There's the question too of where to go and what to do with myself once I'm there. It turns out that leaving is not quite so simple as shrugging off one jacket and reaching for another.

One bright spot among all of this is Mike. We resolve to take things very slowly—a resolve that lasts right up until I drink too much wine and more or less throw myself at him. "Oh, thank God," he mutters as he kisses me back. "I've been going insane for the wanting of you." I'd worried about feeling guilty on account of Nick, but somehow it helps that I know Nick liked and respected him very much: I feel he would have approved. It helps too that Mike felt the same about Nick, that he knew him, knew the oddness of him, his foibles and quirks and startling cleverness, that might have been hard to describe to a stranger. There have been a few disapproving faces who clearly feel I've *moved on* too quickly, but thus far I've managed not to get exercised about that; I can only imagine they are lucky enough to have never lost anybody they're close to. Otherwise they would know that you never *move on* exactly: you take the person you've lost with you. And nobody else can ever tell you how you should grieve.

The chalet party regroups at Robert's funeral. His death, just before Easter, had come as a shock—to me, at least; I'm told Peter had begun to have an inkling that Robert was seriously ill when he transferred trusteeship of the chalet to him. Not that there is an actual chalet at the moment, but there are plans to rebuild one; French buildings insurance is apparently remarkably comprehensive, even covering wildfires. There won't be a chalet party for the next couple of summers but there ought to be one the summer after that. I can't imagine that what they build will be the same, though, in look or in feel, and part of me hopes they won't even try for that. The Chalet des Anglais that I knew is gone for good.

I don't speak to Peter, though I know through the IP office that his patent application is still in process. It's not too difficult to avoid him at first, but as Mike and I become more involved, it begins to require more agility, given their friendship groups overlap as a result of being part of the same department. It's probably more awkward for Mike than for me, though, knowing what he does and yet having to behave professionally. I have the same difficulty with Jana: I can't avoid seeing her in my department. She no longer tries to engage me in one-one-one conversations—she's learned I will simply turn on my heel and leave if she does—but of course we're sometimes thrust together in a group environment. There are moments then when she says something funny or clever or direct, when our eyes would once have met in secret shared amusement, and it's a struggle to school my face into impassivity and keep my gaze from hers, because she's still Jana. She's still refreshingly forthright and funny and efficient. Everything she always was is still there. It's a relief when she goes out on maternity leave.

The funeral is on a cold gray spring day that feels like January rather than April. It's pleasingly well attended and the minister speaks movingly, as does Robert's niece. Peter speaks about Robert's dedication to the chalet and the university more widely—he does well, blending anecdotes with emotion and obvious affection. Like almost everyone, I am tearful by the end, but I always am at funerals—except Nick's. I couldn't cry a single tear at Nick's, perhaps from fear I would never stop.

Afterward we move to a hotel for sandwiches and tea and something stronger for those who want it; enough people are there that it's not too difficult to avoid Jana in the crowd. I caught sight of her at the service and she looked good, as if motherhood suits her. Will was with her, of course, but I couldn't see him clearly. I saw James too, looking very pale and red-eyed, beside a tall man who could only have been his father, but at the hotel he seems to have slipped that leash and I see him in animated conversation with Julie and Akash. Caleb, to whom I'm speaking at the time, keeps glancing over.

"Relax," I say quietly. "I'm sure she's fine."

"I know; it's habit, really." His mouth twists ruefully. "To be honest, he's been much nicer all round since the chalet trip."

"I think it's that he's stopped trying to be Ripley."

"Ripley?" Confusion covers his face. "Like as in *Alien*?"

I laugh out loud. "No, not *Alien*. Tom Ripley." He still looks blank. "*The Talented Mr Ripley?* Patricia Highsmith?"

"Oh." His face clears. "I never read it. Sort of on principle actually: it always seemed like one of those novels that people read so they can show they're the sort of person who reads *The Talented Mr Ripley*."

I laugh again: Caleb certainly has a talent for spotting affectation. "Well, you can always watch the movie instead."

Later Julie catches me at the buffet table. "This is almost like a good-bye party for you."

"A slightly macabre one, but yes. Are these tuna, do you think?" I'm dubiously inspecting some sandwiches.

"Or maybe fish pâté? Are you all packed up?"

"Just about." I put some much-safer-looking ham sandwiches on my plate. "Are you checking that I'm really leaving and you can really have the house?" I tease. Julie and Caleb are both staying on for doctorates and will be renting my house from September. Mike and I are off to Canada. He didn't get the deputy job. Actually, none of the three of them did; it went to an outside applicant. But Mike did get a tenured position in Canada, which at least answered the question of where to go after Oxford. I'm still working on what to do once I get there.

"I'd rather have you in Oxford than the house," she says, and I turn to look at her properly and see the truth of it in those cornflower eyes.

"Oh, honey," I say, my throat almost too tight for words. I wrap my plate-free arm around her in a one-armed hug and close my eyes as I feel her squeeze me back. "Come visit us anytime. We'd love to have you."

We draw apart. "Same to you," she says with a small wobble in her voice. "You can sleep in your own spare room," she quips, and we both laugh. Mike ambles over to join us just as, through the bay window, I spot Will outside. He's pushing the pram gently forward and back across the car park, his chin tucked into his red scarf and one hand on the handle; the other is scrolling through messages on his phone. "Back in a sec," I say quietly to Mike, handing him my untouched plate.

His eyes follow mine to land on Will. "What are you going to say?" he asks in an undertone. There's a slight tightening around his eyes that telegraphs his concern for me; I doubt anyone but myself would notice.

"I don't know." I shrug. "Back in a sec," I repeat, smiling at Julie. Then I turn to push my way through the crush to the door.

Outside I soon wish I'd brought my coat: my thin black funeral-appropriate dress isn't quite up to this chill. "Hey, you," I say as I approach Will.

He looks up from his phone and halts momentarily, then remembers himself and keeps the pram moving back and forth even as his feet have stilled. "Hey, yourself." He smiles, tucking his phone into his pocket to free that arm to hug me. Now that I'm closer, I can see he's very pale, with pouches under his eyes that I don't recall seeing before.

I peer into the pram. With the blankets heaped against the cold of the spring day, I actually can't see anything except a small tuft of dark hair. "She's gorgeous," I say anyway, straightening up. "How's she doing?"

"Thriving." The mixture of pride and awe in his smile makes me want to hug him again. He starts to walk and I fall into step beside him. "She hasn't quite learned that nighttime is for sleeping but we're working on it." He pauses, glancing sideways at me. "You haven't been round."

"No."

"We miss you." He's feeling his way through this cautiously. "Jana feels hurt."

I miss you both too. "Jana knows exactly why I haven't been round," I say tightly.

He nods; for an instant, it seems as if he's going to leave it there, but he suddenly can't help himself. "Look, I know it's not my place, but— Well, it's difficult, I know, when someone has what you want—I know you and Nick wanted kids—but couldn't you at least be happy for us?"

I've stopped walking and my mouth has dropped open. "Is that what she told you? That I'm avoiding you both out of jealousy over your new arrival?"

382

"I . . ." He's stationary now too, except for the arm that powers the pram. "Ye-es," he says uncertainly. "Is . . . is that not it?"

"Not in the slightest. Nick wanted kids, sure, but for my part, I hadn't quite got my head around it."

"Oh. Then . . . why?" he asks, bewildered.

"Because I know." *I didn't mean to say this,* I think. And then, *Is that right? I didn't meant to say this precisely* now, *but I'd begun to realize it had to be said. The reason I couldn't decide is because it's not a decision I should be making for him.* There's a rightness to what I'm saying, what I'm doing. Sofi needs justice; she needs us *both* to fight for it for her. I can't decide alone and neither can I go through the process alone, not successfully. "I know," I repeat.

"Know what?"

"I know what happened to Sofi." His eyes screw tightly shut for a second as if that might block out what I'm saying. "I know Jana walked down alone; I know you only joined up with her somewhere on the path before entering the chalet together. And I know what she did in that time you weren't together."

"That's not true—"

"It is. You know it is."

He starts to walk again, faster than before. "She didn't mean to lie; she just said it because it made things simpler. And just because we didn't walk every step of the way down together doesn't mean she—"

"No. But she did. And I think if you're honest with yourself, you know that."

He stops abruptly, then looks at the pram, then back at me. "That's the mother of my child that you're talking about," he blusters, but it's unconvincing; it's as if he feels he *ought* to be angry. "And my fiancée."

I blink. "Oh, you're engaged now. I suppose I ought to say congratulations."

His free hand moves as if to swipe all that away. Every single one of those sleepless nights shows in his face as he looks at me. "No. You're wrong," he says helplessly. "I won't believe it."

"But I'm not and you do. And I know you: sooner or later you'll have to do something about it. She'll try to blame you when you do, though. We should talk to the police together; it might carry more weight. I have a recording: it's not exactly an admission of guilt, but it does include her threats to implicate you." A recording taken on Mike's phone stuffed into my bra during that conversation outside. "It's not great quality"—padded lingerie is, unsurprisingly, not conducive to good sound quality—"and it turns out it's totally illegal to record conversations in France without consent, but I'm willing to take the chance on any charges." His eyes widen and his mouth opens, but then snaps shut quickly, before any words can escape. I reach out and briefly squeeze his upper arm. "It's good to see you. Call me when you're ready to speak." *He will call me,* I think. I don't know how long it will take him, but he will call me. *I have faith.* I fancy that Sofi does too.

When I'm almost at the door to the hotel, I see Jana in profile looking through the bay window from the inside. We are separated only by a few feet and a pane of glass, but she hasn't seen me; her attention is on Will and the pram and her expression is strangely unreadable. *She ought to be happy,* I suppose. She has what she wanted, at least for now: Will and their life together. *And Will has what he wanted too*: a child, a wife-to-be, a dazzling career—if there has been any professional fallout from his dalliance with Sofi, it's been kept very much under wraps; he ought to be happy too. Even if Jana is held accountable, even if they never marry, he will still have two out of the three, but Jana will have nothing. I can just imagine Jana's scornful vitriol in that scenario: *He's the one who had the fucking affair but somehow he gets everything he wanted, and I end up in this pile of shit? How is that fair?*

It's not, I think. *But you killed Sofi, and that wasn't fair either. And when did you ever expect life to be fair anyway?* I climb the steps quickly before she can turn and see me, for she's still Jana: still every bit as brightly refreshing and compelling as she always was. It's the right decision to leave Oxford.

The following week, I'm at my house, though it no longer feels like mine, clearing out the final odds and ends in Nick's study. After that, and a good cleaning by a professional firm, the property will be ready for the short-lease tenants who are moving in for three months, prior to Julie and Caleb taking it on in September. Winter has finally yielded and I have the door to the back garden open to air the house. A light breeze flits in every now and again, bringing with it the noises from outside—cars passing, a dog barking, a snatch of conversation too indistinct to understand—but there is nothing for it to rustle inside. Almost everything is gone.

Not quite everything: I open an overlooked cupboard to find years of Nick's daybooks, all filled with tiny, dense, near illegible script covering every single inch as if paper were the most valuable of all commodities and any waste a travesty. I flick through them at random but serendipity does not choose to smile on me: none of the pages I glance at have anything about dendrites or solid-state batteries written in his cramped hand. They all go in a box marked *Department*; perhaps one of Nick's colleagues will find something of use in there somewhere.

The last thing to do is to remove Nick's pinboard, which isn't really a pinboard at all but a large laminated rectangle fixed to the wall by drawing pins, to which he stuck pale yellow Post-it Note reminders with cryptic scribbles on them: *Grant application*, *Check Clifford citation*, *Call TP* and so on. I pull them off, one by one, feeling a familiar sadness spread through me as more and more of the laminated white sheet is revealed until it's finally empty, a blank staring space on the wall where once there was a feathered lemon pelt of tasks and reminders. But there is no more to do now.

At last, I dig out the drawing pins with my fingernails, bemoaning the indentations they've left in the painted wall. The laminated sheet curls in my hands as soon as it's released and I belatedly realize it's not blank—at least, not on both sides. I hold it up, trying to see what it is, and then exhale sharply in surprise. It's a poster. An academic poster. On . . . let me see . . . I start to laugh: *Electrolyte Configurations in Solid-State Batteries*. The text starts: *Lithium dendrites are a major obstacle to . . .* There are even three annotated diagrams.

Karma, I think with amused wonder. *Mike may be onto something*. I pin it back up on the wall with the drawing pins, but this time with the content facing me, and take a picture on my mobile phone. Right there and then I send it to my contact at the IP office, copying Peter.

I wonder if he will reply. I wonder what I will do if he does.

A few months later, I'm making scrambled eggs in the (frighteningly orange) kitchen of our temporary apartment in Canada when my mobile rings. I scoop it up and see the caller ID: *Will*.

Will.

I quickly move the eggs off the heat and answer the call. "Hey, you," I say. "How are you?"

"Hey, yourself," he says, and then pauses. The long beat of silence crosses three thousand miles as I wait for him to say what surely must be coming. *I have faith,* I think. *Sofi has faith. We've both been waiting for you.* Then I hear him exhale slowly before he says, "I'm ready to speak now."

ACKNOWLEDGMENTS

I have a confession to make. For many years I thought I would be so much more productive in my writing if the world would just stop for a while; if the demands of ordinary life—be they familial, social, administrative or professional—would cease pressing upon me. Well, the world did stop, in a fashion. The global Covid-19 pandemic happened, and suddenly there were no family events, no social events, no kids' school events, no work events, no sporting events and no travel—no reason (or even, during certain periods, permission) to ever leave the house, in fact . . . and it turns out I didn't write any faster at all.

Now, it's certainly true that all the uncertainty and worry (and zooming and homeschooling) were not in the least bit conducive to either a creative process or self-discipline, both of which are fairly crucial if you're aiming to produce a novel. But I think it was more than that. I've always felt that there's nothing quite like a deadline to concentrate the mind, but novel deadlines are loooooong. They loom large, but from a distance; they're months away—at least to begin with. It can be all too easy to let something so non-immediate slide. I hadn't appreciated the importance of micro-deadlines, such as *I have to write one thousand words before I go to my eldest's athletics event*, or *I need to nail this chapter before my youngest gets home from school*.

Without those, there's a danger that a big expanse of nothing in my diary just leads to achieving . . . nothing.

And so I have a newfound appreciation of all those small demands on my time, that do indeed take me away from writing but in fact also keep me sane and productive, and I'd like to start my thank yous by expressing my gratitude to all the people who tried to keep some semblance of normality going through the tough times, be it by creating outdoor eating spaces, or developing bubble systems so that kids could still exercise in groups, or any number of other efforts which gave us all something to put in the diary even while certain Covid restrictions remained. It was truly important, and much appreciated—thank you.

On a more specific note, I'd like to once again thank my fabulous agent, Marcy Posner, at Folio Lit; without her encouragement, guidance and advice, I would be an absolute basket case, as opposed to the anxious and insecure, but—importantly!—still functional writer that I am today. She is truly a treasure and I am so very lucky to have her. As if that wasn't enough, I also get the added bonus of access to Marcy's interns and assistants, and with respect to this novel I'd particularly like to thank Jessica Macy for her truly insightful notes.

To Kerry Donovan and her wonderful team at Berkley and Penguin Random House, thank you so much for all your hard work, enthusiasm, dedication—and wonderfully creative marketing ideas! It continues to be a real pleasure to work with you all, and I'm enormously grateful for the support you have given my writing career right from the very start. I'd also like to express my huge appreciation of Sarah Hodgson at Atlantic Books, who somehow produced extraordinarily detailed and thoughtful notes despite being handed a desperately short timeframe, and also of the wider team at Atlantic Books who have worked tirelessly to champion my novels. And to the Midas PR team, it's been a pleasure getting to know you and thank you for everything you have done to raise my profile.

Many thanks to Professor Stephen Golding who was kind enough to answer my questions about the chalet, and also to Leigh Innes, who racked her brains to remember details of it—apologies, Leigh, that the Robbo shower explosion wasn't ultimately included in the tale!

I'd like to thank all my friends and family, who continue to be such stalwart supporters of my work and, more importantly, enormously good company! There never seems to be enough time to see enough of you all. And of course I have to particularly thank Matt, Cameron and Zachary, who never fail to make me smile even on the darkest of writing days—all my love, always.

Lastly, I'd like to thank my readers. The one thing we are not short of in this day and age is choice of leisure activities; therefore, it's extremely humbling that anyone would choose to spend their time stepping into the stories I create. I can't tell you how incredibly grateful I am that so many of you do. Thank you from the bottom of my heart.

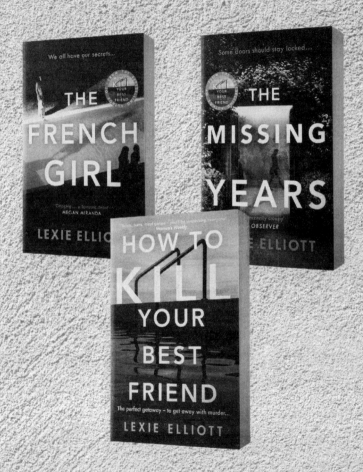